QUEER FEAR

GAY HORROR FICTION

edited and with
an introduction by
MICHAEL ROWE

QUEER FEAR

ARSENAL PULP PRESS

Vancouver

QUEER FEAR

ARSENAL PULP PRESS
103 - 1014 Homer Street
Vancouver, BC
Canada V6B 2W9
www.arsenalpulp.com

The publisher gratefully acknowledges the support of the Canada Council
for the Arts and the BC Arts Council for its publishing program,
and the support of the Government of Canada through
the Book Publishing Industry Development Program
for its publishing activities.

This is a work of fiction. Any resemblance of characters
to persons, living or dead, is purely coincidental.

Design by Solo
Printed and bound in Canada

CANADIAN CATALOGUING IN PUBLICATION DATA:

Main entry under title:

Queer fear

ISBN 1-55152-084-2

1. Gays' writings, Canadian. 2. Gays' writings, American.
3. Horror tales, Canadian. 4. Horror tales, American. I. Rowe-McDermid, Michael, 1962–
PS8323.H67Q43 2000   C813'.0873808920664   C00-910922-6
PR9197.35.H67Q43 2000

For Jean and Don Hutchison, with love.

CONTENTS

ACKNOWLEDGMENTS

No book is the exclusive province of the author or editor. I'd like to thank Brian Lam, Robert Ballantyne, and Blaine Kyllo, at Arsenal Pulp Press for their support of *Queer Fear*, and for taking the leap into an un-quantified literary territory. Working with these gifted and dedicated publishers has been a supreme pleasure, and I count their friendship as a gift.

For permission to use of the beautiful painting on the cover, I thank the artist, James Huctwith, and Dennis O'Connor. The O'Connor Gallery is one of Toronto's most valuable cultural resources, and it continues to showcase some of the finest young artists in North America.

Thanks also to Dean Allen, one of Canada's finest designers, for the beautiful cover itself.

Thanks to some of the editors in the field with whom I've worked, Rod Gudino and Mary Beth Hollyer at *Rue Morgue*, Barbara and Christopher Roden at *All Hallows*, and, of course, the indefatigable Tony Timpone and Michael Gingold at *Fangoria*, who have borne with me graciously during a very difficult year.

Many of the writers in this book are good friends, and I'd prefer not to create a perceived hierarchy by listing them here, but I have to name Ron Oliver and Michael Thomas Ford as being as essential to me on a daily basis as coffee, and who, like coffee, can be counted upon for sweetness and bitterness in equal measure (but mostly sweetness).

Some friends, in and out of the field, have been nurturing of this project, and me, in a consequential way. They include, but are not limited to: James Huctwith, Robert Thomson, Barnaby Ellis-Perry and Douglas Brockway, Christopher Wirth and Johanne Laperriere, Michael Elliot, Lesley Durnin, Bruce Warner and Patrick Burr, John Scarfe and Jason Pace, Louis Amato-Gauci, Jenny Griffiths, Shitij Kapur and Sharmistha Law, John Diduck and Lissy MacKewn, Victor Graziano and Demetra Kourtis, Denise Newton, the Bradbury-Kus family, Anthony Bernardo (who already has books), Matt Glaser, Julian Concepcion, Jane Oliver, Tracy Oliver, and Helen Oliver, Casey Wallace, Gabriella Martinelli, Teri Lorentson, Warren Dunford, Werner Warga, Tasia Hazisavvas, Josh Ezekiel, Angie Moneva, Randy Murphy and Wayne Brown, Tom Armstrong, Howard Aster, Charly Lin and Drew Harris, Duncan Jackman, Graydon Moffat and Ian Russell, Dan Duic,

Nancy and Jay Bowers, Michael J. Garraoui, Rick Andreoli, Tracy Jobe, Stephanie Keating, Jamie Blanks and Simone Chin, Brad Luff, Carsten Stroud, Shaw Madson, Davin Hoekstra, Rick Bryant, Marlon Wurmitzer.

My friend Jon Larson, who brings his exquisite sensitivity and generous talent and intelligence to our friendship, warrants a special thanks.

My extended family among the Little, Shaw, and Davis clans are a consequential force of good in my life, and I thank them for that.

To my life-partner, Brian McDermid, the author of all good things, thank you for being there in the night to catch me with such love when my nightmares wake me up screaming, and for being nice about it in the daylight. Being married to a horror writer involves frequent nocturnal interruptions, and he bears them with startling good-nature, one of the many reasons I love him.

My mother, Penny Rowe, passed away on the morning this manuscript was completed. She celebrated every success of both my brother and myself, and *Queer Fear* would have been a source of pride for her, even if she neither cared for horror or understood it's appeal. My mother believed in the power of literature, and her love of books has been one of her most enduring legacies. I thank her for that, and I thank my father, Alan Rowe, for showing me what grace is.

Lastly, and most importantly, to the writers whose stories glitter on these pages, thank you for giving me such wonderful work, and for sharing your brilliant darkness with all of us.

Like one who on a lonely road
Doth walk in fear and dread,
And having once turned round
Walks on,
And turns no more his head,
Because he knows a frightful fiend
Doth close behind him tread.

– Samuel Taylor Coleridge, *The Rime of the Ancient Mariner*

I have supp'd full with horrors.

– William Shakespeare, *Macbeth*

INTRODUCTION:
IN PRAISE OF QUEER FEAR

Michael Rowe

"It's Halloween. I guess everyone's entitled to one good scare."

– Sheriff Leigh Brackett to Laurie Strode in
John Carpenter's Halloween (1978)

THERE'S A STORM COMING.

The air is paralyzed, sweating ozone. The late-afternoon sky is blue-black and swollen with the sure promise of violence. I like storms. A perfect one can take you to the very edge of creation. In 1818, Mary Shelley, a houseguest with her husband, Percy Shelley, at Lord Byron's rented Villa Diodati on the shores of Lake Geneva, first dreamed of her monster during a furious lightning storm that her husband noted was like the end of the world. "What terrified me will terrify others," Mary Shelley wrote in her "Author's Introduction to the Standard Novels Edition" of *Frankenstein* in 1831, "and I need only describe the spectre which had haunted my midnight pillow."

My partner Brian and I live in a 135-year-old farmhouse on a tree-lined street in a leafy Toronto neighborhood. In the summer, when I draw the blinds against the sun, the house smells like time sleeping. The ceilings are high, and sometimes at night, by candlelight, the shadows seem to move at their own discretion. As a writer, I spend hours alone with the blinds drawn, inhabiting other people's lives. Any reader who has ever lost themselves in a well-written tale of terror on a stormy night will understand what I mean when I say that I sometimes wonder if we don't bring the stories back into the world with us by reading them alone; whether or not they stay contained. A board creaks in an upstairs room even though you know you're alone in the house. A tapping on the glass has to be a branch tortured by the wind. A sigh in the shadows of the far recesses of the next room has to be a draft. The slumped figure drifting just out of your line of sight is a shadow cast by the candles.

You're alone, reading.

Keep telling yourself that as you read the stories in *Queer Fear*. The creatures that live in these pages, monsters, both human and otherwise, are better confined between the covers of the book you are holding in your hands. The authors of these stories, among them some of the darkest jewels of the horror fiction field, have written in the spirit of Mary Shelley's maxim: what terrifies them will terrify you as well.

———————

When I was a little boy growing up in Ottawa, Ontario in the early 1970s, my allowance was twenty-five cents. In those days, that was enough for a twenty-cent comic book and five cents' worth of candy. Remembering my childhood summers, some of the clearest, purest memories are of gold and green Saturday mornings. I would ride my banana-seated Schwinn up Kilborn Avenue to the Kilborn Confectionary, a neighborhood grocery store run by a Lebanese family whom, it seemed, had always been there. The store was air-conditioned in the summer, and faintly scented with pine floor cleaner and some indefinable powdery perfume that I have always associated with that innocent, vanished time. The radio behind the counter would always be playing music – Janis Ian, Bread, The Monkees. It was there in that store, on the creaking metal turnstile racks near the entrance, that I first discovered the field of horror fiction, both in comic book form and also in the form of cheap paperbacks with titles like *The Frankenstein Wheel*, *Dracula's Brothers*, and *Power Through Witchcraft*. The novels cost as much as seventy-five cents, so if my mother wouldn't buy them for me (which was a rarity; my parents believed that reading – something, anything – was better than not reading), I would save up and buy them myself. The comic books – *Tomb of Dracula*, *The Witching Hour*, *Werewolf by Night*, and *Dark Shadows* – I could always afford. I was fascinated by the beautiful, lurid covers, and something in me soared at the power and the magic – and yes, darkness – inherent in the stories. Heart pounding, I would place the comic books and the candy in the basket of my bike and peddle home, wind in my face, pretending that I was flying like one of the night-creatures in my comic books. I would "land" in our driveway, curl up in the porch-swing in my mother's cutting garden in the back yard, and proceed to lose myself in the wash of acid-toned storytelling in the comic book I was reading. My friend Gordie Brown lived nearby, and we would often swap comics. He was a die-hard *Dark Shadows* fan, and he had the best collection of horror comics of anyone I knew. His father had made him a silver wolf's-head cane, like the one Barnabas Collins carried. Gordie also had a large cardboard "coffin" in his basement, which I thought was very cool, for when we played vampire.

What I know now, but didn't know then, was that I was living in what would become a clearly-delineated pop-culture moment. The early seventies coincided with the beginning of the end of a period of grand and garish gothic storytelling that had begun in the fifties, both in fiction and in film. Indeed, the second-last of Hammer Films' Dracula pictures starring Christopher Lee was *Dracula AD 1972*. In 1972, I was ten years old, and my imagination was they key I was using to unlock the world around me.

Around the same time, I was beginning to detect something about myself, my nature, that was at odds with what I was seeing around me in my friends. Although they were still too young to be much interested in girls, neither were they in love, as I was, with Bobby Sherman and David Cassidy. They were interested in war games, fort building, and hockey. My interest in horror comics was a neutral area, a socially-acceptable DMZ where I could rest, observe, and try to figure out what was going on. If I identified with Rachel Van Helsing, the glamorous blonde vampire hunter in *Tomb of Dracula* who, pre-*Buffy*, was fast on her feet and handy with the crossbow (and in love with handsome Frank Drake, Dracula's tormented descendant), no one was any the wiser.

Gene Colan, the artist who drew all of my favorite Marvel Comics characters, had an unerring eye for the male physique. The male characters in Marvel Comics were usually well-muscled, so a pre-adolescent appreciation for big shoulders, strong pecs, and corded biceps was queerly inculcated into my nascent sexual psyche by those comic books in a way that I'm sure Colan never intended when he put his pen to paper. In 1998, when Wesley Snipes fired up the screens in New Line Cinema's action vampire epic *Blade*, all muscle and leather and attitude, it was *déjà vu*, like meeting an old boyfriend. Blade was a character created by Marv Wolfman in *Tomb of Dracula*, issue ten. Seen from the vantage point of almost thirty years, I have to smile. There's nothing quite as queer as having a crush on a comic book character, unless it's wishing you could *be* one.

As childhood segued into adolescence, horror novels and stories were my still my preferred reading material. The perpetual October country of horror fiction was a haven in which to escape what I perceived as my body's betrayals of the norms I saw all around me. My nose was always buried in a book, and there was a certain sanctuary accorded to boys like me. Teachers liked us, and even if our peers didn't, they thought we were "brainy," and left us alone for a little while.

At some point, though, my male and female friends began pairing up. I dated girls for two reasons: the first, a defiant attempt to fit in; the second, a desperate hope that somehow the real magic of the world (as opposed to the magic in the supernatural novels I was reading, which I always knew didn't exist) would touch me, and transform me into an insider with normal desires instead of the perpetual sissy outsider I – and everyone (I believed) – knew I was. As I got older, in the later

1970s, when the market was flooded with horror novels, and film-makers had decided that the market was hot enough to begin to flood it themselves, my friends and I would load ourselves into our parents' cars, and watch movies like *Halloween* and *Friday the 13th* at the mall cineplex, or at the local drive-in. It's hard to think about those movies without remembering what it felt like to be pressed up next to a guy with feathered hair and tight Levis I had a mind-blowing crush on, smelling his soap, Clearasil, and cheap aftershave as we watched slash after slash, especially if his girlfriend had decided to stay home because horror movies were "too gross." Talk about developing a gay horror sensibility. As a dear friend of mine, who grew up to be a great horror writer, recently reminded me, "It was good to be a big old sissyboy ter-rified of a butch monster." He was only half-joking.

At thirty-seven, I can afford to look back at the horror influences of my youth in the seventies with warm nostalgia, with a sense of a more innocent era caught in amber, and perhaps with some awareness that some of the messages contained in those influences were ultimately not all that desirable, especially for a young gay boy fumbling in the sticky darkness in search of a sexual identity. While my peers saw their own sexuality played out on the silver screen (albeit with lethal results), adolescents of my persuasion were left somewhat out in the cold.

The horror films of the seventies and eighties were morality fables of the first order. There were five basic "types," with occasional varia-tions – boys, "good" girls, scantily-clad "bad" girls, virginal and/or homely girls, and "neuter" boys. Boys wanted sex with girls. "Bad" girls wanted to give it to them. When they had sex, they would be killed, and there would be a lot of screaming by the girls as they checked out. The boys, however, never screamed. They shouted UUUUUHHH! or went to their deaths silent, and surprised.

Athough virginal and/or homely girls more often than not sur-vived, "neuter" boys, possessed of bland, sexless tag-along tendencies, were dispatched without a look back. I doubt that many gay boys watching those movies had any doubt at all where we fit into that par-adigm. We rolled with it. Everyone shrieked, but nobody was surprised when the neuter boy was skewered. It all seemed very normal; the way of the world.

The girls in those movies were the eye-candy, spilling juicily out of lacy bras, silky panties, and wet towels. Never the boys, whose pre-Nautilus 1970s bodies remained coyly draped under the sheets as they performed the death-fuck that would earn both they and the girl a pointy reckoning. Girls, or closeted gay boys, who wanted some beef-cake, were out of luck.

Except occasionally.

In 1982, on a pre-university catalogue modeling job, I happened to meet Richard Rebiere, the handsome blond French-Canadian actor who played Greg, the hapless star-crossed jock, in *Happy Birthday to Me*, released by Columbia Pictures the previous year. As part of a series of inventive murders suspected to be the handiwork of the character played by Melissa Sue Anderson of *Little House on the Prairie* fame (the camp possibilities in this film are virtually limitless), Greg is killed, pumped-up and sweaty, while lifting weights.

In a pre-Freddie Prinze Jr/Ryan Phillipe moment in the history of horror films, when handsome guys were not a requirement for casting directors, Richard Rebiere was a knockout.

I had seen that movie several times in 1981, but didn't think it appropriate, on that snowy afternoon at the photo studio in 1982, to explain to him why. Today, I would. So, if you're reading this, Rick, thanks for the memories.

By the time the horror genre was resurrected by director Wes Craven in 1996 with his neo-slasher, *Scream*, the pansexual vampire novels of Anne Rice had long been in the best bookstores in the world. Poppy Z. Brite, a brilliant writer whose elegant novels embraced queer themes with gusto, had become a superstar. Clive Barker, a writer whose extraordinary literary sensibilities have often led him to explore the monster as a beautiful, redeemable outsider, had unleashed the SM-inflected *Hellraiser* in 1987, and, in 1990, *Nightbreed*, a visually stunning and genuinely affecting film about an underground city of monsters who are portrayed as heroes who must battle the forces of "good" for their very survival. Whether it was Barker's intention or not, the film serves, in some ways, as a powerful gay allegory, dextrously illustrating how those society sees as "evil" can, in fact, be intrinsically gallant paladins, whereas the titular guardians of "decency" are often the truest monsters. All of these writers demonstrate how, under the deft pen of a gifted author, a queer sensibility or theme can be focused through the prism of contemporary horror fiction, yielding a result at once terrifying and illuminating.

In 1998, Michael Marano published *Dawn Song*, an award-winning first novel that, for me, stands as one of the most ethereally lovely, poignant, yet terrifying novels of the decade. The protagonist, Lawrence, is a fully-developed and evolved gay man whose homosexuality is an ensemble characteristic to his character, and he interacts with the other characters in the novel without explanation or apology.

The application of this aesthetic by authors such as Marano – and indeed many of the best horror writers working today, some of whom appear in this anthology – may be the foundation upon which a new genre of "gay horror fiction" rises. Unlike the novels of previous generations, gay men and lesbians can conceivably find themselves represented as part of the literary mosaic. It's not politically motivated – the motivation is a natural artistic, and realistic, inclusion based on the new arena in which to develop the well-crafted tale of terror; indeed, the genre may appear only briefly, like flashfire, leaving in its wake a freshly-scorched literary terrain from which newly-inclusive mainstream horror fiction may grow.

Goth culture – now more part of the mainstream than ever – continues to further blur the boundaries, and in many overlapping horror circles, being gay, or bisexual, is cool. Even desirable.

Even horror films, formerly the near-exclusive province of red-blooded heterosexual boys, now feature buff, shirtless *himbos* with washboard abs and tight butts, being rescued by empowered girl-power girls – all of whom still scream, but now sound like they *mean* it, and, more often than not, scream loudest just before they deliver the sort of roundhouse kick to the masked killer's groin that would do Jamie Lee Curtis proud.

In horror literature, vampire fiction continues to be a good barometer by which to measure the acceptability of gay imagery in popular horror fiction. Intrinsically sexual, invasive, and necessarily wet, vampire fiction has expanded the classic Victorian paradigm of evil, corrupt male versus virginal, delicate female to encompass a much wider net of possibilities. In 1996 and 1997, respectively, Thomas S. Roche and I edited two well-received gay-themed vampire anthologies, *Sons of Darkness* and *Brothers of the Night*. The stories we collected in these two books demonstrated how easily gay iconography could be incorporated into horror fiction.

The same can be said, I think, for horror fiction itself. It requires a certain amount of imagination to visualize a world of ghosts, vampires, werewolves, and other night-creatures. Imagination is a stock item for gay people, who have traditionally needed to literally imagine themselves into existence by visualizing a world in which they *could* exist. Concurrently, imagination fuels the ability to relax, and to let an author take you down a long, dimly-lit corridor into a macabre world. There is something operatic about horror fiction that continues, century after century, to strike a resonant note.

The difference today, of course, is that we have a social climate that has evolved beyond the female beauty / male beast strictures that kept horror fiction so mired in a type of sedentary, torpid homophobia perfectly portrayed in 1974, when a popular but dreadfully-written novel called *The Sentinel*, featured a now-hilarious encounter between the protagonist, Allison, a fashion model, and "a bull dyke and her lover," in which Allison delivers a scorching diatribe about ". . . sickness! Masturbation and lesbianism!" then portrays a "lisp[ing]" gay fashion show announcer with a "high-pitched voice," a few pages later.

In those days, we took our monsters where we could find them.

———

Even today, though, the question that I find myself answering even more than anything related to being a gay man, or a gay writer, is this: *Why horror? What is it that attracts you to horror? Isn't there enough horror in the world already? Do you like being afraid? Does violence turn you on?*

The stories in this book aren't an attempt to answer that question, which has more to do with taste, and perhaps a peculiarly suspicious, puritanical reluctance to acknowledge the legitimacy of a literature that isn't a serious moral duty to read.

Never mind that Charles Brockden Brown, the first professional author in the United States, admired by Sir Walter Scott, Keats, and Shelley, was arguably the father of American literature when he wrote *Wieland, or The Transformation*, a gothic horror novel, in 1798.

Never mind the notion that no marginally-aware gay man or lesbian at the beginning of the new millennium is going to have a moment's difficulty differentiating between vampires, werewolves, and ghouls, and the true horror of hate crimes, AIDS, or the abandonment by parents of their gay children. Yes, there's more than enough "horror" in the world – a passing glance at CNN confirms that.

As Robert McCammon, today sadly (for us) retired from horror fiction, but whose *oeuvre* has included some of the best horror fiction of the twentieth century, wrote, "Horror writers are simply trying to make sense out of the chaos."

And yes, there are real reasons to feel terror today. I don't care to be in fear for my life, or for the lives of people I love, but that has nothing to do with reading Stephen King, or Clive Barker, or Robert McCammon, or Douglas Clegg, or watching *Urban Legend* or *Deep Blue Sea*.

Horror fiction incites the same response in the mainstream reading public as erotica does. Both of these "outlaw" genres deal with strong emotion, violence, and a lack of control that is uniquely human. The imagery is often violent. Fear, like lust, is only truly acceptable to the mainstream reading public when it is confined within strict boundaries. In the case of lust, marriage and adultery are okay; rape fantasies and SM are suspect. For its part, horror places the reader squarely in the middle of conflict, invites visceral responses, and doesn't provide the "easy out" of an antiseptic, dispassionate, cerebral literary experience. Like those snobbish Victorian physicians who used to look down on surgeons as little better than butchers, so does a certain element of the literary establishment trillingly dismiss horror as vulgar entertainment for the unwashed.

Among gay men, athough we have provisions in our canon for a variety of sexual and emotional variations on "the norm," I have found, over and over, that open horror fans are a clandestine group, best known to each other. When we meet, there is often a joyous sharing and celebration of our joint histories. Sometimes, for gay "horror people," the path from adolescence to adulthood has that extra dimension of shared cultural flashpoints that our less-imaginative brethren may have missed completely. What we have read, seen, and loved, has made us what we are. This is true for everyone, but it is especially true for the lover of horror fiction.

Ultimately, though, it's about the stories.

We can place gay-themed horror in a myriad of different socio-political contexts, but if the stories don't frighten, disturb, or cause us to question reality as we know it, they're not horror stories. This is one genre, thank God, where it's impossible to hide behind political rhetoric or polemic. I commissioned or selected the stories in *Queer Fear* because they strike a nerve, like a cool hand touching your face in the dark when you know you're alone, and although they may be termed "gay" or "queer" in theme or content, they are horror stories, make no mistake.

The writers you will meet in this collection have, among them, won most of the premier genre literary awards – the Bram Stoker Award, the International Horror Guild Award, and the Lambda Literary Award. Some of them are screenwriters; some are mainstream horror novelists with film-options on their books; some are underground celebrities on the verge of breaking out. Some are making their debuts here in *Queer Fear*.

Lucky you – you can say you knew them when.

They come in a variety of genders and sexual orientations. All are gifted authors who have turned their considerable talents to the stories at hand, with the same aim. Like Mary Shelley, the need is merely to describe the spectre that haunts their midnight pillow.

Like horror itself, it's always personal.

———

There's a storm coming.

The sky outside is now black, and the wind is blowing hard against the windowpanes, making them rattle like old bones. The lamps are flickering, and I think we may lose power. I'd better wrap this up and find some candles to light the coming darkness.

Hold tight. I think all hell is about to break loose.

Toronto, Vancouver, Los Angeles, Toronto
September 1999 – July 2000

THE NIGHTGUARD

C. Mark Umland

AS ALWAYS, HE AWOKE WITH THE HORRIBLE sound of buzzing in his ears and the stench of dead flesh in his nostrils. Gerrard Brown, the old black guy in the next cell, told him it was the dissipation of his dreams, that was all, the scattering of subconscious images. His mind just working things out.

Dreams is solutions, was what Gerrard Brown told him.

But Fred was sure the buzzing was real, and he'd been after the Nightguard *forever* to do something about it. He hated approaching the Nightguard for anything – the man was not a man, he was a monster – but Fred was desperate.

What do you want me to do? the Nightguard had asked him.

I dunno. Spray.

You fuckin' spray.

It was so unflagging, the buzzing was, that Fred sometimes believed he was losing his mind. The dreams weren't working. His brain couldn't work it out. There was no solution. When he sat up in his cot the sound, the drone, dropped a notch, like it was playing some kind of goddamn game with him. Stand up. A minute distraction. Lie back down. A pulsating bombination, a churning in his ears, so steadfast, so relentless, he'd jump to his feet and do a search of the eight-by-ten cell for the thousandth time, probing the dark musty corners, searching for the source, a diminutive piece of carrion maybe, a dead mouse, anything.

A fly strip? he had asked the Nightguard.

The response was ugly laughter.

What's that stuff? You know. Deep Woods Off.

You'll sniff it.

I won't.

But finally the Nightguard had relented, said he'd take a look, but it would cost him. He normally took what he wanted for nothing anyway, but Fred nodded, said *fine . . . fine. . . .*

The big man had entered. He was a good ol' boy in a brown polyester uniform, with protruding ears stuck on a square, meaty head, and a cheek full of Redman. He did a perfunctory search of the cell, shrugged, undid his Sam Browne belt.

Texas has flies, boy.

The Nightguard came back twice that night.

And now Fred lay on his cot, on his side, knees drawn up in a quasi-fetal position. He was naked, save for a week old pair of skivvies. His hair was matted with blood over his right temple and his eye was swollen almost shut. His tongue protruded slightly from cracked lips. A long shadow of bruise ran from his armpit down to his hip. There was a slow trickle of blood leaking from his anus and he could vaguely hear the Nightguard washing his cock in the custodian's closet next door. Voices from other prisoners – people he never saw – echoed down the corridor outside his cell, people talking, whispering, moaning, swearing.

Time passed, and the pain subsided to an intense feeling of pressure. He found himself drifting, falling toward the torment of sleep. Sleep used to be a relief, a limbo of sorts where he lay suspended – caught between two worlds – where darkness was vast and complete and all sounds were dormant, if not dead. Back when he would lie next to Hank in the golden light of a new dawn and listen to his deep breathing, knowing that nothing could ever get to him, to them. Now sleep was a private hell. It was a world containing ripe, swollen bodies, and fat green flies burrowing eggs into dead flesh. A world of decay, of maggots blossoming from a fish-white belly in the heat of the afternoon sun.

Dreams were solutions?

He wondered.

He tried to stretch out on his cot and groaned. He had seized up, his muscles contracting, the wounds coming fully awake. Goddamn that Nightguard. He liked to hit when he came.

And still they buzzed. Out of sight. Hidden in the right angle of two concrete walls, tap-tapping against the rough coolness, sometimes ticking against the tiny barred window.

It was almost dawn. The mornings were difficult for him as he watched that tiny patch of outside – that little square of freedom – turn from black to pale blue to brightness. Shadows withdrew and went into hiding as the sun peaked from the horizon and came forth.

Almost dawn. That meant the Nightguard had a scant hour left in his shift.

And as if the thought had summoned the man, the Nightguard was there, peering through the bars, licking his lips. A fleeting look left and right and then in he came. Three times had not sated him. Fred moaned as he turned over and buried his face into the crook of his arm. His tongue found his own flesh. He licked the saltiness, then bit down as the guard moved over him. Fred clamped his eyes shut.

Please, he thought. *Please stop. Please, please, please*, and then he wished death upon the Nightguard.

Fred was sure that Gerrard Brown had been a young man during the civil war. Fred wondered how old a person had to be before it was no longer impolite to ask their age; surely it was safe to ask Gerrard Brown.

They never seemed to let Gerrard out of his cell. Each morning when Fred was led down the corridor to the showers, he saw him briefly, hunkered down there in the cell. Always only time for a fast nod. Gerrard was a tiny, wizened husk of a man with crevassed, cracked, blue-black skin and a wisp of white hair perched on top of a skull wrapped in aged leather. Fred wondered what a man of 300 had to do to wind up in stir.

"Ahhh," Gerrard Brown had rasped to him once, "how did I know the girl was only thirteen."

Fred had smiled in the darkness while the old man had cackled away.

"Hey, boy," Gerrard Brown now whispered to him from his own eight-by-ten hell. Both men were picking at their morning meals.

"Hey, Gerrard," Fred whispered back.

"That guard. He be gone now, boy."

"Yeah. Shift-change."

"I hear what he be doin' to ya."

Fred said nothing. His cheeks burned.

"Now, I's not the smartest man in the world, but I ain't no fool, yeah? I knows what it is some men like, how some like the ladies, an' others would rather be fuckin' the boys, an' well it sure as shit ain't no one's business but their own."

Fred wondered what he was getting at.

"You go up someone's ass, that be yo' business. Not mine. But I hear what the guard be doin' to ya, an' I'm thinkin' that ain't right. You like the boys, son, I know you do – in yo' sleep you keep callin' out fo' someone name' Hank, an' this feller strike me as someone who ain't just a drinkin' buddy – but rape is rape, know what I mean, boy? Rape is rape an' it ain't right."

Fred nodded in the gloom.

Gerrard paused, almost as if gathering his strength for what came next.

"You want to start thinkin' about leavin' this place," he said. "Get gone befo' real bad things happen. 'Cause in case you ain't noticed, boy, this ain't no ordinary lock-up. You in hell. You in the house of livin' death."

Before real bad things happen? Had he merely been experiencing the warm-up?

"Leave this place, Gerrard? Oh, I didn't know my stay was voluntary. Well, give me the key and I'll be on my way."

"Oh, I gives you a key, boy. Only, my key look like a screwdriver."

Fred didn't understand.

"You gonna unscrew all the hinges and remove the doors, Gerrard?"

Gerrard cackled. "Gonna unscrew somethin', boy. Gonna unscrew what that muh-fuh screwed up. Gonna give him what-fuckin' fo'. But, ya see, boy, he be gone, but he never leaves, you know. He finishes up with you and goes down that corridor when the sun comes up and he waits till it's time to come back. He waits, gives you a lot to think about. Lets ya stew. The way I sees it, boy, beyond that guard is an open door. 'Course, when you come to that door she sure won't be open. But I'll take care-a-that."

Fred said nothing.

"Here's what I sees. I sees a man busted, and I sees a man incarcerated, no judge, jury, no nothin', and ain't nobody knows where he be. This man just fuckin' disappear. They keep him twenty years, ain't no body gonna know. You ain't on no record, boy. You got busted by some bad cops, they take you to this bad place. You here fo' entertainment purposes, you know what I'm sayin'? You here to get corn-ho'ed. That you purpose in life right now. That be my purpose too but they don't want be corn-ho'in no ancient muh-fuh like myself. You understand, boy? You here fo'ever, less you do somethin' about it."

Fred thought about this.

"So," he said finally, "you think I can just leave?"

"I's very observant, boy. I watch. Cock-suckah guard come in, goes up yo' ass, he get crazy on you. He comes, he go out of his mind. *I listen.* Don't always hear him lock you back up. Yo' door sometimes unlocked all fuckin' night long."

"But he goes to the front. Sits at the desk there. And what about the other guards?"

"Don't you be worryin' about other guards. Long as he's on the floor, they be gone. But the Nightguard, he don't go back to his desk directly. No, first he go washin' up. Scrubs the shit off his dick. Then he go up front."

"And then –"

"Ain't no *and then*, boy. 'Cause I take care-a-that. Well, you take care-a-that with somethin' I gives ya"

"And what do you give me?"

"A key."

"A key? The one that uncannily resembles a screwdriver?"

Gerrard laughed. "You talk good, boy. Yeah, you got the idea."

Noise came from down the corridor and the two prisoners hushed up. Fred stared at his food, picked at it, tasted it. Dreadful as always. He ate it anyway and watched three pencil-thin sunbeams angle in through the window. Down the hall somewhere a chant rose up, an obscene plainsong, a string of motherfucker motherfucker motherfucker motherfucker . . . and behind him flies – those goddamned flies – buzzed furiously.

———

There was no guard that night, and the night following, which made things easier for Fred, but light-years from better. He still had the buzzing to contend with as well as those horrible dreams. Dreams of death.

This night, Hank was there, in the dream, strutting about his subconscious, all big-cocked and confident, big greasy gun in hand, some bad-ass strut suddenly appearing in walk.

This was the dream of the day. *That* day. The desert had breathed on *that* day; it was like standing on the skin of a giant. The ground seemed to move, pulsate beneath their feet, but it was the gun really, that big ol' .44, obscenely huge, the motherfucking John Holmes of pistols, that shook the ground, made everything move as it went *boom* . . . *boom* . . . and Fred gaped at that hand cannon and he screamed at Hank to make it stop *booming*, but might as well ask a man to stop *coming* . . . and then the other man, *The Mechanic* they called him, because he was a drug-dealing auto mechanic – but really he was a fucking narc – was falling into the dirt, broken and spent, his head half off.

Hank! What have you done!

Maniacal laughter. Hank is suddenly not of his mind, if he ever was. Hank has reprised his role, one he's performed many times, that of god (a role that Fred too has played rather successfully from time to time), but now Hank is doing a terrible job. His mind is collapsing like a house of cards.

Kill the civvies, Hank, murder till you're blue, but what's the number one rule?

Hank! You can't kill cops!

Why not? What makes them so fucking special?

Hank, Fred says, asking the obvious. *Is he dead?*

Hank answers in the affirmative. The Mechanic indeed is dead. And then some.

Leave him for the flies, Hank says.

The flies. They'll make short work out of any piece of dead flesh out here.

And then The Mechanic's backup team arrives – two unmarked, three cherry-tops, and Hank's weapon booms away some more, and Fred finds his own weapon, a modest little .38, and he blasts away. He tags at least one of them – the spray of blood from the back of the uniform's head is evident – and the man drops undramatically and curls up, dead.

We can't kill cops! Fred screams, still blasting away, maybe catching another one in the skull, not sure.

Fred woke from his dream, the sound of gunshots still resonating. He wondered for the thousandth time what had happened next. It was like someone had punched him in the back of the head. Maybe Mike Tyson, because he'd been out for a long goddamn time and he'd come to not in a hospital but in jail. Goddamn *jail!* Which made what Gerrard was saying make some sense. Skip the hospital, skip court and bail-hearings and procedures and being tried by his peers, twelve of them all good and true, and *then* skip the sentencing. Fuck, man! Do not pass go, do not blah blah blah. . . .

So the cops, all fresh off the set of *Deliverance,* had captured him, probably killed Hank, and conspired together. Possibly they talked about how the criminal-justice-system treated prisoners like vacationers at a Club Med, and how this killer – no, this *cop* killer – was not going to go away to some country-club prison. They possibly all knew of a place that didn't exist, but nevertheless stood, had been abandoned decades earlier, but was still used. Used for their special cases. *Let's send him to the place,* they might have said, nodding and winking at each other. Official report: drug trafficker killed in a fire-fight with police. *One* drug trafficker. Fred bet his arrest-warrant went missing. Case closed.

This man just fuckin' disappear.

Oh Christ, Gerrard, I think you're right. I think things are going to get real, real bad.

━━━━━━━

They had brought him in at night, during a wind storm. He remembered tasting heat and grit, the smell cloying, acrid, sulphurous. And he remembered a cluster of people carrying him, their faces swathed in shadow, his head swathed in bandages. He tried to speak but somehow they prevented him from doing so. Then everything faded . . .

. . . and returned, seemingly in a blink, but it was a day or days later. The windstorm was over. His bandages were gone.

The day had just ended according to the fading light outside his tiny cell window, and that was the first time the Nightguard had come for him. Taken from his cell, he had been led down a dim gray corridor to shower facilities where he was ordered to strip. But instead of a shower he was pushed against the wall and his legs were forced open.

"Cavity check," the Nightguard said while inserting three fingers, *sans* latex glove, into Fred's anus. With his other hand he pulled out his cock, then removed his fingers from the prisoner's asshole and plunged his huge organ ruthlessly in. He rammed it deep, tearing delicate tissue along the way. The pain surprised Fred, caught him off guard. It was like he was being wrenched in two. His face mashed against cold, wet concrete and his scream came out, a great guttural whooping of air. It caught in his throat and he tried to breathe. Couldn't. His vision faded. He thought he might pass out, then figured he wasn't that lucky.

Later, back in his cell, the Nightguard reamed him again, and two more times even later, just before midnight. It went on and on, that first twenty-four hours, and by the end of that time a thick layer of semi-congealed blood had formed around his anus. The pain was obscene, an abomination, and the rent flesh didn't scab over for several weeks. The Nightguard never gave it a chance.

Soon after his incarceration, Fred believed he was alone in the prison. Stray voices echoed up and down the corridor but he began to think that the voices were in his head. The buzzing had started almost immediately, which he was sure was real, but he wasn't sure about all those voices, fragments of sentences, bits of words floating aimlessly, disembodied, soulless. A cough of dry desert wind had more soul. One night, desperate for human contact, he had called out, sending his voice into darkness.

And that was how he had met Gerrard. The old man's rasping voice, cigarette-scarred and hoarse, had come back to him, announcing that indeed he had company.

"Where are the other prisoners?" Fred had asked him.

"Got me, boy. Got me. Got you too, boy, from the looks of it," and

27

the old man laughed, a laugh that became, in this house of horrors, the only sound of comfort.

"How long you in for?" Fred asked him.

"Oh, I's a lifer, boy."

Though he had never received a sentence, Fred believed he was probably a lifer as well.

———————

The next night, as thoughts of what Gerrard had said (*best you be get gone*) moved painfully through his mind, the Nightguard returned. He stood just outside Fred's cell, peering through the bars, eyeing the prisoner like he was some kind of exhibit. Fred didn't meet his gaze, but only sat on his cot, eyes at his feet. Despite the coolness, sweat trickled from his armpits and from his brow, over his swollen face, down his neck, past his chest and wounded ribs.

Grinning, the Nightguard's right hand drifted up to the front of his shirt and his fingers fumbled around for the key that hung there on a chain. Fred didn't have to watch to know what he was doing. It was odd, Fred thought. So old-fashioned, this place. Literally under lock and key, not like more modern facilities he'd stayed in, where everything was opened with the push of a button, everything monitored by roving cameras. This jail-house might have been the last of its kind, an anachronism deemed obsolete years ago. From what he could gather, the building was rectangular. The structure housed what seemed to be twenty or thirty cells, each one segregated by concrete walls on either side. Only the front was open, good old-fashioned bars and a lock that looked like any church key would fit. This undoubtedly was not the case. Fred was sure many prisoners before him had taken to the locks with twists of this and that; a twig pried from the sole of a boot, a cue-tip, bobby-pins smuggled in by relatives, an undercooked stick of spaghetti swiped from their supper plate – all to no avail.

The Nightguard slid his key into the lock and Fred could hear the bolt slide back into its casing. The hinges whined softly as the door swung open. Fred continued to stare at his feet but he listened to the approaching footsteps with mounting fear – no, not fear, it went well beyond that, into that shadowy netherworld known as horror. Sweat washed down his face as though he had just come from running a brisk ten clicks. His wounds ached. His heart pounded. Flies buzzed crazily all around him.

Fred listened to the footsteps stop before him. A hand brushed his chin, then took hold firmly, and his head was forced up.

The Nightguard leered. "Time to move to another recess, boy."

Fred relaxed for a brief moment, thinking the Nightguard meant he was going to move him to another cell. His confusion was fleeting, however, and understanding dawned.

"Please —" he began.

"Open up and say *ahhh*."

He managed to shake his head despite the Nightguard's firm grasp. "No," he said, and the fist came from the man's right; a short, quick jab into Fred's left cheekbone. The prisoner would have fallen back but the guard held him up, hit him again, then one more time, the last punch opening up the skin beneath the left eye. Blood welled, pooling with surface tension before sliding down the side of his face.

"Right, then," the Nightguard hissed, and undid his pants with one hand, his grip remaining fast on Fred's chin. Blood trickled over the Nightguard's fingers.

"Please," Fred gasped. "Please . . . don't . . . please stop —"

"One more word," the Nightguard intoned. "That's all. One more. Then I'll rip your motherfucking heart right out from your skinny little motherfucking chest!" He spat the last word, sending spittle into Fred's bleeding face. "Say ahhh, boy. Say it, or I'll motherfucking *kill* you."

Fred clamped his eyes shut, swallowed, and opened his mouth.

But instead of saying ahhh he said: "I bite."

The Nightguard's eyes narrowed. Mouth became a flat line.

"You're fuckin' *dead*, boy."

The rape had been fast and furious, the Nightguard holding nothing back, and this fresh reaming sent Fred into a level of pain that was nearly blinding. But he wasn't fuckin' dead, and that was something. It just wasn't much.

Afterwards, the Nightguard disappeared through the cell door, his boots shuffling off down the corridor, fading quickly. Then a hollow sound of a different door opening and closing.

The custodian's closet.

Fred lay, listening to his heart pound, his breath coming in and out in great gasps. Spots danced before him. The pain was exquisite. The pain had transcended everything and become something of an art form.

Then there was another noise. Metal on cement. Very quiet, a diminutive scraping, followed by Gerrard Brown rasping something to him, something about —

a key.

A key.

No, Gerrard, he thought, while standing up. I can't. He's much too strong, I'm much too weak, how could I possibly . . . how could I? He limped to the door, pushed it, watched completely unamazed as it swung open.

Getcher cloze on, boy!

He limped back, pulled on grey pants and a short sleeved shirt, and limped back to the door. Limped through it.

Can't do it, Gerrard. He'll snap me in two like a breadstick.

He turned right, looked down.

The screwdriver lay dormant in front of Gerrard's cell.

Pick it up, boy! Pick up the goddamn key!

Can't do it, Gerrard. Nope. Chicken shit, that's me.

Leaning over was a whole new adventure in itself, and he could feel fresh blood flowing down his inner thighs in a sheet.

Won't do it, Gerrard, but the screwdriver was now in his hand. He looked over at Gerrard, just a shadow in his cell, just eyes and a gleam of sweat.

Now what? he heard himself ask.

The closet, boy. Sneak up behind him. Stick it in his ear. Then what you do is get the key around his neck, come back here, unlock my door, we leave together.

Stick it in his ear?

As far as she goes, boy. To the hilt.

I don't know if I can do that, Gerrard, and he turned away from his friend's cell and moved down the corridor.

This had been the way he had come in the first time, he realized, but had not been down since. The showers were the opposite way. This corridor only led to the custodian's closet, the front desk, and the exit. Fred figured all prisoners walked this corridor only once, and it was always in the wrong direction.

The voices weren't any louder down here, but they weren't any further away, either. Wisps of noise, words – angry or desperate – faded in and out. Auditory vapor eddying wistfully by the ceiling, drifting and rolling with great slowness like cigarette smoke.

Where are you people? he thought. What he hadn't noticed before was the anguish that accompanied those words, those fragments of sentences. Complete and utter hopelessness. It was the worst thing he had ever heard.

The custodian's closet on his left. The door cracked a fragment.

Fred used the business end of the screwdriver to push open the door. He moved it barely, five, six inches, no more. He knew at some point the bottom of the door would scrape the cement. Scraping the cement at this stage of the game would be very serious. He'd wind up with those voices.

Fred peered in. The Nightguard's back, big and sweaty, the uniform filthy. Shoulders hunched, torso a giant shifting mass as he scrubbed at the sink.

Fred turned himself sideways. He slipped into the closet, or at least halfway, before stopping. He took a great, silent breath. He didn't know if he could do this, yet he had no choice. The feeling inherent within him wanted to push him back, make him flee.

It was the blood dripping down the insides of his thighs that kept him going.

In the dimness, the Nightguard started to shed his clothing. Slowly he peeled off his uniform, dropping the filthy garments to the cement. Shirt first, then pants. No underwear for the Nightguard.

Fred nearly dropped the screwdriver.

The feeling to flee surged up tenfold

. . . to the hilt, boy . . .

but he held his ground, both repulsed and amazed at what he saw.

The Nightguard's back was a mass of scales, big as saucers, the color of old fingernails. When he moved his shoulder blades the flesh on his back rippled and undulated, the scales scraping and clicking against each other.

More amazement as he watched the Nightguard's wings unfold. They spread out, a small span, maybe five feet. Ugly, drooping buzzard wings.

Fred made a noise. He didn't know from what part of his body, but he was sure it was a horrified gasp, a choke maybe, a noisy swallow to keep the vomit down.

The Nightguard's movements ceased for a moment. The wings drew back. After a long moment they relaxed, spread out again.

Voices. Loud in here, or louder anyway, very clear, yet distant. Someone calling very loudly from afar. Prisoners? What, were they torturing prisoners?

Prisoners. Not likely. Fred had fleetingly come to terms with that. There were no prisoners, just as sure as this was no prison.

And then, standing there, a skinny little killer, armed with nothing but a screwdriver, Fred's eyes happened to drift down, past the undulating scales, down to the massive gray buttocks.

They were difficult to make out at first, but it wasn't the absence of light that made it so. It was pure denial. It was a refusal to see what he was seeing, to disbelieve what was right before his eyes. Attribute it to fatigue, to pain, to sensory deprivation, to good old down-home madness. Ignore it, just do what had to be done with the screwdriver, get the hell out.

But no. Hallucination or not, this was something quite impossible to ignore.

Human faces, a small, sporadic group of them, protruded from the Nightguard's buttocks. They were newborn tiny, but with grownup features; sharp cheekbones, cleft chins, high foreheads that met the slight rise of receding hairlines. The faces were smooth, like porcelain dolls, like faces pushing through a bedsheet.

Fred was paralyzed. He gaped at the scene, at the little rolling eyes and lolling tongues. One looked directly at him and its mouth stretched impossibly wide, its little white tongue flapping.

Voices. Voices all around.

It took him a second to realize that they were calling to him. No. Not to him. To anyone. Anyone that could hear, anyone that could help.

And then Fred broke his paralysis.

He dropped the screwdriver.

It fell to the concrete, landing handle-first, and Fred did what he thought was the impossible and darted down, catching the screwdriver on the first bounce. Now he was crouching and looking up.

The Nightguard stood over him, monolithic in size. Even his cock seemed bigger; a great, thick, grey snake that hung and twitched by his knees, and for a second Fred was sure he saw a forked snake-tongue flick out from the urethra. The Nightguard then turned and in a giant half-step moved to the door, pushing it all the way open.

My God, Fred thought, *he can't see me!*

But then a hand fell onto his head and he was hauled up to his feet, and then off his feet, by his hair. He stared into the Nightguard's face. More changes. The Nightguard's eyes had shrunk, disappeared further into his head. His hair was wet and slick, ears sharpened little nubs. And his mouth had been replaced with a horrible, rotting beak.

No time to think. The faces were screaming, the air was cloying and filthy, the Nightguard's breath in his face like raw, rotting flesh.

The Nightguard clicked its beak. Fred heard scales gnashing together. Wings flapped as a hand closed tightly around his throat.

No time to think.

. . . to the hilt, boy . . .

Knowing there was only one chance at this, Fred brought an arm around to the side of the Nightguard's head and swung hard, aiming at one of those little pointy bird ears.

A chorus of screams . . . a choir from hell . . . and Fred felt himself tumbling to the floor.

Going back up the corridor, away from the exit, was the most difficult thing Fred ever had to do in his life. That, and removing the key from around the Nightguard's neck. The creature had collapsed hard, snapping one of its wings as it hit, and then it had been still. The faces had continued howling, however, and it was enough to push anyone over the edge. But less than half a minute later, they had silenced.

The screwdriver had gone in easily and with no resistance, the metal gliding through what had sounded like brittle cartilage. Fred figured that the creature's weakness, its Achilles' heel, were the ears, and somehow Gerrard had learned this. He'd probably been studying the Nightguard for decades. Perhaps Gerrard had had confrontations with it and had noticed it wince or shy away if he got too close to its ears.

He arrived back at Gerrard's cell.

"You got it, boy?" the old man gasped.

Fred nodded. He was numb.

"Everything all right then?"

Fred shook his head and stuck the Nightguard's key into the lock. The bolt slid open and without saying a word he turned and went back down the corridor, not willing to wait for Gerrard, not willing to wait for anybody or anything. He slipped past the custodian's closet, moving quickly away from it all, from his cell, from the buzzing, from the lifeless form of the Nightguard, toward the front door, toward freedom.

Potter County Hospital, Amarillo, Texas.

There had been a change. Nothing much, the twitch of a facial muscle, or perhaps he had shifted his body slightly.

The young doctor looked down at her patient. White male, comatose since the third of June. That made it nearly four weeks. One month, with a respirator to ensure a constant air supply. It had been touch and go for a while, and they'd gone into his skull to ease the pressure. And now, here he was, making improvements.

The young doctor moved to a large window to the right of the bed. The day beyond was warm and sunny. It was only mid-morning – not unbearably hot just yet. She angled the blinds over the window so that only thin beams could get in. She turned and strode purposefully to the door.

She paused now, very aware of the dangerous territory upon which she was about to tread. Very dangerous indeed . . . and all because her patient, the young man with the head-wound, was coming out of his coma.

Normally a patient's improvements would be considered good

QUEER FEAR

news, but not in this case. The patient, after all, one Fred Mulloch of Nowhere, Texas, was a man who, along with an accomplice, had brutally slain four police officers during an undercover operation. Apparently during the melee the accomplice, Hank Turreau, had backed away from the police, and accidentally shot his partner, Fred, in the back of the head. Fred had dropped and Hank Turreau had gone down with over twelve bullets in him.

But it didn't stop there. Evidently there was plenty more to the two career criminals than just the one incident. They had dealt heavily in narcotics – coke and H – selling to kids, giving away free samples of crack in schoolyards and playgrounds. Also, both were wanted in the shooting deaths of three teenagers in a deal gone bad, and in the accidental execution of a pregnant woman in an elevator. They'd thought she was someone she wasn't.

Class acts, these two.

The young doctor regarded the man. Most of his head was swathed in bandages, and gauze covered his left eye socket. The eye had been the bullet's point of exit after its entry into the head and subsequent passage through the skull. It had been a fluke, a freak happenstance that he had survived. The young doctor had silently wished death upon him. This contradicted her primary function of seeing that all ailing and wounded human beings that came into her care received the best treatment possible, to be sure, but she didn't consider this thing a human being. A human being wouldn't take the life of a pregnant woman in an elevator – a pregnant woman just coming from an ultra-sound appointment, the sex of her baby newly discovered, her life a profound joy since conceiving, her family so happy for her, her stepsister, Jane, who was a young doctor at Potter County Hospital, the happiest of all.

The young doctor took a slow, deep, shaking breath, and casually glanced up and down the hallway. If she was to do this it would have to be now.

She stepped back in, then took one more fast glance outside. Many people were about but no one paid her any mind.

Now she closed the door and hurried over to the bed.

First the young doctor disabled the alarm set up to the respirator. In normal circumstances, if a respirator fails, the alarm sends a warning to the staff.

In normal circumstances.

The doctor then surveyed the respirator, hesitating momentarily before disconnecting the life-giving air supply.

"There," she whispered to the patient. "There you are . . . enjoy hell," and she moved back to the window, reopened the blinds, leaned against the wall, and watched.

34

Behind her, outside, a fly buzzed against the glass.

———

The door swung wide open. Before him was a desertscape of infinite beauty. The sky was a solidified shard of red and purple and it went on for numerous eternities. In the distance, beyond generous scatterings of cactus and pale brown sagebrush and rock bleached as white as old bone, where the horizon kissed the strikingly bleak terrain, a dark shape moved. It drifted and circled, riding the winds, exploiting the elements. It came closer, its wings unmoving. Fred watched the eagle and thought of a word. No, not a word, but a concept. He thought: *freedom*. Freedom. It was a stirring thing, inducing old moldering feelings. Freedom. A hallucinogen for the soul.

A hand fell on his shoulder.

Fred's body became a live wire as he jerked violently and spun around, thinking: *the Nightguard!* but it was only Gerrard, smiling easily up at him.

"Jesus, Gerrard, you had me —"

Gerrard was wearing the Nightguard's uniform. It was too big for him, hanging foolishly from his limbs, as though he were a little boy in his father's closet playing grownup. He still smiled up at Fred, and his hand remained firmly on Fred's shoulder.

"You done good, boy," Gerrard Brown rasped. "Done real fine. Can't tell ya how long I waited. Long goddamn time."

"Gerrard, we need to go!" The need to run, to flee into the desert, was terrific, and he tried to take a step back, but Gerrard's hand held fast, the old mans fingers practically hooked under a bone in Fred's shoulder.

"Ouch! Chrissakes, Gerrard!"

"Long goddamn time," Gerrard repeated. "*Ages*. Understand? Not years, boy, but *ages*. Lifetimes and lifetimes I've been in that cell. Waitin' and fuckin' waitin'. Ever since that guard tricked me, got me in there. But now, thanks ta you, freedom is mine again." That easy smile he had given Fred had changed, shifted somehow. It could still be construed as a smile, but it was far from easy.

"Gerrard?" Fred managed. Behind him, the desert beckoned, displaying its pale colors proudly. It showed off its expanse, showed him just how big freedom was.

"But y'know, boy," Gerrard continued. "Y'know what else is mine now?"

Fred said nothing. He was suddenly afraid he knew.

Gerrard shook him slightly with that grip. "You, boy. You mine, now."

Fred started to scream then. He screamed for his newfound freedom so ruthlessly snatched away from him. He screamed for Hank, wherever he was. But mainly, he screamed for himself.

Smiling, the new Nightguard took him back inside.

Inside the hospital room: flatline.

PIERCING MEN

Douglas Clegg

I

"SEX IS AGGRESSION," SAM SAID.

"Aggression is aggression," Danny laughed. "Once I got so mad, I put my fist through a window. When I was a kid. Maybe I was fourteen. Fifteen."

"Yeah? That must've hurt."

"Weirdly enough, it didn't."

"Once, I got so mad," Sam said, "I took it out on someone I really cared for."

They both laughed about this.

"Once I got so mad, I *wanted* to," and then they laughed louder.

"You like to fish?"

"How'd you know?"

"The fishing poles." Sam nodded toward the open garage door. "In the garage. Dead giveaway."

"You like to swim?" Danny laughed. "The pool. In your backyard. Dead giveaway."

"Sometimes, I swim buck naked back there," Sam grinned. But it was an innocent comment.

It had rained for six days in a row, and southern California had that feeling of quicksand by the time the sun had come out. Then, dryness like a pagan bonfire, the barbecue was lit and spitting with steaks and burgers, and the wives had already noticed the house down the block where no one seemed to live any more, and which Bonnie, who dabbled in real estate, could not sell for the life of her.

He and Danny were standing on the front lawn in Summerland, and Danny's wife Faith was over by the oleanders with Sam's wife Bonnie, pointing out where they'd found the dead cat after the coyotes had gotten to it. Faith had a look on her face that was not her best – she hadn't really liked moving out to Summerland from the city, and now they had to contend with coyotes and the murder of small animals. Still, Danny shot her a smile, and she acknowledged it with a slight, quirky one of her own, ice goddess that she was.

It was mid-summer, the sky hazy with an approaching sunset; the house was older than the one that Danny and Faith had just moved from, and, as Sam, their new neighbor, had told them the week before,

"It's gonna take a lot of digging to get the crap out of that place." Sam was a fast friend, Danny noticed. First, he'd swung by in the minivan with his four-year-old son in the backseat, and a hello that had lingered into a "Let's all go for pizza, the wife'll love meeting you," to bringing over a local gardener to work on the rose garden that had gone to hell under the previous owner's neglect. Then, a beer or two out back by the plum tree, and "A word to the wise, don't get to know the Bartlett's down the street," for reasons that weren't entirely obvious to Danny. But it was good to know another soul in Summerland — it was small-town life, which meant Danny and Faith were not yet part of it, but still Outsiders waiting for acceptance.

Back to the roses, another day, Sam had advice. "You've got to put bags over them, and water them with a hose, right into the ground, at dawn, and then at sunset. Don't water mid-day, and never spray. Get the hose right into them," Sam had said, demonstrating by squatting down and pressing the garden hose almost into the dirt. For the barest second, in the harsh sun, Danny had thought that the hose looked like a snake — and he had a fear of snakes, especially in Summerland where there were legends of rattlers.

The conversation that day had gone from gardening to football to another beer in the backyard to Sam commenting on the master bedroom when Danny gave him the tour, "I can already see where Jeff — the guy who lived here before — had done things to this place to ruin it. But the walls are sound," and then, within two and a half weeks of the move-in, Danny and Faith were having Sam and Bonnie over for steaks. That was how great friends were begun, Faith told him, in places where the sidewalks rolled up at seven, and where the only town drunk was married to the only town tramp.

And Sam — standing in the cloudy smoke of the barbecue, watching the wives talk by the oleanders — somehow had worked the conversation from where in town you could get the best steaks to how, when he'd been twenty, he'd decided sex was a sport, and then he found out that it was fertility later on, only now, in his mid-thirties, it was pure aggression.

"What about you?" Sam asked. "I see you and Faith. You're both young. Good shape. Both of you pretty and smart and on your ways up in the world. Has it died yet?"

Danny took a breath and nearly smiled. He glanced over at his wife who seemed to notice him, and nod, as if giving permission from nearly an acre away to reveal some intimacy. He chuckled. "Sam, that's private."

"Oh, come on," Sam said. "We're all men here. I've been married thirteen years. You've been married, what, five?"

"Six."

"All right, six. I know what happens by the sixth year, Danny. The friendship develops and then, zip-zap, out the window with sex. It has to transform right about then, or the marriage never lasts."

"If you say so," Danny said, turning one of the steaks over. Then he laughed again. "You're joking. You joker."

Sam shrugged. "You meet Faith in college?"

"Right after grad school. Long story."

"Love at first sight."

"Pretty much."

"You know," Sam said. "I noticed something about you, that first day. Not when I drove up here to say hi. Before that. You and Faith came out to look at the house. She wore jeans and a sweater and pearls. You wore khakis and a striped shirt."

Danny squinted. "What?"

"A white shirt with red stripes. I remember details," Sam said. "That steak looks done." He went to the cart by the barbecue to get the long china plate. "Let's start piling 'em on."

2

After supper, they had a really good dessert wine and some boysen-berries in small saucers – Bonnie had picked them from the bushes out by the field at the back of the neighborhood.

"These are delicious," Faith said, her lips berry-stained. "I don't think I've had them before." Faith always seemed to say the right thing at the right time. She had a knack – Danny had noticed this right away with her. She was direct, she didn't flinch, and she knew how to com-pliment. These were all the things he first noticed about her, and they were the things she still had. She was going to make a friend in Bonnie, he thought. That would be good.

Bonnie laughed. "Gordie calls them poison berries."

"You should've brought him."

"Please, we like to have at least one night a week with just the two of us."

"You should have kids," Sam said, too bluntly. He was sitting there, his shirt open, and Danny wished he would just button the damn thing, but he was too polite to say so. Sam was in good shape, but Danny did-n't like to eat berries and see so much flesh from a neighbor. He thought of making a joke of this – maybe it was the wine that made it seem funnier, the wine on top of the beer – but decided it was best to just keep quiet.

A momentary silence. They were in the courtyard, the summer sun still not gone, sitting on the cheap lawn furniture that Danny had managed to grab for this, their first barbeque together.

"Problem is," Faith said with a straight face, "I'm barren."

Then she laughed, and they all did, and it was a funny, funny shock of a joke.

Then, Danny said, "I think we'll wait until we're thirty for kids."

"That's smart," Bonnie said, pointing her finger at him. She glanced at Sam, still pointing at Danny. "This is one smart cookie." She was a bit drunk. They had gone through three bottles before the dessert wine. Bonnie had hair like a nest, all short and wispy and crackling and wrapped around her face, the baby bird.

Danny had his arm around Faith, who nestled further against him, spilling wine and dropping berries. "I want to have three kids," Faith said. "Two girls and a boy."

"That's too many," Bonnie waggled her finger. "Go for one boy and one girl. The perfect family."

"We once had a daughter," Sam added, and then said nothing more. Danny, feeling woozy from the sweet wine, felt as if music had suddenly stopped, and before he knew it, the barbecue was over, and he was in bed with Faith and it was two AM and he woke up needing a glass of water. He went to the kitchen, and looked out the window, over at the house across the street. His head pounded.

You can't drink anymore, he thought. Gettin' old.

He glanced two houses up the street, and saw Sam and Bonnie's stucco house. Their boy's tricycle was in the driveway under the garage light. For a moment, he thought he saw Sam standing there, the red circle of a cigarette in the shadows. Just standing there.

He went and fell asleep on the sofa in the living room.

3

"Sex is aggression," Danny laughed, as they ran.

He and Sam had taken to jogging on Sunday mornings in early September. Sam wanted to keep his weight down, and Danny just liked jogging. Danny had always jogged, since he'd run cross-country in high school, and now, at twenty-eight, he was still in good shape. This made him happy and comfortable, because he'd been an uncoordinated kid and had always been a little plump and too attracted to food. To attract people, he wanted to look good, and he liked the feeling of running rather than team sports. So, here he was, late twenties, still jogging, up and down the sloping hillsides of suburbia wasteland. Sam was older and couldn't keep up – he had just enough weight around his middle to qualify as a love handle, but not enough to ruin his looks; Danny slowed down to keep pace, but the sun threatened along the edge of the distant mountains. Once the sun was out, there could be no more running, because the sun brought the desert down like God's fury.

When they rounded the curve on Baseline, Sam said, "All sex is aggression. I notice that you lost your edge."

"My edge," Danny chuckled. He slowed to a walk when they reached the edge of the orange grove. He stepped off the pavement, and onto the dirt. It felt good beneath his sneakers. They always ended their run with a cool down walk through the town's groves. The orange groves were the only wilderness left in Summerland – once farmed, they now grew wild. The town maintained them to some extent, harvesting oranges for local markets, but they were not tended as they once were. They provided shade and privacy to wanderers, and free fruit to anyone who wished to break the local law and grab it.

"Yeah, your edge. Most guys lose it early," Sam added later, after he'd plucked an orange ("That's illegal," Danny had chided gently). "Not all. Just most."

They shared an orange, Sam hogging the larger segments, and Danny didn't like the way Sam had held the orange sliver up to his lips like he was a baby, but then he felt that heat, and the look that Sam gave him – as he could see into him, as if he knew his secrets – and Danny took the bite of orange in his mouth, the juice biting him.

Danny felt a gentle shiver as he stood there, among the orange trees, and smelled his own sweat from the run, and knew better than to stand there with this man who had created such intimacy so quickly, just as the man had in Los Angeles, the one who brought the overnight package, causing that shivering, that cool darkness within him, that overwhelming feeling of helplessness that Danny only rarely felt in the presence of other men.

When Sam took his hand, Danny felt it was okay, but he couldn't look at Sam. "You're sure?" Sam said, leading him back into a bamboo thicket that grew beneath a clutch of palm trees at the center path between the groves. The thicket was like a child's fort, it could not have been designed better by nature, and who would look there, for two men as they pursued their secrets?

"I guess I've been expecting this."

"It's in the eyes. We always know each other."

"Don't talk," Danny said. And it had begun. "Don't say anything. Don't."

4

The second time, again in the groves, but this time at night, Sam said, at the height of Danny's arousal, "Let go, let it all go, let it out, whatever you have, open it, let it go, release it."

And Danny felt a wildness come out, like the fist through the window, and it was as if his movements in the throes of this uncontrolled heat were part of some primitive rhythm he had never before known.

5

It wasn't until after Christmas that Sam mentioned the college kid. "He's beautiful."

They took a drive into the hills overlooking Summerland, and Sam's son was strapped into the backseat. Danny kept glancing at Gordie, but Sam laughed. "Oh, Gordie isn't going to understand this."

"It doesn't seem right."

"Gordie," Sam said, looking in the rearview mirror. "Whatcha up to back there, peanut?"

"I see birds, Daddy," Gordie said, pointing a wobbly finger out the side window.

"He sees birds," Sam grinned, sweetly. "Okay, so here's the thing. I think the three of us."

"Three?"

"Yeah, you, me, and Joe."

"The college kid?"

"Well, he's nearly twenty-one. He's hardly a kid. Not much younger than you."

"I sort of thought what we have is special."

"Crap. Don't start moralizing. Jesus. What we have is special. This is about sport, baby. We talked about this."

"Not like this. Not like it was real."

"All right, in the throes of fucking," Sam was decent enough to say this one word in a low voice, "you said that you could imagine another guy with us. Wouldn't it be great?"

"It was a fantasy," Danny said. Then, he began feeling ugly. "Pull over."

"What?"

"I want to go for a walk. I'll walk back into town."

"No, you won't," Sam said. But still, he pulled the van to the side of the road. Once the car was parked, he turned in his seat to face Danny. "Here's what you are going to do, Danny. You're going to go invite this young man to your house when Faith goes to her mother's on Sunday, and you and I are going to have a party with him. Just like you fantasized."

"That's ridiculous. You can't tell me what to do, Sam. That's complete and utter bullshit."

Sam turned to glance back at Gordie. "Gordie, cover your ears, please."

"Okay," Gordie said, gleefully pressing his hands against his ear-lobes.

Sam reached across the seat, pressing his hand against Danny's stomach. It created an uncomfortable warmth, and Danny tried pulling away. He wanted to reach for his shoulder harness and seat belt, but didn't. "You will do this, Danny. For us."

"Get your hand off me."

"How's Faith going to feel when she finds out about us?"

"You *sad* –" Danny couldn't finish.

Somewhere in his mind, he had already begun to accept this. Accept that Sam somehow dominated him.

Sometime between that first time among the oranges, to the motel out by the freeway, to the Saturday up on the high desert, to the night in the swimming pool in Sam's backyard, practically under Bonnie's nose, somewhere between knowing who he was on the inside and being unwilling to let it out into daylight, Danny had already accepted Sam's complete ownership.

His protestations were merely for show.

Finally, Danny said, "All right."

Only later, when Danny had gotten a room over in San Bernardino, did Sam cuff him to the bed and begin to slap him too hard, all the while telling him that if he was going to own him, body and soul, then Danny had better get used to doing what he was told.

6

"Well, good news," Faith said, when he picked her up down at the drugstore. She looked great that day, very relaxed, which was a relief for Danny, since Faith had seemed agitated and suspicious – for no apparent reason – since before Thanksgiving. She had pulled her hair back, and he was sure she had gained a small amount of weight, which looked good on her.

"How good?"

"So good it's hard to believe."

"Wow. Something at work?"

"No," Faith said, suddenly losing her cheer. "Oh honey, let's go grab dinner out tonight."

"Okay. What's the good news?"

"It'll wait. How was your day?"

"Uneventful. The usual usual. Too much to do, too few hours, and wishing I was back home the entire time."

She kissed him on his cheek. "That's so sweet. Chinese?"

"How about Mexican?"

"How about Italian."

"All right, baby," he said. "Italian it is."

Over pizza, the noise unbearable with all the teens in the pizza parlor, Faith leaned into him and said: "We're going to have a baby."

7

The college kid looked nearly like Danny, but with shorter hair – nearly a buzz cut – and spindlier legs. He wore a white button-down shirt and jeans and sandals.

"Jack." His voice was scratchy and full of hormones.

"I thought it was Joe."

"Sam calls me Joe. He says I remind him of a Joe."

"Where's Sam?"

"Aren't you gonna invite me in?" Jack asked.

"Yeah, sure," Danny said. He drew the door back, allowing Jack to enter his house.

"You're married."

Danny shrugged.

"Happy?" Jack asked, with a bemused look on his face. He was brash and arrogant. Danny could already tell. In fact, Jack reminded him of some of his frat brothers, who were generally pricks.

Jack walked around the living room as if he were in a showroom picking out furniture. "So this is the place."

"Where's Sam?"

"He's running late. He beeped me. He wants you to make me feel at home."

Danny felt nervous. Danny had run marathons, sat on board meetings with corporate honchos who ate people alive, had gone on Outward Bound and survived a forest for weeks, had taken a journey on a sailboat from Florida to Venezuela through rough weather, but with a young man of twenty in the living room of his own home, he felt as if he were a child about to go to the dentist for the first time.

"How do you know Sam?"

Jack glanced back at him. "How do you think I know him?"

"I –" Danny wasn't sure where to go with this. Better to just wait for Sam to show up. "Want a Coke?"

"How about a drink?"

"All right. Want a beer?"

"How about a shot of vodka?" Jack grinned. Then, he went to sit on the sofa. He was almost a pony of a guy – sturdy and tight and strong and yet very small in some way. Not short. Not compact. Then, Danny knew what Jack reminded him of: a pony ride. He nearly laughed out loud thinking of it.

Danny returned with two vodka martinis; he set one down for

Jack, and sipped from the other. "Maybe I should call Sam."

"That your wife?" Jack pointed to the picture on the wall.

"Yeah," Danny said.

"Have a seat," Jack patted the cushion beside him.

Danny went and sat next to him. He gulped most of his drink, setting the glass down on the coffee table.

Jack leaned back, sinking into the sofa a bit. He put his feet up on the coffee table, stretching. "Nice place, Danny boy."

"Thanks."

"You're probably wondering where Sam is."

"I guess he'll be here."

"Actually, he won't. He wanted the two of us to get acquainted."

"Yeah?" Danny said, meekly. "Cool."

"I can tell you're nervous. I'm a little nervous, too," Jack glanced sidelong at him. Jack was very, very cute. Sweet. Handsome. A pretty boy who was a bit masculine. Danny had noticed his shoulders and his ass, and then could not help but see the outline of thick penis pressing against the front of his jeans. It was a substantial mound.

"I bet I'm more nervous," Danny laughed. The alcohol was beginning to warm him.

"Maybe. So, where's your pretty woman?"

Danny looked at Faith's picture. "She's seeing her mother. Every few Sundays she goes over to Redlands to see her."

"You never go?"

"Her mom and I don't see eye to eye."

As an after-thought, Danny added, "She stays for hours. And hours."

"Nice," Jack said, but it was a different kind of word from his throat than most people made it out to be. It sounded sexual. *Nice.* Then, Jack unbuttoned the top two buttons of his shirt. Danny looked at Jack's throat. He was a muscular young man. He was pretty and muscular and he was already aroused, just by the vodka and the picture of Faith and the sense that he was in this suburban home about to do god knew what but it would involve men's bodies.

That was enough.

"How long have you known Sam?"

"Not long. Long enough. You know."

"Sam's a good guy," Danny said, but didn't really mean it.

"Oh, he's not too good," Jack said. "So, Danny, am I going to have to get you really drunk before you reach into my jeans and grab my dick?"

"Umm –" Danny began, wondering how he could respond.

Then Jack leaned over and whispered something so vile in Danny's ear that it made Danny feel cold and on fire and as if every part of him were melting into some kind of thick liquid, and he saw darkness at the edge of his vision as this demon named Jack whispered these things, over and over again, about what he wanted Danny to do to him, how he wanted it, where he wanted it, how much it would hurt him but the hurt would give him so much pleasure that Jack would beg for mercy and even that turned Danny on; and he felt as if he had become more of a man.

8

"Was it good?" Sam asked. They met for a squash match at the Bally's in Riverside, but Sam didn't really want to play squash. He wanted to sit in the Jacuzzi and find out about Danny's Sunday with Jack.

"It was great," Danny said. "Just great."

"What'd I tell ya?"

"Wish you'd dropped by."

Sam grinned. "I was there."

"You were?" Danny asked, suddenly feeling as if maybe Sam had been hiding somewhere, watching what he had done to Jack, what he had made Jack experience and do and how he had humiliated him and forced him and dealt with him as if he were less than nothing and how it had completely turned Danny on.

"In spirit," Sam winked. "Next time, the three of us, Danny."

"Yeah," Danny said, and that's as far as it had gone until the next time Faith had gone out of town, this time for two days. Her father – who lived in Ojai – had recently remarried, and Faith had to go patch things up between them, but didn't want Danny coming along. "It needs to be me and my dad," Faith told him.

"All right," Danny had said.

"You'll be fine. One weekend alone. You and Sam can drink beer and talk like old bachelors or something."

But, in fact, what Sam and Danny did was invite Jack over again, and this time, it got a little out of hand, because they had two days with Jack, who was more than willing to keep the pain going, the humilia-tion, even the terror – that's how Danny had begun to think of it, as a kind of reign of terror on this twenty-year-old who had seemed so in-nocent, who was just starting life, really, who was not much younger than Danny, just seven years or so, this Jack who could withstand a can-dle flame and pincers and a large instrument that Sam called the Cradle of Judas – and somehow, Jack was inflamed, and Danny was out of con-trol, and Sam was there, a shadow, goading, encouraging, suggesting, but it was Danny's hands on the ropes, Danny's hands tightening the apparatus, Danny's hands reaching in and around and beneath and above until all the openings seemed to split and separate and Danny felt as if he were entering a vast cavern through a sleeve of human flesh and in that cavern, a beast waited for him.

9

"Jesus," Sam said.

"What?" Danny awoke to Sunday morning light through the one open slat of the blinds in the rec room. His face was pressed to the carpet. His hand rested across Jack's back, which was ridged slightly from welts.

"Jesus, Danny, what did you do?" Sam said.

Danny glanced up. He could barely see Sam at all.

"Jesus, Danny."

Danny glanced over at sweet Jack, waiting for the young man's grin, but saw the bubble of blood from the edge of his lips, the eyes nearly sewn shut with fishing line.

And then, the nauseating smell.

10

Sam held his hand over Danny's mouth for what seemed like a half-hour. Finally, when Sam had assurances – given by nods – that Danny would not cry out, he released his hold.

"I didn't do that."

"I went home last night at three," Sam said, measuring his words carefully. "You had Danny in the stirrups, and the wax melting, but his eyes? Danny?" Sam held Danny's face in his hands. Danny's eyes were tearing up so he could barely see.

"Did you lose it last night?"

"I swear, it couldn't have been me," Danny said. "Christ. Poor Jack. Poor Jack."

"Look at him. Jesus, Danny. The barbed wire? Was that from out back?"

"I don't know. I didn't do it. I couldn't have," Danny pleaded, sure of his innocence.

Sam held Danny's hands up. They were scored in shallow red lines, the flesh torn up.

"And that other thing, the way he –"

"Please," Danny wept, pressing his face into Sam's chest. "I couldn't have. I know I couldn't have. You were there."

"It's all right, baby. It's all right. Jesus, Danny, I think you went too far. I think you went over the edge," Sam whispered, and Danny didn't want to ever go back into the rec room or see what had become of Jack, he didn't want to see the fishing line through the eyes, or the wire wrapped around his thighs, or the other devices and instruments – the household items, the things from the garage – the way Jack had just been taken one step beyond what he had desired.

By someone.

It could not have been me, Danny told himself, and believed it. It had to be Sam. Or Jack himself.

But now, they had to deal with concealment.

11

"You took care of it?" Danny asked.

"Don't go into this, Danny. You don't want to know," Sam said.

They were jogging on Sunday night, and Danny had taken Sam's advice and stayed away from his house for the entire day – he had gone to the movies in town, but had a fever the entire time. As they came to the orange groves, Danny tried to take Sam's hand, but Sam would not let him.

"Jack was a good guy," Sam said.

"I'm sorry," Danny said, and it seemed stupid to say it.

"He was a fine specimen," Sam added. They walked through the groves in silence.

12

When Faith was six months pregnant, she finally began showing. "You bitch," Bonnie laughed, patting her stomach, "I was showing in two months. I got so fat. Didn't I get so fat?" she turned to Sam.

The sun was high, and they all sat at the edge of the pool, feet dangling in the water. Faith sat in a chair, and wore a big straw sunhat and movie star sunglasses. Danny slipped into the pool to cool off.

"Yeah, you got fat," Sam said, "but I knew that was good. Too thin and pregnant can't be good for a kid."

"I wish I could hide it," Faith grinned. "But part of me just wants to get really fat and happy with this baby and maybe deal with aerobics classes after it comes."

"You look beautiful," Sam said.

"She does yoga every day," Danny said.

Danny swam to the diving board, and then slowly swam back to the shallow end. He walked up the steps, out of the water, and tossed watched as Sam helped Gordie put on water wings.

Faith said, "I'm glad we moved here. I think it helped me get pregnant."

"It's in the water," Bonnie giggled, like a schoolgirl, and Danny grinned and went over to help Sam because Gordie was struggling to get his flip-flops off his feet.

13

When they were alone, after Gordie was in bed, and the wives had gone for a long walk up to Sunset Heights, they took a shower together to rinse off the chlorine. Danny said, "How did you know him?"

"Danny," Sam said, soaping his back. "Don't."

"I just don't know anything about him."

"That's as it should be."

"Who was he? Sam?"

Sam kissed his neck, and began drawing his arms behind his back, which hurt slightly, but Danny felt he deserved some hurt. "He's gone now," Sam said, kissing his shoulders. "He was just somebody pretty. That's all. He was just somebody pretty."

THE SIEGE

Michael Marano

 I LOOK AT YOU AND WONDER IF I LOVE YOU. We sit, and I see you. We sit, and can do nothing else. The light – the lovely light that entrances so many – touches you . . . mirages you . . . reveals the dusk of your brow and I realize for the first time how much we look alike. Handsome jaw. Handsome eyes.

"Is that why we first became lovers?" you ask, speaking my thought. Speaking my *untrue* thought . . . pulling it from my mind with a sharp pain as if you had pulled a thorn. You know it to be a untrue thought.

The pain you inflicted was an act of healing which will never form a scar.

I look at you, as I have without respite since last night, and am taken by your beauty. I wonder if to be so taken is a thing truly felt. What I feel that I might feel is a sadness unreleased, a sorrow held in a cold urn. I look at you, at the blood on you. It smells of brass corroded by sweat. There is skin on my lips, and I would spit it away, if I could. But to do so would diminish my dignity.

I can hold onto that – dignity. But not love? Not love for you or myself or anything? Together we shall avoid all things. We shall avoid our very selves if we can, split ourselves from ourselves and unknit the fabric of birth.

I would spit the skin away. Would you?

It was for dignity that we were born.

It was for lack of dignity that we died. I am aware of the phone beside you ceasing to ring.

When had it started? We should answer no further calls. Perhaps one who finds us darling wishes us to come for a gin and tonic (when had afternoon come?), for the boring spectacle of civility.

I shift my weight slightly, and hear a broken tooth, caught in the tread of my boot, scrape the polished hardwood floor. Blood has leaked from my clothes, soaked in the fine silk cushions of the sofa we restored.

Darling of us, was it not?

The siege has ended.

And another has begun.

I remember what it was like to cry. The lost faculty of tears pains me as the tingling of a limb long severed. If I try hard enough, I can remember what it was to dream. I wish I could again . . . both cry and dream.

Were I able to dream, I could delude myself that we could wake from this.

But mostly I wish to cry . . . to release what I feel — what I convince myself I feel as an article of a heretical faith — would be a benediction.

"We can have no benediction," you say, "for what we lack so profoundly."

You are not welcome in my mind. Even in my emptiness, you are not welcome. But you are here, with me, in my mind. In my sight. I ache to ache for you. I ache to share myself with you as an act of volition.

I remember the snapping of my neck. Do you? Is my memory part of that upon which you intrude? I remember the sound of cracking bone, the vibration of the break upon the base of my skull, bewilderment and the taste of the basement floor — concrete and mold. I remember your smothering the way I remember ever so vaguely what it was to dream.

I look at you, and remember love.

Can memory, a shared memory, of love be a kind of love?

When I saw you the first time, I knew who and what you were.

When I saw you the first time, we, whose true aspects were then and ever shall be invisible, saw one another. We slipped into mutual visibility. Two pillars of refracted light, revealing configurations of dust motes. Seeing you seeing me had been a moment of completion. Completion is bittersweet. It is the fulfilling of a longing to which you have become accustomed. I welcomed you in my sight. You welcomed me in yours. It had been lonely, to be born of the dead, to have acquired a soul as a mushroom acquires the air from the forest floor, to have not a soul loomed into your mortality.

When I saw you the first time, I knew who and what I was. You defined me in your sight.

History class — had that been irony or happenstance?

You stepped forward from out of the crowd — not from the crowd, but from the moving, featureless blur I had always seen the crowd to be, even when it had been comprised of my "friends." You stepped forward, the first face I had ever truly seen outside of a mirror. You stepped forward, a thing of solidity from out a bank of rain.

We knew each other.

Without a word — dead, yet able to breathe — we sat beside each other.

The rain of the others could have split rock, split the world; we took no notice.

We, splintered by murder – too old to be part of or with those who were so adolescently immortal – joined out of the churn of humanity. Our bonding was a thing of heavy liquidity in the storm, of quicksilver droplets touching in rain.

Of course we would meet in a history class. We are creatures of inevitability. Finality led to our first breaths in this life. History is the point where past and present meet, intertwine, interact. Flesh and memory join in history. We live for having been torn from flesh. We said nothing, for we did not need to. As you sat in that plastic molded chair in the lecture hall, I had been relieved to hear your chair creak, relieved that you were truly a being of flesh, with the weight of mortality.

My return to flesh had been inevitable. For my father, while still a young man, had been unhappy because of the impolite dissolution of his affair with his secretary, and chose to deal with the end of that Cheeverian, clichéd coupling by twisting my head almost completely around while I watched cartoons. He covered the tracks of his suburban murder by throwing me down the cellar stairs, and would tell himself later that I had driven him irrationally over the edge by incessantly pestering him for a popsicle . . . though in fact the offending popsicle – a strawberry confection that would be the last thing I would taste before my tongue lolled out to touch the cold cement upon which I finally died – had been something already in my hand at the initial moment of my murder. But truly, he, with his new pot belly and newly softening muscles, had come home from the termination of his affair with the intent to kill me, with the intent to vent his pathetic flannel-suited anger by lynching me in his un-callused hands. I had been conceived that first innocent time as an act of coercion on the part of my hysteric, Valiumed mother. I was a desperate bargaining chip with which she could refuse him his desired divorce. No child, no chip. Later, better alimonied than she had expected, and in her gin and pill-induced bliss, she would at times not even remember my name.

You knew this, the circumstances of how I died, and drew a crude flight of stairs in your notebook when you should have been writing about Leonardo. You knew this, in the way all know the color of the ocean, even when we have never seen it.

You had been younger than I had been when you died, when your mother, desperate for the accolades and the attention of a tragedy, smothered you with a pillow and covered her crime by shoving a small plastic toy down your throat. She had not been insane, just bored. You had been another accouterment to her housewife existence. You, unlike a new fridge, had required more attention and care than you had been worth. Dead, you were worth much more to her – a cross to bear. Dead, you had brought her a great crop of pity, upon which she flourished, much as a flower does in sunlight. Your mother's next child had been a girl, who, for her own good, had had the foresight and good sense to have born autistic.

I knew this, and drew a crude pillow while I should have written about the Medici. I knew this, as you had known of my death.

No psychopomps had brought us back to this mortal coil, no spirit-animal had whistled us up from the earth. Only Justice had brought us back. Justice – which may be older than God, for how else could He have judged Satan? Justice returned us from exile to flesh, to avenge ourselves upon those who had razed our homelands of blood and bone, those who had rudely killed us in the summer, when the earth is easy upon the spade and funerals are not so uncomfortable. We had been denied the courtesy of interment while the world was not bright and warm.

We are the interruption of earthly creation.

Justice keeps those who murdered us alive, so that we may serve Justice by killing them. We, Second Born, were brought together by Justice. We, Second Born, knew each other, much as Jews in dull and primitive cultures know each other with a furtive glance. History is where the past and present speak and interact. We could have met nowhere else save in a history class. For others, fleshed but only once, Exile from Eden is the Catastrophe to which they owe their bestowment of Original Sin. We are born of the first sin of the first sinners' progeny. It is a sin that is not ours. Can our flesh be ours?

If we had been brought back in any way to breathing life by agencies of this earth, it would have been by the random collision of genes instigated by both pairs of our respective second parents. Justice has its mercy – both couplings that produced us would have yielded stillborns if our vengeance-heavy souls had not been dropped into the wombed blood clots out of which we grew.

My second parents never understood why they never connected with me as they had with my living siblings. You, an only child, as you had been at the time of your death, knew and still know the love of your second parents, though you have never been able to return the courtesy by loving them back.

Those who have besieged us no longer do so. Do I miss them? Do you? Their desirous gaze? Their imaged language?

I look at you. I look at your glance and I long to held by it. I long to be held by you. We no longer reflect each other in the polished stones of our eyes.

I am an absence in your glance. I hate to think – no, it is not thought – I hate to know that you are absent in mine.

"Where shall we go?" you ask.

We have met the inevitable. We have fulfilled it. Existence is a river full of currents and eddies. We have reached the inevitable end of our river. We followed it as one. Our journey became one journey on the afternoon we had met, when we followed the immediate and facile path of living men who find each other.

"It wasn't facile," you say.

No. It wasn't.

"Then say it."

"It . . . wasn't facile."

A dorm room – walls of cinder block.

The first orgasm either of us had had – we shared it on a stiff, un-yielding mattress off which I had removed the pillows out of courtesy for you and your death.

The flow of our blood.

The flow of our breath.

The flow of concocted blood from our loins.

The still and rocky landscapes within us moving as would a draft.

Joined together in the larger flow of our lives, our shared in-evitability bought us to this city where so many rivers meet the sea.

To our "friends" – our social peers we had to take up and keep on hand like tools in a drawer that are used once a year yet are indispen-sable at that one time a year – we were "fashionably queer." To us, we were the only other members of our particular humanity. Around our island was a poisoned silence, a waveless silver ocean that hurt to look upon.

We had encountered others like us as time went on and our hori-zons broadened. We met Sheila, the vapid princess who, within her soul, had been an aged homeless man beaten to death by a Legionnaire in Philadelphia. We shared the bland entertainments of youth with her. One day, we ate together under a tree – three of the Second Born pic-nicking on a college campus as if they were happy youngsters with their whole lives before them – two queens and a fag hag, with spirits older than their bodies.

There is a moment before a summer storm, when out of all the green around you something is drawn out and dimmed.

Such a moment came under that cloudless sky.

Such a moment called Sheila, who looked up from her student newspaper and gave a look like a fawn suddenly startled. For a mo-ment, her face seemed reflected upon itself, as if she swam a still pond. She sniffed the air; we saw, from behind our eyes, the air acquire her.

"I have to go," she said.

We have not seen her since.

Though we had read in the Philadelphia newspapers of the suspected murder of a very old man – a veteran and a Legionnaire about to expire from lymphatic cancer – who had somehow been abducted from an ICU. Police were searching for the man, even though it was almost certain he had died within moments of being disconnected from his respirator.

We knew better.

Justice would keep him alive until its terrible will was done, until Sheila's will was done, amen.

Inevitability had called Sheila away from our sweet picnic façade. She had broken from us as would a piece of ice from a larger floe.

"Where shall we go?" you ask.

No such question had been asked before our arrival here.

Migration had brought us to this city – a faculty, like that which calls birds, had called us to meet the economic migration of our murderers. We knew we had to come here, with the finality and profundity of what had called Sheila to harvest her killer.

Our murderers – each of their own accord – had both come to this, "the Holy City," to retire. An unknowingly shared pilgrimage marking the fulfillment of two separate and distant suburban lives. Charleston, aged city, languid, rising in sea-level barely over a marsh, was the place our murderers had chosen to retire, rather than Florida. Golf had been the deciding factor for both. A happy game to be played in sunshine despite at least one hip replacement between the two of them. Two people, two strangers, both marked by Cain, had both chosen to live their golden years in the same city. You and I, an echo of their crimes (one echo? can two sounds make the same echo?) went toward them. Their crimes called their echoes back.

Charleston is bright and warm, much like the days on which we had been buried. Noon here is a dream. Amid the steeples and streets, one can never truly wake.

Charleston is where many rivers meet. It is where they flow and intertwine and extinguish themselves in the sea. It is where land and sea suspend each other as marsh. We arrived posing as two respectable faggots drawn to the city for its great history, its great culture, its arts scene, its cheap antiques and charming bargains, its legacy of the dashing Rhett Butler, the city's most famous son – who never existed. What could such a pretty myth mean to us, jaded to existence twice?

Charleston is the confluence of many rivers, and what the rivers bear. Dreams and fictions cast into those rivers with the surrender of a coin to a fountain wash here. The place is composed of fictions that many have casually read and forgotten. They clog the air and the minds here as would silt.

"You must love it here!" said the real estate agent who showed us our house. Not an observation. A demand. A toll extorted.

"You must love it here!" said the furniture store proprietors.

"You must love it here!" Politely, we always said we did love it here. The demand, the statement, was an affirmation on the part of those who spoke it. To not agree would have been as rude as interrupting a prayer.

We did not come here to love the place as they did. How could we love the place, amid the screams?

"No, not the screams," you say.

No . . . not the screams. The screams that are not released, the screams that are held inside without respite among the dead. Even discorporate, the dead are denied the catharsis of a scream in Charleston.

"It's the quiet of the screams that deafens," you say.

The ghosts of Charleston are patient. So terribly patient. We – the dead – can see them. We – the avatars – can taste them. We cannot breathe, for Charleston is so thick with them. They are litter left by the inconsiderate. They are ignored, much as Charleston natives ignore visitors who do not fawn over the city as if it were a coddled trophy child. The solidity of their unreleased screams at times seems greater than that of the ancient brick.

It is the dead of Charleston – desperate to have us see them – that lay siege to us. They hunger for our sight. They drink our gaze – clear mountain water amid lowland stagnance. The dead are creatures of dreams unseen in a city that never wakes. They are as invisible as chime notes.

Among the fleshless ghosts, we hunted our murderers. We did so as an act of will. Not in response to a profound call – as Sheila had responded to the call that brought her to her murderer's deathbed – for Justice is in part a creature of time. We know that, now. Justice is cause and effect. The fullness of effect is not always known before Justice is inflicted. We moved among the forested screams. The stone-still cries. We hunted our killers easily; the living eyes of Charleston are talked into blindness.

We stalked your mother to the beach. You knew where she would go. You knew where she would be. Perched upon a pier the pilings of which touched the Gulf Stream, we looked down upon the stretch of cold sand you knew your mother would walk this mild winter day.

And for the first time in either of your lives, you were moved to tears.

Your mother led her autistic daughter along the surf. Gently. So lovingly. What had she become, this murderess, that she could love so tenderly? She still carried her cruelty; we saw it as a brimming urn she held by her heart. Yet she did not let it spill.

She, who is your sister not by any flesh, wore loose clothes that flapped in the wind. Fully grown, she still looked a child. Her hair flew in wild directions. Your mother carried a picnic basket, and your sister not of flesh bore fresh spills and stains upon her shirt – traces of what the basket had held. The beach was empty. There were no accolades to be had. No pity to be bestowed by onlookers who admired your mother for her strength. Just a woman and her ruin of a daughter.

You, unseen by her, gave her the pity for which you had been butchered.

I comforted you that night. I held you to my heart and stroked your hair. The comfort I gave you was too small a hill to rest upon, my body an inadequate homeland.

We hunted my father next, knowing we would not now kill him, but knowing we would have to know why we could not now kill him.

You gasped as you felt me feel a pang of love for the old man, as I saw the now liver-spotted hands that had wrung my neck.

You exhaled softly what you had inhaled as a gasp as you felt me feel jealousy toward the young man who was now his son. Strapping. Beautiful. Glowing with health and vitality, the young man who in flesh would be my brother walked with my murdering father through the banal consumerist landscape of a shopping mall. He did not love his father. That was plain. Filial hatred was etched upon his face. Yet he walked with my father, who plainly loved him. Yet he walked with my father, who limped slightly due to his surgeried hip. Filial hatred meshed with filial duty. You and I, knitted from behind time – who have never walked a visible path save for that which Justice had decreed – saw the injustice we would inflict if we killed my father now. To kill my father would be to destroy this boy; he would become the focus of an investigation that would ruin him, even if he were found innocent. To kill my father would kill part of him; to take away the object of his hatred and his sense of duty would flood him with an ambiguity of feelings he could not tolerate.

You comforted me that night by making love to me. You took away the pain of inaction by desiring me.

As best you could.

Justice would tell us when to strike.

And thus, besieged by the dead, we began our own siege.

And thus we closed ourselves off from Charleston, living in it, participating in it, but always closing ourselves off from the place where the dead were so badly treated. Where ghosts were trinkets used to lure tourists along with gewgaws made of saw grass and plaster. We closed a siege wall around us as we lay siege to our murderers, waiting, always waiting.

We waded into the confluence of Charleston. We waded into the silt of fictions and dreams and lies. We walked among the living and the ghosts.

The dead looked in our eyes and coveted.

Here, a woman in an ancient dress, her gullet full of holes. Her moonlight form rosaried with knots of the pain she had felt in life. She stood upon the street, a thing of February forced to exist against a backdrop of May, forced into invisibility by the eyes of the city that had killed her for loving wrongly. We saw her on a bright corner, as a horse-drawn carriage full of tourists passed her.

We waded into Charleston's indifferent cruelty, "*You must love it here!*" punctuating our stay the way "*Amen!*" does a tent revival.

Commodities, we were invited by *nouveaux riches* belles to behold and marvel the purchases they had made with the money of husbands who saw them as trophies and incubators and little more. We, commodified as furniture queens, marveled.

Here, the mouth of a child gnawed away. The rats that had nested in her unfound body did not follow her in death, did not ghost themselves with her, though the violet she had died picking had. A man with a flayed back walked with her, a man who would have come back as an avatar to avenge himself if he had not died at the hands of so many who had been enraptured by the fiction of *Birth of a Nation*.

We, commodified as educated strangers who had come to Charleston and had learned the truth of how things really are (did we not answer in the affirmative to "*You must love it here*"?), agreed sagely with the city's fat white patriarchs, who would spout their provincial nonsense believing they could create informed opinions about anything, having seen nothing of the world save what they have seen through the fiction of tourism, the fiction of the dream of Charleston they take with them no matter where they go.

Here, a man composed of the sheen of tin. A thing of numb, indifferent fleshlessness, he walks the Battery, walks foolishly upon the stagnant water of the harbor. He is a buffoon in death, as he had been in life. In life, he had been a happy figure, a person of frolicking dementia who ended the jolliness he provided by inconsiderately freezing to death one unseasonable evening. The sheen of his unliving flesh is as cold as the wind that killed him. He sleeps his dead sleep at the very spot in the park where his cold body had first been flecked with dew.

We, commodified as faggots, fell in with the destitute and inwardly exiled gays of Charleston. We saw the broken-down men of King Street, coolies bitter that they had not married the Rhett Butler they had always believed they deserved. We saw the faggots from other places who come to Charleston to plunder fraudulent antiques much as Mr Kurtz had gone to the Congo to plunder ivory. We fell in also with the Charleston queer aristocracy, those who, less because of their sexuality than their caste perceptions, always went elsewhere to indulge their sexual proclivities.

Some went to New York to screw young black men not as an expression of sexual taste or desire, but to express racial contempt, and contempt for the foreign culture of the North. Some went to Thailand to express their contempt for a culture older than theirs by fucking its children. Some kept apartments under false names in San Francisco, simply because they could.

We became conscripted for the sake of Justice to save the life of such a Charleston scion, to keep his damp and earthen soul in his body. We interfered in his acquiring of AIDS by taking his attention away from a drag queen crack addict. We were compelled to interfere, saving the life of this respectable son of one of Charleston's finest families so he could be later punished by the as yet unborn avatars of those he had killed. He was marked, that we could see. His crimes could be read in his eyes. He was marked perhaps for fisting that boy to death in New York? Perhaps for that child whose kidney ruptured in Thailand? Maybe they both would be reborn to take him. Perhaps as twins.

As we led the scion away, we saw on the drag queen's face what she would become. We saw the mirrored unliving shadow of her that would move as a breeze – with the feminine grace she had in life always wanted – down the quaintly cobblestoned streets she worked.

Charleston is a mind set. Its crowded loneliness is an eyesore. We walk amongst its dead, those conscripted to invisibility, those whose screams are stifled with indifference only the living could muster. Besieged, we waited. We could not breathe for the thickness of our fleshless siblings. Ghosts are born of guilt without catharsis. Without redemption. You cannot be rid of a ghost until you own the sin that has created it. To own a sin is to acknowledge history, and Charleston has none. History is where the past and present interact. There is no such interaction here, no more than a foot interacts in a meaningful way with the ground. Charleston has no history . . . for though it loves its past, such love is nothing but antiquarianism. Such love objectifies. Such love is not, and can never be history. Justice is impossible in the drunken fog of such non-history. Our fleshless siblings will never be free. The weight of the air is too heavy in Charleston. The cold places of the North, the dusty attics and the chilled cellars, the shadow eaves and October breaths, they give expiation to ghosts. They provide a way home. Here, the weight of cast-off bourgeois dreams keeps ghosts earthbound. Slaves. The disenfranchised. The refugees who found refuge here only for their flesh, not their souls. The refuse of the brutal agrarian plutocracy based upon stolen labor. The foolish men who, having read the pretty fiction of Ivanhoe, had believed in the chivalry of agrarian plutocracy and who cannot fathom why they did not die nobly, but died shitting themselves, screaming for their mothers.

Incontinent and bloody in the Greys, they are soldiers still of the siege. We would help them if we could. Yet how can you dig a grave for a body already buried in haze? They look and glisten in the moonlight. They hunger to be seen.

The city gets smaller, as Justice makes us wait.

We go to our polite jobs as Boys, such as we are expected to. Yes, we are Boys. Queers are not full men because any challenge to patriarchal normalcy cannot be tolerated. Your female boss finds us "darling" and "clever."

Justice makes us wait.

Justice keeps us unseen for what we truly are.

Who, among the living, is invisible enough to truly see us?

The Call came in the depths of summer.

There is a peacefulness to butchery. Mining. Excavating. The path through flesh is a path of discovery.

We stood from our couches in our living room. The sound of the television passed to nothing; we were not truly watching it. We kept it on at night because the light of the screen reflected on the windows and blanked the faces of the dead who milled, who longed to be seen, who formed themselves out of ether not out of Will, but out of its terrible absence. Will is a thing for the living. Will is the ability to Sin, which we have not. Without Will (truly without Sin?), we stood and calmly took our quarry.

To have been near Sheila when she heeded her Call was to see – as you see in the moment before a summer storm – something drawn out of all the green around you.

We were that which is drawn out of the green. We were drawn out of where we were while still present.

"Where are we now? Where shall we go?"

There is a certainty a child knows with finality – that it must never touch fire.

We knew with the same certainty and finality that tonight was the night to avenge.

We harvested your mother, knowing her daughter was in the care of an aunt in a cooler place. The terrible heat was making the child mad. Dehydrated and sick, she had been packed off. To punish your killer tonight would not punish the autistic child she brought into this world.

We harvested my father, knowing his son was away hiking with friends. The closeness to his father in the heat was making him mad. He went to the mountains. To destroy my murderer would not destroy his son. The boy could let go his filial hatred if he had an alibi not only for those who would investigate, but an alibi for himself; that he could not have saved the man were he with him the night he disappeared.

Out of politeness for my father, and in consideration of his hip, we put him in the back seat of our car. Not in the trunk with your mother.

We, the unavenged dead, dug our graves in their flesh.

The marshes are tannic. The marshes crawl with life that is hungry. We buried our open-fleshed graves in the marshes.

I look at you, and wonder if I love you.

Dried blood upon the lids of my eyes makes it hard to blink. My eyes hurt. The phone has stopped ringing again. When had dusk come?

There should be a difference in weight, for what we have lost.

There is skin upon my lip, and I would spit it away.

Yet we have been spat away this night, we have been left behind like skin.

Our souls, avenged . . .

. . . ascended.

They cast us aside, we fleshy vessels. Justice was served by us, we things of marrow and blood and gristle are empty now. Our souls are free and we wish them back. We are uninhabitable, even by ourselves.

Love.

How can we love while soulless?

I look at you, and wonder.

We are dead. Nothing is held by our gazes. No soul or spirit.

The ghosts crave our glance no more than they would from corpses. They have ended the siege. As I saw them walking away, I realized that if I could still feel anything, I would miss them.

"Where shall we go?"

We have not even graves to crawl in to sleep. They have been dug into our murderers and given to the marsh.

You ask one last time.

We are in Charleston.

We are dead.

We might as well stay.

BEAR SHIRT

Gemma Files

 WEDNESDAYS — ODIN'S DAY — I GIVE MY LAST TALK at five. Afterward, as I walk out, I find the blond kid already waiting: a somber Aryan clone, barely out of his teens, puppy-fat still sleek and pink over his football-ready mass of cultivated muscle. I can tell he's one of Karl Speller's just by looking at him, though his face isn't exactly familiar. Far too young to be one of the disciples I knew, way back when; a late convert, maybe? Fresh lower-middle-class meat, scooped straight out of school, fallen through the deepening crack between liberal cant and so-called "Equal Opportunity" in action? Somebody's —

Karl's?

— second-generation Separatist son, even?

Ick.

Another damn zealot out of the same half-cracked mold, anyway — pure white, not too bright, up all night every night stockpiling weapons and updating websites in the service of the holy Cause. Same philosophy I was supposed to share just because an accident of genetics left me looking like the RaHoWa's unofficial gay pin-up; same not-so-underground "culture" I now spend my days lecturing against, at colleges and universities from Vancouver to Florida.

The University of Toronto is more than a bit off my beaten track, going by these established standards — a bit too close to my former home for comfort, all told. But it had been a long time, and I was invited, and so I came: back to Toronto. Back to where Karl and I first rubbed up against each other.

And now . . .

. . . now, I don't get much time to consider whether or not this may have been a mistake before the kid brings his fist up towards me, held at an awkward angle — and I feel my lips peel back, automatic fight-or-flight reflex kicking in hard; get a sudden, giddy rush / flash of (*gun*), (no *time*), (screw it, screw *him*, just stand there and take it like a *man*, you dumb fucking faggot. . . .)

Because: you always knew this day would come, now, didn't you? In your heart of hearts. Or somewhere considerably —

(lower down).

As it turns out, however, all the kid has to offer is the palm of his hand, salmon-belly soft and city-bred callus-less – plus a dull brass key, half caught in the crease of his life-line.

"Brother Speller . . ." he begins. And I think:

(Oh, be fucking serious.)

Flushing bright, temper flaring – snapping back at the very sound of that long-lost title, sharper than I need to, fear sliding fast into half-embarrassed anger:

"My name is *Hengist*, little boy. Okay? And I am *not* your 'brother.'"

Because, sure, Karl might have pushed me into that fucked-up ritual acknowledgment of his – hand-fasting 'round the fire, calling me his "shield-brother" in front of the whole camp and daring anybody else to say different. And sure, I might have gone along, like I went along with most of Karl's suggestions –

(– to a point, anyway.)

But: doesn't mean we were ever married, him and me. Doesn't mean I *took his name* like some housewife from the fucking 'burbs, or anything. . . .

The kid's eyes stay steady under those blond brows – eyes pale as Karl's, brows almost white as Karl's. Karl's chosen spawn, staring calm at Karl's chosen . . . what?

Mate? *Friend?*

(fuck-)

–Buddy?

"Brother Speller," the kid repeats, calm enough to lull and freeze – a cheap postpube imitation of Karl's manly Fuhrer rasp, Novocaine-sting over sandpaper-rub – "left us this. And he told us it was for you. *Mister* Hengist."

━━━━━━━

When I turn my forearm over and look down, exposing the smooth inner flesh, I can still see Berkana – the bear-rune – imprinted just where the skin is thinnest: the slightly raised, black outline of two side-long triangles on a stick, a Nazi letter "B." Comes complete with a sense-memory of it going on, faint buzz and hot metal stink as Karl held my arm out to the tattoo artist's gun, fisting my reluctant hand hard. Like he was helping a fellow soldier face down some battlefield surgeon – to stay brave while his bullet-wounds were packed with gunpowder and set alight, in tiny explosions of righteously-earned pain.

And speaking of pain, I remember *that*, too. Like getting stung by a bee, only worse. Longer. More intense.

But then, that was Karl for you: pure intensity, constantly moving back and forth between himself and everything he touched. Including –

(me).

It's a complex rune, *Berkana* – one of twenty-four, hallucinated from fallen willow-twigs by the great over-God Odin while he hung nine days and nights on the World-Tree *Yggdrasil*, a sacrifice, himself to himself. The FUTHARK alphabet, Viking wisdom reduced to sketchy little bite-sized chunks, each one a mess of contradictory implications. So scratch 'em into stones, throw 'em down on a scraped-out hide, read the results and draw your own conclusions . . . and if you don't like the way your future seems to be turning out, so what? You can always cut yourself a handy mouthful of foxglove variant – belladonna, lady's mantle, laurel leaves, whatever – chew on it a while, and make up something better.

Berkana's direction is the east: Spadina, Mimico, cottage country. Its bird is the swan, its color blue (like Karl's icy eyes, or my own), its tree the beech. It's the rune of birth, of creativity – children, or new ideas. A marriage –

(or *re*marriage)

– in the offing.

And even now, after I've had every other trace of that crazy man I once thought I loved lasered from my body . . . a demure swastika on either hip, palm-sized, like handles; an elaborate iron cross above my heart; Karl's name like a half-collar across the back of my neck, where the first big visible knob of the vertebrae nests, so he could read it aloud while he plowed into me from behind . . . I still force myself to look at Berkana every day. The bear-rune. The sign of Karl's chosen totem. The ancient, meaningless symbol that bound us together, then tore us apart.

I do it to remind myself why I left him, in the first place – why I ran away, and hid, and haven't seen him since, even assuming he was still anywhere he *could* be seen. And I do it to remind myself just how much, how oh so very much indeed, I once wanted –

– to stay.

So – stones on hide, falling, shifting; rune-magic, poetry, and probability conjured together from the empty air. Berkana *in* air, first reading out of a possible four. Exciting family news quite probable. A birth or a new venture a distinct possibility.

I recognized the kid's key, of course. Last seen – Christ, ten years earlier, on a chain around Karl's neck, swinging hypnotically between his pecs as he labored back and forth above me. Grunting low, right in my ear; saying, over and over:

Oh, baby. Oh, Lee, baby . . . you're it. You're . . . the one.

The bulky weight of him, all over me, making me ache and strain with secret heat: big hands, big muscles, big, rough head. Mica-fine blond stubble of cheek, chin, scalp abrading my inner thighs as he rooted and lapped at me impatiently – forcing me open, willing me wet and slack enough to take all of him in one slick thrust. Karl never had any of the hang-ups my other nominally-straight tricks clung to; never thought twice about enjoying every part of me he could reach, as long as it made us both moan and snarl and sweat together. From the minute we met, he treated me less like some uppity academic fag he was way too cool to kiss than a long-lost brother, rediscovered at last in the very heart of the enemy's camp – some fellow warrior who'd fallen amongst thieves and picked up bad habits, not that he didn't like the result.

"Key to your heart?" I suggested, flicking idly at it, as we lay together after our first encounter. He snorted.

"Ma's folks left her a cabin, up Gravenhurst way. I go there, sometimes."

"To get away from it all."

"Yup." A pause. "That, and find my bear."

Uh –

(– 'scuse me?)

My key, then, to Karl's cabin. Where I'm heading, by car, even as we speak – even as I cast my mind back further still, remembering how we first met: at a faculty do, earlier that same evening. I was there alone, bored and horny and single, just one more Media Studies TA backing up the prof of the moment in return for some help with my never-ending thesis; my duties included Pop Culture and Literary Antecedents MMS301, which mainly involved showing up and grading papers.

Karl, meanwhile, was ostensibly "there" with Nini Machen – Barbie's thinner and far less smiley twin turned program student rep, the female equivalent of those straight guys you hear about all the time who think lesbians only exist because none of these poor, deluded girls has met *them* yet. She'd already tried that tact on me, only to be rebuffed. And now that I'd been officially erased from her personal radar screen, it just made it all the easier for me to sidle over and cast Karl the narrowed, flirty eye – which he noticed, eventually. And, eventually . . .

. . . returned.

Big and blond and peach-fuzz pink-and-white all over – he looked like me times two, the cartoon super-hero version, cut and solid, utterly unrufflable. Every fetish made flesh, every neo-fascist dream come true. Son of a bitch made my knees knock, and I'm not a knees-knocking kind of guy.

When Nini turned her attention to the Prof, we drifted to the door, swapping names as we went: Karl Speller, Lee Hengist; Lee, Karl. He smiled when he heard my last name – good Swedish stock, fair-skinned and fuckable, with no fear of contagion.

(Not racially, at least.)

"You're a fag, though," he said, a minute later, shattering my initial assumptions. "Right?"

No particular revulsion in his voice, just a seemingly genuine interest – a relief, coming from somebody who looked like they could crack my skull and eat my brains for breakfast.

I nodded. "And you're . . . not?"

A shrug. "I do what –"

(*who*)

"– I want." A pause. "You clean?"

I swallowed, mouth suddenly dry. "I've been, uh . . . tested...."

"Negative." At my nod: "'S'good. Ma always says condoms are a Jew plot to keep us from breedin', but I just hate the way the damn things feel. That, and I like bein' able to – *taste* –"

(– what I'm . . . eating.)

Hunger boiled off him in a wave, too pure to even seem intrusive. He was up against me, looming, so close all I could breathe was his hot musk. I'd never felt so small, so slight, so patently unable to defend myself. Or so – weirdly –

– desirable.

I fisted my hands and gulped, through growing dizziness. Stammered, annoyed by my own inarticulateness:

"Uh, I don't, I don't go bareback, that's just *dumb*. I mean, you do two friends, and I do two friends, and HIV takes five years plus to even show up on the chart, so –"

Karl just looked at me, knitting those no-brows, like I was the cutest, dumbest little thing he'd ever seen. Making me . . . blush.

"But – you're not gonna *be* with anybody else, Lee," he said, finally.

Simple as that: no one. Never.

(Ever again.)

I reddened. "Say what?"

Dick going: yes! Brain going: *nut*. And everything in between slapped suddenly awake, tentatively *up*, from the rising hairs on the back of my neck to the crawling skin of my balls, my widening nostrils, my fluttering pulse.

An hour later, we were back at my place, with him already in me deep enough to hurt. And me, already –

– pulling him deeper.

There are a lot of bears to choose from, but the one Karl had in mind was – naturally enough – the biggest aside from long-extinct *Arctodus simus*, the prehistoric short-faced monster bear, which ranged from six feet at the shoulder on all fours to fourteen standing up. Under the skin, Karl believed he was a Grizzly: *Ursus horribilis*, "The King of the Brutes," 2,000 pounds, able to run thirty miles an hour, and survive four bullets in the heart just long enough to suck the marrow from your bones.

He reeled off statistics like they were love-talk, or family anecdotes: told me how bears eat each other, adult and child. How fights between bears lead to broken jaws, shattered teeth, lost eyes. How the female bear is called a sow, the male bear a boar. How female bears won't have sex while raising their young, which can take two to four years.

"Thought you were a cat, y'know, first time I looked at you," he murmured that night, into the sweaty side of my neck. "But now I think maybe . . . maybe *you're* a bear, too."

(Uh *huh*.)

Nini aside, you see, Karl wasn't faculty – but he *did* teach: White Power cant, liberally admixed with a highly personal form of Viking shamanism. The first he'd inhaled, almost literally, with his mother's milk; "Ma" was Verena Speller, called Vee, currently serving twenty-five to life on a particularly grotesque beat-down that turned into a full-scale race riot – payback for Karl's father, Grand Wizard of Klan North, who died of a heart attack after getting into a fist-fight with the Holocaust survivors' group protesting his initial public appearance. Karl, a toddler at the time, could no longer remember seeing her outside of a contact visits room.

"She knew what she was doin'," was his only comment, the one time I asked about it. "Ma's a soldier. She knew the risks."

We went to visit once a month, after Karl and I had become an item. But I usually stayed out in the car, because Ma had "issues" with "my kind"; she was old-school to the bone, and didn't want to be anywhere near the narrow faggot ass of any white guy who wasn't doing his level best to replace the race. Karl was safe enough, though – he'd already done *his* bit, and then some, sowing his seed with nine good Aryan wenches he'd met through ads in the backs of Heritage Front hand-outs. He got baby, toddler, pre-teenage pictures through the mail and took them in for Ma to coo over, destroying them ritually at each visit's end to keep the guards from confiscating them.

And every time, he left saddened in a way that made me sad just to witness it: revolted, horrified, shaken to his unshakable core by the spectacle of his mother stuck behind bars, penned and prowling restlessly, as a lioness confined in a stall built for dogs.

"They're never gonna put me in a cage," he told me, with equal emphasis on all parts: not them, not me, not a *cage*. Not *ever*.

Oh, no.

I kept my opinions on the subject to myself, for then. Things had already gotten complicated enough once news got around, and my friends started telling me I was screwing Hitler. I'd scoff: *Rommel*, maybe. After all, he'd never said anything too repulsive to bear without response about non-white people around *me*. . . .

And was that rationalization? Bet your ass. And did I need it, just to make my own behavior endurable, and still dream myself moral?

Not –

– as much –

– as I *should* have.

I told myself what Karl told me – that he didn't really give a damn about "the Cause," about paramilitarism, neo-Nazism, racial Separatism, any kind of *ism*. That all he really cared about was the grail he pursued to the exclusion of virtually everything else: the maddeningly elusive goal of evolution – or *deevolution* – into his own "natural" animal form.

It was the second part of Karl's creed, the one he'd been left to come up with all on his ownsome . . . a Frankenstein faith patched together from romance and ritual, mythology and madness, snips and snails and old wives' tales. Put simply, he aspired to remake himself into a *berserkgangr*, or berserker – a bestial warrior-poet, Odin's champion, intoxicated with blood-mad ecstasy, who could wade into battle naked except for his totem animal's flayed hide, the ritual bear-shirt.

Pretty nutty, huh? So much so that even other Aryans considered Karl cracked. To the Far Right Christian Coalition he was a renegade, an unrepentant pagan, maybe even a devil-worshipper. Straight-up paramilitarists, meanwhile, thought his time would be better spent fighting the good fight on a battlefield the rest of them could share – down here on earth, where the usual weapon of choice is rocket-launchers, not shape-shifting.

But Karl didn't care what they thought. He truly believed this state of holy fury was the true nature of every white man – *his* true nature. What he wanted to be. *Could* be, with just a little more . . .

. . . application.

Go out into the woods, find your bear, kill it and wear its skin – into battle. And then –

"Battle?"

"Find a fight, get in it; shit, baby, what'd you think I meant?"

(I mean, this ain't *rocket* science, here.)

"Okay: skin, battle. Because. . . ?" I prompted.

"'Cause that's how you change." A pause, while I took this in. Adding: "Won't work if it's not *your* bear, though."

"And you know this — how?" I asked. He just shrugged. And replied, simply —

"'Cause it hasn't worked yet."

(. . . *yet*.)

———

Skirting the lake, Karl's key was already pulse-warm beneath my shirt; I hadn't driven this route for two presidencies, but it's not like I had to check the map. So I sit, letting the engine's drone pull me past an endless panorama of long-forgotten sense-memory material: grey walls of rocks, green-brown blur of trees — reflected light lapping back and forth, setting sun gone liquid all along the shore. Berkana in water, my tattooed rune's next logical reading made flesh. Synchronic or coincidental, sports fans?

(*You* decide.)

The books agree, mainly: a time for self-assessment, for inward thinking. A time to relax, and count your blessings.

And: (ten years) I think, as I take the next hill. (Three with Karl, seven without.)

Ten . . . whole . . . years.

(Christ.)

Because sure, I know you must all be saying to yourselves, right about now: the sex sounds good, but there has to have been *something* else to keep Lee with this nutcase after the lovin' was done, smart guy that he obviously is. Right? I mean, let's not fool ourselves — freak sex, good or not, is kind of like pure Scotch: you can only drink it every day for just so long, before your insides spring a leak.

So what was I doing, exactly, while those initial years flew by — besides letting Karl have his wicked way with me anytime he wanted, that is? Well —

— not . . . a lot.

But lest you think I just lay there and took it the whole damn time, I might as well mention the other primary component of the whole Lee / Karl melange — the not-so-hidden character flaw Karl sniffed out in me that very first night, and lovingly nurtured every subsequent second we shared: my aforementioned temper, which tends to range — on a daily basis — from simple finger-snap snarkiness to outright barfight-picking piss-artistry. I've struggled with it all my life, and turning out gay has neither helped nor hindered, especially since the men I sleep with usually seem just as uncomfortable with my sudden flare-ups as those few women I forced myself to get jiggy with ever were. More so, in fact – because most guys don't really know *how* to deal with rage, except by producing some of their own.

Not Karl, though. He didn't want to be placated, or reassured, or soothed. Culturally, conflict was his medium; he expected it, required it.

Hell, he reveled in it.

"'Anger management problems,'" he repeated, after I – reluctantly – let slip the reason I still saw a psychiatrist twice each week. "You."

I felt heat boil across my face, jaw to hairline. "Yeah, *me*. So?"

"Like when you get riled you go all psycho, that it?" I stayed silent, as he continued, teasingly: "C'mon, seriously – like you can't think? And you see red? And when some guy keeps comin' after you, you start wantin' to rip his guts out with your bare hands?"

Teeth gritted: "Something like that, yes."

He chuckled, deep in his throat – came in close, doing that looming thing again. But this time, my blood was up. I showed him my teeth, all white and sharp . . . and he just laughed again, even harder, at the sight of them.

"Naw, don't think so" he said. "Little pretty kitty fag-boy you? Be serious." Leaning closer, showing me his: bigger, whiter, sharper. "Believe *that* when I –"

– see it?

(Well . . . okay.)

And then, with a growl, I was on him – had him on his back, struggling, before he even had time to count his losses. We went at it hand to hand, no holds barred. I kneed him hard in the groin; he roared but sucked it up, cracking me across the jaw so hard I bit my own lip. Finally, as I hissed blood, he got his knees between mine and spread them hard, pinning me. I raked his face, so he flipped me, bit into my nape, and gave a flesh-smothered crow of surprise and delight. Rumbling, while I thrashed beneath him –

"Ah, now – that's better."

I bucked up like a hard-rode horse, made it to my knees – then froze as he slipped into position, humping me higher, drawing a helpless moan. So quick, for all his bulk. And the touch of him, raising hairs where I barely knew I had them – so raw, so rank, so right. So utterly, unnaturally goddamn . . . natural.

"This," he told me, firmly, "this's how it should be. Way you're feelin', that ain't something you *manage* – that's an ancestor-gift, Lee, pure and simple. The very best part of your heritage."

Trying to unseat him, and failing miserably. I gave one last half-hearted flail, one last hoarse groan, then managed:

"This's me getting pissed, that's all. Nothing more, nothing –"

A snort. "That's your *bear*, Lee, lookin' out through those baby blues. Sayin' hi to mine . . ."

(. . . the way bears do.)

All hot breath and hunger, carrion-rank, honey-sweet. Grappling and snuffling. All claws and jaws and *blood* in every part of me, pumping me hard enough to pop on contact. Making me feel alive in a way I've never felt since: Not then, not now. Not before. And sure as hell not –

(after)

"Oh, shit," I hissed, finally. "Just . . . shut the fuck up and fuck me, you fucking freak."

Another grin, into my spine. "Whatever you say –

(shield-)

– brother."

Karl didn't just accept my unsociably low tolerance for annoyance, he encouraged it; we'd fist-fight as foreplay, go straight from making bruises to licking them. While all around him had been trained to try and *keep* their tempers – keep them on a leash, keep them in check – if Karl felt it, you knew it. It was like breathing to him, like sex. Like prayer. For Karl, rage was a means to its own end, its own energy and its own purpose: a negative rush, infinitely destructive and potent. It was meditation, masturbation, sex and drugs and rock and roll, all rolled up into one. An in-body out-of-body experience. Losing yourself.

Or, maybe –

– finding yourself.

"These guys I run with," he said, "they're weekend warriors, mostly. Talk big, sure, but ain't nothin' under their skin worth the lettin' out. *You*, though...." He paused. "You could go all the way, you wanted to."

"All the way where?"

Well . . .

. . . that'd be the question.

(Wouldn't it?)

Wherever Karl went, I suppose, all those years ago. Wherever he left me for, after I – finally –

– left *him*.

I try not to think much about that last night we spent together, if I can help it. That time we went up alone, just the two of us, with no disciples invited – when we built a fire so big it felt like we were cooking in our own sweat and fucked in every splintery corner of the house Karl's grampaw built, till we were both so hot and tender we could barely move. And then, when everything was at its peak . . . when Karl, who never drank, had already downed what seemed like a potentially fatal load of fermented honey-mead he'd bought from some fellow Viking-obsessed freak in the Society for Creative Anachronisms, and made me match him slug for slug from a couple of dirty steins . . .

. . . then, if I force myself, I can just about barely remember what it felt like to find him pulling me outside by my hair, holding me upright against the wind and pointing me towards the trees. Crooning so low I could hear it move through his chest and into mine, like some subsonic earthquake-warning; pressing a *knife* – a goddamn knife, serrated blade long as my femur – into my limp right hand, and telling me:

C'mon, Lee – tonight's the night. Can't you feel it comin'? My –

(*our*)

– bear.

Naked, sweating, barely upright. His fist on my hip, over that left-side swastika – fingers spanning my thigh, nudging my half-hard cock. Steering me by it, practically, like it was a magic wand that'd make me do whatever he wanted me to . . .

(. . . whatever . . . I wanted to.)

Because here's the truth, all right? It was never what Karl wanted that scared me. It was the part of me that desperately *wanted* to be what he wanted – to do whatever it took to keep him with me, on me, *in* me. The insatiable part. The angry part. The –

(*bear* part)

That voice, murmuring – was it even coming from him, anymore? Or from somewhere deep inside me?

So c'mon, baby. Into the woods, knife out. And I'll get mine, and you'll get yours, and we'll be together, always –

Hunt together. Kill together. *Eat* . . . together –

(– forever.)

And at the last second, the very last second possible . . . I turned, and I dropped the knife, and I punched him in the face, so hard I broke a knuckle. And then I took off, running. And I have never looked back, never. Not *ever.*

———

. . . till now.

———

Say it with me, once again. Right *now.* Which is when I find myself turning sharp off this last, gravel-paved trace of road – eyes burning, neck stiff, limbs fatigue-cramped, with memory still lodged bone-deep and burning sharp in every part of me, like too much lactic acid after a long, hard race. When I pull over into the trees at the bottom of Karl's hill, turn the engine off, get out, kick my joints awake again. . . .

Then look up, squinting into the sun. And easily spot, even through seven years' worth of encroaching overgrowth, the door of what that blond kid says Karl's *will* says is (from this moment on) "my" cabin.

The key still works, albeit with a rusty click. Inside I find a homespun panorama of decay – wood-rot and silence, dust rising like ghosts, screen-doors black with caterpillar corpses, cobwebs laden deep with mummi-fied flies. That oil-lamp we used to see by, its wick only half-burnt, waiting for a match's kiss; that unvarnished pine table-and-chairs set Karl once bent me across, splintery as ever. That same fireplace, full of cold ashes.

And everything I touch, everything I don't – just, plain, everything – still smells . . . exactly . . .

. . . like Karl.

Musty, musky. Earthy as a cave. Like somewhere you can sleep all winter, hibernate till spring – live off your own fat and dream, *willing* yourself into another shape by the time you finally wake.

(And how the fuck can that be, anyway? After seven *years?*)

I feel a shiver go up my spine at the very thought of trying to an-swer that particular question, quick and cold as the phantom lick of long, grooved tongue.

Because: it's been quite the ride for me, one way or another. And now that it's finally over, I find I have almost no idea –

(good *or* bad)

– why I ever actually bothered to come back up here again, in the first damn place.

Dust on the floor, dirt smeared black on the dimming windows. That earthy scent. Berkana *in* earth, third reading of four: unsafe foot-ing, shifting ground.

The rune-books' advice? Hold back a little. Take stock. Try "not to be so pushy," because –

(*things*)

– could rebound on you.

Jump–cut, moment to moment; lost time, skittering sidelong be-tween action and reaction. And suddenly, it's later – maybe *very* late – with the oil-lamp's shine joining a shifty play of firelight across the dusty floor . . . a huge, blood-warm, spark-leaking blaze I must have worked at least a whole half-hour to build, being the woodcraft-un-friendly little city mouse that I am.

(Late.)

The fire, the lamp. And me, looking down at something laid out across my lap, all big and stiff and . . . *furry*.

Something with a hood-like, floppy, shaggy head.

Something that smells, worse than the cabin around it. Worse even than my own stink of cold-sweat incredulity.

Something with empty eyes, and sleeves – their seams sutured fast with dried gut – that end in claws.

Something I know – must be –

(Oh, go on ahead and say it, Lee, baby. You *know* you want to.)

The bear-shirt, itself.

(Karl's . . . bear)

– or what little's left of it, at least. After he finally got through with it.

(Ah, *shit.*)

I feel my eyes sting, my head buzz; feel my inner arm hum with sympathetic pain, my Berkana tattoo puff rug-burn raw, just like it did the day Karl let them draw it on me. Make it to my feet, swaying slightly, and watch this terrible artifact I hold unfurl to brush the floor beneath me; Jesus Christ Almighty, but the fucking thing's fucking huge. Big enough –

(– for two.)

Questions reeling through my head, answered practically in their moment of asking: so where'd I *find* this particular haphazard master-piece of outsider art, anyway? Must've been in that open closet by the bed – the one that looks so very familiar, 'specially when I squint. And why am I having so much trouble forming these questions in the first place? Well, the empty bottle by my boot might hold a key, rolling to clack against a few of its similarly empty buddies as I stagger back to-wards said closet, trailing Karl's precious shirt in the dust – but barely make it to the bed before this subtle numbness in my face and hands spreads southward, felling me onto its rumpled sheets.

And yes, that *is* me crying openly now, all salt and snot. Me knot-ting tight into a wet-faced human ball, kicking off my offending Docs, shucking the rest of my trendy clothes to crawl inside this dead animal husk; me, slicking this unsanitary parody of a fur coat over my own naked skin and hugging it to me, sobbing.

I think about Karl, and wonder: was it just too much for him, in the end? My desertion? This latest – last – failure? Or a self-image-de-stroying combination of the two, that awful morning after . . . cold light of day, the hard death of a lifetime's dreaming, cut with blood-stink and mead-hangover?

Bear-grease on my cheeks, mixing with my tears. Bear-head pulled down over my nose like a mask, toothy jaw flapping to knock against my chin. And Karl's spoor shedding everywhere it touches, marking me with his scent – its sheer bulk so like his, warm and heavy on all my most intimate parts. As I think, hysterically:

(Got me under your skin, Karl, baby – down deep in the heart of you. So deep, I'm really . . .)

. . . a part of you.

(Just like you always said I was.)

I still don't know where he went, and maybe I never will. But – wherever he is, *this* isn't with him. Which means it sure as hell can't be where –

(or *what*)

– he wanted so desperately to be.

And the sad fact is, I think I know Karl well enough to know that if he couldn't be what he wanted, then – in the end – he'd probably rather be . . .

. . . nothing at all.

So I cry myself to sleep, and dream my own dead dream – face-down, tapped out, crushed flat under ten years' worth of retroactive anger and bitter regret. I dream of one more reading, the final one available: Berkana in fire, hot and close as this cabin, sliding swift towards incineration like one of those volcanic islands off Iceland's coast, the kind that rise and fall in a flood of lava and a matter of days. Danger, Will Robinson; you don't know as much as you think you do, not by fuckin' half. So pay attention to detail, or pay –

– the price.

Rune-knowledge, hard-learned, flickering in and out like light through the Yggdrasil's narrow leaves. But paying attention's not exactly top of my list, right at this very moment. Instead, I find myself slipping down fast into a morass of memory crossed with fantasy – "feel" the bear-shirt part beneath Karl's phantom hands as his stubbly profile glides quick across the sweaty small of my back, leaving a trail like the scratch of an open matchbook-cover all the way up my spine. Submerged, swamped, moaning and drooling in my drunken daze, I "hear" him snort and snuffle between my shoulder blades as he pulls me up by the tail, rooting and spreading and puppeting me around in that way he's always liked best. "Feel" my mouth come open as he thrusts inside, coring me, and think:

(Oh Christ, Karl, *Christ* . . .)

Christ, but I've missed this, you could-be-dead-for-all-I-know Nazi nutbar of mine – missed *doing* this, *with* you –

But: it's not true, and I know it, even as the charge begins to build. It's just my fume-filled mind tricking me, my body looping back into those painfully pleasurable patterns of hurt and hunger it knows so well. And the idea that I could be such easy prey, even for my long-lost

75

lover's ghost . . . the mere idea of me overtaken by dumb ecstasy, ruck-ing the sheets and howling, then sagging forward like I've just been dis-emboweled: a corpse myself, skinned and gutted and left to soften like the splayed remains of some —

(bear's)

— last meal.

Jesus, it all just makes me so damn . . . *mad.*

And I come awake, mid-spurt, amid smoke and mess and oh *fuck*, are those *flames*? Fucking cabin's on fucking fire, how the fuck did *that* happen — like I kicked the oil-lamp over in my sleep and it hit the rug, spread and sparked across those bare pine boards where my boots fell and shit, can't believe I'm gonna have to run *barefoot* through this crap — slamming hard into the wall where I think the door should be and bouncing, spinning into that filthy screen, my Berkana-arm punching through in a spray of wounds, broken metal threads already hot enough to cauterize on contact —

Stumbling out into the cold night air, with pine-needles stabbing the soles of my feet; turning back, squinting and gasping, to see the whole damn thing engulfed beyond saving. Shivering in the bear-shirt, clutching myself. Thinking —

(Hey, look, boys 'n' girls . . . a real live Viking funeral, just like on TV. Everything Karl ever had, gone up in flames —)

— all except me.

More questions, though, as the ash flutters upwards: where're my glasses? Inside, of course — unsalvagable by now, mere melted slag. But . . .

. . . I can still see.

And that smell, mounting, that back-of-the-throat strong stink — that must be me too, right? Burnt hair, burnt flesh, burnt bear-hide. Looking down to confirm it and seeing the charred palms of my hands poking from the bear-shirt's paws, my shins already swollen with wa-ter-blisters . . . but why can't I *feel* it? And — what — is that —

(*other*)

— smell?

At which point I turn again, further, towards the first shadowy rim of trees, and see the bear come out of the woods.

Five feet at the shoulder. Twelve standing up, clawed hands tenta-tively drooping inward, childish as a Tyrannosaurus' vestigial clutch. Its fur is sandy, touched with dull hints of gold; its muzzle matted with blood and honey, underbelly-fur shaggy with burrs. I can smell its breath from here, even over myself, over the fire: old bees, fresh car-rion. Honey-sweet blood-reek.

The bear is huge. The bear seems hungry. And its tiny eyes, so dull and atavistic, which widen almost beyond the limits of their narrow orbits as they turn my way — as it catches my (familiar?) scent, and moans with goony ursine lust —

— are blue.

(Karl.)

Karl, in *his* shirt, in "his" bear. In his *natural animal form.*

(That bastard.)

Because if this is Karl's shirt I'm wearing . . . and that's *Karl,* then . . .

. . . I have been seriously screwed.

Find your bear, kill it. Wear its skin —

Yeah, okay, got it. But once you put it on, once you change —

(as is becoming *more* than obvious)

— you can't ever take it off again.

Which makes this not Karl's shirt, then, at all. Made *by* Karl, for certain-sure, back when he still had hands — imprinted with his musk, his enticing flavor, before he traded his tender human skin for the far less permeable coat he now wears. But not on his own behalf. No.

Because just like he said that night I ran away and left him — holding his knife, alone in the darkness — this bear whose hide I wear now, *this* bear was meant —

(— for me.)

The final puzzle-piece, gut-feeling intuition made explicit. Bears are predators, omnivores, opportunists, pure and simple; they tend not to think strategically, if they think at all. And in the wild, just like everywhere else, the only animals who lay traps for other animals . . . are humans.

Giving that kid the key, making him wait. Making *me* wait, and brood, and convince myself I wasn't thinking about Karl at all — even though I rarely thought of anything but — for seven long years. Then sending it to me, and sending me up here, where the trail was strongest — where my memories would finally rise up, break their floodgates forever, knock me down and drag me under like a dark, sweet, dreadful tide —

(Bastard, you *bastard,* you)

— but that's no good. Gotta stop that, right fucking now, before the final phase of Karl's plan kicks into gear. Before he provokes me into battle.

(Fuckin' "battle.")

Yeah, that'd be about his style, that racist son of a racist *bitch.* I mean, what's the definition of Valhalla — Viking heaven — if it isn't getting to fight the same worthy opponent . . .

(and that'd be me)

. . . over and over, world without end, amen?

Which is why, to be frank, I'd be a hell of a lot more worried about these burns of mine if I couldn't already feel them healing.

So I stand here trying to rip the shirt off, before my own inner grizzly has a chance to really sink its hooks in me – but goddamn it all, I just can't. Feel it sealing fast, the claws clicking in and binding to my fingers. Feel my broken knuckle ache and blaze, a white-hot arthritis-flower just about to bloom, like it's going to rain and never stop. Feel my mind getting bear-slow, bear-petty. Bear –

(angry)

Yeah. 'Cause my blood's up, and I'm panting, and that bear –

(*my* bear?)

– if I didn't suspect it was physically impossible, I'd say that bear was fuckin', well, *smirking* at me.

And: ah, but Lee, that treacherous little inner voice whispers teasingly, soft as rot – if you really didn't *want* to wear it, then you never should've put it *on*. You know what I'm sayin'?

I mean, if the shirt fits. . . .

(Oh, fuck *you*, you fucker.)

Lowering my head, lips peeling back over teeth, all sharp and white – sharp*er*, whit*er*. Feeling blood in my head, my face, my heart. Feeling my cock jump, bone-harden, and my pulse pound like a war-drum. And wondering, with what might be my very last – intelligible – thought: is this how they felt, the *berserkgangrs*? When they chewed the edges of their shields flat and bloody, then tore off their mail to reveal the fur beneath? When they threw their swords aside and ran into the fray, like they were finally going home after a long, long journey in the upright, lying, divided world of men – biting, clawing, changing, gratefully – as they went?

History in motion, good Swedish stock. "A part of my heritage."

(The very *best* part, to be exact.)

I feel my jaw seize up, shallowing – my words deform, as a groove carves itself down the center of my tongue. And snarl, with my last human breath:

"Well, fine. You want me back this bad, huh? C'mon on ahead, motherfucker. C'mon and –"

(– *take* me.)

LITTLE HOLOCAUSTS

Brian Hodge

 THERE MUST'VE BEEN SIGNS FIRST. THERE ALWAYS are — subtleties we're afraid to imagine go any deeper than one day's mood. So I don't suppose it was until our latest funeral that I broke down and admitted that something inside Jared was truly changing, and not for the better.

This one had been particularly rough on Jared. Neither of us had been strangers to funerals over the past few years, but this time it was for an earlier lover of Jared's, amicably parted from after a growing realization that all he and Terry had in them was the honeymoon.

People — lovers, especially — have a million ways of changing on you, most of them bad. Not inherently, maybe, but bad for *you*. Because you couldn't or wouldn't follow along.

You'll hear people say that only the dead don't change, but obviously they've never thought this through, because to the dead change comes naturally, as they seek their return to earth and air and water, while we survivors who loved them manage to forget all the flaws that kept things interesting. Remake them into idealized versions that we'd never be able to tolerate if they came walking back through the door this way, so perfect we'd eventually want to kill them all over again. *You . . . you've changed*, we'd accuse them, feeling somehow betrayed.

Terry had died at home — the virus, what else? — his current lover helping the nurses and hospice volunteers care for him. It's where we gathered after the funeral, his brownstone apartment with vintage wood as solid as a bank vault and laid out shotgun-style, one long chain of rooms full of friends, acquaintances, strangers. Everybody was welcome, except for those righteous fuckers who'd showed up at the cemetery to gloat in the distance, toting picket signs.

SODOMITES REPENT, that was one of the gentler ones. Some of them got almost as ugly as the faces underneath, eyes frightened and angry, prissy mouths crinkled tight like drawstring purses.

"And those are the ones with the nerve to claim they're made in God's image?" Jared had whispered hoarsely in the cemetery.

"I'd always pictured God as better looking," I said. "That doesn't make much of a case for omnipotence, does it?"

He appeared not to have heard me, staring at this wretched Greek chorus. "But what if they are? What if they really are?"

At Terry's apartment we threw our coats atop the pile already on the bed, Jared lingering over all the sleeves that seemed caught up in some pointless struggle for supremacy. I wondered if he was remembering being in this same bed three years earlier, maybe recalling a conversation or some good night's love.

"*Déjà vu?*" I said.

Or maybe he was thinking that here was where Terry must have died. Jared pushed hair back from his eyes, saying, "It's felt like *déjà vu* all afternoon. I'm just getting way too familiar with days like this."

"We're here, we're queer," I murmured, "we're dropping like flies."

"And you're not helping any, with your laughter from the gallows," he said, so I just held him, limp and unresponsive even when I squeezed along the back of his neck, where he liked it, and would ordinarily flex back into my hand like Voodoo, our cat. "Was it this way for you when Serge died?"

I stiffened. "What way?"

"Remember that picture from Vietnam? Of that Buddhist monk? He'd set himself on fire in the middle of a street and just sat there burning. Didn't move. Well . . . like I wish I had the kind of control he must've had, not to feel the flames," Jared said into my neck. "*That* way."

"Serge was different. You can't compare the two."

And Jared knew better. Serge and I weren't broken up; not exactly. Serge hadn't been sick. I felt something stir down deep, like the rusty scraping open of a hatch on a ship long sunk, and hurried to slam it shut again. In its saltwatery grave.

"Serge . . . Serge wasn't the same at all."

"This isn't a good day to split hairs," Jared said. "Not if they're both dead when they shouldn't be."

We joined the others, who wandered from room to room in a kind of subdued humor, by turns warm, then mordant, everyone here instinctively craving each other's company and heartbeats. I'd not known Terry, never even met him, and so spent awhile staring at a picture that Jared pointed out, contrasting the vibrant guy on Kodak paper with the one I'd first encountered in his coffin. Had I not had Jared's word on it, I doubt I'd have made any connection.

An hour later I went looking for Jared after I hadn't seen him for a while, and found him alone in the middle of the kitchen, the final link on the chain of rooms.

"You doing okay?" I said to his back.

When he finally turned, he had a look on his face I wasn't braced for, a look that balled up its fist and sucker-punched me right in the heart. He pointed across the room, where he must've been staring for too long, toward the floor along the back wall, near the door, where you'd probably set something too large to fit in the trash can until you could run it out to the dumpster. It was an unused box of Depends. The way Jared pointed it out, looked at it, the box embodied all the loss and sorrow and indignity that had ever escaped Pandora's.

"Diapers," said Jared, like an accusation. Approaching tears. "That's what it comes down to? Goddamn diapers."

Whenever he came to the next town, the stout man in the soot-grey top hat spent a few days getting to know it from the inside out before plying his varied trades. By strolling its streets and alleyways, by poking amongst piles of rubble with his lacquered walking stick, by sniffing over puddles of spilt blood, both psychic and sanguine, he made of each town a lover from whom he could ferret out prizes most delicious. In tipping his nose to a breeze he might sort its complex mélange into component threads – here, garlic; there, despair; further along, mingled excrements of men and machines.

Such habits served sentiment more than utility now. The world held no more surprises for him, and frontiers were illusory. Cities all smelled the same, the populace of one burning and burying, pissing and shitting, in equal measures to those of the one before and the one to come. He could expect nothing else so long as they in their millions sucked from the same monstrous tit.

He missed the land's Byzantine variety of the old days, or as he remembered them to be – time *did* possess a peculiar gilding. Three hundred years hence, he might very well look back on these present days with nothing but fond nostalgia. *Great gods!* he would marvel, *but back then how they knew how to suffer!*

And they did. Boom times, these, everywhere he went.

He'd trod here before, fuzzy on how many decades ago, but long enough that he scarcely recognized it now. How the city had grown; how the city continued to do so, beyond all sensibility, a body sprouting brick and iron tumors in frantic abundance, beyond the needs of healthy expansion. Arteries of thought and commerce met, only to choke one another. Idled factories sat scabbed with corrosion, dead hearts presiding over the decay of a system they'd once nourished, while tenements suppurated, spilling infections into the streets.

As they had sown, so would they reap, and reaping time had come.

The pack which set stealthily upon him one evening he likened to maggots squirming from the fetid cavity that had hatched them. He listened to them jeer him, his appearance, his obvious differences. It was English they spoke, but no English he'd heard the last time he'd walked these lands, a newer dialect sprung up that would set the Queen to spinning in her grave.

That they wanted his money became quite apparent, regardless.

"Don't be absurd," he told them. "I've very little use for the currency of the realm."

They glanced at one another, translating.

"Dead man walking," one decided. "Only he don't *know* it yet."

He counted two guns drawn and another displayed in the waist of one's baggy trousers before he showed them an avuncular smile, gave his face a half-turn, and lifted his walking stick to tap its pewter head upon the ruddy padding over his cheekbone, below his widening eye.

"Now if you'd take a moment from your busy schedules to look in here, we can wrap this up in a trice."

His eye continued to bulge, window to the soul flung wide. He thought of all and nothing, the vast repertoire of his days an open book. He bent his soul into a kind of parabola, on which they might focus through pupil and metacosm, and see reflected back at themselves a thousand-fold what each had cast toward it – all their loathings and hungers, resentments and fears.

It was absurdly simple. They did most of the work. And God alone knew what each one saw. Mischief-makers such as these were doers, not talkers, wasting no words to tell of terrible wonders.

Two of them soiled their trousers and ran. One turned his pistol on his friend a dozen times over, even while the fallen body twitched on asphalt; the final bullet he'd reserved to put through his own mouth. Another fell to the ground screeching, then hooked his long fingernails back to gouge out both offending eyes.

The man in the grey top hat lowered his bulk to his haunches, beside the blind and whimpering brigand. Like Jack Horner seeking plums, he plunged his thumb into the runny well of one ruined eye socket. There he left it, while visions came and went, until he was satisfied: if the dead ones had lives and histories comparable to this one, he clearly had done them a favor.

"Terribly sorry I came too late. Dreadfully sorry," he said. "But in your case there was really nothing left to save, you see."

He tidied his thumb on the boy's jacket, then righted himself and straightened his dingy frock coat. From a breast pocket he produced his card, dropping it onto the writhing boy's chest. It was color of ivory and, bordered with filigree, read:

Hieronymus Beadle, Esq.
Conjurer of Visions
Extractor of the Psychometric Arts
Trader in Souls

And so announced to the asphalt harvest, he went upon his way in search of a warm fireside, soft cushions, and whatever passed for mulled wine in this place of ignoble rot.

By the time of Terry's funeral, Jared and I'd had a couple of good years together. Career waiter and career video store manager; the tail of the world had somehow eluded our grasp. At least Jared was still giving it a good chase. Most of my running now was in circles, five miles each day and ending right where I'd started.

I'd noticed him a half-dozen times in the video store before we'd exchanged any deeper words than when his tape was due back. Mid-twenties, a generous handful of years younger than I, and with round-lensed glasses and dark messy hair looking as if he could be equally at home in a law library or aerobics class. Danielle, my favorite co-worker, finally got tired of my doing nothing.

"Let's take a peek in his subconscious," she said, and pulled up his rentals on the computer. I was happily intrigued to find mostly Japanese animation, Kurosawa samurai films, and everything we had in stock directed by Ken Russell and Sergio Leone.

The afternoon he asked if we had a copy of *El Topo* that we weren't letting on about, I was smitten. Jodorowsky's horrifying symbolist western that somehow veers into socio-religious parable – the boy was no fluff-monger. He said he'd looked all over the city for *El Topo*, and I had to tell him that he'd finally stumped the band, that it wasn't distributed domestically.

The instant he left the store, I phoned a grey market service in Miami for a rush-order VHS dub off Japanese laserdisc. I had it in hand two days later when he returned his current rental, and invited him to a private screening. If he was interested. Since he was such a good customer, with such commendable taste in film.

Several nights later, atop rumpled bedsheets, with our first taste of each other still on our lips, Jared said it had been the only VCR date he'd had where the other guy hadn't popped in a Jeff Stryker or Danny Sommers video, something like that.

"When you see *Beach Blanket Boner* coming on again, it gets a lit-tle obvious," he laughed.

Jared laughed a few weeks later when his lease was up, and I sug-gested he move in with me, saying all I wanted was a cheap way to en-liven my apartment's brick walls. For years he'd been trying to break into comics, with marginal success and rarely better than token pay-ments. Within days of the move I was surrounded by prototypes of brooding existential loners, sketched in shades of gray, who wandered vaguely recognizable wastelands.

He laughed when he showed me all his rejection slips from the better-paying costumed hero markets, saying that the art was only for killing time until he became headwaiter at his restaurant.

He laughed while he told me about being on his own since he was eighteen, when his father kicked him out after finding a porno maga-zine. "If it'd been hetero," Jared said, "he probably would've taken me out to get drunk instead, maybe even buy me a whore if he could've found one cheap enough."

He laughed when he told me about the former friends in high school who'd beaten him up for being too honest about himself when it wasn't what they wanted to hear.

But by this time I was noticing how forced his laughter could sound, a worthy try but no longer good enough to fool me, like the unnerved and tuneless whistling of someone lost in a cemetery.

And that's the way it sounded, more and more, until the day it stopped altogether.

———

"*There's this guy. . . .*"

No man wants to hear anything starting like this, tiny words that send heart and stomach skittering into sick panic. While you knew all along you were irreplaceable, everyone else knew better.

"*There's, um, this guy. . . .*"

Jared pulled it on me at one of the sidewalk tables in front of the beanery where we came for cheap, spicy meals served in crockery that would steam your face and warm both hands. A coterie of pigeons would always gather near occupied tables, to glean crumbs from the crusty bread served here.

"*There's, see, there's this guy. . . .*"

It would be one of the last fine days of autumn before the killing frosts of winter took hold, the late afternoon sunlight golden even when the best it had to shine on looked otherwise run-down and cor-roded and ready for a renewal that would never come, because those with the power to decide these things knew that such places were easier destroyed than lived with.

"There's this guy," Jared tried again, then drew into himself as though he couldn't bear to say the rest.

I wondered if this wasn't some rebound thing, triggered by issues we'd gotten into last week, with Jared still smarting over Terry's funeral and seeking . . . what? Reassurance in a world that offered him none?

He'd interrupted my 200 daily sit-ups and suggested, since we seemed to be getting along so well, with an eye to far tomorrows, making it as official as we could. A same-sex union ceremony? Lots of couples were doing them, even if they legally wouldn't hold the breath expended on the vows.

"It's not the legality of it," he'd defended. "It's the thing itself. It's the ceremony that counts. The statement we'd make."

I'd thought of when we first realized we had something going. Got ourselves tested for the virus, passed six months of fidelity, then got tested again, praying for a rerun of dual negatives, then putting the condoms away afterward in relief. This was all the ceremony we needed. All the statement. A phony marriage seemed like a hoax to play on ourselves. Why pretend to join some club that wouldn't have us for members?

And it surprised me how much bitterness I heard in my voice, how much rage I thought I'd sunk to the bottom of my ocean, until it might break itself down into complete apathy over everything I was denied, that so many others took for granted. Say, walking down any street with someone I obviously loved, and not having to care who realized it. I listened to myself, hearing everything I'd never meant Jared to think was directed at him; said I was sorry.

But once you've laughed in someone's face, he'll remember the sound forever, and only a saint can overlook your best reasons.

"Serge isn't coming back," he'd told me. "I'm the one you're stuck with now. I guess. I'm the one you have to settle for."

There's this guy.

My Brazilian black bean soup cooled in its bowl.

"Does he have a name?" I asked.

"Probably."

"'Probably.' Well, that's good. Two years, and you can still surprise me over a bowl of beans. Jesus. I never took you for the toilet tramp sort."

Jared blinked at me in genuine surprise. "That's the kind of conversation you think we're having?" He shook his head. "I haven't sucked off anybody in a toilet. I haven't gone cruising the park, I haven't even gone cruising the personals."

"Then what kind of guy am I supposed to think you're talking about? You're not the Jehovah's Witness sort, either."

He didn't answer, was somewhere else behind his eyes. Then he leaned back to watch the pigeons strutting on the sidewalk, sleek heads bobbing as they pecked at promising tidbits.

"I've never understood why so many people hate these birds," he said. "Calling them rats with wings. What aren't they seeing?"

He was shredding bits of his bread; sowed a generous handful across the concrete. Wary, the pigeons lifted off a moment with a great snapping of wings, then settled back again to feast.

"They're not just grey," he went on. "Look at those colors around their heads. All those different purples. Lavender. Greens, on some of them. Those are beautiful colors. So maybe they shit on statues, what's to hate?"

"Jared," I said, "I don't want to talk about pigeons now."

He nodded, sweeping more crumbs toward the birds. "There," he told them. "Go shit on a statue for me." Then it was my turn.

"You know one thing I've always envied about you?" he said. "It's the way you can deal with pain. You lock it up and once it's in the box, you never open that box again. You must have skin like an alligator inside."

"Jared . . . " I said. "You're giving me way too much credit for something I'm not even sure I'm flattered by."

"Don't be ashamed of it. I wish I could cope like you, with all the things that are wrong. I look in your eyes, then I look in the mirror, and I don't see the same quality. I wish I could, but I don't."

"If you've got something to tell me," I said, "quit dancing around the subject and *tell* it. Who have you met?"

"Aren't you listening? I haven't met anybody."

A pair of sluggish flies buzzed into his bowl of red beans and rice. Impassive, he watched them crawl and feed; seemed capable of watching until their eggs hatched a new generation. "Everybody has a breaking point," he murmured.

And when I told him he wasn't anywhere near his, that he was stronger than this, Jared didn't even look at me as if to say *How would you know?* It made me question my credibility. If I conveyed nothing — no confidence, no faith, no belief — because nothing worth conveying was left. If, in experiencing most of the same intimate plagues that life had brought to Jared, the better qualities that were part of my essence hadn't been burned away. Or worse, by my own hand been locked beyond retrieval.

"I'm tired of hurting," he said. "Tired of letting everything hurt me, just taking it, because there's nothing else to do, until I don't have anything left inside for it to grind down. So. . . ."

"There's this guy that I've heard about. Walks around looking like something out of Charles Dickens. I don't know what he is, or where he comes from . . . but he's supposed to make the pain stop."

I went with Jared as he sought his deliverer, not because I necessarily believed in rumors he'd heard, or because if they were true I believed myself capable of dissuading him from rash acts, but simply because I'd convinced myself that he'd be safer this way. The streets could be dangerous; he shouldn't walk them alone.

Like Serge had.

Up streets and down alleys, inside bars and outside liquor stores, beneath neon and through shadows . . . we followed a winding course of anguish the same as we'd follow a stream. Where it was created and where it deepened, where it bottomed out and where it became a roaring cascade that swept everything before it.

We talked to hustlers who leaned against graffiti-thick walls or smoked between tricks under the trestles of the elevated train. Talked to runaways who warmed themselves over fires built in rusty oil drums. To castoffs who made homes in boarded-up warehouses, or factories where smokestacks held their last stale dying breath, beneath a sky that still looked irreparably seared.

"Never heard of him." This we got most often, a relief to me.

"Oh yeah, I heard of that guy." This, too, sometimes.

And: "Hey, I think I saw him. He's a killer."

"Right. Some kind of saint, right?"

"Fag. Fags."

"You just missed him, by, like, a day."

Never enough to discourage Jared from continuing. Just enough to keep me from feeling sure this was mere rumor.

There seemed to be no end of places to look, and if we began to think we must have covered them all, then we'd find more. More sprawl, more shadow, more derelict hulks etched against sooty new horizons. It made me recall something I'd been told by one of the street people I used to see all the time near the video store, for whom Danielle and I would sometimes buy sandwiches.

The city grows at night, he'd told me. On its own. That's why so many people can pass a spot for the hundredth time and look at some building as if for the first . . . even if logically they know, from the way it looks, it must've stood there crumbling for sixty, eighty, a hundred years. The only thing they can figure is that it has somehow escaped their notice until now.

The city grows at night, and that's why people can drive past some spot on their way out of the city and think, wait, last week didn't it all used to end right around here? So they decide their memories must be playing tricks on them again, and knit the changes into the way it's always been.

Then, most of them don't give it another thought, he told me. But a few can still feel the city's growth pains in the deepest places inside their dreams, and even those who don't remember on awakening, at least awaken with a growing dread of the city and its demands, realizing that it'll never be satisfied until it's consumed everything there is to be had, making slaves of all who live there. Feeders, and those fed into the maw.

He told me these things one day on my lunch break, then lived another month. Died of acute alcohol poisoning two blocks over, in the alley behind a Thai restaurant. But his face was gone, I heard. Rats. And maybe it's only creative hindsight, but now I swear he told me these things like a man who'd already heard his death searching for him, stalked for dreaming too deeply and brushing dust from the wrong secrets.

He'd said the city had sorted out long ago who it could use to maintain itself, and who would taste best between its teeth.

But why listen to paranoid drunks, anyway?

Hieronymus Beadle recognized intent as soon as he saw them coming, moving with trepidation through the musty Welsh pub until they could see him near the back, sunk comfortably into his chair and drowsing by the fire. During his sumptuous weeks in the city, his waistcoat had grown frightfully snug, buttons a-popping and threads a-straining.

"Sit! Sit!" he bid them. "Been expecting you, I have."

"How's that?" asked the older of the pair, the more prickly; clearly the skeptic, the sniffer out of charlatans.

Mr Beadle gestured toward the fire. "I've been watching the news, of course."

He could unfailingly spot those who'd made a concerted effort to find him, and such was this pair, if the elder against what he thought to be better judgment. But if that wasn't love, Hieronymus Beadle didn't know what was. Always most touching, when they came two by two.

"Wine?" he offered, showing them the stemmed glasses ranked before the fire, glowing like purplish orbs. "There's no place left to serve it mulled. Criminal, that. I'm forced to do it myself, but if you'll look 'round at the sad state of disrepair here, you'll understand why they're only too happy to allow me the indulgence. Cloves and cardamom, cardamom and cloves. They smooth and mellow, they round off the bite."

"Jared," said the skeptic. "The man's an escapee."

"Perhaps. But is it a true escape after the jail's fallen to ruin? Of course not – it's opportunity seized. Now. Seize some chairs, why don't you? They're not half uncomfortable."

When they moved to sit, he leaned forward as if to shake the skeptic's hand, catching him by surprise and clenching tight.

"Don't mind me, just browsing," he told the man, whose lean and startled face had begun to show the true lines of age and of character, and harder times in sorrow's forge. "You're possessed of a fitness mania to prolong the illusion of youth. You've a cat named – Voodoo, is it? – whom you feel you've quite ignored as of late. Your favorite sexual act is mutual oral, but you've never bothered to dig deep enough to understand why. Shall I tell you?"

Always a treat, shocking doubters into silence.

"I'll take that as a tacit affirmative. Somewhere very, very deep within you, the act you call sixty-nine satisfies a yearning for wholeness in creation. Reminds you of the uroboros, the snake swallowing its own tail. Much more apropos, I say, betwixt two men than man and woman. You're each half the world to the other then, yes?"

"It's like that, yeah," he said, dry-throated, and yanked his hand free.

"How. . . ?" said the one in need. Jared.

"Psychometry, plain and simple. A gaudy parlor trick, though, telling present and past. But the future, now, if I could only have managed that one, why, the world would've come to me instead of the other way around." Hieronymus Beadle smiled, eyes crinkling above plump cheeks. "Still, here you are. You've met me halfway, at least. Tell me what carries you through yonder door."

But he knew already. Spend a few weeks anywhere, and whispers inevitably churned like an undertow to draw out seekers of relief from the torments of existence. They came looking precisely like this Jared: miserable with hope, before the court of last resort.

"I take souls, gentlemen," he began, sparing himself the need of listening to questions heard a hundred thousand times already. "I'm no devil, I wreak no sulphurous damnation. A humble peddler, am I, a tinker of flesh and spirit. A dying trade, but all I know to practice, and ironically, more needed today than ever before. I take souls. They're never missed, for with them goes the *capacity* to miss them. It's not unlike the snipping of a giant nerve that connects one to a gangrenous appendage. And just as the amputated limb may be burnt without bringing further suffering in the flames, so too will that troublesome soul wither quite on its own, unfelt. I take souls, and give peace in return."

"And what do you do with them then?" asked the skeptic.

"None of your bloody business."

Hieronymus Beadle sipped his wine, folded hands over belly, and watched them argue. Once he'd provided his services for kings and princes, sultans and emirs, who'd feared themselves in danger of attack by malign sorcery. They'd paid him fabulous sums for the safekeeping of the stuff of their hearts and dreams, until enemies could be rooted out and destroyed. Quite the comedown, this, for so few believed in true magic anymore, motivated only by hopes of an end to suffering. He refused to blame them. It had been a cruel century, overall.

The argument was over, and Jared unswayed.

"Can you . . . do it here?" he asked. "Now?"

"Good heavens, no. Don't be absurd. Souls can't be handed over like wallets. They can't be stolen. They must be surrendered willingly, because they cling to the flesh they know, and must be coaxed and bullied into quitting the familiar. Rather exhausting, the process, but then, peace must often be preceded by a war."

"And is there any other . . . cost?"

"To you? Oh, no. The overhead's already been paid." Hieronymus Beadle now regarded the skeptic. "And you, sir? Is there naught I can do for you? Because if you'll pardon my bluntness, I caught quite the potent whiff of soul's gangrene from you, as well, a few minutes ago. Serge, was that the name? Indeed it was."

Mr Beadle watched him wriggle on temptation's hook.

Some days he felt there to be no honor left in what he did, what had once been a noble trade, suffering no master but his own soul and the short-term dictates of royalty. Never had he dreamt back then that he would one day dance to corporate tunes played by wealthy pipers in their steel towers, overlooking kingdoms of rust and ruin. Serving the beasts they had created, this new generation of city fathers paid bounties in hopes of cleansing each malignant landscape of those who did not fit its dream of what it should be. Purity had always struck him as such a bland and petty goal, yet they worked so tirelessly to achieve it.

He told himself he was still providing a valuable service. In such an age as this, wasn't one's soul a liability, after all?

"Sweet peace, good sir?" he said to the skeptic.

"I don't suppose you can . . . remove the gangrene, and leave the limb, can you?"

"I fear not. It's to be all or nothing. Rather like severing one's spinal cord."

The man shook his head, as if it took some effort. So close; so very close. Still, Hieronymus Beadle was heartened to see one slip through his grasp. Hope for the future, and all.

"Go to hell," the man said, then clung to his Jared in final appeal, which fell upon deaf ears and a heart already starting to scale.

The next morning was the first in more than two years that I woke up alone. Voodoo, curled in a black and white ball at the end of the bed, didn't count. I've often envied the way cats can sleep with someone, yet still sleep alone.

I laid my hand on Jared's side of the bed, then stood before the window, staring out at streets and signs, at other buildings and other people who stared in turn, all of us framed alone and dead-eyed in our windows like portraits left subtly incomplete.

Jared. He was out there somewhere. Or maybe he was now Jared in name only, no longer the real Jared who delighted in obscure movies and liked his chest bitten and drew apocalyptic anti-heroes making their ways through worlds that had been leveled around them by war-heads or disease or neglect. Maybe that's why he hadn't yet come home, maybe never would. He'd become his own character.

I moved away from the window and lingered before a cluster of his sketches inspired by the title character of *El Topo*, the movie that had brought us together. Slim-legged, in black, wearing a rider coat that hit him above the knee, this was your archetypical wandering gun-slinger, rendered in sharp, scratchy strokes of Jared's pencil. Mostly he roamed the starkest deserts and canyons and blasted city streets. But in one he stood contorted in anguish as bullets splattered his blood onto a wall behind him, already shaded with stains from corrosive rain, while the shadow he cast upon it stood in contrast, the essence of balance and calm.

There was nothing like this in the movie, although I could guess what Jared had been drawing inspiration from: the scene in which *El Topo* has met the first of four Master Gunfighters, a man who can no longer be wounded because he's learned to render his flesh impervious to gunfire.

"I hardly bleed," he explains. "I do not resist the bullets. I let them pass through the emptiness of my heart."

When Jared and I watched the movie, I suspect that each of us was too afraid to tell the other how deeply we connected with that line. Wishing we could learn such a trick, and teach it to friends and allies, and others whom we loved, so we could at least sharpen our edge against a city that had decided it could do without us.

Our only regret being that, for some, we'd still be too late.

———

When Serge died, killing him might not have been the initial intent, but things like that so easily get out of hand, it may as well have been premeditated. He was cornered one evening near the mouth of an alley by some cock fascists, four of them, one for each of the cardinal points, so there was no direction to run. Their fun was strictly casual for the first few minutes, using only their fists. Then they got serious. Started in on him with a length of pipe that turned up in the alley.

Somebody who later watched the police inside the yellow-tape corral said that the homicides stood around with coffee, joking over Serge's body. They already knew who he was; a couple of the uniforms on the scene had rousted him with some younger guy a few days earlier, after we'd had an argument. They'd been in a car near his favorite coffeehouse. Now one of the homicides squatted down, inspected Serge's pipe-broken jaw, used a latex-gloved hand to waggle its huge, grotesque skew, and said, "Looks like this cocksucker just didn't know when to say when."

Four years later his murder remains unsolved. Infer from that what you will.

When newer friends, people who'd never met him, would chance across a picture of us together and ask whatever became of Serge, I usually said he'd moved back down to Tampa. Couldn't stand the cold winters here, the way they seem to start in October and end in April. Used to be I could tell they knew I was lying, that they'd caught the throb of some raw nerve that had escaped cauterization.

Eventually, while I'd told Jared the truth, no one else suspected otherwise.

Sometimes I go scratching at the wound, to make sure I've not forgotten how to feel it. But I have to dig very far down, because only the most deeply concealed nerves still feel flayed and raw, like the tendrils of sea anemones scraped with a wire brush. The rest, my public nerves, must've become as encrusted as the city.

I used to think this was something to aspire to.

Used to think it was what I wanted . . . so that somebody else would be forced to look me in the eye someday and tell me how I'd changed, except he wouldn't speak it like an accusation; rather, with admiration, for all I could withstand.

———

A few afternoons later I came home from the video store, and he was back. I'd had days to anticipate and dread and rehearse the moment, but had wasted them, too fearful of even contemplating it.

He must've heard me on the stairs, was there waiting as soon as I came through the door. He hadn't forgotten how to smile, but it seemed a reflex, as if he might've forgotten why he'd want to.

"So, it's . . . done?" I asked.

He nodded.

"What's it like?"

"It's . . . different. But different isn't bad."

"Did it hurt?"

"Hurt . . . pain . . . those really aren't part of my vocabulary now. So I'll just say no." Jared seemed profoundly calm and thoughtful, and when I asked how Hieronymus Beadle had done this thing to him, he recounted it as if telling me about something that had happened to someone else that he'd heard about secondhand.

"He took me to a warehouse, I think it must've been. All you have to do, really, is look in his eye, but that's where any sense of time falls apart. I know I walked around some afterward, but I still don't know how long I've been gone.

"You just look in his eye, and he won't let you look away, no matter how much you want to. He's taking everything you hate most about yourself, and that scares you about whatever might be ahead, and turning it right back at you. Taking you through it all, but a hundred times worse than you dreamed it could be . . . until you just . . . give up. Then he kisses you, and it feels like he could suck away every breath you ever breathed. And then you sleep. Or I did.

"But I think it's solved a lot of the problems I was having. I think I'll be easier to live with now."

Jared shrugged, turned away to leave me wondering what life with him could possibly be like now. What life might've been like elsewhere, in a place that never existed but we'd spoken of just the same, where bigots were few and the diseases all had cures. We used to joke about it, our own private Israel, a queer homeland.

But on second thought, that'd just make it easier for all the righteous fuckers, who brought picket signs to funerals, to raise their own air force and deploy bombers.

I followed Jared toward the bedroom, where he'd disappeared, and halfway down the hall I stooped to pick up a pair of feathers. Small and pale grey, they took me back to that day at the beanery when Jared had told me of the man he needed to find, and how he'd fed crumbs to pigeons, asking why they were so hated by so many.

The bedroom floor was dusted with them, so many feathers a pillow might have been ripped open. But pillows don't bleed. Live birds do. Feathers and tatters of flesh lay clumped about the room. Wet pawprints were tracked everywhere, while here and there larger heaps of meat were still intact enough to recognize, with bent wings and scaly stick legs. The tiny strewn organs glistened bright red, the pocks of shit a chalky white.

Jared was sitting in the middle of the mess, before the open window, through which a cold autumn breeze was blowing, scattering feathers like chaff.

"Look what I can do," Jared said, as he watched Voodoo burrow his fangs deeper into the cavity of a shredded abdomen. "Nothing. I can do nothing."

———————

One reason I've always enjoyed talking with Danielle at the video store is her accent. She originally came from Alabama, and there's something about a Southern accent that can infuse sorrow with enough whimsy to make it tolerable. She once told me that lesbians didn't get beaten up in her town, the same as boys were, because they presented too keen a challenge to most red-blooded hetero guys, who knew they had the proper cure between their legs.

"So I started carrying this big old dildo in my purse, about two sizes past horse," she'd told me. "And whenever one of these guys'd tell me I didn't know what I was missing, I'd pull out Mr Ed and tell the guy if he could top this, he was on."

She was one of the few I'd told the truth about Serge, so filling her in on Jared made sense to me, and then it made more sense to keep going and tell her that it was a temptation to take to the streets again. Hunt down that peculiar man in his top hat and walking stick, and let him work his anesthetizing magic on me, too. And then it would no longer matter that the flesh I loved and fit best with was now emptied of the stuff that had first made it so appealing. Such terrible temptation.

"I never told you about when I came out to my family, did I?" Danielle asked.

I told her I didn't think so.

"When he found out about me, my daddy called me an accident of birth," she said. "Scarcely said a word to me for the next two years. Didn't even want to look at me, and us in the same room, why, you'd think we were strangers. And I suspect I suddenly was, to him. An accident of birth. Got so I played it for a joke, and I'd stand all quiet-like around a corner, lying in wait for him to come face to face with me, so I could see him squirm, just like a wiggle worm on a hot sidewalk."

I wondered which was worse: someone who abandons you in the

flesh, or one who does it while remaining under the same roof.

"But I see things a little different now," Danielle admitted. "We're all accidents of birth, every one of us. Born in the wrong place, or at the wrong time. In the wrong body, or to the wrong set of people. No matter who you are, there'll be something not right. So that all just becomes part of the game, then – there's no malice in it. And the rest of the game? It's putting those things as right as you can."

She reached down to hold my hand. Lifted it up, kissed it, put it back where she'd found it.

"But you don't go throwing away what's not broken," she said, "not unless you got something better to take its place. Nature does abhor a vacuum, you know."

I told her I'd try to remember that.

Danielle liked the fit of her own body just fine, so there'd been no accidents there.

But sometimes I still wished she was a guy.

I don't see Jared anymore.

He left a couple of days after the thing with the pigeons. If it hurt to see him go, it was only because it was a physical echo of what had already happened. Jared was gone before he ever walked out the door, maybe even before he'd heard of the strange man who traversed the worst streets and called to those in pain, offering them an easy way out. Maybe he was gone long before any of it, part of him beaten to death as surely as Serge had been.

So I don't see Jared anymore.

A few nights after he left, I went to sleep wondering what Hieronymus Beadle did with the souls he collected, and in a dream I saw him strolling ponderously away from the city, bloated almost to the point of bursting with his cargo. He walked and sweated blood and walked and mopped his brow and walked until the city lay far behind. At a copse of trees, he stopped, stripped the clothes from his swollen body, and strained and shuddered. They poured from within him like a sickness, those souls, something between liquid and vapor, seeking safety in the ground below; some anchor to cling to. Then, much slimmer, his reservoirs depleted, he put his clothes back on and strolled onward, with purpose, while from the ground on which he'd voided grew rose bushes. The petals were so perfect they nearly resembled faces, and seemed to scream when another man came along, with white hair and a leathery patrician face, and snipped each bud from its stem. He'd toss each one over his shoulder, or drop them to the ground, and when he was done and the bushes were bare, he smiled while a herd of coarse-bristled, tusked pigs burst from deeper within the trees. They squealed and rooted and stamped and slashed, until every last blossom had been devoured, and then, grunting, they lumbered back into the shadows while the white-haired autocrat patted their crusty dark hides.

I was shaking when I woke up, as though I'd seen something I wasn't supposed to. It was a long time before I could get back to sleep, or even wanted to, afraid I might see Jared on hands and knees, fueled by regret and emptiness, rooting in the piles of pigshit, saying, "I know it's here. I know it's here someplace."

━━━━━━━━

But I don't see Jared anymore.

He's around, though. I've seen the writing on the wall.

It was weeks before I made the connection, entertaining the notion that the painted silhouettes which had begun appearing on building walls had come from Jared's hand. No two were the same, black silhouettes as crisp as shadows thrown by someone who could have been standing right next to you, but wasn't. Each one looked tensed, as if startled by the coming of something that cast no shadow of its own. There was one on our building, one on Terry's. One inside the alley where Serge had been murdered. Others, and I wondered if they'd been chosen at random, or if they too had some special significance.

Now and then I'd hear people talk about them, wherever people lingered, and the silhouettes were spoken of with great curiosity. Where they'd come from, what they meant. Everyone loves a mystery.

But no one else had been privy to the things that Jared found most significant when he looked at the world. No one else had sat with him one evening while he paged through a book, horrified and fascinated by photos shot fifty years earlier in the wastelands of Hiroshima and Nagasaki, of the silhouettes of human beings that had been seared onto walls at the instant of the bomb blasts.

What if those were their souls, he'd wondered, souls yearning in that instant of sublime and blinding violence for some record of their passing, even as their bodies were vaporized.

It gave us something to think about.

And now, every day, I look at the silhouette he painted on the side of our building, hoping I'll find it gone. Hoping against all rationality that in the night it will have peeled itself free of the bricks, and gone seeking the flesh where it so rightfully belongs.

But even if I get my wish, what a long search it has ahead.

The city grows at night, and I don't see Jared anymore.

THE SOUND OF WEEPING

Thomas S. Roche

AS MIDNIGHT APPROACHED, QUINN WANDERED the corridors of air-conditioning and frozen death, noting check marks in triplicate on his clipboard, stroking the top of his mace canister, muttering Hail Marys under his breath, and dancing nervously when he crossed the path of the too-young and too-beautiful boy. He did not feel what he thought he felt. The television echoed down the white-tiled halls, casting the bleating screams of the unfortunate damned into the morgue's frozen air. Quinn listened to the wails of the walking dead. *John Doe #743, 11-14-99, Russian River, Gordonville.* He heard the groans of the dead as they were assaulted with pick-axes and knives and baseball bats, knowing that under no circumstances could those who walked in death be defeated. For at the end of this road of life lay the eternity of oblivion, where all the deeds one performs in life remain alive – walking, stiff-limbed, through the world of the living. The screams of zombies filled Quinn's ears as he neared the drawer where the beautiful punk boy lay fine and private. The moans of the victims throbbed in his soul as he touched the smooth metal of the drawer's handle. He heard the crunching sounds as bones were cracked and flesh rent by the unforgiving blows of the risen. He did not feel what he thought he felt. He did not feel what he thought he felt.

He did not feel anything at all.

Quinn had seen the boy brought in on a gurney, bagged and tagged already, locked safely away from Quinn's too-curious eyes. When he first took the job half a year ago, Quinn had been thankful that local health ordinances required bodies ("empties," the ambulance drivers sometimes called them) to be zipped away in bodybags before they ever crossed the threshold of Quinn's world. They were quickly locked in drawers to await autopsy. Then that bastard Coltrane came along. He had moved from San Francisco, the big city, the city of Sodom, the city of Gomorrah. And the town of Gordonville was, to him, a hick-town paradise where he afford a house with his lover – but also, more importantly, where he could be the most outrageous guy in any room. Sure, Gordonville was more liberal than most small towns, which was, perhaps, why Coltrane felt comfortable wearing, quite contrary to the policy of the ambulance company, a large pink triangle patch sewn on the front pocket of his navy-blue fatigues. And why he felt it necessary to torment Quinn endlessly.

Coltrane had seen something in Quinn's eyes, something that Quinn himself hadn't seen – or prayed he hadn't seen. Coltrane *thought* he saw in Quinn's eyes the flicker of lust that spelled a brother. And so, as older brothers typically did, Coltrane tortured Quinn.

Of course, Coltrane probably didn't think of it as torment – Quinn knew this. "Charliegirl." "Miss Charlie." "Girlfriend." "Mary-Charlie," which soon merged into "Mayor Charlie" without losing any of its cheekiness. And finally, "Mayor Charlie of the City of the Dead." Charlie felt a little pleasure at hearing that last one – at least it was vaguely ominous. But Trane soon started back at the beginning of the list with "Charliegirl."

Bastard.

With any of Coltrane's so-called "friends" from the city, such teasing would have been jauntily returned, and the sparring would have ended in a good-natured feeling of camaraderie. Obviously that was what Coltrane expected to happen in Quinn's case. Except that Coltrane was sadly, pathetically mistaken, unforgivably off the mark. Quinn did not ever, under any circumstances or in any surroundings, feel the things Coltrane thought he felt.

Such things simply did not occur, and if they did they were to be dealt with swiftly. Mother had been very clear on that. Such things were fine for Sodomites like Coltrane or his big-city cronies, they were even fine for neighbors and perhaps distant acquaintances. But such things were simply not possible for children of Sarah Quinn, and she had made that abundantly clear to the young Charlie Quinn, particularly the time she had caught him and cousin Jimmy playing in the closet. Oh, how clear she had made it.

Jimmy had been taken away, and Charlie Quinn never saw his cousin again. In the magical thinking of childhood, Charlie thought that his cousin had been taken away to Hell, having confused the evangelical ranting of his mother and the dream-logic of cartoons and Christmas specials. The one time Uncle Karl and Aunt Betty had visited again, when Charlie was twelve, Jimmy hadn't come along, and nobody asked about him. The visit had been stifled and uncomfortable, the adults sipping coffee in the living room while Charlie shifted uncomfortably on his chair. Karl and Betty left after half an hour of nervous small talk about politics and distant relatives.

It was perhaps three months after that when Charlie screwed up his courage and asked his mother whatever became of Jimmy. By that time he was old enough to know that Jimmy had certainly not been taken away to a children's Hell. Charlie was a little embarrassed that he had ever thought such things himself (luckily, he had never told anyone). So he posed the question, and received a terse, pinched reply. Jimmy would indeed be going to Hell. But he hadn't gone there just yet, Sarah Quinn told her son. He was living in San Francisco.

Quinn usually read the Bible or a prayer book during his long watch as morgue security. It mingled nicely with the TV, gave him something to do during commercials or if the all-night horror-movie marathons got slow. Channel 38 showed all-night horror movies, Fearsome Freddy's Fangtastic Feast, hosted by that used-car salesman who used to be a bit-player in low-budget horror movies. Quinn liked the horror movies, because they scared him just a little – just a little – which took his mind off how ridiculous the Bible was. Quinn read it every night, because he couldn't get interested in anything else except horror movies and the Bible. But Quinn didn't believe in God or Jesus – not really. Certainly this disbelief was a much greater obscenity than anything Quinn might have thought of doing – if he had thought such things, which he didn't. To himself, Quinn rationalized his Bible study in one of two ways.

First, it made Mother happy, and kept her off his back. She would quiz him every morning on the chapters and verses he claimed to have read, and if he couldn't answer her intelligently she would launch into a rambling discourse about how her only son was doomed to Hell. Which Charlie didn't necessarily believe, but once Mother got started he was certainly in Hell for twenty minutes or so.

But the second reason Quinn studied the Bible, and the reason that was more confusing to him, was that he really did wish for salvation – he ached bodily to feel the hand of God. Quinn had stopped believing in God somewhere in adolescence. But part of him wanted to believe there was a divine intelligence watching his every move. Because it was a goddamn lonely universe out there.

The night it happened, it was the classic '60s zombie flick *City of the Walking Dead* on KTCA 38. "One of the greatest horror films of all time," Fearsome Freddy had cackled. "Your own little reminder of

Halloween in May. And after the show . . ." Fearsome Freddy rubbed his hands together in his trademark fashion – the way he had done it in *Bride of the Nightmare* and *Lord of Terror Castle*.". . . after the show we have a very *ghoulish* surprise for you, Fear-fans. A very ghoulish surprise, indeed."

And Freddy laughed, a wicked, Satanic laugh, one which, after many months of late-night horror marathons at the security station in the morgue and the horrible thing that had happened earlier, Quinn found oddly comforting, oddly soothing, oddly pleasurable – oddly familiar.

What had happened earlier that night, the "horrible thing," was this: that annoying bastard Coltrane had crossed the line. Quinn, in response, had crossed one, too. He was still pretty embarrassed about it, and he was scared about what Trane might do to get back at him.

With Quinn's help, Coltrane had been pulling the gurney out of the back of the ambulance, while Trane's partner Sanders finished up the paperwork. Quinn really wasn't supposed to help them move the bodies, but at eleven o'clock at night, nobody would know or care. But rather than quickly wheeling the boy into the morgue for processing, Coltrane leaned over and started to unzip the bag.

"You've got to see this one, Charliegirl. OD down by the river. Probably heroin. You won't believe your eyes. It's a fucking shame for a beauty like this to go. And so young!"

"Coltrane, *don't*," spat Quinn irritably.

Coltrane unzipped the bodybag and Quinn fought against the impulse to look at the body. It would satisfy Coltrane too much, and that was the last thing Quinn wanted to do.

"Isn't she a beaut?" asked Coltrane with a smile on his face, looking at Quinn. And, despite his determination not to satisfy the smug bastard, Quinn looked down at the boy.

Quinn would have sworn his ears started ringing when he saw the dead boy's face. Drained of blood, it had the ivory quality that only a few corpses get. His lips were full and blue, thicker in death, even, than in life. The boy wore one silver earring which flashed behind the translucent curtain of his blue-black hair. The smooth, pale skin, which only made his face more beautiful, contrasted with the tangled curtain of the boy's hair. Framed in black, the face looked like that of a velvet-robed monk – holy and beatific in prayer, in contemplation.

The boy was so beautiful it hurt Quinn's eyes to look. Quinn could feel an ache in his throat, and he wanted to weep for the lost little boy.

The kid looked like one of those punk-rock hustlers who worked the river, having run away from home in Iowa or Kansas or something and come to California to make his fortune. Why the hell they chose Gordonville was anybody's guess, and certainly not Quinn's. They usually ended up working the truck stops – boys and girls both. The boy appeared to be about sixteen.

"Didn't you close the eyes?"

Coltrane shrugged. "Sorry, girlfriend. I did, but they do that sometimes. They just open up. Won't do any good to close them again. If somebody claims the body, they'll take care of it when they autopsy him so the parents don't have to look into their son's baby-blues. If not . . ." Coltrane sighed. "Then it's ashes to ashes."

Glaring, Quinn reached out and gingerly closed the boy's eyes. The feel of the boy's flesh against Quinn's fingertips was chilling. Quinn stared for a second at the boy's face – eyes now closed, as if in sleep. He felt his heart pounding.

"Zip him," said Quinn, but Coltrane did not.

"Zip him up," Quinn repeated, louder this time.

There were tears in his eyes and he couldn't figure out why. It was pissing him off, in fact. He wanted to smack Coltrane for showing him the boy – didn't that prick know that death wasn't something to fucking laugh at? Except that Quinn couldn't really convince himself of that, since he laughed at the jokes sometimes, too. But this time it wasn't funny.

"Zip it!" growled Quinn angrily. But Coltrane chose that moment to deliver the words that crossed the line in the sand between him and Quinn.

He said it lovingly, his voice rich with sarcasm and want: "He was sitting when he went – you know what that means, don't you? And he's tall and thin, and look at that nose . . ." Coltrane laughed. "I wouldn't mind getting twenty minutes alone with this one, myself. How 'bout you?"

Quinn did it before he even knew what he was doing. He reached over the boy, grabbing the lapel of Coltrane's shirt, and as he held Coltrane he lashed out with his fist and socked the smug bastard in the face. Quinn had never hit anyone in his life, but it seemed like beginner's luck – Coltrane went down. Quinn was still holding his shirt, and Coltrane was a much larger man than Quinn – maybe six-two, maybe two-ten to Quinn's five-six, one-forty. Once the blow had been delivered, it was like everything happened slow-motion. As Coltrane went down, he reached out, grabbed Quinn's belt, and dragged Quinn with him, pulling the younger man right into the gurney, right up against the splayed body of the punk boy, whose flesh felt cold even through the bodybag. And as Coltrane went down, the gurney tipped and spilled, bringing Quinn down with it. Quinn landed on top of the boy, whose chest gave way as Quinn's knee came down on it, and whose lips therefore uttered a strangled squeal of post-mortem pain or ecstasy or despair or longing, or maybe simply mourning, as his eyes popped suddenly and unexpectedly open, as if the boy had just awakened from a nightmare. He stared upward, alive but frozen in the instant of his passing, as Quinn struggled to get off of him.

───

Coltrane knew he'd been out of line, and he'd let the incident pass. But he wouldn't be making jokes with Quinn any more, that was for damn sure. "Your problem's that you're a fucking homophobe," Coltrane hissed, as he and Sanders wrestled the punk boy back onto the gurney and zipped the bodybag closed. "You're a fucking homophobe."

"Yeah, and you're a fucking faggot," said Quinn.

───

The cheesy music blaring from the television grew louder as Quinn floated down the corridor, his rubber-soled shoes oddly silent on the white tile. He could feel his heart pounding as screams echoed through the halls. He could feel the tightness in his crotch that he tried not to think about. He wasn't getting hard. He didn't feel anything.

Screams. Sobs. Breaking glass.

He knew the TV would cover the sounds of what he was doing if somebody happened in. In case Coltrane came back. Not that Quinn was going to do anything. He just wanted to look. Just a little. Just a quick look. The boy had cool hair, that's all. Not that Quinn was interested in hair, at all. Not at all. But his was cool, he just wanted a look. Just a moment. Just a moment to look at the boy.

Quinn was surprised to hear himself muttering Hail Marys under his breath. He cursed.

Moaning, crashing, another scream. Violins, louder and louder.

The handle of the drawer felt cold in Quinn's hand through the rubber. Quinn had put on rubber gloves. Why had he done that? He was just going to look at the boy. . . .

The drawer slid open noiselessly.

Screams, moans, screams, cries, a wet, splashing sound.

Somebody weeping.

The zipper felt as if it were greased, it came down so easy. Quinn looked at the boy's beautiful face, and he could feel the blood pounding in his ears. The boy looked alive. His eyes open, his parted lips swollen and blue, as if he were wearing blue lipstick, like the boys Quinn had sometimes seen down by the river liked to do. Blue lipstick . . . and such full, thick, beautiful lips.

Quinn got the zipper down halfway. Without knowing what he was doing, he leaned forward. . . .

Such beautiful lips. . . .

Screams, screams, screams, the sound of weeping.

The boy's swollen, cold tongue was easy to tease out of the open mouth. Quinn tasted its sourness, the sharpness of whiskey. He felt his hand moving down. . . .

What was that? What was that he was feeling in his hand? Was it his own, or the boy's? Quinn could feel himself shivering as he touched it, whoever's it was, and it seemed so big, bigger than it could possibly be. Quinn shivered, and he knew he was going to come. And the boy –

Wails, crashing, splintering wood, screeching violins, the sound of weeping.

Quinn screamed.

All around him, the drawers which held the dead had begun to slide gradually open.

Moans, the sound of weeping. A chainsaw. Breaking bone.

Underneath him, under the boy's drawer, another drawer came out quickly – it was the one with the German tourist in it – and Quinn tripped, fell on top of the boy, gasping.

The boy's arms came up, around him, cold, stiff, his limbs frozen as if in premature rigor-mortis. Quinn screamed, squirmed, tried to struggle as the boy's hard cock pressed against his thigh. The drawers, all around him, were coming open, and in them the dead were sitting up, reaching for him, moaning, wailing, weeping – the boy moaned.

Yelling, gasping, moaning. The sound of weeping.

Sobbing uncontrollably. The boy's hands wrapped in Quinn's longish hair and pulled his face down. Quinn could feel the boy's cold tongue in his mouth, as the myriad walking dead crowded around him and he heard the television going dead.

"Charlie! Charliegirl! You know you shouldn't be watching that shit, it'll rot your brain! Charlie? Charliegirl! Don't tell me you're still pissed at me! Are you? Charlie?"

Quinn clawed at the boy's cold hands, trying to pull them from the tangle of his hair; the boy's grip was unbreakable. He felt the stiff arms of the boy pulling, dragging, forcing him down. He felt the hands of the dead touching him as they crowded around.

"Charlie! Yoo-hoo, Miss Charlie! Mary-Charlie – holy goddamn *shit!*"

Quinn could feel the cold hands ripping at his clothes, tearing, yanking, unfastening. He could feel the cold fingers prodding at him, curving around his hardness. He could feel the boy forcing him down. Feel his naked flesh against the boy's hard cock.

"Charlie! Quinn! Charlie! Jesus Christ!"

The boy pulled Quinn fully into the drawer, so that Quinn sprawled on top of him, their bodies mirrored, their legs and bellies and chests and faces pressed together. Quivering, Quinn sobbed, in fear and despair and something else he could not define, in release and pleasure as the boy's cold dead body sucked the heat from his. As he heard the footsteps of the dead and felt their touch on his flesh –

As, slowly, the boy reached out, grasped the edge of the drawer above theirs –

And with one smooth movement, pulled the drawer closed.

"Charlie! Charlie! What the hell –"

Screams.

The drawer slammed shut, the boy kissed Quinn, deep, his cold tongue probing. His cock pressed against Quinn's body. It was cramped in here, but Quinn didn't mind.

Wails. Screams. Moans, gasps, a wet, warm slurp. The sound of weeping.

Quinn, without knowing why, hungrily kissed the boy back, and he could hear the sound of his own weeping in the tiny, cold, cramped space, but oddly, Quinn did not feel sad or lonely or frightened – maybe for the first time in years, maybe for the first time ever.

Outside, in the night, there was a scream.

"HEY, FAIRY!"

Edo Van Belkom

 HE HAD JUST STEPPED OUT OF THE BAR AND ONTO the sidewalk when he'd heard the call.

"Hey, fairy!"

It made him stop where he stood, the faerie within him curious to know who had called him and slightly fearful that he'd been discovered.

The faerie had been inhabiting the man's body for less than a month. It was a commensal relationship in which the faerie was free to explore the man's world while the man – his host – neither benefitted nor suffered from it. And even though the faerie shared and sometimes even influenced the man's thoughts, this host, like every one before him, was completely unaware of the faerie's existence. The faerie often thought of the humans he inhabited as trolley cars in perpetual motion. He was free to hop onto any one of them he pleased and could ride them for as long as he liked. When he grew bored, he would simply jump from one train to another, leaving the familiar behind in favor of something new.

But although his present host was providing him with a very comfortable existence – a respite, almost – the faerie had grown tired of him and had already begun looking for a new one.

Someone different . . . more exciting.

He turned to face his accuser.

"Yeah, I'm talking to you, faggot!"

Oh, that, mused the faerie.

———

Joey Fleck and the boys were looking for some fun.

They'd been shut out at the bar, and Mark had even had a drink poured in his lap by some bitch who thought she was hot.

Four bouncers and a couple of cops made sure they left the place without any trouble, but that had been an hour ago and six blocks away. There weren't any cops around now, and nobody would care all that much if some homo got his fucking ass kicked.

"Where do you think you're going?" said Joey, as he picked up his step to catch up with the faggot who'd just come out of the St. Charles.

Mark and Serge kept pace with Joey, one on either side of him, both laughing like school kids.

The faggot was trying to ignore them, like if he pretended that he didn't hear them, then maybe they'd go away. Fat chance! Joey had been getting the cold shoulder all night and no fuckin' way he was going to take shit like that from some take-it-up-the-ass homo-fucking-sexual.

"I said, where do you think you're going? Asshole!"

Mark and Serge ran ahead, grabbed the faggot by the arms and moved him off the sidewalk and into an alley where the light was bad and people knew enough to stay the fuck away.

Joey approached the faggot slowly. He was a short guy, but still looked solidly built for his size, like he worked out. And even though Joey would never say as much, he thought the guy was good-looking, the kind of guy who – if he wasn't a fucking faggot – probably wouldn't have to leave a bar like Maxwell's holding his own pecker in his hands.

"I'm going home," the faggot said. "Now if you just leave me alone, please. I'll be on my way."

"I'm going home," said Joey in a high-pitched falsetto. Then he lowered his voice: "Home to your butt-buddy?"

"No, just home," the faggot said, his voice tinged ever-so-slightly with fear, like he knew he was about to get the fucking shit kicked right out of him.

It gave Joey a good feeling. The bitches in the bar could laugh and turn their backs on Joey Battistuzzi, but no way this faggot could get away with it. Joey Fuckin' B. was in control here, and the faggot knew it.

There was a crazy look in the faggot's eyes that was giving Joey the creeps. "What the fuck are you looking at?" he asked.

"Nothing," the faggot shrugged, trying to look away.

"You calling me *nothing?*" said Joey, tilting his head to one side and looking up past the faggot into the starless night sky as if he couldn't believe what he just heard.

Mark and Serge started laughing again, knowing – like Joey did – that it didn't matter what the guy said, it would all be turned back against him and eventually lead to a beating. But what could you expect? The guy was a faggot and he had it coming to him.

The faggot just shook his head, keeping his eyes on the ground, afraid to look Joey in the eye. In a minute he'd probably offer them money or something, or just beg them not to beat his ass. And then he'd probably start crying, which always made Joey laugh. Fuckin' faggots couldn't even take a beating like a man.

"You think you're too good to talk to me?" asked Joey, slamming his palms into the guy's shoulders and sending him reeling backward onto his ass. He moved forward and towered over the fallen faggot waiting for an answer. But of course there was no real answer to the question – a "yes" was the same as a "no" since either one would suggest the faggot felt himself superior in some way.

The faggot said nothing, but his body was beginning to tremble, like he was afraid.

"So you think you're too good to talk to me?"

Finally, the faggot said, "No."

Joey shook his head like he'd just heard some bad news. "You know what your problem is, asshole? You got a big mouth."

"From sucking too much cock!" said Serge and both he and Mark laughed.

Joey tried to keep a straight face, but couldn't help snickering at the line.

———

The faerie watched the scene unfold with rapt interest.

When he'd chosen this particular one as his new host, the man's sexual preference hadn't even been a consideration – in fact, he hadn't even known what it was at the time.

Previously, the faerie had been living in the body of woman whose frequent sexual encounters with both men and women had been interesting at first, even exciting, but which eventually became boring and repetitious. Then one morning as his host walked down the street following another of her one-night stands, she came upon an old lady who had tripped on the sidewalk and was in obvious pain. To the faerie's chagrin, his host walked right past the woman without even a glance to see if she needed help.

Even worse was the fact that his host was not alone in her indifference. Everyone was walking past the old woman, some even stepping over her as if she were an unpleasant mess on the sidewalk. But there was one young man who finally came to the old woman's aid. He knelt down beside her, asked if she was all right, and used his cell phone to call for an ambulance.

The faerie had found his new host.

But while kindness and compassion were comforting qualities in a host, they weren't much use here. This situation called for brute force and savagery, of which his host had none. And yet, the man was managing to maintain a fairly brave front, especially considering that his mind and body were wracked with fears of being disfigured, crippled, even killed by these three thugs.

Well, there was no way the faerie could allow that to happen.

Doing nothing while his host received a beating was absolutely unacceptable. And so the faerie decided to help level the playing field by wiping away a bit of his host's fear and replacing it with a little self-confidence.

If the three men were lucky, or smart, they would resolve this situation without coming to blows.

The faggot got up off the ground, dusted himself off, and said, "If you let me go now, I – uh, I won't press charges."

All three of them stopped laughing. "What?" said Joey.

"I said, if you let me go now, I won't go to the police. I won't say anything to anyone."

"You want me to let you go?" said Joey, wondering how the guy figured he was in a position to bargain.

"Yes."

The guy's got some balls, Joey thought. Have to give him credit for that. Too bad it isn't going to help him any. If anything, it's gonna get him beat even harder. "Just let you walk right out of the alley like nothing happened?"

"That's right."

"And if I don't?"

"Somebody might get hurt."

"Ooo-hooo-hooo," howled Mark.

"It might even be you, asshole," said Serge.

Where the fuck did this kind of talk come from? wondered Joey. The closer this guy was to getting his ass kicked the more attitude he had. "So you're going to hurt me?"

"Maybe."

Serge and Mark were giggling, but Joey didn't think it was all that funny. For some reason he was starting to get a bad feeling about this guy. Usually when they picked out a homo he'd start begging for them not to hurt him almost right away, and eventually he'd end up crying like a baby until Joey got so disgusted, he'd give the guy a kick in the nuts and tell him to get lost. This one had started out that way but he seemed stronger now. He was talking like he could take all three of them and Joey wondered if maybe he had a gang of faggot butt-buddies hiding in the shadows somewhere, just waiting for a sign.

Joey took a look around, sizing up the situation. Even though it was dark in the alley there really wasn't anywhere to hide. Obviously the guy was bluffing, and Joey had almost fallen for it. That pissed him off even more.

Joey paused for another moment as if he was thinking it over. Finally he just shrugged and said, "Yeah, okay."

"What?" said the faggot.

Joey could see the relief on the guy's face, like it was really over. Like all they were doing was scaring the shit out of him. . . . See if he'd pee his pants or something. "Go on," said Joey, slapping a hand on his shoulder. "We were just messin' with you. No hard feelings, all right?"

Mark and Serge held back their laughter long enough to nod in the direction of the street.

"Really?" said the faggot. "I can go?"

"No," said Joey, balling up his right fist and swinging it as hard as he could at the faggot's face.

———

Even the faerie was surprised by the blow. His host's nose had been crushed by the force of it and several bone splinters had been pushed dangerously close to his host's brain.

It had all happened so fast.

His host had tried to reason with them, had politely asked to be let go. And they'd agreed . . . only to hit the man when his defences were down. Even now the other two were holding him while the big one pummeled his face and body with his fists.

And for what?

Because he was different.

Preferred men over women.

It just seemed so . . . small.

Three against one.

And the one wasn't fighting back.

The faerie decided to change all that.

———

"You'll be sorry you did that."

Joey stopped the beating, his fist hesitating behind his head like a hammer waiting for a nail.

"What?"

"I'm going to make you pay."

Joey lowered his fist and just looked at the faggot. The guy's nose was caved in and he was missing a few teeth. His lips were split open and his face was already starting to swell. How was he able to talk?

And the voice . . . it wasn't the same one as before. A few minutes ago the guy had sounded soft, like air coming out of a hole in a tire.

Now, his voice sounded deep and throaty, as if it was coming from somewhere deep inside of him.

It had Joey a little spooked.

"Come on, let's get out of here," said Serge, still holding the faggot down but looking out into the street like that's where he wanted to be.

"Yeah," said Mark. "He's busted up bad enough."

"Shut up!" cried Joey, giving Mark a slap in the head.

"You're afraid of a little fucking homo talking tough!"

"You can't run from me," said the faggot.

Joey looked down at where the faggot lay in the alley, his eyes opening wide in amazement at what he saw. The faggot's nose and teeth were all back in place and his lips were healed over. Joey took a hard swing at the faggot's head and hit him just under the right eye. He could feel the cheekbone shatter and the eye socket turn wet under his knuckles.

But when he pulled his hand away, the guy's eye was winking up at him and the guy was fucking smiling . . . smiling as if the tables had been turned, even though Mark and Serge were still holding him down.

"Fucking macho-homophobic-pussylicking straight boys," said the faggot.

Joey hit him again. Mark and Serge started whaling on him, too, but it didn't seem to be doing any good.

It was like punching a bag of sand.

"Is that the best you can do?" said the faggot with a bit of a laugh. "'Cause now it's my turn."

Joey reeled back for another swing but the faggot's foot came up and caught him in the nuts. It was like getting hit by a baseball bat. Spikes of pain shot up like fireworks from between Joey's legs and his stomach heaved as if he was going to barf.

Mark and Serge reached over to hold on to the faggot's legs, but as they did the guy's fists flew up and caught each of them on the chin. Mark was able to shake off the blow, but Serge was thrown backwards, landing on his back a couple of feet away.

Mark threw a few punches at the faggot but they didn't do a thing to stop him from taking another swing at Mark's chin. Only this time the faggot hit him with an open hand, his thin straight fingers piercing the skin and slicing up under his chin like a knifeblade. Then he curled his fingers around Mark's jawbone, grabbing it like a handle and using it to pull him down to the ground.

Joey felt Mark's blood splatter across his face and a second later he was spewing chunks of the quarter-pounder he'd had a few hours ago onto the alley floor.

The faggot stood up, looking huge from where Joey lay on the ground. The guy's face was a mass of angry shadows, and it looked like he was just getting started. "What's the matter with you guys?" he said. "Three of you can't take one little homo-fucking-sexual."

Joey couldn't stand anyone talking to him like that, no matter how bad off he was, so he spit a mouthful of puke onto the guy's shoes.

But that only seemed to make him more mad, because a second later the faggot's puke-covered shoe smashed into Joey's forehead, snapping his head back and sending him spinning deeper into the alley.

"Three against one," he said, turning around to face Mark and Serge. "That seems fair, doesn't it?"

He took a step and kicked Serge in the gut as hard as he could. The air whooshed out of Serge's lungs with a grunt.

"Or maybe four against one would have been better."

Mark tried to get up then, tried to scramble out of the alley, but the faggot wouldn't let him. "Where do you think you're going, shit-for-brains?"

The faggot kicked Mark in the ass, sending him sprawling onto his stomach. Then he was pulling down Mark's pants until they ringed his ankles like he was taking a shit.

"Hey, nice equipment," said the faggot grabbing Mark's cock and balls. "Maybe I'll take them as a souvenir."

"C'mon, man," pleaded Mark. "I didn't want to hurt you. It was all –"

The man's words were cut off by his scream as the faggot dug his fingers into his flesh and ripped his nuts from his body like he was pulling fruit from a tree.

Somebody's gonna hear that, thought Joey. But even if they did hear they wouldn't be coming around to see what was going on, would they? No, they'd be too afraid to enter the alley, and they'd wait until morning instead.

Mark managed to get to his feet. He swayed back and forth in the mouth of the alley with his hands over the wet patch between his legs, holding it like he was trying to keep his guts from sliding right out the hole in his crotch. He stayed on his feet for a few seconds, blood oozing between his open fingers and streaming down his legs, then he just fell forward, not even putting his hands out to break his fall.

The faggot must have been worried about another scream attracting attention because when it was Serge's turn he just walked up to where Serge lay, stood over him for a second or two, then drove his knee down into Serge's neck. There was a crunch of breaking bone and a single yelp – like a dog that's got his tail caught in a door – and then nothing.

Joey wanted to run, but he couldn't even stand up. Instead, he got up on all fours and began to crawl toward the dark end of the alley where there was a door. Maybe he could crawl through it and get away.

"Nice view, buddy," said the faggot, coming up behind him. "After all we've been through, I would have thought you were the last one who'd want to take it up the ass."

"Up yours!" Joey managed to say, teetering on an arm and two knees long enough to flip the faggot the bird.

The faggot laughed. "No, my friend. It's going up yours."

Jesus, thought Joey, he's going to do me up the ass right here in the alley.

But that wasn't the faggot had in mind at all.

He grabbed Joey's right hand – the one he'd used to give him the finger – and yanked on it, pulling Joey flat onto his stomach. Then there was a foot pressing against Joey's shoulder and his arm was being pulled . . . hard. It was being twisted, too, to the point where things were starting to break.

Joey could feel the tendons in his shoulder being stretched, then the muscles too and finally the skin. And then there was a tearing sound, like a tire being slashed open, and a loud snap, like a dry piece of wood being broken in two.

And then his arm was gone.

His shoulder felt cold. Wet.

The darkness of the alley began to grow even dimmer.

The faggot was pulling at his pants now, pulling them down.

And then something big was pressing against his asshole, pushing to get in.

More tearing sounds and then a feeling of being stretched wide open.

Penetration.

And a hint of laughter.

Joey looked down between his legs and saw the bright red nub of his upper arm – the part that had been ripped from his shoulder – jutting out from between his legs like some huge phallus. The arm was bent at the elbow and the other end – the end with his hand – was buried deep inside him.

His only thought was that there was no way he wanted to be found like this, and so he reached down between his legs with his left hand and grabbed his right arm.

He pulled on it once, before the darkness overtook him.

The faerie felt strong and alive.

He wanted to do more to these men, tear them into little pieces, pound them into the ground, but there was no point to it now. Besides, he couldn't remain in the alley forever. Someone was bound to come along at some point.

So he wiped the blood from his hands, leaving the shadows behind and walking down the street toward the subway. But even though he wasn't far from home and the ride would be a short one, he wondered how he'd be able to sit still for it when his entire body was coursing with energy and in desperate need for more action.

When he reached the entrance to the subway and the stairs that lead down to the trains, the faerie hesitated.

He wasn't done riding this one yet.

Maybe he'd walk.

Take the long way home.

And that's when he noticed the shadow-stained park across the street. It stretched out across the city for several blocks and it was as black as night. It would only take him about ten minutes to walk it, but if he were lucky, there would be some little shit lurking in the shadows, or behind some tree.

He checked the traffic, then headed for the park, walking slowly, whistling a tune.

THE SPARK

William J. Mann

 NORMAN GILLETTI COULD ALWAYS TELL WHICH ones were really in love. They were the ones who slow danced to "Stairway to Heaven" even when the music speeds up. You know how it goes. It starts off slow and the boys dance with their arms hanging over the girls' shoulders, but then it gets faster and most of the couples break up and start dancing on their own. Except for the kids who are really in love: they stay holding on to each other and move real slow even when the music gets fast.

"Clare Aresco is so fucking hot," Stick Guthrie told Norman, watching Clare and Dave Wysocki barely moving on the dance floor, faces buried in each other's long auburn hair, chest to chest.

"Yeah," Norm agreed.

"Can you imagine what that feels like?" Stick asked.

"What?"

"Her tits pressed up against you like that."

Norman thought about it. "Yeah," he said. "Must be great."

Stick shook his head. "It's giving me a hard-on just thinking about it."

"Really?" Norman asked.

"Shit, yeah. See?" Stick thrust his groin out at his friend. He was wearing very tight, maroon corduroy pants. There was a vague outline of an erection pointing toward his navel, slightly off to the left.

"I can't see in here," Norman lied. "It's too dark."

"Aah," Stick said, dismissing him.

It was dark in there. The Dance Committee for the Class of 1979 at Sacred Heart Academy always made sure the lights were turned down really low in the gym. That way the kids could make out behind the bleachers. It was always the same kids on the Dance Committee: Pattie Marino, Nancy Barbagallo, Dave Wysocki, Clare Aresco. Norman looked out onto the dance floor: yep, Clare was gone all right. Probably letting Dave Wysocki feel her up under the bleachers this very minute. But that was okay: they were really in love.

"I hate this whole fucking place, this whole fucking school, and whole fucking town," Stick said suddenly. "What's left in this place for us? These miserable dances and nothing to look forward to when we graduate."

Stick was always saying things like this. They were older than a lot of their classmates. Both had turned eighteen months ago, and they were edgy to get on with it, get past all this. Norman didn't know what kind of a job he'd get next year after school was finished. College was out of the question; his mother couldn't afford it, even with loans. There weren't many jobs in town, especially since the last thread factory had closed two years ago. Norman didn't like to think about Stick moving away without hi, but he figured that's probably what would happen.

"Stairway to Heaven" was finishing . . . *and she's baa-baa-ing a sta-baa-way to hebb-heb-run. . . .* That was the big song of the night. Most of the cool kids would leave now. "You're The One That I Want," the song from *Grease* by Olivia Newton-John and John Travolta, was coming on (*ooh, ooh, ooh, honey*), but only a few kids were still dancing. The geeks, thinking they looked real cool in their flared polyester pants and silky flower print shirts, and their girlfriends, in tight dresses and real tall spiky-heeled shoes. One girl did look a little like Karen Lynn Gorney, but Norman still thought she looked silly.

"Whatsa matter, Norman?" he heard over his right shoulder. It was Clare Aresco, coming out from behind the bleachers. "You've been standing there all night."

"Just waiting for a good song, I guess," he said.

She giggled. "Or were you just too afraid to ask me to dance?"

He laughed. She heaved her big breasts up and then down, her nipples poking through the tight black Danskin. She shook her big, feathered Farrah hair and smiled again. "Right?" she asked.

"Naw, I know you're Dave Wysocki's girlfriend," Norman said.

"That's right," Dave said, coming up behind them. Dave was almost six feet, with broad shoulders, great butt (so the girls said) in tight, shiny pants, feathered hair like David Bowie. He and Norman had both turned eighteen on the same day, but that's where the similarities ended. "That's right Galatti," Dave repeated. "Clare's my girl." He gave Norman a nudge that wasn't mean, that was probably even meant to be friendly, but it was nasty nonetheless. Nasty because Dave Wysocki – track star, rock singer, deep voice, lifeguard at the Franklin Davis resort – was cool. Norman Gilletti – five-six, baby-fine face fuzz he hadn't yet shaved, curly, unkempt hair like a white boy's Afro, supporting player in the school's musicals – was not.

Norman just laughed when Dave gave him the nudge.

"See ya later, Norman," Clare smiled, as Dave grabbed her tiny waist and pulled her close to him.

As they walked away, Norman watched both of their butts.

Then he saw him.

"Oh, God," Norman said.

"Hey, Norman," he heard Stick saying to him from behind. "Me and Larry are going out in the back to get high –"

But Norman wasn't listening.

"Jesus," he said. It was the kid again. He was out there on the dance floor, dancing by himself, just swaying back and forth, his eyes closed, not at all in time with the music (*I got chills, they're multiplying, and I'm looo-sing control . . .*). Clare Aresco and Dave Wysocki walked past him, their arms around each other's waists. The kid seemed to sense it. He opened his eyes, stopped his dancing, and without a second's hesitation followed them out the door.

"Jesus," Norman said again.

"So do you want to come?" Stick asked again.

For a moment, Norman didn't hear him. Then it registered. He knew what might happen if they got high. It had happened before, once with Stick, and once with Larry, though he doubted any of them had told the others. Norman sure as hell hadn't. He hadn't even talked about about it with Stick or Larry, after it happened.

But he couldn't just go, not with that kid following Clare Aresco and Dave Wysocki. "I can't right now," he said.

"Why are you being weird?"

"Leave me alone," Norman said, and he followed the kid out the door.

Brother Finnerty, talking with Sister Mary Patrice, arched an eyebrow at him as he walked past. "Leaving for the night, Mr Gilletti?" he asked.

"No," he said. "I'm trying to catch up with somebody."

In the parking lot, he saw Clare getting into Dave's car. "Hey," Norman called.

"You're a strange one, Norman Gilletti," Paulie Marino said. Nancy Barbagallo laughed.

———

The first time Norman ever saw the kid was the day little Petey McKay disappeared forever. "Remember Petey McKay," Mothers would tell their children. "Remember what happened to little Petey McKay."

Norman Gilletti remembered what had happened to little Petey McKay all those years ago. "Now you stay in the backyard," Norman's mother told him, tying his hood under his chin. "Don't go so far that I can't see you from the window."

Norman's mother didn't go out much. She would sit at their Formica-topped kitchen table and smoke her cigarettes, one after the other, looking out the window, occasionally waving at her little boy when he would look up at her from playing on the swings. He would ride first one swing, then the other, then ride back and forth on the teeter-totter, then climb the three metal steps to the top of the slide and wave to his mother. Usually he got stuck halfway down. The slide wasn't very slippery.

Norman's cheeks were getting cold. It hadn't snowed yet, but his mother had said it might snow late tonight. He was sitting midway down the slide, not moving, and he started to pick his nose. He heard a hard rapping on the window pane. Inside, half-covered with smoke, was his mother's face, and she was shaking her head no. He stopped picking his nose. He looked up through the yard. All the leaves were off the trees, and the grass was a dull shade of gray. Down the street were the woods: bare and cold, deep and dark.

Little Petey McKay wasn't really so little: he was fat, with hard, round cheeks. He was actually a year older than Norman. They rode the bus home together from St John the Baptist School. They would get off at the bus stop down at the end of their street together. Norman and Petey and Susan Fletcher and Todd O'Brien and Karen Syzmanski. Petey's house was four down from Norman's, the closest to the woods. Petey was at the bottom of the slide. "Hey, Norman," he asked. "Wanta come over to my house?"

They weren't really friends. Petey had never asked him that before. "I dunno," Norman said.

"I got a new bike," Petey said.

Norman's mother rapped on the window. She could hear everything. She nodded her head yes. She raised her index finger. One hour, it meant. Be home in one hour. So he just tagged along after Petey, down the cold street to his house. Petey grunted as he struggled to raise the door to his family's garage. Inside, sparkling new, was a blue banana bike, with its long seat and very cool handlebars.

"I bet you don't know how to ride a bike yet," Petey said.

Norman shook his head.

"Wanna see me?"

"Okay."

Petey climbed, with some difficulty, over the seat. He steadied himself.

"Petey?" came his mother's voice. She appeared in the doorway that led from the kitchen into the garage. "Petey? Come in for your snack. Who's that with you?"

"Norman," Petey told her.

"Norman Gilletti? Oh, hello, Norman." Petey's mother pressed her face against the screen door. It made her look really ugly. She was fat, too. That was where Petey got it, Norman guessed. Norman watched

Petey's mother with fascinated eyes. Her face looked big and bloated pressed up against the screen.

"I just want to show him how I can ride my bike," Petey said.

"All right, but just one spin," Petey's mother said. "After that, come in for your snack. I've got it all prepared."

Later, after Petey disappeared, Norman would ask his own mother, "Do you think they threw his snack away?"

"Oh, hush, Norman," his mother had said, covering her mouth with her hand.

"Son," Norman's father said, stooping down in front of him, "are you sure what you told the police officer was true? You didn't make any of it up?"

Norman shook his head.

"Joe, Norman wouldn't make anything like this up," his mother said.

One look silenced her. Norman had seen his father do that before. "Norman," his father said again, "if we found that boy, the boy you said offered Petey the candy bar, would you be able to recognize him again?"

Norman nodded.

"Oh, it's so frightening," Norman's mother cried.

"For God's sake, Regina, you're just getting the boy more upset than he already is," Norman's father complained.

Petey had gushed: "Watch me, Norman!"

The fat little boy huffed and puffed as he rode his bicycle down his driveway and into the road. Norman walked down to the curb to watch him. "Bet you wish you could ride a bike like me," Petey called.

Norman nodded.

Petey swerved into the middle of the street. A car honked at him. It startled him, and his riding got very shaky. Finally he fell against the curb on the side of the road. The bike slipped out from under him. Its back tire spun madly.

"Ow!" Petey cried. He had scraped himself against the asphalt. A scratchy patch of red throbbed on the underside of his forearm.

That's when the kid came out of the woods. He was about Petey's age, or maybe Norman's. Norman couldn't tell. He was asked later to be as specific as he could, but he couldn't give them many details. Except that the kid had big, round eyes, and Norman had liked the way he looked.

"What do you mean?" the policeman had asked him. "What do you mean you liked the way he looked?"

"I dunno," Norman said. "I just liked how he looked."

"Hey," the kid said.

Petey looked up at him.

"Can I ride your bike?"

Petey stood the bike up and got a real tough face.

"No," he said.

"Come on," the new kid said. "I'll give you a candy bar." And he held out a chocolate bar.

Petey considered. Then he turned to Norman: "Go on home, Norman."

"I want to see him ride," Norman said, pointing at the kid.

The kid looked at Norman and winked. If Norman remembered anything, it was that wink. "I liked the way he looked," he insisted to his father, who finally just shrugged and went to bed.

"Go on home, you little baby," Petey shouted. Norman turned and ran. But at the corner of his street, he looked back over his shoulder. Little Petey McKay was walking away with the kid, who was pushing the bicycle while Petey ate his candy. They were heading down a trail that led into the woods.

"And that's all you know?" the policeman asked him, after Petey had been missing for five whole days and Norman finally told his parents about the kid with the candy bar.

"Yes," Norman said. "That's all I know."

———

They called him Stick because he was so long and skinny. So was his dick, Norman knew, because he'd sucked on it, that one time they'd both gotten high when Larry wasn't around.

Now they were listening to Blue Öyster Cult, sitting in Stick's Trans Am and smoking weed.

"This is harsh stuff," Stick said.

Stick took a long drag. The car was filled with thick, sweet smoke. Norman figured he usually got more high from the second-hand smoke than he did from his own tokes. He wanted to get very high tonight.

They were out behind the factories, long boarded up, left to rot. This was where Norman had sucked Stick's dick the last time. Stick turned off the car but kept the Cult playing softly. "Aw, man," he said, and put his head back, rubbing his crotch. Norman was instantly horny. He'd been horny all night, actually. He bent over the emergency brake that separated their bucket seats and pulled down Stick's zipper. "Aw, man," his friend moaned. Up popped Stick's whopper, really long, more than eight inches, but really thin, like the circumference of a quarter. Norman eagerly took the head into his mouth and began sucking. "Aw, man," Stick said again.

There was nothing like this, Norman thought. He managed to get the whole thing down his throat, feeling it slip down there like a thin hose. He lapped his tongue up and around the underside, pulling off to bite the tip with his lips shielding the teeth. "Aw, man," Stick kept saying, over and over, each time emphasizing the word "man" more: "Aw, man."

Norman didn't say a word. He just kept sucking, his nose crushed into Stick's sparse, dry pubic hair, which smelled faintly like marijuana. Then, all at once, headlights flashed across them, big white circles that illuminated the inside of their car, then disappeared.

"Who is it?" Norman whispered, sitting up like a bolt.

"Aw, man," Stick said, pushing Norman's head back and stroking his dick. "They're gone. If you don't wanta do it. . . ."

"No," Norman said. "I do." He went back to work. But he was uneasy. Uneasy about seeing the kid follow Dave and Clare. Uneasy about those headlights. His eyes were on the window each time he bobbed up from a plunge down on Stick's shaft. Even though the windows were getting all fogged up, Norman watched for movement out there.

"Jesus!" he said, ripping his mouth away from Stick's dick.

"What the hell – ?" Stick started.

"Somebody's out there," Norman said.

"Hey, don't get out," Stick said.

But Norman was already out. He stood by the side of the car, peering into the dark night, no moon or stars to assist him. He heard the snap of a twig: a squirrel? Or that kid? That kid who killed little Petey McKay and Norman's own father and probably now Clare Aresco and Dave Wysocki, too.

"I know you're out there," Norman said into the darkness.

There was nothing.

"Get the fuck back in here," Stick was saying. "What the fuck do you think you're doing?"

"I know you're out there!" Norman shouted.

"Norman, Jesus," Stick whispered.

"Something's going to happen," Norman said to Stick in the car. Then he slammed the door and ran off past the deserted factories toward the street. The road curved sharply here, a dark stretch of forgotten road. Headlights again, swinging across Norman and then piercing through the darkness ahead of him. A car swung around the curve. Norman fell back into the shadows, his heart suddenly in his ears. He knew who it was. The car's brake light went on full force, big red eyes burning holes into the night in front of him. He heard the screech of tires, smelled the burning of rubber. He heard Clare scream, just as the sickening crunch of metal against tree hit him like a slap in the face.

He reached the curve. There, wrapped around a tree – literally, not figuratively – was Dave Wysocki's Duster. The red stripes down the sides now looked like lightning bolts, all bent and zig-zaggy. The front tires were still spinning, just like little Petey McKay's bicycle wheel. Another car skidded to a halt some yards away. Paulie Marino and Nancy Barbagallo got out, running toward the accident, screaming. Paulie rushed around the twisted wreck to the front of the car.

"Call an ambulance! Call an –" he cried, but he couldn't finish. Norman heard him throw up, retching all the beer he'd secretly consumed that night, foul-tasting bile that burned its way out of his guts and up his throat before splattering onto the dried leaves on the side of the road. Nancy Barbagallo started to scream.

Norman looked through the shattered window. Yeah, it was them, all right. Clare's large breasts were bared and bloody, her nipples a lot bigger than Norman had ever imagined. Her head was turned completely around. Her eyes were still open. Dave had been thrown forward, his head through the windshield. His beautiful butt, still perfect and probably still warm in those tight, shiny pants, was draped across the steering wheel, pointing up for everyone to see.

And when Norman turned around, he saw the kid – grown up now, with those same big, round eyes – leaning up against a tree, his nicely defined arms folded across his chest. Norman realized he was the most beautiful boy he'd ever seen. He gave Norman the wink.

The sirens came over the hill.

The day his father fell off the roof while he was fixing the antenna and split his skull open on the driveway was the second time Norman saw the kid.

Norman was twelve. The kid looked about the same age. Norman recognized him by the eyes, sitting across the street watching Mr Gilletti up on the roof.

"Dad," Norman called up to his father.

"Norman, don't come up here. It's dangerous."

Norman wished his father would stop treating him like a child. The aluminum ladder rested securely against the side of the house. Still, he was unnerved by the presence of the boy across the street, just sitting there cross-legged in the neighbor's yard, staring up at Joe Gilletti.

"Dad," Norman insisted in a whisper-yell. "It's the kid who I saw with Petey McKay that day."

"With who?" his father called down.

"Across the street, Dad. Do you see him?"

But of course his father didn't. And he didn't see the first rung of the ladder either, just moments later. The whole ladder slipped out from under him, and Norman watched, spellbound, as his father gracefully spun once in the air and then smashed against the driveway.

The coroner later said he died instantly. Snapped his neck while smashing open his skull. Norman didn't think so. He thought his father was still alive until the boy ran over, and placed his hand on his father's heart as if checking for a pulse.

That's when Norman believed his father died.

"He's dead," the kid said, looking up at Norman.

Dad's brains leaked out onto the kid's sneaker. Norman was stunned. "It's dangerous up there," he said blankly.

The kid winked. Even in that moment, Norman's heart fluttered when the kid winked at him. Of course, by the time Norman's mother came screaming out the front door, the kid was gone.

———

Now, sucking Stick's dick out behind the school, Norman was positive that the kid had killed Clare and Dave as well, probably running them off the road.

"You wanna move to New York when we graduate?" Stick asked.

"You mean, you and me?" Norman asked, raising his head. "Like get an apartment and get jobs and get out of this town, you and me together?"

"Yeah, that's what I mean."

"That sounds totally cool," Norman said, swallowing Stick's cock again.

"You *like* to do that, dontcha?" Stick asked the back of Norman's head.

Norman pulled off in a hurry. "What's that supposed to mean?"

"I dunno." Stick's eyes glistened. "Just that when Larry does it, he doesn't get into it like you do. Come on. Keep goin'."

Norman gave his friend a hard look, then resumed his work. That was the first time Stick admitted that he and Larry also fooled around.

They were behind the school, the Monday after the dance and the deaths. School had been let out early, after Brother Finnerty announced over the intercom that "our much beloved brother and sister, David Stanley Wysocki and Clare Annette Aresco," had died. They had been welcomed into the arms of Christ, Brother Finnerty intoned.

Norman had been pretty upset all weekend. "No," he told the police. "I didn't see anything." What was he supposed to say? Nancy Barbagallo did ask him, after she stopped screaming. "Where did you come from?" she said.

"My mother's womb," Norman told her, turning from her drippy mascara eyes and walking back to Stick's car. Which wasn't there, so he had to walk home. Which was a long walk, at least forty-five minutes. Which left his mother frantic with fear.

Norman was thinking about this when Stick finally shot his load into his mouth, a big, salty gush. It took him by surprise, and he gagged a bit before swallowing it down. He burped a few times.

Stick was zipping up his pants when there was a knock at the driver's side window. It was all foggy, so Stick rolled down the windows a bit.

It was Brother Finnerty.

He didn't say anything at first. He just let his large brown eyes peer through the crack in the window.

"What are you boys doing in there?"

"Nothin'," Stick said. "Just talking."

"School's been let out for an hour now. You're not supposed to be hanging around the parking lot."

"Yeah, okay," Stick said, rolling up his window.

"Just a second," Finnerty said. "Mr Gilletti. Is that you?"

Norman's ears perked.

"Why don't you come to my office for a minute?"

It struck him, as he followed Brother Finnerty in through the back door, that maybe Nancy Barbagallo had said something about him being at the accident scene. And maybe that was good. Maybe he should tell somebody what he saw. What he'd seen all his life.

But Brother Finnerty didn't want to talk about the accident. That wasn't why he called Norman in.

"But I've got to tell you," Norman insisted.

"Tell me what?"

So he told him. About the kid, about Petey McKay, about his father. They were in a private "meeting room," as the brothers called them. Tiny little cubicles with one chair and a window seat. Norman sat in the window seat and Brother Finnerty chose to sit beside him, ignoring the chair. It was a little tight. They were looking into each other's faces.

"I've seen the devil," Norman said.

"Well, Norman, I —"

"You don't believe me."

"Look Norman, I think you should —"

"Well he's gonna keep coming around. He's gonna kill more of us —"

"Norman." Brother Finnerty's voice was hard. Norman was silent. "I think the deaths of Dave and Clare have upset you. As they have all of us. It was a terrible tragedy. The deaths of others often make us

123

unsure of where we are, or where we're going. It takes away that sense of security that we have, especially when we're young, when we think nothing is ever going to happen to us, that we will never die."

"Well, I saw him," Norman said. "And he's still out there."

"Death always is," Brother Finnerty said. "That's the one inescapable fact of life. But Christ taught us that we can triumph over death."

"How?"

Brother Finnerty laughed. "Haven't you been paying attention in religion class, Norman?"

He patted him Norman's knee. "We can triumph over death by accepting the Word of God, and Christ as our personal savior. That is the way we live forever." His big brown eyes bore down on Norman and he smiled.

"That brings me to the reason I asked you here."

"What's that?" Norman asked.

"I've been watching you, Norman. I believe you have – the spark."

"The spark?"

"The spark to join us. Here. As a Franciscan brother."

Norman was dumbfounded.

"Every once in a while, I'll notice a boy. I'll get a sense that he has what it takes. Because it's hard work. The devotion to the order is a devotion to God. Put your faith in Christ and your fears will go away. We hold special weekend retreats at our order's sanctuary in upstate New York."

"You want me to become a brother?"

"I'd like you to consider it." Brother Finnerty patted him on the knee again. "At least come with us on the retreat. There will be other boys your age, from other schools around the region."

"Boys who have – the spark?"

"That's right," Brother Finnerty smiled. "Only very few have the spark. It's a great gift, Norman. It is a shield against the temptations of the world. What do you say?"

"I don't know."

"Will you consider it?"

Norman shrugged. "I guess I could do that."

"Then get back to me." Brother Finnerty gave him a quick hug. "Now run along home. And be careful when you're on the road. Please be careful."

Norman saw Larry standing by his car as he walked back out into the parking lot.

"Where've you been?" Larry asked.

"Talking with Brother Finnerty."

"Well, I want to talk to you." Larry looked angry. Sometimes he got like that.

"What?" Norman asked.

Larry was smoking a cigarette. He just started smoking. Nancy Barbagallo had gotten him started. "I know what you and Stick do," Larry said, taking a deep drag on his cigarette and holding it in. He was holding it up in the air, the way Nancy did it, between his fingers.

"So what? You do it, too."

"I tried it, I admit. But I didn't like it. Stick says you like it."

Norman didn't respond.

"And I would have thought that we were good enough friends for you to tell me."

"Tell you what?"

"You're gay, Norman," Larry said, gesturing with his cigarette. Norman noticed that Larry had just gotten his hair cut: parted in the middle, feathered back. He looked like Steven Shortridge on *Welcome Back, Kotter*, the blond kid who replaced Travolta.

"What are you talking about, Larry? I'm not gay."

Larry blew smoke over the roof of the car. "Please, Norman, don't deny it."

"I don't know what you're talking about," Norman said. "But I know I'm not riding home with you." He turned, shifting his knapsack on his back, and walked away through the parking lot.

He heard Larry get into his car with a long, "Oh, pleeeeese."

So I'll walk, Norman thought to himself. What a fucking asshole Larry was. If there had been anything glass around, Norman would have smashed it. But there was nothing but tall grass and wildflowers in the field he was walking through. The field led up to Asa's brook, where there was a section narrow enough to cross. From there he'd scale the hill and cut through a corner of the woods, and he'd be practically home. It'd take him a little more than half an hour, he figured.

It was a cool day. The leaves hadn't really started to change color yet, but in some of the trees that ringed the field Norman noticed a fog of red: hardly noticeable, but it was there. The tall grass was mostly yellow and grey, occasionally specked with a wild chrysanthemum, or a dying black-eyed Susan. At one point, he thought he heard someone behind him, but there was no one there.

Crossing the brook, he got one of his sneakers wet when he slipped on a rock. The hill winded him a bit, but he managed. At the top of the hill, the woods looked cold and dark. He knew his way through them, although it had been a long time since he'd ventured into this place. There was a path that took him down another hill and up again. These were the woods where Petey McKay had disappeared forever.

Norman remembered Petey's fat mother, crying at the police station. "Oh, you bad, bad boy, Norman Gilletti," she had said, and Norman's mother had tried to shield him from the woman's wrath. "How could you say there was another boy when there wasn't? No little boy could take away my son! Only a devil, I tell you! A devil!"

The voice caused him to shout out loud, a sound that must have been very primal, because it just came, without him thinking about it. He was pretty deep in the woods now, about to ascend the hill that led him to his home. He was terrified to turn around.

"Is that what you think I am? A devil?"

Norman turned slowly. It was him.

The kid smiled, his big round eyes twinkling. Something shifted inside Norman's gut.

"Or maybe," the boy asked, "*the* devil?"

Norman stood his ground. "I suppose you've come for me now," he said, swallowing.

The kid laughed. "I thought maybe. You could fall climbing that hill up ahead, break your leg. You'd lie there for days. Calling and calling. But nobody would hear you. Finally you'd die. It's going to get cold over the next couple of nights."

"Is that how Petey died?"

"Which one was he?"

"How come you never spoke before?"

The kid shrugged. He was wearing a blue-striped shirt, just like the one Norman had at home in his drawer. It had short sleeves, but the kid's arms filled them out much better than Norman's stringy limbs did. And a nice butt. The kid had a nice butt, nicer than Dave's.

"Well, I'm not going to die," Norman said.

The kid laughed. "Sure you are. Everybody does. It's the one inescapable fact of life."

"Well, too bad. I'm going to triumph over death."

The kid laughed harder. "How? By accepting Christ as your personal saviour?"

"No," Norman said. "By doing this." And he lunged at the kid, the first time in his life he ever initiated physical violence. He'd been the recipient of it once, in seventh grade, when one of the older boys started pushing him around. Norman had fought back, and gotten a bloody nose. But he'd never started a fight. His mother said that was good, that it showed he had a good head on his shoulders. But Norman knew he was just plain chicken.

This time, however, he surprised himself. He threw his arms around the kid's waist and wrestled him to the ground. The kid fought back savagely, trying to knee Norman in the groin, but Norman never knew how fast he could move. He got his hands around the kids neck and started to choke him. He pinned the kid's shoulders down with his knees.

I'm not going to die, you asshole!" he shouted. "I won't. I'm young and I have my whole life ahead of me. I'm not little Petey McKay and I'm not my father and I'm not Dave Wysocki or Clare Aresco. I'm not going to let you get me! I'm going to graduate and I'm going to move away, me and Stick, and we're going to get the hell out of this town and we're going to make it, become whatever we want to become!"

That's when the kid's eyes rolled back in his head and the whites began to leak blood. The kid made a gurgling sound, and his mouth fell open to reveal fangs, big, sharp ones, like a German shepherd. A foul smell rose up from between his lips, the worst smell Norman had ever experienced, like bad eggs and tuna fish and dead fish all mixed into one.

Norman pulled off the kid and stood up. The kid just lay there, not moving. Slowly, his skin started to turn blue.

His bloody eyes had closed, but his lips continued to move, just barely. He spoke in a whisper. "I've got a better idea," he said. "You go on. Run along home. Go ahead and graduate. Move away. Do all the things you want. It's going to be grand and glorious for you. Then you'll see me, on the dance floor. I'll be the one who looks so good you won't be able to take your eyes off me. You'll recognize me – oh, you'll recognize me. But I'll get you anyway. Maybe I'll get Stick first, then maybe Larry, too. How's that? Maybe Larry and then Stick? You like Stick best, don't you? I'll save him for last. But I'll get all of you. Oh, yes, we're going to have so much fun."

Then he was quiet. His skin turned completely blue and then shriveled up, like Saran Wrap in a frying pan. All that was left were his bones. A wind kicked up all of a sudden, scattering old leaves all over the skeleton.

Norman knelt down. The bones were brittle, dry, and dirty, as if they had been there for a very long time. And they were much too small for the kid he had just choked.

It was't the kid, not anymore. "Petey," Norman said, pulling back. Then he turned and ran as fast as he could up the hill.

At the crest he slowed down and caught his breath. He'd be home in a few minutes now. Mom would make some soup for dinner, and then maybe he'd call Stick and they'd go out and get high. He wouldn't think about the kid anymore. Never again. After all, nothing could happen to him.

He had the spark.

SPINDLESHANKS (NEW ORLEANS, 1956)

Caitlín R. Kiernan

 THE END OF JULY, INDOLENT, DOG–DAY SWELTER inside the big white house on Prytania Street; Greek Revival columns painted as cool and white as a vanilla ice cream cone, and from the second-floor verandah Reese can see right over the wall into Lafayette Cemetery, if she wants to – Lafayette NO I, and the black iron letters above the black iron gate to remind anyone who forgets. She doesn't dislike the house, not the way that she began to dislike her apartment in Boston before she finally left, but it's much too big, even with Emma, and she hasn't bothered to take the sheets off most of the furniture downstairs. This one bedroom almost more than she needs, anyway, her typewriter and the electric fan from Woolworth's on the table by the wide French doors to the verandah, so she can sit there all day, sip her gin and tonic and stare out at the whitewashed brick walls and the crypts, whenever the words aren't coming.

And these days the words are hardly ever coming, hardly ever there when she goes looking for them, and her editor wanted the novel finished two months ago. Running from that woman and her shiny black patent pumps, her fashionable hats, as surely as she ran from Boston, the people there she was tired of listening to, and so Reese Callicott leased this big white house for the summer and didn't tell anyone where she was going or why. But she might have looked for a house in Vermont or Connecticut, instead, if she'd stopped to take the heat seriously, but the whole summer paid for in advance, all the way through September and there's no turning back now. Nothing now but cracked ice and Gibley's and her view of the cemetery; her mornings and afternoons sitting at the typewriter and the mocking white paper, sweat and the candy smell of magnolias all day long, then jasmine at night.

Emma's noisy little parties at night, too, all night sometimes, the motley handful of people she drags in like lost puppies and scatters throughout the big house on Prytania Street; this man a philosophy or religion student at Tulane and that woman a poet from somewhere lamentable in Mississippi, that fellow a friend of a friend of Faulkner or Capote. Their accents and pretenses and the last of them hanging around until almost dawn unless Reese finds the energy to run them off sooner. But energy in shorter supply than the words these days, and mostly she just leaves them alone, lets them play their jazz and Fats Domino records too loud and have the run of the place because it makes Emma happy. No point in denying that she feels guilty for dragging poor Emma all the way to New Orleans, making her suffer the heat and mosquitoes because Chapter Eight of *The Ecstatic River* might as well be a cinderblock wall.

Reese lights a cigarette and blows the smoke towards the verandah, towards the cemetery, and a hot breeze catches it and quickly drags her smoke ghost to pieces.

"There's a party in the Quarter tonight," Emma says. She's lying on the bed, four o'clock Friday afternoon, and she's still wearing her butteryellow house coat, lying in bed with one of her odd books and a glass of bourbon and lemonade.

"Isn't there always a party in the Quarter?" Reese asks and now she's watching two old women in the cemetery, one with a bouquet of white flowers. She thinks they're chrysanthemums, but the women are too far away for her to be sure.

"Well, yes. Of course. But this one's going to be something different. I think a real voodoo woman will be there." A pause and she adds, "You should come."

"You know I have too much work."

Reese doesn't have to turn around in her chair to know the pout on Emma's face, the familiar, exaggerated disappointment, and she suspects that it doesn't actually matter to Emma whether or not she comes to the party. But this ritual is something that has to be observed, the way old women have to bring flowers to the graves of relatives who died a hundred years ago, the way she has to spend her days staring at blank pages.

"It might help, with your writing, I mean, if you got out once in a while. Really, sometimes I think you've forgotten how to talk to people."

"I talk to people, Emma. I talked to that Mr . . ." and she has to stop, searching for his name and there it is, "That Mr Leonard, just the other night. You know, the fat one with the antique shop."

"He's almost *sixty* years old," Emma says; Reese takes another drag off her cigarette, exhales, and "Well, it's not like you want me out looking for a husband," she says.

"Have it your way," Emma says, the way she always says "Have it your way," and she goes back to her book and Reese goes back to staring at the obstinate typewriter and watching the dutiful old women on the other side of the high cemetery wall.

Reese awakes from a nightmare a couple of hours before dawn, awakes sweating and breathless, chilled by a breeze through the open verandah doors. Emma's fast asleep beside her, lying naked on top of the sheets, though Reese didn't hear her come in. If Reese cried out or made any other noises in her sleep at least it doesn't seem to have disturbed Emma. She stares at the verandah a moment, the night beyond, and then she sits up, both feet on the floor and she reaches for the lamp cord, but that might wake Emma and it *was* only a nightmare after all, a bad dream and in a minute or two it will all seem at least as absurd as her last novel.

Instead she lights a cigarette and sits smoking in the dark, listening to the restless sounds the big house makes when everyone is still and quiet and it's left to its own devices, its random creaks and thumps, solitary house thoughts and memories filtered through plaster and lathe and burnished oak. The mumbling house and the exotic, piping song of a night bird somewhere outside, mundane birdsong made exotic because she hasn't spent her whole life hearing it, some bird that doesn't fly as far north as Boston. Reese listens to the bird and the settling house, Emma's soft snores, while she smokes the cigarette almost down to the filter and then she gets up, walks across the wide room to the verandah doors, only meaning to close them. Only meaning to shut out a little of the night and then maybe she can get back to sleep.

But she pauses halfway, distracted by the book on Emma's nightstand, a very old book, by the look of it, something else borrowed from one or another of her Royal Street acquaintances, no doubt. More bayou superstition, Negro tales of voodoo and swamp magic, zombies and grave-robbing, the bogeyman passed off as folklore, and Reese squints to read the cover, fine leather worn by ages of fingers and the title stamped in flaking crimson – *Cultes des Goules* by a Comte d'Erlette. The whole volume in French and the few grim illustrations do nothing for Reese's nerves, so she sets it back down on the table, makes a mental note to ask Emma what she sees in such morbid things, and, by the way, why hasn't she ever mentioned she can read French?

The verandah doors half shut and she pauses, looks out at the little city of the dead across the street, the marble and cement roofs dull white by the light of the setting half moon, and a small shred of the dream comes back to her then. Emma, the day they met, a snowy December afternoon in Harvard Square, Reese walking fast past the Old Burying Ground and First Church, waiting in the cold for her train, and Emma standing off in the distance. Dark silhouette against the drifts and the white flakes swirling around her, and Reese tries to think what could possibly have been so frightening about any of that.

Some minute detail already fading when she opened her eyes, something about the sound of the wind in the trees, maybe, or a line of foot-
prints in the snow between her and Emma. Reese Callicott stares at
Lafayette for a few more minutes and then she closes the verandah
doors, locks them, and goes back to bed.

———

"Oh, that's horrible," Emma says and frowns as she pours a shot of
whiskey into her glass of lemonade. "Jesus Christ, I can't believe they
found her right down there on the sidewalk and we slept straight
through the whole thing."

"Well, there might not have been that much noise," Carlton says
helpfully and sips at his own drink, bourbon on the rocks, and he takes
off his hat and sets it on the imported wicker table in the center of the
verandah. Carlton the only person in New Orleans that Reese would
think to call her friend, dapper, middle-aged man with a greying mustache and his Big Easy accent. Someone that she met at a writer's con-
ference in Providence years ago, before Harper finally bought *The Light
Beyond Center* and her short stories started selling to *The New Yorker* and
The Atlantic. Carlton the reason she's spending the summer in exile in
the house on Prytania Street, because it belongs to a painter friend of
his who's away in Spain or Portugal, some place like that.

"They say her throat, her larynx, was torn out," he says. "So she
might not have made much of a racket at all."

Reese sets her own drink down on the white verandah rail in front
of her, nothing much left of it but melting ice and faintly gin-flavored
water, but she didn't bring the bottle of Gibley's out with her and the
morning heat's made her too lazy to go inside and fix another. She
stares down at the wet spot at the corner of Prytania and Sixth Street,
the wet cement very near the cemetery wall drying quickly in the
scalding ten o'clock sun.

"Still," Emma says, "I think we would have heard something, don't
you, Reese?"

"Emmie, I think you sleep like the dead," Reese says, the grisly pun
unintended but now it's out and no one's seemed to notice anyway.

"Well, the *Picayune* claims it was a rabid stray," and then Carlton clears
his throat, interrupts Emma, and, "I have a good friend on the force," he
says. "He doesn't think it was an animal, at all. He thinks it's more likely
someone was trying to make it *look* like the killer was an animal."

"Who was she?" Reese asks, and now there are two young boys,
nine or ten years old, standing near the cemetery wall, pointing at the
wet spot and whispering excitedly to one another.

"A colored woman. Mrs Duquette's new cook," Carlton says. "I don't remember her name offhand."

The two boys have stooped down to get a better look, maybe hoping for a splotch of blood that the police missed when they hosed off the sidewalk a few hours earlier.

"What was she doing out at that hour anyway?" Emma asks, finishes stirring her drink with an index finger and tests it with the tip of her tongue.

Carlton sighs and leans back in his wicker chair. "No one seems to know, exactly."

"Well, I think I've had about enough of this gruesome business for one day," Reese says. "Just look at those boys down there," and she stands up and shouts at them, Hey, you boys, get away from there this very minute, and they stand up and stare at her like she's a crazy woman.

"I said get *away* from there. Go home!"

"They're only boys, Reese," Carlton says, and just then one of them flips Reese his middle finger and they both laugh before squatting back down on the sidewalk to resume their examination of the murder scene.

"They're little *monsters*," Reese says and she sits slowly back down again.

"They're *all* monsters, dear," and Emma smiles and reaches across the table to massage the place between Reese's shoulder blades that's always knotted, always tense.

Carlton rubs at his mustache and, "I assume all is *not* well with the book," he says and Reese scowls, still staring down at the two boys on the sidewalk.

"You know better than to ask a question like that."

"Yes, well, I had hoped the change of climate would be good for you."

"I don't think this climate is good for anything but heat rash and mildew," Reese grumbles and swirls the ice in her glass. "I need another drink. And then I need to get back to work."

"Maybe you're trying *too* hard," Carlton says and stops fumbling with his mustache. "Maybe you need to get away from this house for just a little while."

"That's what I keep telling her," Emma says, "but you know she won't listen to anyone."

The pout's in her voice again and it's more than Reese can take, those horrible boys and the murder, Carlton's good intentions and now Emma's pout, and she gets up and leaves them, goes inside, trading the bright sunshine for the gentler bedroom shadows, and leaves her lover and her friend alone on the verandah.

Saturday and Emma's usual sort of ragtag entourage, but tonight she's spending most of her time with a dark-skinned woman named Danielle Thibodaux, someone she met the night before at the party on Esplanade, the party with the fabled voodoo priestess. Reese is getting quietly, sullenly drunk in one corner of the immense dining room, the dining room instead of the bedroom because Emma insisted. "It's a shame we're letting this place go to waste," she said and Reese was in the middle of a paragraph and didn't have time to argue. Not worth losing her train of thought over, and so here they all are, smoking and drinking around the mahogany table, candlelight twinkling like starfire in the crystal chandelier, and Reese alone in a Chippendale in the corner. As apart from the others as she can get without offending Emma, and she's pretending that she isn't jealous of the dark-skinned woman with the faint Jamaican accent.

There's a Ouija board in the center of the table, empty and unopened wine bottles, brandy and bourbon, Waterford crystal and sterling silver candlesticks, and the cheap, dimestore Ouija board there in the middle. One of the entourage brought the board along because he heard there was a ghost in the big white house on Prytania Street, a girl who hung herself from the top of the stairs when she got the news her young fiancé had died at Appomattox, or some such worn-out Civil War tragedy, and for an hour they've been drinking and trying to summon the ghost of the suicide or anyone else who might have nothing better to do in the afterlife than talk to a bunch of drunks.

"I'm bored," Emma says finally and she pushes the Ouija board away, sends the tin planchette skittering towards a bottle of pear brandy. "No one wants to talk to us." The petulance in her voice does nothing at all to improve Reese's mood and she thinks about taking her gin and going upstairs.

And then someone brings up the murdered woman, not even dead a whole day yet and here's some asshole that wants to try to drag her sprit back to earth. Reese rolls her eyes, thinks that even the typewriter would be less torture than these inane parlor games, and then she notices the uneasy look on the dark woman's face. The woman whispers something to Emma, just a whisper but intimate enough that it draws a fresh pang of jealousy from Reese. Emma looks at her, a long moment of silence exchanged between them, and then she laughs and shakes her head, as if perhaps the woman's just made the most ridiculous sort of suggestion imaginable.

"I hear it was a wild dog," someone at the table says.

"There's always a lot of rabies this time of year," someone else says and Emma leans forward, eyes narrowed and a look of drunken confidence on her face, her I-know-something-*you*-don't smirk, and they all listen as she tells about Carlton's policeman friend and what he said that morning about the murdered woman's throat being cut, about her larynx being severed so she couldn't scream for help. That the cops are looking for a killer that wants everyone to *think* it was only an animal.

"Then let's ask her," the man who brought the Ouija board says to Emma, and the blonde woman sitting next to him sniggers, an ugly, shameless sort of a laugh that makes Reese think of the two boys outside the walls of Lafayette, searching the sidewalk for traces of the dead woman's blood.

There's another disapproving glance from Danielle Thibodaux, then, but Emma only shrugs and reaches for the discarded planchette.

"Hell, why not," she says, her words beginning to slur together just a little, "maybe *she's* still lurking about." But the dark-skinned woman pushes her chair away from the table and stands a few feet behind Emma, watches nervously as seven or eight of the entourage place their fingers on the edges of the metalgray planchette.

"We need to talk to the woman who was murdered outside the cemetery this morning," Emma says, affecting a low, spooky whisper, phony creepshow awe, and fixing her eyes at the dead center of the planchette. "Mrs Duplett's dead cook," Emma whispers, and somone corrects her, "No, honey. It's *Duquette*. Mrs Duquette," and several people laugh.

"Yeah, right. Mrs Duquette."

"Jesus," Reese whispers, and the dark-skinned woman stares across the room at her, her brown eyes that seem to say *Can't you see things are bad enough already?* The woman frowns and Reese sighs and pours herself another drink.

"We want to talk to Mrs Duquette's murdered cook," Emma says again. "Are you there?"

A sudden titter of feigned surprise or fright when the tin planchette finally begins to move, circling the wooden board aimlessly for a moment before it swings suddenly to NO and is still again.

"Then who are we talking to?" Emma says impatiently, and the planchette starts to move again. Wanders the board for a moment and members of the entourage begin to call out letters as the heart-shaped thing drifts from character to character.

"S . . . P . . . I . . . N," and then the dark-skinned woman takes a step forward and rests her almond hands on Emma's shoulders. Reese thinks that the woman actually looks scared now and sits up straight in her chair so that she has a better view of the board.

"D . . . L," someone says, and "Stop this now, Emma," the dark woman asks. She *sounds* afraid and maybe there's a hint of anger, too, but Emma only shakes her head and doesn't take her eyes off the restless planchette.

"It's okay, Danielle. We're just having a little fun, that's all."

"F . . . no, E . . ." and someone whispers the word, "Spindle, it said its name is Spindle," but the planchette is still moving and "*Please*," the dark woman says to Emma.

"S . . . H," and now the woman has taken her hands off Emma's shoulder, has stepped back into the shadows at the edge of the candlelight again. Emma calls out the letters with the others, voices joined in drunken expectation, and Reese has to restrain an urge to join them herself.

"A . . . N . . . K . . . S," and then the planchette is still and everyone's looking at Emma like she knows what they should do next. "Spindleshanks," she says, and Reese catches the breathless hitch in her voice, as if she's been running or has climbed the stairs too quickly. Fat beads of sweat stand out on her forehead, glimmer wetly in the flickering, orangewhite glow of the candles.

"Spindleshanks," she says again, and then, "That's *not* your name," she whispers.

"Ask it something else," one of the women says eagerly. "Ask Spindleshanks something else, Emmie," but Emma shakes her head, frowns and takes her hands from the planchette, breaking the mystic circle of fingers pressed against the tin. When the others follow suit, she pushes the Ouija board away from her again.

"I'm tired of this," she says, and Reese can tell that this time the petulance is there to hide something else, something she isn't used to hearing in Emma's voice. "Somebody turn on the lights."

Reese stands up and presses the switch on the dining room wall next to a gaudy, gold-framed reproduction of John Singer Sargent's *The Daughters of Edward Darley Boit* – the pale, secretive faces of five girls and the solid darkness framed between two urns – and in the flood of electric light, the first thing that Reese notices is that the almond-skinned woman has gone, that she no longer stands there behind Emma's chair. And she doesn't see the second thing until one of the women cries out and points frantically at the wall above the window, the white plaster above the drapes. Emma sees it, too, but neither of them says a word, both sit still and silent for a minute, two minutes, while the tall letters written in blood above the brocade valance begin to dry and turn from crimson to a dingy, reddish brown.

When everyone has left, and Emma has taken a couple of sleeping pills and gone upstairs, Reese sits at one end of the table and stares at the writing on the dining room wall. SPINDLESHANKS in sloppy letters that began to drip and run before they began to dry, and she sips at her gin and wonders if they were already there before the reckless séance even started. Wonders, too, if Danielle Thibodaux has some hand in this, playing a clever, nasty trick on Emma's urbane boozers, if maybe they offended her or someone else at the Friday night party and this was their comeuppance, tit for tat, and next time perhaps they'll stick to their own gaudy thrills and leave the natives alone.

The writing is at least twelve feet off the floor and Reese can't imagine how the woman might have pulled it off, unless perhaps Emma was in on the prank as well. Maybe some collusion between the two of them to keep people talking about Emma Goldfarb's parties long after the lease is up and they've gone back to Boston. "Remember the night Emma called up Spindleshanks?" they'll say, or "Remember that dreadful stuff on the dining room wall? It *was* blood, wasn't it?" And yes, Reese thinks, it's a sensible explanation for Emma's insistence that they use the downstairs for the party that night, and that there be no light burning but the candles.

It almost makes Reese smile, the thought that Emma might be half so resourceful, and then she wonders how they're ever going to get the wall clean again. She's seen a ladder in the gardener's shed behind the house and Carlton will probably know someone who'll take care of it, paint over the mess if it can't be washed away.

In the morning, Emma will probably admit her part in the ghostly deceit and then she'll lie in bed laughing at her gullible friends. She'll probably even laugh at Reese and "I got you, too, didn't I?" she'll smirk. "Oh no, don't you try to lie to me, Miss Callicott. *I* saw the look on your face." And in a minute Reese blows out the candles, turns off the lights, and follows Emma upstairs to bed.

A few hours later, almost a quarter of four by the black hands of the alarm clock ticking loud on her bedside table, and Reese awakens from the nightmare of Harvard Square again. The snow storm become a blizzard and this time she didn't even make it past the church, no farther than the little graveyard huddled in the lee of the church's steeple, and the storm was like icicle daggers. She walked against the wind and kept her eyes directly in front of her, because there was something on the other side of the wrought-iron fence, something past the sharp pickets that wanted her to turn and see it. Something that mumbled and the sound of its feet in the snow was so soft, footsteps in powdered sugar.

And then Reese was awake and sweating, shivering because the verandah doors were standing open again. The heat and humidity so bad at night, worse at night than in the day, she suspects, and they can't get to sleep without the cranky electric fan and the doors left open. But now even this stingy breeze is making her shiver and she gets up, moving catslow and catsilent so she doesn't wake Emma, and walks across the room to close the doors and switch off the fan.

Reaching for the brass door handles when Emma stirs behind her, her voice groggy from the Valium and alcohol, groggy and confused, and "Reese? Is something wrong?" she asks. "Has something happened?"

"No, dear," Reese answers her, "I had a bad dream, that's all. Go back to sleep," and she's already pulling the tall French doors shut when something down on the sidewalk catches her attention. Some movement there in the darkness gathered beneath the ancient magnolias and oaks along Sixth Street; hardly any moon for shadows tonight, but what shadows there are enough to cast a deeper gloom below those shaggy boughs. And Reese stands very still and keeps her eyes on the street, waiting, though she couldn't say for what.

Emma shifts in bed and the mattress creaks and then there's only the noise from the old fan and Reese's heart, the night birds that she doesn't know the names for calling to one another from the trees. Reese squints into the blacker shades of night along the leafy edge of Sixth, directly across from the place where the police found the body of the murdered cook, searches for any hint of the movement she might or might not have seen just a moment before. But there's only the faint moonlight winking dull off the chrome fender of someone's Chrysler, the whole thing nothing more than a trick of her sleepclouded eyes, the lingering nightmare, and Reese closes the verandah doors and goes back to bed, and Emma.

THE PERPETUAL

David Quinn

THE VAMPIRES OWN THE HIGHWAYS NOW. *Forever at rest in motion, forever foraging, they are perpetual, The Perpetual.*

I stopped typing, put another cigarette in my mouth, lit it from the spent one, crushed that – and talk about perpetual – continued to type:

At the command of the Emperor, the Imperial City's slaves flattened the Earth to make her roads. Now, our highway miles match the number of the Holy Roman Empire's at its peak. No coincidence The Perpetual have lived among us the ones they feed upon, and cull to breed their own, the ones they call the Limited since the Roman Ways were built. Our roads are their veins. Here flows the life of the beast itself. All roads end in the same place, though time and distance may seem to alter the neophyte traveler.

When we're gone, our crumbling asphalt monuments will be our coliseum. Future anthropologists will confuse them for churches. And the Perpetual will outlive our interstates, two-lanes, and freeways, of course, evolving to travel with speed upon whatever comes after.

I didn't even hear Michael enter my office. Well, the small bedroom we converted into my office when we built our craftsman bungalow two years ago. Hope he was amused, catching me completely unconscious banging lines of text into the PC, smoking, scratching my head, naked but for my underwear.

"Brett," he said, "when would be a good time to finish talking about the –"

I don't hear what comes after "the." That sweet-faced, sexy man who looks to you like Tom Hanks in one of his chubby roles is Michael, my lover. I'll stand by him, but he knows me well enough to know that if I'm in here, it's never a good time to talk to me about the anything.

And I've lived with a professional social worker long enough to know that the pissed-off look I give him isn't just for him. He pisses me off, sure, but it's just one of those moments of friction. Eight years of living together, we're surviving each other's company in hundreds of minor ways. Some people call that survival love.

The growling sound I'm making at my man says I need peace, not love. Peace to write. But I know that's a lie.

The truth is, I can't get this film treatment into gear, so just living

in my own skin is pissing me off. I am hung up on this intellectual con-
ceit, comparing decadent America and Rome, hung up on the idea of
vampires in our veins, hung up on highway dreams. Why? Where will
that take me?

*The born-again trucker, the hitch-hiking hustler, the fugitive husband, the
runaway wife or child cast like a die, the travelling sales pitching hack. All roads
end in the same place, the lost soul. Feel the wind in your hair, ride blind,
hurtling into promised land.*

*The Perpetual own the highways now. At first, we forgot time and dis-
tance. We could travel forever. We forgot what we felt, for we could drive through
anything. A memory of feeling is no substitute for feeling itself. A scent cannot
be described without rendering it in the language of another scent. Am I writing about vampires or am I writing about something that's missing?*

Piece of shit film's never going to funded, anyway. My director, the
last closeted, low-budget auteur in North Hollywood, hasn't a clue why
he wants to put leather-clad vampires on the highway, but he'll know
what he wants when he sees it. Right. What's needed is for me to quit
jerking off conceptually and get some fucking leather-clad blood-ad-
dicted night-things moving down that fucking highway!

I think of the anti-hero of the film, the scarfaced Perpetual rider
named Black Jack Mojo, and the way Michael's smiling at me, I just
want to smash his face.

"I'm kinda working, kinda spinning my wheels here, Michael."

"Well, now that you're stopped, give me a minute."

"How many times do I have to tell you? If I am awake, Michael,
I am working."

"If you're awake, babe, you're smoking. Let's let a little air in here."

"Leave that! Is that what this is about? Shit, it is, isn't it? You will
turn any conversation into a public service announcement, won't you?"
I sneer, lighting up.

Here's another reason this film will never get funded. Women will
never get the character, and the popcorn doesn't sell without women.
My closeted director can't see that only a man could love and hate
Black Jack Mojo enough to go along for his ride. Woman are attracted
to the feminine in their celluloid obsessions. Even in their leading men.
Of course, that's as invisible to most people as the micro-second of
darkness between the frames of the movie running past them at
twenty-four shots a second. Only a man who truly gets men could lust
after Black Jack Mojo. There's nothing to him but brutal man. Nothing
in him but destructive man. Nothing left in his wake but scorched earth
and you will love it, man.

A barely perceptible jagged scar rivers down Michael's forehead
and lips, white and hard against warmer tones in his flesh. In a certain

light, or when his blood is up, you can't miss it. Makes me want to kiss it long and hard enough to wipe it away.

The scar was engraved there by four punks, with bottles and boots.

This didn't happen in the Bible belt, nor in a trailer park in Kansas Klan Kountry. This happened at an Ivy League University that will go unnamed. Michael, the class valedictorian, on his way to graduate studies in social work, delivered a commencement speech against bigotry of all kinds, quoting, "Set your house in order." In typical late '80s sensitivity backlash, the fucking queer got what was coming to him.

I mention the scar because Michael's blood is up tonight, and everything seems close to violence, every moment of the day.

And The Perpetual, immortals who cruise the highways, are only at home in speed and feeding their blood-addiction. And to know them, you must know Black Jack Mojo, the gravedance runner. Mojo is eroticized power, self-destruction, the ocean in winter, an ice-blue shark thrashing in shallow water. His skin barely contains the muscles underneath; anarchic driving force threatens to tear through. His teeth grind as if he could gnaw through his own life. He leaves a road deep red. You don't want to see his flat black Thunderbird in your rear view mirror. This motherfucker just loves to play with his food.

"Brett, just try to hear my loving intentions, here. I refuse to be a nag."

"Oh, right! Michael, I let it go when you didn't want to play hitchhiker with me. Give me a break."

"Brett, how can you compare – look, fantasy's fine, right place, right time, but –"

Hitchhiker. A rocks-off game, but just a game.

When Michael and I first got together, passion's heat made me want to live dangerously – dangerously within, that is, the safety of the first monogamy I had ever experienced that didn't chafe like Weight Watchers for the perpetually horny. Michael had indulged me. He'd pick me up, pretending I was an anonymous hitcher. I used a code name. Fred Flintstone. He was Barney Rubble. Carnal cavemen, a little sardonic humor amidst our primal, no-holes-barred sexual slam. I still get hard just seeing parts of the Pacific Coast Highway and the 101. You don't know what sucking and fucking can be till you master them in a speeding car.

Now Michael's scar is furious.

"I wouldn't still be here if I didn't love your nasty, rutting slut side, babe, but role-playing feels silly, sometimes," I said. "I mean, I can get off just on you, on us, on what we have come through together. Do you know how rare this is, what we have, between two people? Authentic commitment, in action, whatever comes? Well, of course you do. None of the couples in those movies you write get to stay together.

That kind of survival would be too hard to believe, wouldn't it?

"Smoking hasn't made you a rebel bad boy since you were twelve, pistolero, it just makes you look like an idiot. I quit, and I smoked two packs a day. You can, too. You have a death wish, fine, but fulfilling it by smoking is beneath you, babe."

Why couldn't I just give in? Admit he's got the right idea, just supremely fucked timing? This isn't like the time Michael wanted to adopt a baby. So some innocent kid could get bashed at school, too.

"Hey, excuse me, am I one of your clients?" I said. "Shit, nothing harder on the addict than living with a recovering addict. You quit smoking, great! I will, too! Leave me the fuck alone!"

"I'll leave you alone. Don't go to sleep till we finish this, that's all."

I stand up. My underwear's on the floor in one push. Hit the road. Get away from him before you throw him down the stairs. Hit the road and maybe you can break through.

———

Time was, I guess we would have talked the breakdown through till we ended up in each other's arms, sweating and exhausted. I take a long time getting dressed to ride the bike. Zipped into one-piece leathers and my boots, black–dyed polished cow from neck to ankle, my hard-as-nails swagger says fuck you and your loving intentions, Brett, I'm going out. But I say, "I'll be all yours when I've got some more of this into the word processor, and to do that, I've gotta clear my head."

The garage: my bike's a refurbished late '50s Triumph Bonneville, azure blue and pearl grey in color, heavy enough to be real, but light enough to let you feel the road. Though disqualified from official statistics for political reasons, it was unofficially "The World's Fastest Motorcycle" in its day. Not as predictable as a rumbling Harley amongst the leather boys, but it suits me I like style with my 650cc vertical twin cylinder speed, and something warm throbbing between your legs is always a decent start for the night.

I jam the machine to life. The Triumph shakes the garage with a concrete ring.

"Flintstone, you certain you want to ride tonight?"

If that's a seduction, it's not enough.

"Research. I'm writing about highways at night."

"Be sure to bay at the moon and suck blood while you're at it."

"I would, but there's no moon tonight."

California Route One, the Pacific Coast Highway: 600 miles from L.A. to San Francisco, even a little beyond, and at its best, it is dark rugged rocks and mountains on one side, deep black ocean on the other, and a stretch of blacktop winding in between. The wildest winding drive starts where the PCH splits from the 101, near our home near San Luis Obispo from here to Monterey is the prettiest stretch of riding on the planet. I wouldn't take on this set of twisties at night if I didn't know the road.

First part of the run is thirteen miles of four-lane interstate. I open up the throttle and move through the gears, running as fast as I can through the turns, but not beyond myself; I'm looking for that click that comes, that settled feeling when rider, bike, and road are one. I know that sounds all Zen and zooey, but it's real. And I thought that's how The Perpetual would feel.

Black Jack Mojo's just one of many names-heir to freedom, balled up in speed, all-holy negation, and creation in the void at the edge of the bitch cunt world!

I take the time to feel out the surface a little some moisture, but some sand, too. Only one other car shares my road: old Mercury, by its headlights, back so far I only see it on the straights.

On the straights, I love to jam. I shoot a look at the nacelle, check the speedometer pushing 100, and a black hulk of a car vaults past me, passing way too close.

I swear it's a Thunderbird, built when the bird still had thunder! I open the throttle in anger and get air. I lay the Bonneville down around another turn, sit up straight fast, try to grab some distance –

But the T-bird, or whatever it was, is gone.

Black Jack Mojo's off the road, having a few teenage wanderers for a midnight snack. Imagine the charnal chaos of the T-bird's cockpit. The girl's throat, cleanly punctured with a metal oil-spout, hisses and splashes hot bubbling fuel all over Jack Black's mouth, chin, and chest. Gushing, he presses the pedal to the floor.

"Little bitch cured my blues, boy. Wanna know what I got for you?"

The boy's screams are submerged in Black Jack's music as The Perpetual lets him get a good look just before he impales the boy's wet and tangled head into his lap. The little fuck's right eye comes free on the silver prong of his wide leather belt, the socket welling with its own juices. Black Jack begins to fuck the angry hole.

"Listen, don't think you ain't appreciated. I've had a bellyfull of junk food – you are going to be like dining on moist, velvet-ribbed mushrooms, every day! You, little bitch, are gonna be adored!"

I shoot up a rise and there is the Pacific, stretching out forever, so black and alive it shines. At Morro Bay, which still feels like the prehistoric volcano it used to be, especially at night, the fortunate rider re-enters winding two-lane blacktop, a hundred miles of twists and turns.

It's gorgeous, but if you ride beyond your limits, deadly. You don't just point a fine-tuned machine at a road like this and squirt. Every turn, you have to feel where your weight has to be, and slip into the right gear, without thinking, just by feel. This must be what The Perpetual feel this must be the only thing they can still feel.

I shift my weight, pop the clutch, grab just a little brake in flow through the twists, sweetly. Black Jack Mojo is no longer fucking with me, and the sweat inside my leathers begin to wick away. That car might have been an old '70s Thunderbird. It might have been black. Might even have been flat black – the car I gave Mojo in the film, Mojo of The Perpetual, my highway star vampire. But if I'm being followed by my own fictional nightmare, it's synchronicity, a good story to tell the RATs at the next Riders' Association of Triumph run. I downshift and negotiate another twist. And it all comes back to me, whether I like it or not.

Black Jack bellows as he feeds his scarred brown cock into the fresh hole in the noisy animal, thrashing to the screaming, pumping to the beat. He'll never get over how scalding the brain feels against his cold meat. Maybe later, after he's good and buzzed on the blood, he'll skull-fuck the boy's mate, too.

Nothing like having the road to yourself on a Sunday morning. He rolls down one tinted window, hollers, "Yabba dabba fucking doo!"

Devouring the Limited just isn't enough for Jack Black. He's developed a hunger for his own kind. If human blood gets you hard, and gets you high, what passions will the blood of the Perpetual stoke? He'll find his sister, he vows, add her head to the trophy seat. He'll take on the ancients in the adopted city of his father, the place Mojo, more at home with the Bible-black night Pacific, or a desert showered with stars, loathes the "skyless sewer," New York.

Freed by death to create his own life, Black Jack lives by a Providence that is brutal. Everyone is abandoned. Live to reap.

Deep braking, I scrape around a bend, a little too fast. Stupid! If the story comes to me, I should pay attention, but not at the cost of my life. Two points of rubber meet two points of road, that's the knife edge between me and oblivion. Helmet's reinforced alloy. Gloves have kevlar palms. Leathers, reinforced back support – but all that and fairy dust won't save me if I high-side over the fork and smear a squid patch for a quarter mile of Pacific Coast Highway. Gotta keep the rubber side down, as the old RATs say.

I calm down, enjoy the road, and remember. I remember what I heard when the black hulk cruised by me.

There's a wet metal music when we ride with Black Jack, booming undertow soundtrack. Kinetic lust and annihilation throb and a voice from a hunger forever young wails:

> Don't say a word
> Hold me if you dare
> You say we're lost
> I say half-way there
> I'll follow you down down down

The gravedance runner's T-Bird almost runs me down.

I am thinking clearly, now. I remember. I can see the scarring, the body work where the car had been resurrected from Black Jack's joy ride crash and burns.

"Sometimes I like barbecue."

Fuck synchronicity. Maybe I didn't make this up, I wonder, rocking around a bend. I made this shit up, didn't I? To get my director excited, but more than than, to find out what if might be like to release myself from responsibility for other people, cut free of any concern in the fucking world?

Why else would I even think about getting inside the head of a 500-year-old parasite god? Or Black Jack is real. I know about him. I can feel his lust.

And he can feel mine.

The Triumph straightens up as I enter a quarter mile straight, and there's the Thunderbird's headlights, staring me down. Any minute now, I'll see his fucked face, a mixed-up map of scars. His face is fucked. Just can't quit the kick of walking aflame from crash-and-burn wrecks he likes to cause, spraying himself with the hissing, steaming blood of toasted survivors.

His headlights shoot toward me.

My nacelle speedometer reads 115 MPH and nothing in me wants to do anything about that. I imagine I can see his ice-blue shark eyes in his melted candlewax flesh. I catch fire as the bike explodes into the Thunderbird's grille, but Jack Black's laughter erupting from my throat startles me to consciousness. At first we lost the sensation of tasting. Finally all sensations . . . only a memory. But the fresh essence of the Limited, the living, or the dying, I should say, refuels that well of feeling if only for the time it takes a cigarettes to ash.

"Another fucking day in paradise, boy!" I scream, a living ghost on fire.

I am Jack Black Mojo.

I am Perpetual.

I own the highways now.

And I am limited. Like, right now, I want to watch Michael sleeping.

Just outside Cambria, I take the turn-off to Moonstone Beach Drive too fast, feel the bike sliding, going over, imagine myself about to head into a wreck that will trash the bike and make a leather bag job out of me. I look over the beach, quiet.

I'm shaking as I light up. Not from cold – adrenaline. I imagine myself descending into that fiery crash, alive for a final, single scream, destroyed and consumed by the hottest fucking vampire I'll ever imagine. What the fuck was I thinking? Almost killed myself just to put myself in emotional harm's way, in the direct path of fear – or hope?

I know I'm sounding zooey again, but the last one was the sweetest drag I ever tasted. House might have room for a dog. I got to get some of this on the computer.

Four cigarettes left in the pack. I set it down on a flat black rock and jam my bike back to life.

GENIUS LOCI

Becky N. Southwell

 HERB FOSTER IS SEATED IN HIS USUAL WICKER chair on the veranda of the Mary Lamb Institute. The white clapboard building, more rest home than psychiatric asylum, sits high on a hill in Northern Vermont's version of the middle of nowhere. Foster sips water from a paper cup and watches a Cessna seaplane in the distance. The Cessna circles the lake once then cuts a diagonal across it, streaming a wispy thread of human remains out one window. The ashes hesitate in mid-air for a moment as if the body is reluctant, even now, to give over to death. Then a gust sneaks up and scallops the ashes into the air and they disperse, then disappear. The plane turns toward the Institute and flies past with a growl, close enough that Foster can read the words "A Wing And A Prayer Scattering Service" painted on its right flank.

Foster, normally not a talker, surprises himself by turning towards the old man seated in a rocker a few feet away. "You believe in ghosts?"

The ancient man doesn't reply, just stares straight ahead, with glaucous eyes like marbles. Foster wonders if he's blind and resists the urge to raise his voice.

"That's how I ended up here. Because of a ghost."

The man cocks his head slightly, interested. "You're thinking I'm crazy, right?" Foster waves his paper cup. "I know — you can't swing a dead cat in this place without hitting forty guys who'll tell you they ended up here by mistake, and God help me if I sound like one of them." He thinks he detects a small smile on the old face. "All right, then. It was the first weekend of June, 1985. I had just turned eighteen. A guy died a grisly death in a bathtub. It was in all the papers, a reporter's wet dream. Maybe you remember it?"

The man continues to stare straight ahead but Foster senses he's listening. He proceeds to tell his story.

━━━━━━

That first weekend in June, 1985, started as innocuously as any other, except for the unseasonable electrical storm headed towards Vermont. It was expected to be the worst storm in thirty years, if anyone was counting. And the meteorologists spewing perky doom from the TV certainly were.

For Foster, the weekend was supposed to be notable for one reason, and one reason only; the '77 Firebird he and his cousin Benny had been lovingly restoring for over six months was finally getting a new transmission. Well, maybe not *new*; it was slightly used, but it was a good one. Mr McAlister, who owned one of the many auto repair shops in the industrial part of Scarsdale, had been holding the trannie for them for months while they saved up enough cash. McAlister was a good man and was giving them a damn good deal some might call foolish. But he'd been eighteen once himself and obsessed with restoring an old '48 Chevy Fleetliner (in which he'd gleefully lost his virginity with young Mary Margaret Hannigan). So he understood.

Benny was picking up the transmission that afternoon and bringing it over to Foster's mother's house, where they stored the Firebird because Benny's parents didn't have a garage and his father was prone to shooting beer cans when he was drunk. The plan was to install the transmission over the weekend so that on Monday they could drive the Firebird – the pussy-mobile, Benny called it – up to camp where they were working maintenance for the summer. Benny had tried hooking them up at a co-ed camp where he said getting pussy would be like shooting fish in a barrel but all those jobs filled early, so they'd had to settle on Camp Moccasin for boys.

The truth was – and Foster's truth lay well hidden in the dark recesses of his mind but he wasn't stupid, he knew it was there – the absolute truth was, the idea of a boys' camp was all right with him. Not because he was a homo or anything but because Benny's constant pussy-talk made him a little queasy sometimes. Who *wouldn't* be turned off girls hearing "creamy-cunt" stories day in, and day out?

No, a boys' camp would be fine. At least he'd be spared Benny's constant harassment over why he wasn't hooking up with this chick or that chick. Though truthfully, and again, he was willing to be truthful here, hanging out with one hundred guys all summer would definitely pose its own problems but it was nothing he, Foster, couldn't handle. Or hadn't handled before.

He walked into the living room where his mother lay on the couch, snoring in front of the TV, and took the burning cigarette from between her fingers. He stubbed it out in an ashtray, and then looked out the front window for the millionth time, wondering what the hell was taking Benny so long with the transmission. He hoped nothing was wrong. Like McAlister had suddenly decided 600 bucks wasn't enough after all.

That's when the phone rang.

"Herb!" The voice was jovial, loose. As soon as Foster heard it, his knees buckled and he had to sit down. "John Holt here."

"Yeah, hi." Foster managed to talk around the lump gathering in his throat. "It's, uh, *Foster*, actually. Nobody calls me Herb except my Mom."

"Okay, *Foster*. I'm calling because I need someone to come up to camp this weekend and help me with some last minute things." Foster pictured John sitting with one arm behind his head, the way he had for the entire job interview, with a smile on his handsome face that reminded Foster of nothing if not Sylvester the Cat. "I'd pay you a hundred bucks for two days. What do you say?"

Something twirled around the base of Foster's spine, like a mouse running in circles around a column. For the director of the camp to call him, a maintenance guy, something was up. Imagining what that *something up* might be sent the mouse spinning. Suppose John wanted – ? Suppose he *didn't*? Benny would kick the shit out of him for sure for not helping with the transmission, for bailing at the last minute to go hang out with someone Benny had called "a fuckin' *fudgepacker*, you can *tell*, man." Well, Foster could deal with the ass-kicking; he was used to *that* by now, his cousin had a famous temper plus four years and forty pounds on Foster. But the *names* Benny would call him, maybe for the rest of the summer – Benny was *not* known for letting things go – Wilma, Mary Jane, fudgepacker, faggot. Those names could worm their way into his gut like nothing else.

Well, fuck him. Fuck Benny.

"I'll do it."

"Really? Great! I'll pick you up tomorrow, ten AM. Don't worry about a sleeping bag. There's a guestroom with a bed and plenty of covers." John sounded so wonderfully in charge, Foster relaxed a little.

They hung up and Foster sank back into the armchair in his mother's living room, where she still lay snoring on the couch. He wondered if it were his imagination, but something about the way John had said, "bed" and "plenty of covers" made Foster picture a yellow Tweety Bird feather sticking out of the Sylvester smile. And if he were going to be *totally* honest, the image was a little thrilling.

The next morning, John picked him up at ten AM sharp in a black Ford Taurus that smelled of new leather. Foster rested his head back against the seat and winced. Benny had given him a couple of lumps last night after hearing about his weekend plans. Benny had called him a queer, Foster had got in one good pop to the nose – guaranteeing Benny double black eyes this morning – and his cousin had come at him like an insane gorilla, wrestling him to the ground and banging his head against the driveway until Foster's mother finally came out in her bathrobe and, screaming, sprayed Benny with the garden hose until he stopped.

Under the darkening sky, the trees had that hushed look trees always take on right before a storm. Foster tried to keep his eyes off John and at the forest slipping past but it kept making him car sick. But looking forward meant a constant, maddening awareness of John just inches away; one hand draped casually over the wheel, the other resting on his thigh which looked for all the world like steel poured into denim. Every time John moved, running his hands through his hair and licking his lips, a simultaneous gesture he made every few minutes, Foster's skin would prickle and his heart would race.

They'd left Scarsdale almost three hours ago; traveling up Vermont's I-95, over to the 6, finally turning off at Spencer, which was the last town they would see for the rest of the drive to Friar's Lantern Lake. Three hours and Foster was so worked up by now beads of sweat were prickling his back. He ached to put a hand on that thigh, just to feel it. And on the bulge he'd caught a glimpse of before. Carved into those tight jeans as it was, who the hell *wouldn't* notice it?

On a man as good-looking as John, with that shampoo ad hair, and cowboy jaw line, Foster would challenge anyone's eyes to behave themselves.

To hide the nervous blabber of his thoughts, which he was sure were bouncing around the soft leather interior of the car, Foster looked out the window and saw something that pulled him upright.

"What the hell is that?"

Out there in the dark forest not twenty feet from the highway, a light bobbed eerily between two trees, like a ball of fire.

"Swamp gas," John said. "Peculiar to this area right around camp. No one knows why."

It was then that Foster noticed something. The mouse had been quietly circling the base of his spine for several minutes, and now it was quickly growing uncomfortable. John slowed and turned the car onto a dirt road.

"Here we are."

Foster's stomach heaved.

He stared at the sign. The paint was fresh. Red letters on a white background.

CAMP MOCCASIN FOR BOYS.

Foster's heart started to race. He knew, suddenly, he had to get out. Get the hell away from this place. Before he could say anything, the trees around him started to move. They stretched their limbs down toward the car, jostling with each other, as if trying to see what was inside. Spindly twig fingers scratched at the window. The trees murmured in high-pitched voices like excited toddlers babbling and poking at a present. The limbs started to bang, in unison, trying to break the glass. Foster tried to scream but couldn't. A jagged black branch broke through the window by his ear. Before he could bat it away, it snaked itself around his throat and squeezed as if it would crush the life out of him. Then everything went black.

When he came to, John was shaking him and shouting.

Foster opened his eyes. Blinked. The trees around the car stood erect again. The murmuring had slipped away. He drew a ragged breath while his heart skipped around in his chest.

What the hell just happened?

John's eyes were like saucers. "Jesus, are you all right?"

He looked around at the woods, which were quiet other than a slight wind rattling the leaves. He was fine. He swallowed a mouthful of bile and jiggled a finger in his eardrum. "I'm okay – sorry I scared you."

"Christ, you looked like you were having a heart attack!"

"I don't know. I guess I wasn't feeling well and –"

"Why didn't you tell me? I could've pulled over!" John's eyes were concerned, not just for Foster, but as if maybe this whole thing wasn't such a great idea after all.

Foster unrolled his window and sucked in a fresh gust of air. "Seriously. I'm fine. Let's forget it, okay?"

John shot him a glance, then shrugged and threw the stick shift back into drive. He drove slowly, swerving around potholes in the dirt road, and glancing over at Foster a few times as if trying to decide something.

They pulled up to the director's cabin and made it inside before the first drops of rain started to fall. The cabin was actually a house, two stories high, with a mildewy smell, brown shag carpet and furniture from the seventies.

It's happening again, Foster thought, miserably.

He could hear John upstairs, unpacking. He pulled his jacket tightly around himself and looked out the window at the waves slapping the dock. It had been five years since anything – the voices, the panic attacks – *anything* at all had happened. He'd been diagnosed, given a prescription for pills that he dutifully took every morning – had taken *this* morning, he would swear on it – and it had all ended as quickly as it began. No harm, no foul. So why now? Why again? And – the thought snuck up on him and hissed in his ear before he could squelch it – what *next*? There had been a few times where he hadn't just heard things. He'd seen things, too.

Suddenly, Foster knew he wasn't alone. He knew that if he turned around, he would see it. Standing quite close. For one thing, a smell had quickly grown up around him. The unmistakable smell of rotting flesh. He recognized it from the time he'd had to scrape the neighbor's cat off his mother's driveway where Benny had – accidentally – backed over it with his truck.

There was a dry rustle. Foster spun around.

Nobody there.

Only the ugly furniture and the thick smell like moldy fruit cling-ing to the air. Thunder exploded in the distance and Foster was up the stairs before he could even tell his feet to move, throwing John's bed-room door open with a bang.

"Jesus!" John threw the sweater he was folding into the air. "What the hell are you doing?"

"Nothing. I just – I was wondering if –" Foster's voice trailed off.

John's mouth tugged up at the corners. "Afraid of the storm?"

"No. Of course not."

"Good. Because I need you to go down to the circuit box in the rec hall. Take the keys hanging on the hook by the front door. There's an umbrella and a flashlight in the front hall closet, too. When you en-ter the rec hall the circuit box is by the stage. Open it and flip all the red togs to the left. That'll give us power." John smiled a smile that re-minded Foster for all the world of his mother on a good day. "I'll make us some spaghetti while you're gone. You like spaghetti?"

For a quick moment Foster wondered if John regarded him as a kid, somebody to feed spaghetti to. And maybe hot chocolate later. The realization gave him a pang. "Yeah. Sure. Thanks."

Foster was relieved to step out of the musty cottage and into the fresh air. Rain pelted his umbrella, drowning out the doubts crowding his brain.

The woods around him were an almost phosphorescent green. The trees were just normal trees again. Anything else was his imagination, which his mother had always said was too wild for his own good.

As he walked further away from the cabin his sense of dread abated. The thunder and lightning were still at a distance, but the rain had kicked up all the sweet forest smells and with each breath he felt calmer. He shook his head hard to silence the voices elbowing for room in his mind. This was two days alone with John in the middle of nowhere and he was *not* going to let himself fuck it up. Anyway, it was probably just his medication. Maybe after taking it for five years, his mind was adapting to the dosage and he needed that shrink down at St. Joseph's to up it a little. Bad fucking timing. But he wouldn't let it wreck his weekend.

His musings were cut short by the sound of men marching. He heard their boots crunching down in unison, heard the sergeant call out an order. He looked around at the forest but the sound seemed to come from further down the path.

He kept walking and the sound grew, a steady noise like 10,000 cows chewing their cud in perfect unison. He followed the bend in the path and stopped dead in his tracks.

Fifty feet ahead, the rec hall loomed large and dark against the bruise-colored sky. Faded green, with a row of black windows, the hall seemed to hum with an energy he could *feel* as surely as he couldn't see it.

Genius loci. The thought came from nowhere.

The pervading Spirit of a place. He'd just read the expression in a book recently and had to look it up. Staring up at those cavernous windows, he understood what it meant. They were watching him with a kind of intelligence. As if at any moment they might blink. Or was it – was it something *behind* those windows that was staring out at him?

The marching continued from inside the hall. He begged his feet to turn around and take him out of there but they disobeyed and started to move forward, as if he were being pulled.

And he knew with chilling certainty that he was.

He reached the door. It swung open of its own accord. And the marching ceased in unison.

Terrified, Foster stared into the hall. He sensed hundreds of eyes peering back at him but he could see nothing, his flashlight barely gouged a hole in the utter darkness. He felt a pull. And he was hauled inside.

The door slammed shut behind him, and locked with a resounding click. His flashlight caught the circuit box and several light switches to the left of the stage. All he had to do was unlock the box with the small marked key, flip the red togs to the left and reach over for the wall switches. They'd light up the whole place. Enough to dispel the darkness, the *real* darkness that was here.

He felt the eyes staring, awaiting his decision. He didn't dare reach for the door handle behind him. Instead he shoved himself forward, fast, towards the metal box. Tried inserting a small key into its hole. Wrong one. His flashlight slipped through his sweaty fingers and clattered to the floor with appalling volume. Tears gouged his cheeks. He tried another key. It *worked*. He threw open the box, smacked the five red togs to the left, leaned over in the darkness to the switches on the wall and felt his fingers press into a clammy arm. He let out an involuntary cry. A hand grabbed his wrist, very hard. The stage lights switched on.

A trickle of hot piss ran down the inside of his thigh.

Foster knew he was looking at a young man who had been dead for a very long time. He couldn't have been more than seventeen; with a terribly pale, gaunt face and milky-grey eyes. His soldier's uniform hung off his skeletal frame. He looked exactly like one of those black and white pictures Foster had seen of Holocaust victims at school, where the cheekbones threaten to push through the skin.

Foster could feel the dead man's icy fingers even through his thick logger's jacket. As if reading his mind, the dead man let go.

"You can see me. Can't you?" The ghost spoke in a raspy Southern accent, staring at Foster as if *he* were the spectacle.

Foster nodded and the ghost pulled his lips back into a smile, revealing a row of teeth as yellowed as the old radio knobs Foster had installed in the Firebird just yesterday.

"You can hear me, too."

"Yeah." Foster heard himself answer. He touched the back of his hand to his nose. The smell coming off this boy was putrid. Foster glanced down. Blasted through the boy's middle was a clean hole where his guts should be. One of his arms hung at an odd angle. The boy patted himself down with his other arm and asked if Foster had any cigarettes.

"No. Sorry."

"Damn." The soldier hoisted himself up onto the stage with his good arm. "You got a name?" The ghost sounded so casual, as if this were something that went on every day, ghosts and flesh-and-blood people shooting the shit together. Then he realized. The soldier's uniform. The marching. He remembered a pamphlet on Camp Moccasin mentioning it had been turned into a basic training camp during World War II. The awful fear that had, literally, wrenched the piss out of him was replaced with a wave of sympathy.

"Foster," he answered.

"Foster?" The boy's tone was eager. "I knew a Foster in Company 'C.' Relation?" Foster shook his head. "I'm Leverette Jerome. Call me Levy."

Levy dropped the smile, looked around, leaned forward and hissed; "You know what this racket's about Foster? Huh? 'Cause I been racking my brains and I don't get it. One minute I'm in France. Next minute I'm back at basic training with my guts shot out and my arm all fucked up and no one'll tell me nothing."

Foster looked around, unsure of what to say. "I don't know."

Tears sprung to Levy's eyes. "Last thing I remember, our battalion's hiding out in this French town, Maisongoutte. Me and this kid McCaffy get sent ahead to scout out this abandoned church to see if we could tuck in there for the night. We make it all the way inside, check upstairs and down. I step out to give the 'all-clear' signal and *boom!* two krauts come 'round the corner and start firing. I don't remember nothing else till I woke up. Found myself back here at basic training. Can't move my arm. . . ." He lifted it with his working arm and let it drop back down. "My insides. . . ." He glanced down at the hole in his stomach then quickly looked away. "No one will look at me or answer my questions." His voice breaks. "It's like I'm invisible."

He drags the sleeve of his good arm across his nose. His voice is hollow and bitter. "I tried to leave. But I can't get past the fucking front gate."

He gives Foster a hard stare. "You know what this place is? It's a puppy mill for young soldiers. The captains change but it's always the same, groups of boys getting moved through. You should see them, kids as young as nine! Tell me, is Hitler chewing through our men so fast we gotta send *kids*? I mean, Christ, just sending 'em off like you're drowning a bag full of kittens. And this latest captain, he don't care. He's a real prick, thinks he's a fucking prince!"

Foster tried to speak but Levy grabbed his arm. The chill from those dead fingers spread like cool wet slime across Foster's skin. "But it's all gonna end. 'Cause I got you now."

The mouse did a slow circle around Foster's spine.

"Don't get me wrong, I tried killing the Captain once myself. Sharpened my ten-inch hunting knife and slit his throat while he was sleeping. Pushed the knife straight down to the pillow, thought it was all over. Imagine my surprise when the Captain walked into the rec hall bright and early next morning like nothing had happened. Just a little red mark around his throat like a necklace and I heard him say he hadn't the foggiest idea how he'd got it. So you see?" Levy breathed his rotten deadman's breath into Foster's face. "He's not a man. He's some kind of demon. But I had a strong feeling about you, soon as you got here. You're going to get ridda him; you're the one that's meant to do it. They'll shut this place down. You'll be a fucking hero." The radio dial teeth revealed themselves again in a crooked row.

The fingers released him and Foster stepped back and rubbed his arm hard, trying to rid himself of the feeling, like icy cold snot working its way through his pores.

This was crazy. He was sitting here listening to a ghost, for chrissakes. What the hell was wrong with him? And what the hell did he feel so fucking scared for? This thing wasn't *real*, not flesh-and-blood real. It was a fucking *vision*, like the projection of a slide thrown up on a wall. It might talk and move, but by god it wasn't alive. It wasn't a thing to be *feared*.

"I'm not killing anybody," Foster said with as much belligerence as he could muster. "That's crazy. And this isn't what you think. This isn't bootcamp –" The hand shot forward, grabbed him around the throat, and squeezed.

"*Don't you say no to me!*" The voice boomed, filling the hall, competing with the storm outside. Several lights over the stage exploded and a chair flew two inches past Foster's head and crashed to the floor. Suddenly, Foster was lifted up by the neck, his feet swinging in mid-air. He couldn't breathe. "*You understand?*" The ghost shook him like a doll, rattling his teeth, then started to fade. Foster was fainting. The fingers released. Foster dropped to the ground.

The dead man pushed his pale purple lips so close to Foster's they nearly touched. "It's real simple." The voice hissed, "Either you kill the Captain. Or I kill you."

The door to the hall crashed open. Foster was hauled to his feet and half-carried / half-shoved by a force that felt like two giant magnets, one pulling him forward, one pushing him from behind. He was tossed out into the rain, landing hard in the spongy grass. The door slammed shut behind him.

Foster staggered back to the director's cottage. He was shaking so hard, the doorknob slipped from his fingers several times before he managed to open it. He stepped inside the cabin, shut the door behind him, and slid to the floor.

The living room lamps were on. John walked down the stairs, two at a time. "Foster? What took you so long?" Foster managed to stand up before John rounded the corner. He tried to speak but his jaws were slamming together like a pair of plastic wind-up dentures. When John saw him his face dropped. "My God, what happened to you? You're freezing. What the hell were you doing out there?" The large arms wrapped around him and John led him upstairs to the guest room.

Foster tried to tell him, no, don't keep me here. Take me, us, home. Back to Scarsdale. Away from this place. But he couldn't find the words to speak. John lay him on the bed, covered him with a blanket. When Foster woke up, John was taking his temperature. He removed the thermometer, stared at it, and frowned.

Foster croaked, "I'm fine."

"Well, according to this, you're dead. So let's assume it's broken." He tossed it onto the nightstand. "I don't know what you were doing out there for an hour but you better get warm before you catch pneumonia. I filled the tub. Go get in."

"John –" Foster sat up and felt fat tears slide down his cheeks.

John's eyes narrowed, concerned. "What is it?"

Foster tried to tell him everything. From what happened the moment they drove into camp. To the rec hall. Levy. The order Levy had issued. John's face kaledeiscoped through seventeen different emotions as Foster blurted his story, ending on a strange mixture of disbelief and anger.

"Please," Foster breathed heavily, "you have to believe me."

John's eyes softened a little. He paused for a moment before he spoke like he was choosing his words carefully. "I don't know what's going on with you. Maybe this is hypothermia, I'm no doctor. So let's just get you warm, okay? And we'll worry about – everything else, later. All right?" His voice was so reassuring, Foster allowed himself to be led into the bathroom, stripped, and lowered gently into the envelope of water that made him shudder with its blessed warmth.

He lay his head back against the tile and breathed deeply. He opened his eyes and saw John slide a hungry gaze over his naked body. They stared at one another. Foster's cock hardened. He felt a flicker of embarrassment but John cut it short by kneeling by the tub and touching his mouth to Foster's, tenderly at first, then harder, probing his tongue past Foster's teeth.

Foster drank him in, not quite believing this was really happening. John slipped his hand under the water. Foster moaned and pressed his head back against the tile. He yearned to take John in his mouth, take him right in and swallow him whole. Without breaking the seal of their kiss, Foster moved up on his knees and fumbled with John's jeans. Foster shivered. This was everything he had imagined and fantasized about.

John lifted Foster out of the tub, and onto the bath mat, pushing him down onto all fours. Foster's hands splayed against the cold tile. John ran his hand down Foster's back.

Another voice clashed with his ecstasy, pulling him momentarily down to earth. A voice hissing in his ear. Levy's voice. Foster ignored it and leaned into John, begging for more, begging for the man to fuck him, arousal tinged with the slight fear of the unknown. But he knew he could trust John. He was ready. Then the bathroom door crashed open.

Leverette screamed, "You fucking faggot liar!" and kicked Foster down on the tile. John covered his face with an arm too late as a fist slammed into his mouth, smashing his head against the wall. Foster got to his feet and tried to grab Levy but the ghost threw him out of the bathroom with one hand. "I don't need you anymore, you little pussy!" Then he picked John up and dropped him into the bathtub.

The radio sat on the toilet tank, its cord snaking into the wall over the sink. Levy grabbed it. John's eyes flew open wide, he made a panicked gurgling sound and scrambled to get out of the tub.

Foster yelled, "No, Leverette, *please!*"

Leverette flipped the radio on and matter-of-factly dumped it into the bath. There was a flash. Then John's body danced under the water like a mad mannequin. He hissed and popped, blisters raced over his skin. Leverette stood over him and watched, without expression, for what seemed an eternity.

Finally, Leverette reached over and caught the writhing cord, unplugged it, and tossed it onto John's body.

Foster lay on the carpet and vomited.

The following day, Joss, the groundskeeper, found the body. It was he who testified that he'd seen Foster acting strangely in the rec hall, talking to himself in the middle of the storm.

The old man on the veranda of the Mary Lamb Institute slapped one knee. "What was the old coot doin' out in the rain?"

Foster shook his head, incredulous. So the old man didn't care about the sex, in fact acted like he hadn't even heard that part. Wonders never cease. "He was checking to make sure the windows of the canoe shack were closed. Which was next door to the rec hall. He saw the light was on and saw me through the window, 'talking into thin air' I believe was how he put it."

"He didn't see no soldier?" His listener shakes his head at the horror of it all, making his jowls quiver. "And now yer in here. 'Cause of some infernal ghost soldier." The man turns his haunted eyes toward Foster, who realizes he isn't blind after all. "Unbelievable bad luck, boy."

Looking through a window, gazing at Foster intently, is a nurse. She has been standing there for several minutes, watching him talk animatedly to an empty chair. She shakes her head. This will have to go on his chart. This is exactly the kind of thing the doctors like to know about, even though she hates feeling like she's ratting on the patients. Especially one as sweet as Herb Foster. She remembers the bottle of lithium in her hand she is supposed to be bringing to the nurses' station, and hurries off down the hall.

Sixty miles away at Camp Moccasin, a group of boys gathers in the rec hall for evening vespers. One of them, seated near the back is looking around, confused. He cocks his head, wondering what that hidden sound is, beneath the camp songs.

It sounds so much like marching.

GOODBYE

Michael Thomas Ford

THE FIRST ONE IS WHITE. WHITE LIKE SNOW. White like ice cream. I catch it in the field behind the barn, in an empty Miracle Whip jar with holes punched in the lid. After I screw the top on, I sit in the tall grass and watch the butterfly crawl up the side, its wings flapping silently against the glass. When it gets to the top, I blow through the holes – gently, so its wings won't break – and it falls to the bottom.

When I get back to the house, Edward is sleeping in a chair on the porch. I pull his tail a little to wake him up. He opens one green eye, and I show him the jar with the butterfly in it. He pads the jar with a black and white paw, interested only for a moment, and then goes back to sleep, turning his belly up to the sun.

My mother opens the screen door and comes out. She's carrying a pot with a geranium in it. She is wearing her red gardening gloves, and bits of black soil cling to them like ants. The geranium is red like the gloves, and it smells sweet. My mother puts the pot on the table next to Edward's chair, then moves it to a place with more shade. I hide the jar with the butterfly behind my back.

She waters the geranium with the yellow watering can. Water splashes onto the leaves, turning them dark green, and then drips off. "Isn't it beautiful?" my mother says. "It's from your grandmother's house. They were her favorite."

I run into the house before she can say anymore. It is cool and dark after the warmth of the sun, and I stand for a minute in the hallway, making sure that my mother isn't coming after me, as she usually does, asking what's wrong. When she doesn't open the door, I go up the stairs to my room. But instead of going in, I go down the hallway and climb the narrow stairway to the attic.

Once I am there, I shut the door and look around me. There are so many things. Things piled everywhere. I close my eyes so that I won't have to look at them. Very slowly I walk to the window, feeling my way along the narrow path through the boxes and trunks. I stop when I come to the rocking horse. When I feel its mane under my fingers, I know it is safe to open my eyes again.

I am standing in front of the window. The window is big, big enough for me to stand up in. It was built to start seedlings in, because the attic is warm all year round. But now that my father has built the greenhouse, it's just a window again.

There is a screen on the outside of the window, so that air can come through, and two more screen doors on the inside that shut and lock, so that the cats cannot get inside and dig up the seedlings. The window looks out over the back garden, and sometimes I sit in it and read. Nobody ever thinks to look for me there. They think I'm still afraid to come into the attic.

I unscrew the top of the jar, and the butterfly crawls onto my hand. His feet tickle my skin. I shake him off and he flutters onto the screen. I shut the inside doors and watch as he flies about in the window box. He travels from the screen to the wall and back again.

When I go back downstairs, my mother is sitting on the porch reading. She hears me push open the screen door, and puts her book down. "Come sit down," she says.

I walk over and sit next to her on the porch swing.

"Do you know what today is?" she asks.

I watch a spider that is crawling along the arm of the swing. It is little and grey. "Grandma's birthday," I say finally. The spider jumps off the swing and hangs by a thin piece of silk. I blow on the string, and the spider scurries back up again.

"That's right," my mother says. "That's why I put the geranium out here today. Geraniums were her favorite."

The spider is going down again. The web spins out behind it silver and silent. When it gets down to the porch floor, I think about stepping on it, but I don't. If you kill a spider, it will rain.

My mother gets up and pulls a dead leaf off of the geranium. "I thought maybe we could walk back to the cemetery later and take some flowers."

I look for the spider. It is creeping across the floor, and Edward is poking at it. I don't want to go to the graveyard, so I just shake my head. When I look back, the spider is gone and Edward is washing his face. My mother sighs, but she doesn't try to make me go. I remember what my father said the day of the funeral, when I wouldn't go into the church: "Why does he have to be afraid of everything? You raised him to be a sissy." I remember that, and that the macaroni salad my aunts brought to the house had cold, hard peas in it.

I leave my mother and go back to the field behind the barn. It is early afternoon, and there are butterflies everywhere. They are feeding on the Queen Anne's lace and blackberry blossoms. They do not notice me, and I catch dozens of them quickly. Big ones, yellow like butter, that sit on the rippling grass with their wings folded up like sailboats. Orange ones with black spots that rise up and away like flames when I walk through the flowers. And handfuls of the little white and blue ones that scurry all over the daisies like laughter. I am very careful not to touch their wings and smear the beautiful dust.

I put them all in jars, and put the jars into a wagon I found in the barn. It is old and red, and the wheels squeak badly. Soon there are rows of jars – Miracle Whip, Jif, and Pierson's Classic Dill Pickles – filled with jumbles of yellow, white, and orange wings.

It is hard pulling the wagon through the tall grass, and I am tired when I get back to the house. Carefully, I load the jars into a cardboard box and take them to the attic. It takes three trips before they are all there. Twice I have to hide from my mother, but she doesn't see me.

When the jars are upstairs, I take them one at a time and empty them into the screened-in window. It is difficult to do because every time I open the doors to put more butterflies in, the ones inside want to come out. But I get them all in. When I shut the door for the last time, I stand back and look. In the window are hundreds of butterflies. The sun shines through them, and they are a living wall of stained glass, moving about like a kaleidoscope over the door screens.

While I am watching the butterflies I hear the porch door open, and I know my mother is leaving. I go downstairs and look out the window. She is standing in the backyard holding a bouquet of wildflowers.

She starts walking down the patch that goes to the old cemetery on the hill. I slip out the door and follow her, staying in the tall grass so that she doesn't see me. The path is narrow, and it winds down through the field before turning up the hill. In the field I see some butterflies and I think of the ones in the attic. *Soon*, I think.

My mother is quiet. She stops and picks some black-eyed Susans. They look like great burning suns mixed in with the other flowers in her hand. When we reach the top of the hill, I stop. The cemetery is just beyond the trees. I walk as far as the first gravestone, but I don't follow my mother as she goes in.

Instead I stay behind the trunk of a big tree and watch as she walks to the grave. She scatters the wildflowers around the grave. Then I see her mouth moving.

My mother stays for a few minutes and then leaves. I follow her back to the house, wondering what it was she said as she stood beside the grave.

After dinner, I sit on the porch steps. It is dusk and smells like rain. Out in the grass, Edward is chasing fireflies. I see a tiny bright light glow in the darkness, then Edward's shadow leaps up to put it out.

Soon there are many fireflies. They float lazily over the lawn, flickering warmly in the summer night. I follow one of them and when it flashes again I catch it in my hands. When it glows, the light shines out from between my fingers.

I put the firefly in the Miracle Whip jar. I catch one after another. When I have enough, I screw the top on. Inside the jar, the fireflies take turns glowing. Sometimes they forget whose turn it is, and they all light up at once. Then the jar looks like a lantern.

I take the jar into the house. My mother and father are in the living room watching television. I go through the kitchen and up the stirs. In my room, I grab a paper bag from under the bed and run up to the attic.

It is dark now, so I don't need to close my eyes. I stand in the doorway listening. It is quiet. I shake the jar of fireflies, and they burst into soft light. Holding them in front of me, I can see my way to the big window. The butterflies are quiet, but when they see the light they begin to fly around. Behind them the clouds are black against the blue of the moon.

I set the jar of fireflies on a box and sit down. For the first time, I really look at the things around me. They are my grandmother's things, brought here after she died. In the darkness they are wrapped in shadows, gifts from the dead waiting to be opened.

I lift the cover of a dusty trunk. Inside there is a layer of brittle paper that crinkles when I touch it. Underneath there are old photographs. The one on top is of my grandmother holding a baby, my mother. The next is of my grandfather and grandmother on a beach somewhere. There are many more – my grandmother on vacation, in the costumes she wore on stage, laughing with people whose names I don't know.

I come upon one that is different from the rest. It is of my grandmother in a long dress standing in a garden. She is holding a Chinese umbrella and smiling at the camera. She is very young. As I look at it, I think about how I ran to her after the first time another boy at school called me one of the names I've heard so often since then. "It's good to be different," she said. "You don't have to be like them."

I take the picture and put the others back. It is how I think she would have looked on her birthday. It is how I want to remember her. Closing the trunk, I turn back to the window. The butterflies are beating their wings against the screens.

I put the photograph beside the jar. I open the paper bag I have brought and take out the cake. It is a seed cake, very small and sweet with honey, my grandmother's favorite. I bought it at the bakery in town, with money my father gave me for collecting the eggs from the hen house. The woman who sold it to me smiled as she said, "Your grandmother used to get one of these every year on her birthday," as if she were sharing a secret. I lay the cake on a chipped blue plate from another box and put the plate on the box beside the other things.

I turn and run to the window. The butterflies are waiting. I grab the window catch and turn it. The screen doors swing open into the attic and wings flap wildly around me as the butterflies rush out.

A wind blows in from the garden. The butterflies, white and blue in the moonlight, swirl around the attic like bits of paper in a storm. I stand in the middle of the madness, watching them flutter ghost-like around me. "Butterflies are the souls of the dead," Grandmother once told me. "They carry messages back and forth between us and the other side, so you must be careful never to hurt them."

There are butterflies everywhere. They dance all around me, sometimes landing on my hands or tickling my face with their feet. Some of them are flapping above the jar of fireflies, attracted by the glow. The big yellow ones glide slowly, riding on the wind from the window. The little blue and white ones scatter over and around the boxes of Grandmother's things in groups of three and four. The orange ones are harder to see. They come flying out of the shadows, and I see them for a moment in the streams of moonlight before they disappear again.

Several of the butterflies land atop the cake. They perch on the edge of the plate, their wings slowly opening and closing, their tongues darting out to taste the honey. More and more gather around the cake, climbing over it, eating. I sit on the trunk and watch.

After a while, I stand up and go to the window. I fumble for the springs at the top of the outside screen and feel them beneath my fingers. The screen comes out easily, and I look out towards the hill. The moon is waiting full over the graveyard, blue and patient, watching the dead.

The butterflies begin to fly out, first one by one and then in groups of two and three. I feel them all around me as they tumble out into the night. They fall into the moonlight and ride the wind to the hill. Rolling on the breeze, they are a river of gently moving wings, rising and falling silently.

When all the butterflies are gone, I take the jar of fireflies from the box and unscrew the lid. They, too, fly out over the garden in a long, flickering string. I watch their lights until they disappear beyond the field. Then I look down into the garden.

My grandmother stands beside the rose bush. She is wearing the long dress and carrying the Chinese umbrella. She is young, and happy. She looks up at me, watching her from the attic window, and she smiles.

For the first time since her death, I cry.

TABULA RASA

Robert Boyczuk

So we beat on, boats against the current, borne back ceaselessly into the past.
— *F. Scott Fitzgerald,* The Great Gatsby

"YOU'RE DEAD." PETER WAGGED THE DAMNING slips of paper he'd pulled from the toque at Barry. "Five minutes to pack your things and leave the cabin."

Barry, the first man overboard.

Daniel watched the soon-to-be drowned man, sitting cross-legged on the floor before the hearth, his bulk eclipsing the fire, a thumb-sized wine stain on his shirt, zipper half-open, eyeglasses at their usual cant. Naturally he was the first to go.

Barry attempted a smile.

"Honestly, Peter," he sniffled through his incipient cold, the susurrus of breath whispering from his nose. "I just got here." Incredibly, Barry had once been Daniel's lover. Daniel couldn't have said why exactly. Pity, perhaps. Or more likely a sense of gratitude. Barry had stuck by him when, some years ago, Daniel had spiraled into an alcoholic despondency. While all his other so-called friends, many of whom now sat in this rough semi-circle around the fire, had expertly vanished.

"You agreed to the rules. We all did." Peter stretched out his long legs, the antithesis of Barry: tall, athletic, handsome in a vaguely dissipate way. Dressed in casually expensive clothes of such quality that, as someone had once pointed out, one was expected to recognize them without the benefit of the usual designer labels. "I trust you'll see yourself out."

It had been Peter's idea. Who else? A game called Lifeboat. Justify your continued presence on a raft in the middle of the ocean, your meager supplies dwindling. Each round of rationalizations to be followed by a vote: who should be thrown overboard?

"Four minutes left."

But the game itself wasn't the crowning touch. No. It was the group Peter had assembled. He'd lured Daniel and his new boyfriend, Marcus, up here with the promise of a quiet weekend, crowing about the beauty of the countryside, the romance of a rustic cabin. An ideal setting for budding paramours. But said nothing about the others. Daniel scanned the circle of faces – and felt nauseous. All his former lovers. A testimonial to his mistakes, to a past poorly spent. Marcus was unaware. He was too young, too new to the community, unacquainted with Daniel's checkered past. And the others seemed oblivious too, ignorant of this connection, perhaps because Daniel had always been discreet in his affairs.

Except with Peter. Fucking Peter. How could he be doing this?

"Buh – but, it'll be dark before I reach the highway." Barry foundered. He raised an arm, running it under his nose and dragging the offending mucus onto the sleeve of his moth-eaten cardigan, spilling a bit of his wine onto the area rug. Peter scowled. Daniel, sickened and embarrassed, looked away. He didn't want to witness this; he wanted Barry gone. Wanted them all gone. Or, better yet, wanted to leave himself. With Marcus. But what could he say without looking like a fool?

"The mob has spoken." Peter held aloft the slips of paper in one hand and the toque into which they deposited their votes in the other. "Five for tossing you out of the lifeboat. Three for Jason."

"Bitches," Jason hissed.

Daniel burned. At Peter. At the game. At being suckered into coming up to the cabin. He curled his hands into fists. Fuck Peter. He *would* leave. And to hell with them all!

Daniel felt fingers touch the back of his hand, startling him. "Daniel?"

Daniel glanced to his left, at Marcus – and went utterly still. Light from the fire played across the planes of Marcus' face. Across sculpted cheek bones, roman nose, skin as flawless as marble. Christ, he was beautiful. Striking as Michelangelo's David. No, Daniel decided. More striking.

Because he was real.

Daniel's heart twitched in that miserably clichéd way. Love. It embarrassed, mortified, and excited him. It made a hash of his life. How could *he*, of all people, be in love? Fifty-eight years old, a once handsome man in decline, an acknowledged cynic. In love for the first time – with a boy toy half his age.

Peter, more than Daniel, was skeptical about the notion of love. When Daniel had confided his infatuation with Marcus, Peter had scoffed. Mocked him mercilessly. And, had it not been his own miserable heart in a vise, Daniel would have joined in. Yet here he was, stupid as a schoolgirl, in love with Marcus. In love with his youthfulness, his naïveté. Aching to reclaim that innocence. To forget his misused past. Daniel wanted a new start. A blank slate. *Tabula rasa.* And up here, away from the affectation of the city and its petty concerns, in the clear, bright air of the country, Daniel imagined it might be possible, the two of them walking, hand in hand, in the breathless winter calm of the forest. . . .

Only Peter's malicious game had ruined all that.

"Three minutes."

Daniel swallowed, suddenly giddy. Barry, somehow on his feet now, trembled in the midst of the circle. He gestured at the front window where large, lazy flakes lit on the pane. Outside, scotch pines, boughs drooping with accumulated snow, ringed the cabin, an incongruously picturesque scene. "I . . . I'm not sure I have enough gas to make the highway."

Daniel almost laughed.

"Sorry, old man."

Barry searched the ring of faces for an ally. "Don't make me go."

Daniel watched them, one by one, stare back impassively: Martin first, then his partner Rick, chewing nervously on his fingernails; Kurt who'd crossed his burly arms; and Jason who stuck out his tongue. And then Barry turned to Marcus. Daniel caught his breath. Two pair of eyes, locked: Barry's hopeful, entreating; Marcus' . . . what? Sympathetic? Impassive? He couldn't tell. Then abruptly, Barry was looking at him.

"Daniel?"

Shamed, though not sure why, Daniel stared at a fascinating swirl in the rug just beyond the banded toes of his hiking socks.

"Daniel?"

"I'm sorry." Quietly. Had he even said it aloud?

"I'll leave in the morning." Barry spoke to Peter this time. "When the snow stops."

Daniel looked up. Peter had moved over to the fireplace. One by one he let the slips of paper drift from his hand and into the flames, chanting as each piece flared: "No. No. No. No. No." He checked his Rolex. "Two minutes."

"What if I won't go?"

Jason sucked in his breath; chairs creaked as Kurt and Martin sat up.

Won't go? Barry refusing? It seemed incomprehensible. Daniel watched Peter for a reaction. Had his face flushed? Or was that a trick of the flickering light?

"As I see it, you've no choice."

"I won't." Barry glanced out the window as if there was something out there that unnerved him more than Peter's scorn. He was trembling. "I'm not going."

Daniel followed his gaze: in the few moments that had passed clouds had knit overhead, darkness spreading over the trees that circled the cabin, hardening their edges, inking out the gaps between them, making the snow they bore look filthy.

"One minute."

"You can't make me leave."

"Yes, I can." Peter flipped open the lid of a vintage cigar box on the mantle. From it he withdrew a small, pearl-handled revolver. Barry stared at the weapon, open-mouthed.

"Every good lifeboat should be provisioned for *all* emergencies."

"Does it really work?" Kurt asked, lifting his bulk from his seat, towering over them like a grizzly.

"You've got to be joking." Rick, perpetually agitated, stood also, pushing past Kurt. Barry looked at him gratefully, as if Rick had just thrown him a lifeline. "It's too little to do any real damage. You'll want something bigger."

Jason tittered nervously; Barry's fleeting expression of hope collapsed like a cheap tent in a windstorm.

Peter waved the pistol towards the door. "Time's up."

His eyes moving from Peter to the lowering sky outside, Barry edged back, caught between Scylla and Charybdis. "You wouldn't shoot me." His expression was akin to that of a rabbit Daniel had once seen, forlornly dragging its crushed hindquarters off the gravel shoulder of a country road into a weed-choked ditch.

Peter cocked the gun. "Get out."

"Wait." The word popped out of Daniel's mouth.

Peter looked mildly curious. "Yes?"

"Let him stay. Just for the night."

"And why should we do that?"

"He's our friend, for God's sake."

"*Your* friend. I never much liked him."

"For God's sake, Peter, if he doesn't make it to the highway it'd be just like shooting him."

"Then perhaps I should save him the trip and shoot him right now."

"Jesus, it's just a game!"

"And it's my fucking cabin! If you don't like the rules, you can leave. With *him*." He sneered. "Maybe that's what you'd like to do, hey? Leave with your fat *friend*. Then if the car breaks down, you two can cuddle to stave off the cold. It's not like you haven't cuddled before."

Daniel's cheeks burnt; the others stared at him in incredulity.

"Daniel and *Barry*?" Jason was positively elated. "This is *too* much."

Marcus stiffened; he pulled his hand away from Daniel's and turned to stare at the fire.

"It's not true," Daniel blurted out, struggling to keep his tone light. "Jesus. I mean, really. Look at *him*."

The color drained from Barry's face; he seemed to deflate. Daniel felt sickened at his betrayal. He tried to hold Barry's gaze, but couldn't. Barry picked up his parka from a chair and tugged it on. His duffel lay slumped over at his feet. Cinching shut his duffel, Barry hoisted it. The dead weight swung from his hand like a condemned man from the gallows. He opened the door. Wind gusted around the edges of the screen door, rattling it, chilling the room. Barry looked back. "Love makes us do cruel things." He spoke to Daniel alone. Then to everyone else, "Fuck you all."

A blast of icy wind, the slam of the door.

"And to all a good night!" Jason said, laughing too loudly at his own joke.

An engine coughed twice, started, snow squeaking under tires, the sound quickly fading, lost in the trees and scrub and the hills, under the incalculable weight of snow that smothered them.

Part of Daniel's past was gone. Despite his self-loathing, he experienced an undeniable surge of relief. Hopeful, he tried to catch Marcus' eye, but Marcus stared resolutely at the fire, his expression set like stone, ignoring Daniel.

Jason snorted. "Good riddance!" He looked to Peter for approval.

But Peter merely turned the revolver over in his hand, admiring it, then placed it back in the cigar box and shut the lid.

Jason fidgeted. "Now that Barry's gone we don't have to play that stupid game anymore. Right?"

Peter arched his eyebrows slightly in a patrician gesture. "Wrong. The next round will be tomorrow morning after breakfast. And we'll have another round after each meal." Surveying the surviving castaways, he smiled. "Now, who's for another glass of wine?"

As Daniel peeled carrots for dinner, Marcus sidled up to him. For a full minute he stood at Daniel's side, silently watching the slivers of orange raining down into the sink.

"Did you cuddle?" Marcus' question was low, almost a whisper. At the other end of the cabin the rest of the group sat around a folding table in front of the fire, talking, laughing, sipping Chardonnay and absorbed in a game of whist, the latest megrim of the theatre crowd. Barry had been gone less than an hour.

"What are you talking about?" Daniel tried to hide his apprehension, continued the rhythmic slicing, the jangle of the peeler filling the silence.

"Did you fuck him?"

"No."

"Then why are your hands shaking?"

Daniel stopped peeling, rested his hands on the edge of the sink to steady them. "For God's sake! We're friends. That's all." From the corner of his eye he caught a glimpse of Peter watching them. He fought to calm himself.

"You know I'm a jealous person." Marcus said it matter-of-factly, like he was describing his height or hair color. "I told you when we first met that I couldn't stand being around your . . ." he hesitated, searching for a word, ". . . your *past*."

It was true. He had almost broken up with Daniel over it. Marcus made no secret of feeling threatened by Daniel's older and "more sophisticated" friends. Especially by his former lovers. The community was lousy with them. They were in night clubs, in restaurants, at the theater. So, after a few awkward incidents, Daniel had steered Marcus away from those places and people. Of anything that might jeopardize their relationship.

Marcus picked up a small paring knife. "The thought of you with Barry makes me crazy. . . ."

Peter leaned towards them, no doubt straining to hear.

"Well, we weren't together." Daniel wished it had never happened. Could almost convince himself it hadn't. "Besides, he's gone." Daniel resumed peeling. He smiled wanly. "Drowned."

Marcus ran the blade back and forth, like a tiny saw, along the tip of his finger. "Is there anyone else here I need to worry about?"

Daniel shook his head. He couldn't bring himself to frame a lie in words.

"You sure?"

"Yes."

"Okay." Marcus put the knife down. A small cut welled blood on the tip of his finger. Marcus stared at it for a moment, then wiped it carelessly on his pants. Leaning forward, he put his hand on Daniel's shoulder, gave him a peck on the cheek, then sauntered over to watch Daniel's ex-lovers play cards. Peter nodded to Marcus, then turned and winked at Daniel. He returned his attention to the card game. Daniel stared at them, the group absorbed in the game, like a small, exclusive club. On his shoulder a single drop of blood seeped into the fabric of his sweatshirt.

Christ, he thought, what a mess.

Peter had lined his former lovers up like ducks in a row. And all Daniel could do was wait and hope it came to nothing. His past rushed towards him like a runaway freight train and there wasn't a damn thing he could do about it.

One AM.

Only Kurt and Daniel remained up. Everyone else had gone to bed. Outside, relentless flakes of snow obliterated everything. Even the row of cars, parked no more than a ten meters away, had vanished. It was as if they been walled in.

Daniel didn't mind being alone with Kurt. Of them all, he'd been Daniel's most thoughtful lover: steady, gentle, undemanding. And in the big man's contemplative silences Daniel had always found comfort. Once, Kurt had even declared his love. Why, Daniel wondered, did I end it with him? The answer came to him as soon as he'd framed the question: because he never loved Kurt. He was merely comfortable with him.

"Can't sleep?"

Kurt's voice was a low, baritone murmur; it startled Daniel from his reverie. Daniel turned; Kurt stood behind him holding the slim volume of poetry he'd been leafing through. The faint odor of scotch was unmistakable.

"A touch of insomnia, that's all." He couldn't tell Kurt he'd been avoiding his room, the empty space next to Marcus. The guilt of his lies. He glanced to the back of the cabin and the short hallway leading to the rooms. It was hard to tell because of the shadows, but the door to room he shared with Marcus seemed to be open a crack.

"I hate this snow," Kurt said, snapping shut the book and tossing it on the couch. "It's as if the world's been erased."

Like Barry was erased, Daniel thought. Instead he said, "It'll look beautiful in the morning. The trees, the hills, the lake."

Kurt shrugged. "Maybe. But I hate not being able to see where I am. Get my bearings." The two stood side by side, staring out the window at the blankness. "When I was a kid, I never got lost. My friends and I would go on hikes and they'd listen to me because I always knew which way was home. But this snow . . . it's messing me up. Like it's jamming my radar or something."

It was the most he'd said all day. Daniel shifted his weight, uneasy at Kurt's sudden garrulousness. It's just the booze, he thought.

"I know the lake's out there. Normally I could point to it, even through a blizzard, and be certain that I was right." He raised his arm and straightened it like a compass needle, pointing out the window, but his arm arced back and forth uncertainly. "Only now, I'm not sure." He let his arm drop. "It's weird, but I get the feeling that out *there*, there is no direction." The lines on his forehead deepened. "It scares me."

Scared?

Kurt was the last person Daniel had expected to be scared. But now that he'd said it, Daniel could see the tension in him, the rigidity of the way he held himself, almost coiled, as if preparing for flight. "You'll feel better in the morning." It sounded strange to Daniel, coming out of his mouth, this attempt to comfort Kurt who'd always done the comforting.

"I don't want to lose the next round, Daniel." Kurt's voice was hushed. "If I have to leave, I have this feeling I'll never find my way back. I know it sounds stupid. I know there's only one road out of here. But I can't shake this feeling."

"You won't lose. Jason will. Everyone detests him."

"But what if I do?"

"Peter likes you. He wouldn't make you leave." Daniel smiled up at the big man in what he hoped was a reassuring way. "Besides, he couldn't make you leave if you didn't want to."

"I'm not so sure." He looked at Daniel. "I'm not so sure what to make of anything anymore." Kurt turned towards the fireplace; it was a moment before Daniel understood what he was staring at: the cigar box.

Daniel reached up and put a hand on Kurt's broad shoulder, felt him try to suppress a twitch. "Peter's cruel. But he's not crazy."

Kurt shrugged away his hand. He walked over to the box and flipped open the lid. He tilted it to show it was empty.

Daniel stared. "Peter must have taken it," he said, not sure who he was trying to convince. "Probably put it away. Because of Jason. You know how he'd want to play with it. And end up shooting himself or someone else in the foot."

"Guns scare the shit out of me." Kurt dropped the box back onto the mantle; the lid fell shut. "So I was watching. Peter didn't go near the box. No one did. Except Marcus."

The wall clock ticked loudly, once, twice. "You saw him take the gun?"

Kurt shook his head. "As far as I could tell, he only looked." Relief flooded Daniel. "But if he was good with his hands, like a magician or something. . . ."

It felt like an icy lump had congealed in Daniel's stomach. Marcus, in an idle moment, had once shown him a parlor trick, making Daniel's comb disappear. Daniel had watched closely a second and then a third time, but couldn't tell how he'd done it. Could he have taken the gun? Christ, why would he want to take the gun?

Kurt had moved over next to Daniel; his fingers circled Daniel's upper arm, thumb easily meeting forefinger. He was speaking quietly, but urgently, most of his words lost on Daniel. ". . . you know about him?"

"What?"

Kurt squeezed; Daniel felt blood throbbing where fingers pressed into his flesh. Kurt leaned in until his chin almost touched Daniel's forehead; thick fumes from the scotch curled into his nostrils, seeped into his brain. He felt drunk on Kurt's breath.

"Marcus. We all know you've just met him. What do you *really* know about him?"

Nothing, Daniel thought. Not a goddamn thing.

"Why would he want the gun, Daniel?"

"He doesn't have the gun. You said so yourself."

"Maybe." Kurt darted a nervous glance around the cabin, as if he was afraid Marcus had, until this moment, stood unnoticed in a corner. He lowered his voice. "I know what Peter's up to. Why we're all here." He shook his head. "Jesus, this is a new low, even for Peter."

Daniel tried to pull away; his efforts were futile. "I don't know what you're talking about."

"Don't give me that bullshit!" His eyes blazed. "It's *you* he wants to humiliate, Daniel. It's *your* lovers he's assembled."

"You're crazy!"

"If Marcus were the jealous sort. . . ." His grip tightened.

Daniel's eyes teared up; blood sang in his ears. "Jesus!" he gasped, "let go of my arm!"

Kurt stared at his fingers wrapped around Daniel's forearm as if he'd just become aware of them himself; he released his grip. Daniel squirmed away, headed for the bedroom on wobbly legs. "For Christ's sake, he didn't take the gun," he said, over his shoulder. "It's not him." He listened for the creaking of the floorboards, for Kurt's steps, but the big man didn't follow.

"Wait. . . ."

Daniel paused, his hand on the doorknob; there was something plaintive in Kurt's voice, a tone wholly inappropriate to him. It dug into Daniel like a barbed hook.

"For the sake of what we once had, please don't let Peter throw me overboard."

He glanced back at Kurt: the big man stood, his back to the window and the implacable snow, his shoulders slumped, arms hung at his side, fingers half-curled around nothing, looking for all the world like a small, frightened boy.

"You're drunk. Get some sleep." Daniel pulled open the door. He stepped into the dark room, dragging the door shut behind him – and almost collided with Marcus. He caught his breath, his heart hammering wildly.

"Jesus! You scared me!"

Marcus was naked; he frowned but said nothing.

Daniel's eyes adjusted. Enough light came through their uncurtained window for Daniel to make out the smooth surfaces of his body, the sinewy muscle, the flawless skin. Perfect as a Greek statue. The beginning of an erection disquieted him.

"What was that all about?" Marcus' voice was as cold the storm outside.

"Nothing," Daniel answered quietly, pushing past him, the skin of his hand tingling where it brushed against the warmth of Marcus' thigh. "Nothing at all." His heart still beat fiercely against his ribs. What had he heard? Daniel wondered. Could the sound of their voices have reached him? Daniel caught himself glancing at Marcus' hands, half-expecting to see the gun. But his fingers were curled around nothing, forming loose fists.

Daniel turned his back, felt Marcus' eyes on him as he pulled off his clothes, sharply aware of the contrast of his own body, mottled with moles and tufts of odd hair, his skin beginning its irreparable sagging. The image was like a plunge into icy water. What was left of his erection subsided. Climbing into bed he lay on his side, his back to Marcus. For a time there was silence, then the bed creaked as Marcus settled behind him.

He didn't take it, Daniel told himself. Kurt's worry about the gun was nonsense. Hell, for all he knew, Kurt had taken the gun. Or maybe it was another of Peter's mind games. Maybe he'd never really put the gun back in the box to begin with.

Fingers lightly touched the hollow of Daniel's side, just below his ribs. Daniel's desire stirred. Marcus' hand drifted around to his stomach, then crept down his abdomen, fingers circling his rekindled erection.

"I love you," Marcus whispered. "Do you love me?"

"Yes," Daniel whispered. He shivered and closed his eyes, falling into thoughtless pleasures where words became unnecessary.

Drifts had climbed the trunks of trees, wrapping around them like mufflers; branches hung low with their burden of snow; pristine white blanketed the ground. An altogether beautiful winter scene. Just as he'd told Kurt it would be.

"He's gone," Daniel said.

Martin, a chef by trade, flipped an omelet expertly. "Who's gone?"

"Kurt."

Rick poked tentatively at bacon with his spatula; unlike Martin, he was useless in the kitchen. There was a time Daniel's apartment had filled with the marvelous aromas of Martin's breakfasts. Of the breakfasts they had cooked together. He missed those. But Martin had been hinting more and more strongly about his feelings for Daniel, feelings Daniel did not reciprocate. What choice did he have? He had to break it off before it had gotten messy. An obscenely short time later, Martin and Rick started dating. Now, they were inseparable. But early in their budding relationship, out of spite at Martin's remarkable emotional resilience, and with Peter's encouragement, Daniel had once seduced Rick. Since then, the small man couldn't hold Daniel's gaze without turning crimson; for months after, he'd clung to Martin like a frightened child in Daniel's presence.

"I just assumed he got lucky." Jason leered at Daniel. He and Kurt had been sharing a room. "He didn't use the bed last night. His bag is still sitting on it." Jason paused between mouthfuls of jam-smeared toast he was supposed to have been preparing for the group.

"Maybe he went for a walk." Martin turned his attention back to his eggs.

Daniel looked outside. In the light of day, the weather didn't look nearly as bad. The tail end of the lake had become visible where it licked the shore. "His Rover is gone." In front of the cabin were two empty spots in the line of cars. Barry's had filled with snow, erasing any evidence that he'd once parked there; not so with Kurt's, thick, tumbling flakes softly rounding the edges of a recent depression. Daniel guessed he couldn't have left more than two hours ago.

"Okay, so he went for a drive."

"He's not coming back." Daniel turned. They all stared at him. Except for Marcus, who sat alone on the couch, legs crossed, a yellowed magazine open in his lap. A vague memory plagued Daniel: of Marcus sliding out of bed in the pre-dawn light, walking silently to the door of their room. Or had it been a dream?

"How do you know?" Peter's question conveyed curiosity but little concern. He sat at the card table snipping slips of paper for future rounds. Next to blank ballots lay the toque in which they placed their votes, Peter's small nod to anonymity.

"He talked about it last night." Daniel imagined Kurt's Rover plunging into the whiteness, the snow coagulating around him, Kurt losing himself on that lonely road.

"That's odd," Jason said, nodding at the coat rack. "His coat's still on the hook."

Daniel looked; there was no mistaking Kurt's large hound's-tooth overcoat.

"Why would he do that? Go without his coat or bag?" Martin poked half-heartedly at the solidifying eggs.

Peter shrugged. "It happens. Despair. A sense of hopelessness. Who knows, perhaps he felt betrayed." He looked at Daniel, then at Martin. "Just like you must have felt when −" He paused, raised his hand to cover his mouth in mock horror, looking from Daniel to Rick to Martin. "Oh dear! I'm afraid I've said too much."

Rick's face colored; he stared at his feet. Martin seemed confused. "What are you talking about?"

"Suicide," Daniel said quickly. To his right, Marcus had gone still, although he never lifted his eyes from his magazine. "Peter thinks he threw himself overboard while we were all sleeping."

"Oh."

Bacon sizzled. Martin looked uncomfortable, but Daniel knew him well enough to know he wouldn't press the issue. If nothing, he was circumspect. Later, perhaps, when he and Rick were alone.

Marcus frowned and flipped pages of his magazine roughly with his right hand, exaggerating the sound. His left hand lay next his thigh, clenched in a fist. Daniel looked at Kurt's coat, then turned his attention to the scene outside the window.

He'd been wrong. Despite the illusion of improved visibility the morning brought, the snow hadn't really let up at all. If anything, it had grown worse. The weather still crept towards them, down the hills and across the frozen lake, closing in on them with the inevitability of fate.

⸻

Over post-breakfast mimosas, Peter announced the start of the second round of the game.

The session moved quickly, the arguments brief and to the point: Peter alluded to the handy survival tips he'd picked up during his brief, ignoble stint in the Boy Scouts; Martin, not his usual voluble self, briefly touted his culinary skills with whatever seafood they might catch; as a teenager, Rick had worked a fishing sloop one summer, and claimed he could supply Martin with a steady supply of fish; having once read a survivalist book, Marcus declared himself capable of rigging up a solar water collector; Jason promised to satisfy every sexual whim of whomever might survive this round. He leered at Peter.

And then it was Daniel's turn.

He felt disoriented, couldn't think. Kurt's disappearance hung over him like a pall. He glanced at Marcus who stared back blithely.

"Well?" Peter tapped his pencil on the arm of his chair; he looked bored.

Daniel couldn't come up with what he felt was a convincing argument. "In a cramped boat," he began, "disputes are bound to arise."

He stopped. "About food. Water."

"Relationships?" Peter added.

Daniel ignored him. "You need me because you need a level-headed mediator whom everyone can trust to impartially resolve disputes." To his own ears his argument sounded weak and irrational.

Peter handed out the slips of paper and pencils. To Daniel's surprise, he passed the toque to Marcus. "As the newest member of our *esteemed* group," here Peter paused and glanced significantly at Daniel, "you can collect the votes."

Marcus took the hat with a stiff nod; a tic had developed in his right cheek.

They scribbled, then dropped their votes in the hat as Marcus held it out. Daniel couldn't meet his gaze when he deposited his.

Marcus reached in and unfolded them one by one.

Jason. Jason. Jason. Jason. Jason. Jason.

Six votes against. Marcus smiled.

"Bullshit!" A vein throbbed on Jason's forehead. "I didn't vote against myself!" He looked desperately at the circle of faces. "You're all out to get me!"

His outrage was no surprise; histrionics were his stock in trade. Although Daniel had extricated himself from their brief relationship in the privacy of Jason's house, Jason had engineered a public scene the next day, accosting him in an outdoor café, making it clear to anyone in earshot that it was he who was dispensing with Daniel. He ceded Jason his small spectacle, hoping that it would be the last he'd have to endure of him. Until this weekend, he'd been largely successful.

"You cheated!" Rising, Jason snatched the toque from Marcus' hand, turning it inside out. It was empty. Quivering like an agitated terrier, Jason glared at Marcus. "He rigged it!"

"We all watched him. He didn't do anything." Peter smiled, clearly amused by the turn of events.

"You shit!" Jason pointed his finger at Marcus. "I voted against *you!* Where's my vote?" He swung around to face Daniel. "They're both in on it! Daniel's still trying to spite me! For the way I humiliated him when we broke up!"

Daniel's temper flared; he wanted to smash Jason in the mouth, to hammer the words back down his throat. But it was too late: Marcus stared at Jason with narrowed, baleful eyes. Daniel swallowed, looked down at the table, his anger dissipating as quickly as it had risen, fear washing it away. Marcus knew. Christ, what would he do?

"It's not fair!"

Peter rose and walked over to the mantle; he rested his hand significantly on the cigar box. "You're history."

Jason shook with fury; for a moment Daniel thought he might make more of scene than Barry had. That he wouldn't have the good grace to depart with what little dignity he had left. But then he stomped off to his room, collected his overnight bag and exited with only the slightest of whimpers. He didn't even slam the door.

Just like that, another part of Daniel's past was gone.

A few minutes later, someone remarked they hadn't heard Jason's car start. As it turned out, no one had.

Peter, mixing up the day's first batch of margaritas, eyed Daniel. "Be a good chap and check to see if his car is gone, will you? I don't much care for the thought of him lurking around outside."

Daniel went to the window. "It's gone."

"Good."

Three empty spaces. Barry, Kurt, Jason. Jason's was a fresh wound; Kurt's had almost filled in, his tire tracks now merely shallow ruts –

Daniel blinked, looked again.

There were no new tire tracks on the drive. No tracks at all leading from Jason's spot. But his vehicle wasn't there. It was as if the hand of a malicious god had plucked his car from the earth and hurled it into the void. Daniel's stomach knotted. When he turned, he found Marcus observing him from the far end of the couch – as distant from the other members of the group as was humanly possible – with a steady, uninflected gaze.

"Good riddance," Marcus said, his words echoing Jason's own after Barry's departure. And then he crossed his arms and turned to stare out the window at the approaching wall of white, willing it – or so it seemed to Daniel – to hasten towards them and smother the past, erasing it forever.

"Why shouldn't we throw *you* overboard?" Peter rolled the stem of his wine glass between his fingers, as if he were rolling around the question. He observed Marcus through the bowl, the legs of his Chardonnay descending in long, parabolic arcs.

It was early afternoon, and the third round was drawing to a close, Marcus the last to justify his continued existence. He hadn't spoken to Daniel since Jason's departure, had studiously ignored him, even when Daniel had tried to catch his attention. Still on the couch, away from the card table, he stared outside as thick flakes of snow blew across the

177

porch and ticked on the window-sill, growing miniature drifts. Visibility had shrunk to twenty meters.

"I'm with Daniel," Marcus answered, as if that was more than enough, never taking his eyes from the scene outside.

Daniel was astonished.

"That's it?" Martin asked.

Marcus turned to face the group. "Yes."

"It's your funeral," Peter said. "Time to vote."

Marcus rose and walked to the table to collect his slip and pencil. They all scribbled, cupping their hands to hide what they were writing. Daniel thought about Jason's altered vote. About the missing tire tracks. About Kurt's disappearance. He moved his pencil, but left the slip blank, putting a tiny crease in the corner with his thumbnail. Picking up the toque, he stuffed his vote in. This round he'd volunteered to be enumerator. Daniel held out the toque to the others. One by one they deposited their votes, Daniel watching them carefully, making sure their hands stayed well outside the hat. He removed the slips and read out the names: two Ricks, one Martin, one Peter and one Daniel.

The slip bearing his name had a tiny crease in the corner. He felt sick.

"Well," Peter said, looking at Marcus strangely, "it's not exactly the result I expected. But tyranny of the ignorant, and all that."

Rick blanched, unprepared for the outcome. He'd arrived with Martin and had probably not contemplated having to leave without him. They'd driven up in Martin's SUV, and now Martin would have to shuttle Rick to the bus station – really a bus stop outside a general store – forty miles away.

"I think the snow's letting up," Daniel lied. "The 4X4 should be okay."

Marcus rose, went into the kitchen and began rooting around in the fridge.

"Sorry," Peter said. "You know the rules."

Rick looked like a lost child. No one said a word.

In silence he collected his kit and slouched to the door; Martin joined him a moment later. Daniel watched from the corner, his arms folded over his chest; Peter still sat the card table where he shuffled and dealt himself a hand of solitaire, cards clicking in the silence. It was a solemn, almost mournful, air. In the kitchen, Marcus sliced onions on the cutting board, making himself a sandwich.

Martin and Rick pulled on their boots and coats. Martin opened the door and stepped out. Pausing on the threshold, Rick looked back and, affecting a false bravado, said, "See you all in hell!" The door banged shut behind them.

Daniel hurried over to the window, watched Martin climb into the driver's side of his 4X4 while Rick loaded his suitcase in the back seat. Daniel didn't want to take his eyes off them for a second, afraid that if he did . . . what? They might disappear? It was absurd. Yet he couldn't shake the fear. He watched as Rick climbed in next to Martin.

He felt a familiar touch on his shoulder; he twisted away, snatching his overcoat from a hook.

"Going somewhere?" Marcus asked.

"I need some air."

"It won't matter."

Daniel buttoned his coat, pulled on his boots, his sense of urgency growing.

Marcus gripped his shoulder with surprising strength. "Don't go."

Shrugging free of Marcus' grip, he hurried out the door. Martin was backing out, his vehicle leaving crisp tire prints in the snow. The temperature had dropped, and the snowfall blotted out everything beyond a radius of a ten meters. Daniel shivered, his breath unfurling before him. The windows of the 4X4 were lightly fogged; but Daniel could make them out, Martin holding the wheel with his left hand, working the clutch with his right, Rick sitting next to him fiddling with the radio. The car backed into the drive until its nose pointed towards the road that climbed into the hills. It wasn't two meters away. Daniel raised his hand to wave goodbye.

Martin waved back.

Then he leaned forward and rubbed a small circle on the fogged windshield. It clouded over within seconds. He rubbed again with no better results. Everywhere else, the gray moisture coating the windows thickened. Martin became less distinct, Rick a dark blotch on his other side, flicking the controls on the front panel, perhaps trying to get their blower to work. Martin reached towards his door. He seemed to be pressing the window button, but the window didn't budge. Daniel lost sight of Rick altogether.

The hum of the engine changed as the 4X4 slipped into gear. The car lurched forward uncertainly, like a novice driver was at the wheel. Only Rick's hands weren't on the wheel. They were flat on the plane of the window, trying to pull it down; then his fists pounded the glass, the meaty part of his palms leaving momentary smears that fogged up as soon as he pulled his hands away. Muffled sounds reached Daniel, the revving engine, the pounding, what could have been screams. A plume of exhaust filled the air as the car slowly accelerated away.

Helpless, Daniel stood rooted.

The 4X4 moved up the road, fading. The horn tooted twice, the way one would signal a cheery goodbye. And then it was gone, lost to sight, thick sheets of snow folding around it like a shroud.

"Love you." Marcus stood next to Daniel as if he had materialized there; he stuck his hands in the pockets of his overcoat. "You love me?"

Cold crept into Daniel's coat underneath his collar; wind made his eyes tear up. Shivering, he wrapped his arms around himself.

"Please, Daniel, I need to know."

"Yes," he whispered, the porch seeming to spin beneath his feet. "Of course I do."

Behind him, the screen door banged shut. Marcus was gone, the space next to Daniel empty, as if Marcus had never been there in the first place.

<hr/>

"He's had plenty of time to drive to town and back," Peter said. "Let's get on with it."

Marcus dried the last plate and placed it in the dish rack. Dinner had come and gone. The portion left for Martin had long grown cold, been wrapped and tucked away in the fridge. Daniel stood by the window, staring at the white that pressed in on the cabin. Beyond the edge of the porch nothing was visible. It was as if they floated in a void, with no proof the rest of the world still existed. "Let's give him just a few more minutes." He had no plan. No ideas. Other than to defer the start of the next round as long as possible.

Marcus took a seat at the table opposite Peter; he eyed Daniel.

"No," Peter said. "Get your wrinkly ass over here."

I'll tell him, Daniel thought. What I saw. What Marcus did.

But he knew Peter wouldn't believe it.

And even if he could convince him, what then? Try to escape like Kurt had? At the thought of leaving Marcus, Daniel's resolve crumpled. He hadn't the will. I love him, he thought. And am frightened of him. He tried to smile at Marcus, to reassure him, that whatever had happened, or was happening, was okay. But Marcus only stared back without expression.

"Martin's dead," Peter said decisively. "One of those couple things, I suppose. You know, one partner dies and the other follows shortly after with a broken heart." He stuck his finger in his mouth and made a retching sound. "Too clichéd. But Martin was never one to shy away from cliché." He smiled. "But then love makes fools of us all. Doesn't it?"

Marcus stared blankly at Peter. Without malice, Daniel wanted to believe. But couldn't.

"The next round begins now. If you don't want to play, then pack your things and leave."

Daniel felt dizzy; beneath him his legs worked, managed to negotiate the distance. Then he was sitting. The toque lay in the middle of the table.

"You go first."

He'd looked at Peter, about to plead for another delay – and realized, up close, how etiolated Peter looked, hunched over, hands in lap, eyes sunken and dark. As if he hadn't slept in days. "Jesus, Peter, you look like shit."

"Fuck how I look." Raising his right had from his lap, he pointed the snout of his gun at Daniel. "State your case."

Daniel was transfixed.

"Perhaps you'd better." Marcus' voice was even, unperturbed, as if he were urging a trip to the market.

Peter had had the gun all along. It wasn't Marcus, hadn't been Marcus. Daniel opened his mouth and snapped it shut; his mind raced in maddening circles. He couldn't take his eyes off the small dark "O" of the weapon's bore.

"Last chance." Peter cocked the gun.

"Don't! I . . . I don't want to die!"

"Not terribly convincing, but okay."

That hadn't been his reason. Daniel wanted to stop things, or at least slow them down. Instead, the scene seemed to accelerate, unfolding with horrifying speed.

"Alright," Peter said, "my go." He smiled crookedly. "So here's why I shouldn't be cast overboard, Daniel: even though you may not know it, I love you."

Love you? Daniel was astounded.

"Isn't that stupid?" Peter shook his head, as if at his own folly. "I don't suppose that's enough. But it's all I have." He swung the gun on Marcus. "Your turn."

"I love him too," Marcus said. "And I think he loves me."

Peter nodded, as if he understood. But what the hell did he understand?

"Time to vote." With his free hand Peter pushed the slips of paper towards them.

Marcus scribbled; Peter did the same, writing awkwardly with his left hand, using the butt of the gun to keep the paper from moving. They put their votes in the toque. Neither made an attempt to hide what they'd written from Daniel: they'd voted against each other.

"I . . . I don't understand." Daniel felt like he was in shock.

"Vote." Peter swung the gun on him.

"That's what it's always been about," Marcus said. "You have to choose."

"Do it!" Perspiration had collected on Peter's forehead; he ran his finger up and down the trigger.

Daniel looked from one to the other, Peter's eyes tinged with madness, Marcus' unfathomable. Then he stared at the empty slip of paper. The pen was leaden in his hand. Peter reached across the table, placing the metal snout of the gun on Daniel's temple.

"You'd best do as he says, Daniel."

Jesus fucking Christ. They were crazy, both of them.

"Make your choice." Peter ground the barrel into Daniel's temple.

"Please," Marcus said. "For me."

Cupping his hand so they couldn't see, Daniel scrawled in small letters his own name, *daniel*, and added his slip to the hat.

"Now empty it," Peter said, the pressure from the gun unrelenting.

Daniel reached for the toque and upended it.

A slip fell out, then another. Then half a dozen all at once, more and more, hundreds of slips fluttering from the maw of the hat, falling like thick clotting flakes of snow, until a mound formed in the centre of the table. Still more slips tumbled out and accumulated in drifts, swirled, slipping over the edge to float into Daniel's lap and then tumble gently to the floor. And each slip was identical, inscribed in large, black letters with the same name, over and over: PETER.

Daniel heard a strangled gasp; the gun tumbled to the table, settled into the rat's nest of paper. He turned. Peter was gone, his seat empty.

He and Marcus were alone at the table.

The snowstorm dwindled, then petered out altogether. The world was fresh, unsullied. A clean slate.

Daniel stood at the side of the cabin, gathering logs from the woodpile until his arms were full. He turned. Sunlight glittered on the new fall, stung his eyes, making it bearable only for the briefest time. In front of the cabin the cars were gone, all of them, even Daniel's. As if they never existed. There was no sign of the drive or of the service road. Trees had filled in those spaces.

Is this the same world or a new one? Daniel wondered. There was no way of telling.

He trudged back through the drifts and climbed onto the front porch. Shouldering open the door, Daniel stamped the snow from his boots, walked the logs across the room and piled them on the andirons. Marcus sat in the corner, a blanket over his shoulders, playing with the gun, spinning the cylinder idly, his breath forming tenuous clouds. The electricity had gone with Peter. As had their phone and everything that ran on batteries. Daniel tore pages out of old magazines, crumpled them and shoved them under the logs along with the bit of kindling they had. He struck a match. Even though the lights wouldn't work, the logs caught obligingly.

"There," Daniel said wearily. "That should help."

They had enough logs to keep themselves alive for two weeks, maybe more; if they rationed, the food might last even longer.

"Do you love me?" Marcus asked.

The constant question was an annoyance, a background hum that wouldn't go away. But Daniel smiled obligingly and answered, "Yes."

It was the new game. That love would sustain them, keep them from vanishing like the others. It was their lifeboat.

"Promise?"

His steady assurances had done nothing to ameliorate Marcus' need. To blunt his jealousy and fear. He's scared, Daniel thought. Been scared all along of not being loved.

"Of course I do."

Marcus scrutinized him, seemed to be weighing the sincerity of his words; Daniel tried to smile reassuringly.

It's not his fault, Daniel tried to convince himself. Not completely. Didn't I wish for it too? For them all to go away? Hasn't he only been doing what I'd wanted all along. . . .

Marcus turned, stared out the window, spun the cylinder again.

"And me?" Daniel asked, his heart tripping in his chest. "Do you love me?"

"So much it hurts."

Daniel let out his breath. He wanted to believe Marcus. After all, he was still here, the smell of burning wood in his nose, the spreading warmth of the fire creeping into his legs, a tingle in his arms left over from the weight of the logs. Alive. But would Marcus love him forever? Or was it only a matter of time before Daniel, too, would vanish, another distasteful memory erased?

A man in love, it seemed, must learn to live with uncertainty.

YOU CAN'T ALWAYS GET WHAT YOU WANT

T.L. Bryers

 ALEX STALKED DORIAN DOWN A NEARLY DESERTED street. He knew that he wouldn't be noticed if he didn't want to be. He had been watching Dorian for a long time and he knew exactly what he was. Dorian's height, his dramatic clothes, and his strong, beautiful features gave him away completely. Alex tracked him out of a dark after-hours club in hopes of getting a phone number and maybe, if he was really lucky, something more. He never imagined he would find what he really, secretly wanted. He hadn't expected to ever find the creature that haunted all his fantasies.

He never thought that he would find a real vampire.

The first time Alex followed Dorian, he had watched in utter shock as Dorian picked up a homeless man from where he had been sleeping and callously tossed him against the wall. His shock had given way to fascination as Dorian ripped open the bum's neck with his teeth, and started to feed on his blood with the hunger of a wild animal. He watched Dorian completely drain the man, then leave the mangled body in a lump on the pavement.

That had been over three months ago. Since then, every night that Alex could get downtown, he watched him. He studied Dorian's every movement, and every night, he became more and more enraptured. Alex watched him take more victims. Some were vagrants, killed with precise and mechanical movements, and some were beautiful young boys like Alex himself; each of the boys were carefully seduced, and then ravished, before they were killed.

Now Alex was sitting in the same after-hours club watching him again. Dorian was fraternizing with a brood of kids in dark clothes, standing against an equally dark wall. Alex marveled at what a stark contrast he was to the others in the room. He was so refined-looking, almost majestic. The other boys were all dressed in expensive leather and crushed velvet or torn fishnet, next to them Dorian's allure was unmistakable. He stood at least six-foot-four and was wearing a simple, tailored black suit. Alex guessed it was probably something Italian. When Alex looked down at his own clothes he sighed. Somehow now the skin-tight black jeans and plain black shirt that clung tight over his frail body didn't seem appropriate attire. He wondered if he would be able to impress him. How would he stand out from every other boy in the room? He wanted so much to find the courage to talk to him. He had waited all his life for this opportunity. When he was a kid, he had fallen for the likes of Christopher Lee and Bela Lugosi, and now he knew that he was in love with *this* man, who clearly was so much more than a mere *man*.

He longed so much to be with him. He wanted to kiss him, to touch him. He wanted to have Dorian inside him. He thought that they could share so much.

He wanted to become a vampire, too. Then they could be together forever.

Alex downed the last of his rum and coke in one quick gulp. The alcohol made him feel more sure of himself. He had to talk to Dorian tonight, and tell him everything he felt. Alex walked over and tried hard not to appear as drunk as he felt. There was a certain urgency and determination in his movements as he approached the creature of his dreams.

Dorian was a good five inches above him. Alex felt small and weak under his sturdy gaze.

"Hi," Alex said, flashing a shy boyish grin that had always worked for him in the past.

"Hello," Dorian replied. To Alex, Dorian seemed to size him up in a single glance.

"Can I, uh, buy you a drink?"

"No, you can't. I don't drink."

"Oh right, of course you don't." Alex looked down at his feet and shuffled nervously, cursing himself for his own stupidity. "Is there maybe something else I could do for you then?" he asked.

"What did you have in mind, little one?"

"I don't know. What do you want me to do for you?"

"I have many desires," Dorian replied. "What can you offer me?"

Alex fumbled with the rings on his hand. He didn't know what to say, and he wasn't use to being this forward.

Dorian laughed and wrapped his arm around Alex's shoulders. "Why don't we go back to my place? I'm sure that if we put our heads together, we could figure something out."

Alex's heart raced, and he nearly fainted from excitement.

Dorian's house was a small one-storey, set back in the low-rent district of town. Alex thought a vampire should have more elegant living arrangements. He pictured a large gothic mansion with high peaks and stone gargoyles guarding the entrance. This place seemed to be so ordinary and plain, but he wasn't about to mention anything about that now. Instead, he stood in the doorway and fidgeted with his jacket. He wondered if Dorian could smell his anticipation.

"This place is nice," said Alex. He was too nervous to think of anything clever to say.

"Let's not spoil this by talking, all right?" Dorian's voice was so soft that Alex had to strain to hear it. Dorian's strong hand felt like ice when he took Alex's and led him towards the bedroom. Dorian kissed him deeply. Alex was only vaguely disturbed by the taste of Dorian's mouth. It tasted like a mixture of cloves and old pennies.

Dorian pushed Alex onto the bed and started to tug at his clothes, almost ripping to get them off. Once Alex was completely naked, Dorian stood above him and smiled.

"Is this what you wanted, little boy?" he asked, and laughed. It sounded to Alex like music.

"Yes!" Alex moaned, unable to control his lust any longer. "Yes, I want *you*. Please, please fuck me."

"Good," Dorian said, " I like it when my boys beg."

The lovemaking – and Alex thought of it as lovemaking, not just fucking – was unlike anything he had ever felt before. He could scarcely believe that this was actually happening to him. He reveled in Dorian's body: his taut, muscled chest, his tight, smooth buttocks, his solid arms and legs that held onto Alex so tightly that he thought his heart was going to be crushed. The intense emotion he felt was so nearly over-powering that Alex had to fight back the tears.

As the first waves of orgasm washed over him he screamed out, "I love you."

Dorian collapsed on the bed, still buried in Alex's supine body.

Alex tentatively wrapped his arms around his new lover and held him as close as he could. He wanted this moment to last forever.

"I know what you are," Alex whispered.

Dorian raised his head and looked at him.

"I've been watching you and following you for months," Alex continued. "I know what you are, and I love you for it. I want to be with you forever."

Dorian smiled. "You know what I am do you?"

"Yes, yes, I do," said Alex, beaming with a child's excitement, "and I've waited for this for so long."

"Good," said Dorian, adjusting himself on the bed. "Then you'll be expecting this."

Alex sighed and closed his eyes. His entire body tensed with painful anticipation as he bared his neck to his savior and awaited the kiss that would grant him eternal life.

Dorian reached for the heavy silver candlestick on the bedside table, and, with one fluid motion, swung it hard, connecting with Alex's skull in an explosion of red fire and black stars.

Alex woke to a ferocious world of pain. He hadn't known such pain could exist.

Dimly, he became aware of his surroundings as the hot white light poured over him. He was still naked but he was no longer in the soft confines of Dorian's bedroom. The air here was old and stale. A damp, musty odor filled his nostrils and choked at his lungs. Everywhere around him he smelled rot.

He was fastened to a large wooden cross with thick leather straps that didn't allow him to move more than an inch in any direction. Fear and confusion flooded through him. His entire body began to shake and he felt bile rise in his throat. He gagged and coughed and spit down his chin and onto his chest.

"Don't bother trying to scream, little boy. Nobody will ever hear you." The voice came from somewhere deep in the shadows beyond Alex's line of sight.

"Dorian?" Alex's own voice was weak, barely audible.

"Were you expecting some else?" Dorian stepped into the murky light. His teeth, very long and very white, gleamed in the darkness of the room.

"Why?" Alex coughed again and blood trickled over his lips. "Why are you doing this?"

"Why?" Dorian replied. "Because this is what I do, that's why."

"But I thought —"

"What?" Dorian brought his face very close to Alex's. "What did you think? Did you think this would be something romantic and beautiful? Did you think that you'd walked into an Anne Rice novel? You yourself said you knew what I was. Or did you think that with you it would be different? That we would have some tragic little love affair? That after one night of fucking I would realize that I couldn't exist without you and I would make you like me and that we would go on and be happily ever after just like a fucking fairy tale? Is that what you thought?"

Tears streamed down Alex's cheeks.

"Is that what you dreamt about year after year?" Dorian asked cruelly. "Fantasized, lying in your bed, in your parents' basement, playing with yourself, wishing you had the courage to admit that you wanted to be with men instead of women? Did you worry that they would all laugh at you? That if they knew they would hate you even more than they already hated you? And didn't you pray to whatever god it is you kids pray to nowadays that maybe, just maybe, someone — or something — could take you away from all this?"

Alex was sobbing now. "I love you."

"You fucking kids!" Dorian laughed. "You play your dress-up games, and you want to live and love forever. You make me sick." Dorian walked slowly in front of him. "I don't know what love is. I'm not your savior. I'm not your 'Dark Prince.'"

Dorian pressed his lips next to Alex's ear and whispered to him.

"I'm the monster hiding under your bed."

Alex's entire body tensed and trembled.

"I'm what goes bump in the night."

Dorian took a step back and paused, looking at Alex.

"I am," he said simply, "everything that you've ever feared."

Dorian's nails slashed into the smooth skin of Alex's chest. Alex screamed in pain, rearing up and thrashing against the leather straps. Five deep lines of blood appeared on Alex's chest and trickled down his stomach.

"There comes a time right before a man dies," Dorian said, dropping gracefully to his knees. He began to lap at the blood dribbling from Alex's hips and thighs. "It's the moment when he realizes, without any uncertainty, that he is going to die. He stops fighting, and a kind of spiritual calm comes over him. He makes his peace. He no longer fears." Dorian stood up and cupped Alex's quivering face in his hands. He shrugged. "At least that's what I've heard. Have you reached that point, Alex? Do you no longer fear me?"

Alex whimpered like a child, his body convulsing.

"No . . . please. . . ."

Dorian kissed him gently. Alex felt, rather than saw, the full, sharp teeth behind Dorian's lips. They felt huge. Alex closed his eyes tightly and turned his face as far away as the strap holding his head in place would allow. He made a sound that might have been a scream if he'd been willing to open his mouth.

"Good," whispered Dorian. "I'm glad you haven't reached that point yet, Alex. The fear makes everything taste better."

THE BIRD FEEDERS

David Nickle

 THE BIRD-SONG DIDN'T JUST WAKE SIMON; IT yanked him up, like a fish hook caught in his jaw. There was none of the sweet and atonal tra-la-la you expect from dainty little garden birds; this song was a jazz-trumpet-cracking-on-the-high-notes, thrash-metal-guitar-shriek kind of a ditty and it left Simon blinking and gasping on the ancient mattress. The sheets had tangled between his legs through the night, and he clutched at them now, squeezing and tugging the sweaty cloth. Simon stared up at the farmhouse's watermarked ceiling. He took a breath and closed his eyes.

"Cock-a-doodle-doo."

He said it to no one in particular. Simon was alone in the bedroom; Zoly, who had brought him here the night before, had apparently risen earlier than he and was nowhere to be seen. Simon wasn't surprised at that; he was what you would call a "night person," and didn't like to get up before noon if he could help it. Most of the time he could get away with it; Simon was nineteen years old, fair-haired and smooth-skinned, and the gentlemen with whom he consorted tended to cut him a little slack as a result.

So he wasn't surprised at Zoly's absence; but he was a little disappointed. Simon would have liked him here now – if for no other reason than to rub down the gooseflesh that had cropped up on his arm. Maybe say *Jeez, Simon, it's just a fucking bird* and maybe give him a hug. Zoly didn't owe him that, of course. It was too early – so early they hadn't even fucked yet, so early that Simon hadn't even figured out how to pronounce Zoly's unpronounceable last name. It one of those phlegmy east-Euro names, weighted down with a big stack of consonants front and back that make a sound like hawking when you put them together in your mouth.

Walter had introduced the two of them not forty-eight hours earlier. Walter introduced Simon to a lot of the guys Simon went with since he'd come to town. And although Simon hadn't seen any money from Walter over the past eight or nine weeks, Simon had a pretty clear understanding of the transactional nature of their relationship. Walter had established that relationship with Simon from almost the moment they'd met.

Simon had met Walter his third night in the city. It was February, and the streets were thick with slush, and Simon didn't really know anybody. He'd tried one of the homeless shelters – but the first night he hadn't made curfew so got turned away, and the second night he got in but, surveying the company and accommodations, wished he hadn't made curfew. So by the third night, Simon found himself faced with the dim prospect of spending another night on the street. As the evening wore on, he settled under an overhang across from a coffee shop on King Street.

In less than an hour, Walter showed up. He was dressed for business – a blue woolen overcoat, expensive shoes slipped inside rubber covers and crisply-pressed black pants. He still had his grey-flecked beard – but it was clipped short and tidy. Very businessy. He came out of the coffee shop with two steaming cups of hot chocolate, kneeled down beside Simon, and held one forward.

"Want one of these?" he asked.

"Fuck, yeah," said Simon. He was bone-cold and hungry and thirsty, and the hot chocolate would have dealt with all of those problems in at least a small measure. He reached forward, but Walter pulled it back.

"Whoa there, kid," he said. "Do you think this comes for free?"

Simon shrugged. "You're offering," he said.

"No," said Walter. "You weren't listening. I asked if you want it. You haven't asked what I want in return."

"Didn't think that was part of the deal," said Simon.

"It's always part of the deal," said Walter. "Get up and come with me. It's too cold."

The deal with Walter involved a lot of introductions – never, as it turned out, to hot young guys who were dead broke, new in town and all on their own like Simon. The guys Simon got to meet were much older, with a sag in their ass and a bulge in their wallet – closet fags who looked at Simon's crotch with a kind of blunt hunger their straight-life wives could never satisfy. Simon would go off with the guys – sometimes in a car, sometimes to a bedroom, and more often than not just to the extra-deep Jacuzzi tub in Walter's can – and do them. It didn't usually take long, and once in a while Simon would get off, too. Usually, Simon felt as though he were counting time with these guys, and he didn't give them more than a thought.

The thing with Zoly was different, though.

For one thing, Walter didn't want Simon to come to his place to do the deed. They were going to Zoly's place – his restaurant. This in itself was a step up for Simon.

Walter picked Simon up just past nine at the Second Cup down the block from him, with barely a word, and took him to a taxi cab. He asked Simon three times if he was feeling okay. Each time Simon said sure – although the third time, he was beginning to wonder if he really was feeling okay. Walter didn't seem to be, but Simon didn't feel the nature of their relationship allowed him to ask.

Zoly's restaurant was on a side-lane near the highway, taking up the greater part of a converted warehouse that faced the undulating wooden fence of a wrecking yard. Although there was no sign out front or back, according to Walter the place was widely known as Zoltan's.

Simon had paid close attention – one of his big dreams in coming down to the city was renting a loft in an old building like this – one big room he could do anything he wanted with and hot young neigh-bours who partied all the time, and an elevator that worked with a lever instead of buttons, that you could stick between floors for an hour if you didn't know how to work it.

There was no elevator to Zoltan's. It was on the ground floor, and Simon and Walter went in across a concrete loading pad and through loading doors wide enough to pass a truck, and from there straight into the kitchens. Simon had bussed table in some places back in Windsor, so he thought he knew kitchens – but he'd never seen anything like this. The place was a cavern – it actually had catwalks running along the walls, and what seemed like dozens of thick-shouldered men in white kitchen-frocks were manning those catwalks. On the floor was a maze of counters and cutting-boards and gas ranges tended by more of the men. At the far end, a great stainless-steel door loomed like a bank vault. From its handle, Simon recognized it to be an immense freezer door. It was nearly as big as the loading doors they'd come in.

All of that would have been enough to impress him. But what caught Simon's eye and held it was the fire-pit at the kitchen's centre. It was a square of glowing red charcoal, rimmed by a two-foot retain-ing wall of blackened cinder-block. The whole thing was maybe eight feet on the side. Above it, a giant ventilation unit hummed and rattled as it sucked the ember-smoke up through wide duct-work straight to the kitchen-cavern's ceiling.

Zoltan – Zoly, as everyone called him – was standing on the edge of the fire-pit, stripped to the waist, thrusting the coals to and fro with a long metal rake. Walter started to point him out, but Simon didn't need him to. Zoly was old – older than some of the men that Walter had brought around – but he had a sinewy body that gleamed like pig-iron in the ember-glow.

Zoly saw them, too, and waved a leather-gloved hand. He hollered something that Simon couldn't understand, and one of the other men came forward and took the rake from him, resumed where the boss had left off. Zoly splashed some water in his face and on his chest from a tub at the fire-pit's far corner, and strode across the kitchen floor.

"Hey, Zoly," said Walter. "Here's —"

Zoly looked at Simon. "Yes," he said. He stepped up to Walter and gave him a rough embrace. Walter stepped away, and Simon noticed Zoly had left a torso-sized sweat-stain across Walter's shirt.

"Good-looking kid," said Zoly in that indefinable accent of his.

"Zoly, Simon, Simon, Zoly," said Walter. "Simon's new in town."

"Not that new, I hear," said Zoly.

Walter shrugged, and Simon smiled. "Hey," he said.

"Hey," said Zoly. His eyes travelled up Simon's torso, stopped about collar-bone level. Then he blinked, and he smiled himself and met Simon's gaze straight-on.

"You're not one of those goddamned vegetarians, are you? This is a meat place."

Simon shook his head. "I like meat," he said.

Zoly nodded brusquely, and turned to one of his men — a shaved-bald guy working at the nearest range — yelled something in that same east-Euro talk he'd used to hand off his rake, and clapped his hands together. The guy nodded, reached into a tray and flipped a purple-red thing about the size of a baseball glove onto the range-top fry-pan. Simon couldn't identify it, but from the way it sizzled and smoked — and smelled; the fragrance flooded Simon's hungry mouth with saliva — yeah, it was meat. "Walter's not feeding you, is he?" said Zoly.

Walter started to say something, but Zoly held up a hand to silence him. "You stay with me for awhile, okay?" he said to Simon.

Simon didn't know what he would have said. He'd been staying at a shelter on the nights he could, on the streets others, and only very occasionally at Walter's place. He shouldn't have felt he owed Walter anything; but at the same time he felt Walter deserved some kind of fealty. Walter had given Simon's life a shape when he landed in town. Who knew where he'd be now, if not for Walter? And that was worth something, wasn't it?

It would have been a wrenching decision, but Walter spared him having to make it.

"Okay, then?" he said to Zoly. "I'm out of here."

"Later," said Simon to Walter. But Walter didn't seem to hear. Simon tried to meet his eye, but Walter wasn't biting. And as Walter turned his head away, Simon caught a look in his eye that Simon hadn't quite seen before. And then Walter was gone, hurrying out the loading-door exit, leaving Simon alone with Zoly. And Zoly's guys — a number of whom who were just then congregating around the freezer doors. Zoly put a hand on Simon's shoulders and guided him to the far side of the kitchen, where a set of double doors led into the dining room.

"So, Simon," said Zoly, slyly, as the lock on the freezer door clanked open behind them. "You better be hungry."

Tentatively, Simon slid his fingers into the back pocket of Zoly's jeans, but Zoly reached around and yanked his arm out.

And that was the other thing that was different between Zoly and Walter's other fags. For once, it seemed like Simon was the hungry one, and old fag Zoly, the one content to wait.

As the shock of waking wore off, Simon felt the hunger again. And not just for Zoly this time — Simon could have used some food. He was famished.

"Hey, Zoly!" Simon tromped down the stairs to the farm house's living room. The room ran the length of the house — which meant that, all-told, five tall windows admitted the grey-purple light of the storm-threatening sky. They made wide and dismal bands across the farm house's ancient floorboards. "Zoly! I'm up! What's for breakfast?"

Still no one answered. Tentatively, Simon walked over to one of the five windows and peered out.

The sky was shifting darker at the horizon, where black-forested hills climbed like a crater-rim. As Simon watched, lightning flickered against it. Nearer, but not too near, Simon could make out a low line of lights on the hilltop across the concession road. Nearer still, a wind blew up dust in the farmhouse's empty driveway.

The driveway shouldn't have been empty. Zoly's car should have been there.

"Shit." Simon turned away from the window, looked back on the indistinct shadow he cast across the floorboards. He stared at it — at the old farmhouse floorboards, the floral wallpaper etched with the ghost-white squares of pictures long-gone; indelible scars against decades' worth of light. This place was old. Older than you saw in the city — or at least the parts of the city where Simon spent time.

And it was, he realized, so bare as to seem vacant. The only furniture in the farm house living room was a couple of old chairs and a corner table with an oil lamp on it. More watermarks made continents on the broad white ceiling. The bedroom upstairs was better-appointed — but only just. Simon shivered, and buttoned his shirt up the rest of the way. He tucked it deep inside his jeans, so the fabric stretched against his shoulders like tight suspenders. Where the fuck, he wondered, is Zoly?

He was about to leave the room, head for the kitchen and maybe find some breakfast, when the bird sang again. It sounded as bad now as it did the first time. Big and loud and shrill in his ear. Simon felt prickling up his neck like a frozen caress; it seemed to pull from sleep all over again. But of course, he was already awake. So Simon could only conclude it was something else in his skin the scream awoke this time.

As the song came, the five bands of light on the floor flickered dark – like something was rushing past them, occluding the storm-light in one window, and another and another, and then two more. At the last window, the shadow lingered an instant; long enough for Simon to discern a man-shape, arms raised and blurred with the motion and the diffuse storm light into wings. But it only stayed that long. When Simon turned, the window was empty.

———

Zoly drove them up here after the restaurant closed. Simon slept most of the drive; Zoly had fed him a big pasta dish, rigatoni in a cream sauce, mingled with strips of a dark, pan-fried meat marinated in honey, and long, purplish mushrooms that tasted like wine. Simon ate the food in Zoltan's dining room, among a half-dozen other patrons who lingered there. They were all men who were older and uglier than the worst of the ones Walter had brought for Simon. And they were ugly in the same way. Their eyes had a golf-ball bulge to them, covered with age-darkened lids rough and supple as car-seat leatherette. That, combined with their too-wide mouths, thin lips, and dry, old-men's skin, made Simon think of lizards more than men. But they dressed well – in finely tailored suits made of funereal dark fabric. And they knew their table manners.

In his dusty black jeans and open-necked shirt, Simon felt out of place – far, far beneath these ugly old guys. He was amazed that Zoly had even let him show his face.

And his food was different from theirs as well. As he looked around, Simon noticed that he was the only one in the room eating the pasta. The other diners ate from plates of meat piled in front of them – turkey-sized drumsticks; large, breaded schnitzels; thick steaks with melting balls of butter in their middles. The tiny potatoes on their plates seemed mere afterthoughts, garnishes. As they finished, their automotive-accessory eyelids would quiver in a kind of transported ecstasy, an almost sexual release. Then they would ruin the effect with an appreciative belch.

For Simon, though, the pasta concoction was enough. By the time they left – an hour after the last patron passed through Zoly's small front door, and just as the kitchen staff began to filter out the broader loading doors to the back – Simon was positively torpid.

"You can sleep on the way," said Zoly, as he got behind the wheel of his car. "It's a few hours away we're going – to a farm I share with some fellows."

"You live there?" Simon asked.

"I haven't been there in too long a time," said Zoly.

Simon only had a fragmentary recollection of the drive to the farm. He remembered the highway heading north of the city, empty but for them and the transport trucks, red-lit giants that roared past them at impossible speeds. Zoly told him stories during this portion of the trip; of time spent in Budapest, where he studied "the vagaries of the Hungarians" as he put it (Simon assumed he was referring to their cuisine); of his travels in "the side-alleys" of Asia (again, though he didn't say it, Simon guessed he picked up a few wok-cooking tips on the way); and of a marriage ended badly, whether in Hungary or Asia or here, Zoly did not say.

Zoly spoke quickly, never pausing to ask Simon his opinion or to counter with stories of his own. After awhile, Simon felt himself going so disconnected from the narrative that it seemed as though Zoly was not speaking English anymore, but his own, consonant-crowded language. Simon did not stay awake for long after this.

He awoke two or three times more. Once, when the car's suspension jostled through a hole on a dirt road and the car's doors rattled with the impact of flying gravel. "Where are we?" he'd asked sleepily, but Zoly, lit only by the dim red lights of the dashboard, had simply laughed. And once again, in a state of inexplicable terror that caused Simon to grip at the door-handle like a lifeline. After he caught his breath, he recognized the cause of his distress for the nightmare it must have been and quickly calmed himself back to sleep – but for an instant, he swore they were flying through the night air, Zoly having dozed and driven off the edge of a high cliff.

Simon tromped back and forth on the porch, looking for the shadow-man. "Hey! Who's there!" he yelled. The air outside was heavy with coming storm – the leaves on a nearby copse of trees were turning their pale underbellies to the sky and a low breeze tickled the seed-laden tips of the field grass across the road. Soon, the whole valley would be drenched in rain and lightning would crack into the ground. "Come on out!" he shouted. "I'm not going to hurt you or nothing!"

"Didn't think you would."

Simon shivered. The boy's voice had come from behind him, from the door he'd just exited. He turned around. The boy was there all right – standing at the base of the stairs, part in shadow. He wore big Kodiak work boots like Simon hadn't seen anyone wear since he was a kid; a pair of unfashionable, saggy-assed jeans; and a button-up flannel shirt that was half-untucked. His hair was light-colored and cut really short, and he wore sunglasses even though it was dark inside. Simon shivered again. He'd been on the receiving end of more than one beating at the hands of boys who looked like this.

"Come inside," said the boy. "Quick now."

Simon was instantly suspicious. He could scope the plan all too clearly: Farm Boy here waits until he sees the car's gone, sneaks over to take some crap out on the old faggot's boy toy of the week. Which is as easy to do inside as it is out – easier, because there's no chance of witnesses inside.

Simon took a step back, off the porch. "What's your hurry?" His foot crunched in the sandy gravel.

This seemed to upset the boy unduly. He stepped forward as well, and bent down as to look behind Simon, and above. "Jesus fuckin' Christ! " he hissed. "Inside!"

"Okay," said Simon. He set his other foot on the gravel and stepped back. The hot storm-wind played across his shoulders. "This place isn't yours. Come on out."

Simon thought he was going to run upstairs or into the kitchen or something. Farm Boy had shifted into the kind of stance that suggested he was going to bolt. Simon was half-right. Farm Boy was bolting, but not deeper into the house. He started towards Simon fast, and for an instant Simon went back to his original thought: the kid was here to beat crap out of a queer, and while he wanted to do it inside where no one could hear or see, outside in plain sight and hearing would do in a pinch.

Simon turned to run, but he didn't get far. Two steps, and Simon's legs were pinwheeling in the air. Looking down, he saw ground bobbing up and down about a dozen feet beneath his shoes. About the same time, the pain in his shoulder registered, and he understood: his feet were out of the equation; the only thing holding him up was the hook that had apparently jammed itself through his left shoulder. He dangled from it, like a doll. There was a sound over his head that reminded Simon of sailcloth in a strong wind. Hot air that stunk like shit drove down on him like a rain. He tried to look up, but found he could not – whether from the force of the wind or the smell of it, the angle of his shoulder or the pain of it, or just his own terror. He looked down helplessly, as Farm Boy looked up at him. He was reaching for something in his back pocket. Simon screamed Zoly's name.

And above him, the bird sang back.

————————

The rain on the roof made a sound like automatic gunfire. It was loud enough to wake Simon up. The pain in his shoulder was enough to keep him awake.

"Zoly?" he whispered. It was dark. There was a smell like cigarettes in a urinal. The pain in his shoulder was like the noise from one of Walter's old men waking up beside him: it got more insistent and un-pleasant as consciousness wore on. Simon shifted, and the pain got a bit better – he was sleeping on a couch, and his bad shoulder had been pressing against it.

"Who's Zoly?" said a voice from the dark. Simon thought he might recognize it, and as recognition came so did the sliver of memory: Farm Boy with a big black sling-shot, drawing it back with a ball-bearing in the loop; a flash in the air; a deafening scream overhead, and a lightness in his belly followed almost immediately by hard contact with gravel; and flapping just above the ground, not a dozen feet from him –

A bird.

It was big – as tall as an ostrich, with the same kind of furry feath-ers you'd see on an ostrich coursing up and down its back. But it had a beak like a raptor-bird, a great chitinous hook big as an axe-blade. And it had wings. The wings were immense – they were feathered with the colors of an oil slick, and extended more than a car-length down either side of its body. Flapping, they stirred dust-devils like the wind from a helicopter, and sent a lazy breeze of bird-stink Simon's way.

Simon tried to move away, but he was too weak. It felt like the worst hunger he'd ever felt, but in retrospect Simon thought it was blood loss: the gravel around him was dappled with large dark spots like shadows. The great bird turned an eye to him – a black golf-ball set into a socket that seemed a perfect circle. Its beak opened, and the folds of flesh around its throat vibrated, and it screamed again as it landed, and took a step toward him –

"Zoly the guy who brung you?" asked Farm Boy in the dark.

"Um. Yeah," said Simon. As he blinked, he could make out shapes in the room. One of them moved, so he thought of that shape as Farm Boy addressed himself to that. "Last night – I think."

"It would have been last night," said Farm Boy. "Zoly's no more."

"What?"

"Bird got him."

Simon processed this a moment. Dashing old Zoltan dead?

Something like grief passed over him like a cold wind. The chill of it surprised him — shit, he'd just met Zoly the night before — until he identified it for what it was: not grief, but fear.

"Like the one —"

"That almost got you? Yeah. Like that."

"Fuck."

Farm Boy snorted. "Better him than you. Old faggot got what he deserved, ask me."

Simon changed the subject. "How — how bad's my arm?"

"You're fuckin' welcome." Farm Boy came over and bent over Simon. A hand detached itself from the shape and rested on his bad shoulder. Simon suppressed an urge to scream. Farm Boy snorted again. "Not as bad as it pro'ly feels. I seen guys walk away from worse. You just got a couple of claws broke through the skin. "

"Really?" Simon reached up with his good arm and took Farm Boy's hand off his shoulder. It was strong and the skin oily, seasoned deeply with grit, fingernails bitten to the quick. He held it.

"Feels like my arm got ripped off."

"Um, yeah." Farm Boy disengaged his hand and stepped back. "It'll start to feel better quicker than you think."

"Right." Simon winced. "So where am I? Who are you?"

This time, it wasn't a snort from Farm Boy, but a full-body laugh. "Second one's easier. I'm Terry. First one's a big fuckin' question. Let me ask you this: where'd this Zoly faggot tell you you were going?"

Simon had meant: where am I right this minute? But he answered Terry's question anyway. "To a farm that he owned with some guys. North of the city. We drove —"

"Huh. What city?"

Simon told him.

"Really." Terry moved off into shadow. "You live on the street there?"

"Not on the street." Not exactly, thought Simon.

"With your parents then? Have your own place? An apartment with a bunch of guys? Your girlfriend maybe?" Terry didn't wait long for Simon to answer. "Don't bullshit me. You lived on the street. He wouldn't have brung you if you didn't."

"Yeah," said Simon.

"So nobody'd know you'd gone — nobody'd call the police when you didn't turn up, right?"

"Right." Simon felt himself getting impatient. "So where am I? Right now?"

"Right now?" A crack of dim grey light spread itself across the room. "You're in a shed in back of the faggot's place. Some guys are coming with a truck soon. Collect us. Take us back."

"Okay, back where? The city?"

The crack widened into a rectangle of grey. Rain was coming down in thick sheets, and it obscured details – but Simon could see the rear of Zoly's farm house. Terry stepped into the light, and then, seemingly without a care, outside. Simon drew in a breath – what if the bird came back?

"It's okay," said Terry, guessing at Simon's anxiety. He was still wearing his sunglasses. "The birds hate the rain. Fucks up their wings."

"Are we going back to the city?" said Simon again.

But Terry was gone in the falling rain before Simon finished the question.

Zoly dead. Killed by a bird. While Simon slept? Simon thought that must be how it happened. Zoly steps outside for a cigarette or a doob or something, looks up at the country sky with all those stars you never see in the city, stars you can lose yourself in. And then the stars go black and the wind whips up and there's a scream out of hell and that's pretty much all. Simon couldn't believe how bad he felt about it. He didn't think he would have been too broken-up over news like this about any of the other men Walter had brought by. He might have felt bad about Walter. And maybe, as he thought about it, he'd feel the same kind of bad. With Zoly dead, Simon felt like he'd been cut loose in space – floating in darkness, with not even the stars to tell him where he was.

Just him . . . and the bird.

Simon got himself off the couch when he heard the engine outside. Terry was right; his shoulder hurt to move, but otherwise it was feeling better already. And his legs seemed to work fine once he was on them. He stepped over to the door and peered out.

It must have been the truck that Terry was talking about.

The truck was actually a deep blue panel van with tinted windows and no license plates. Its lights cut twin swathes through the rainfall as it wheeled around the front of Zoly's farm house and stopped. Simon made his way outside as the side of the van opened. Two figures climbed out and disappeared around the front of the house. The rain had let up a little, but it still struck Simon like ice. Looking up into that rain would have been too much, so Simon hunched over and kept his head low as he ran to the house's back door.

Inside was a mess. Terry and one of the two from the van were half-way through rifling through the drawers in the kitchen. The third was evidently inside the walk-in pantry – a tin can slid out the door and across the linoleum floor every second or two. Terry looked up, saw Simon and grinned a bit.

"Hey," he said. "Know if there's any more food around here? Like in the basement or something?"

"I just got here myself," said Simon.

The other guy in the kitchen was stockier, and a bit older-looking than Terry. He had thick black hair that curled close to his head and too-large eyes. He turned away from the cutlery drawer and fixed those eyes on Simon. "Holding out on us?" he said.

Simon swallowed. He resisted the urge to bolt. Or attack them. Or something. These guys were robbing Zoly's place, for Christ's sake!

"What −" Simon shifted his shoulder and flinched. He had to do something. "What are you doing? This is Zoly's shit."

The sliding cans stopped, and the third farm boy − skinny with freckles and long red hair and an odd limp − stepped out of the pantry. He was carrying, Simon saw, a broom handle, and he looked about ready to use it when Terry put up his hand to stop.

"Easy," he said. "This is the guy I was telling you about. He's not going to hurt anyone − bird fucked up his shoulder, see?"

The two others seemed to accept this, and Terry turned to Simon.

"And you − forget about Zoly's shit because there's no more Zoly. Bird got him, all right? Birds'll get all of us if we don't look after ourselves. So if you know where any more food is, you'd better speak up."

Simon thought again about Zoltan's, and the big bowl of pasta he'd had there last night, and the coal-pit and the meat and the immense freezer. The men in dark suits who ate large cuts of meat in the warehouse-restaurant's dining room.

"Sorry," said Simon. "I don't know."

The curly-haired kid threw up his hands, so that Simon could see them both at the same time.

"Asshole's holdin' out," he said.

"Nah. He's just fuckin' useless," said the red-head, and turned back to the pantry.

Simon just stared. One of the curly-haired kid's hands, he saw, was mutilated − missing the thumb and forefinger. And the other one was limp. And here in the dimness of the unlit kitchen, Terry was still wearing his sunglasses. Simon wondered how many eyes he'd find under those sunglasses. Two? Simon was betting on fewer.

Now Simon thought about his own wounded shoulder, and the ostrich-sized bird that had been in the process of carrying him away when Terry had zinged it with his slingshot. And he wondered, for the first time in a really complete, facing-it kind of way: what was with that evil fucking bird?

So he asked it: "What's with the bird?"

Terry shrugged. "It eats us," he said. "That's all we know for sure."

———

Patches of piss-yellow light appeared in the sky as the boys hurried back to the van. Although no one had explicitly invited him to do so, Simon followed. The bird hated the rain and the rain was starting to let up; Simon's shoulder hurt badly enough that he didn't think he could draw a slingshot like Terry's, even if he had one; and he was pretty sure that Terry and his pals knew more about the bird than the fact that it ate them and hated the rain.

Simon got into the back of the van along with Terry, while the other two took the seats up front. The van was dark and crowded in the back; they'd piled what swag they'd found at Zoly's place against the bare metal walls, along with various other objects: a shovel, an old electric heater, a claw-backed hammer, a broken chair. A couple more boxes of tin cans. It all rattled mightily as the van lurched forward.

Terry patted Simon on his thigh. His lips curled into a half-smile. "You're a lucky little fucker, you know that?"

Simon grunted. It certainly didn't seem that way. But the curly-haired boy up front shouted his agreement. "You could'a been torn to shit," he yelled.

"Bird in the wild," said the red-head. "It won't stop for nothing."

Terry nodded. "Take you to the top of a tree, pin you there, start at you with its beak and claws. At the end of it –" He made his teeth snap together. "No chance."

Simon frowned. "So where are we going?"

Terry grinned now. His hand, still on Simon's thigh, gave him a little squeeze. "You'll see. We like to surprise the new ones."

"Virgins," said the red head from behind the wheel.

"Virgins," said Terry. His hand withdrew. "Right."

Back in Simon's home town, he'd heard that word used to describe guys who'd never taken a swing at a queer boy.

Simon looked away – and when he sensed Terry was distracted, he took hold of the handle of the hammer on the van's floor, and pulled it to his side.

———

Simon used the fifteen-or-so minutes of their little road trip to start work on his theory of "What the Fuck is Going on Here." Early on, it took shape to be a pretty bent theory – but it had been a pretty bent thirty-six or so hours. Simon was still working it out when the van pulled to a stop – outside a huge barn structure covered in rusting corrugated steel. The rainstorm had passed, and Simon could tell this made his new pals nervous. Sure as shit, it made him nervous.

Red-hair cracked open his door, and he and the other two immediately pulled their shirts up to cover their mouths and noses. Not having been warned, Simon didn't – so the stink hit him full force. It smelled like the wind from under the bird's wings, but far worse. Simon gripped the hammer in one fist and held his nose with the other. The others laughed – the sound of country boys laughing at the city kid fucking up his first cow-milking. But Simon screwed his eyes shut as it dawned on him: the bird-shit stink was mingled with the same smell from Zoly's restaurant. The unique smell of his meat cooking. Simon uncovered his nose and sniffed again. The boys had stopped laughing.

"Come on," said Terry, looking up. "Better get inside."

Simon followed. They crossed the muddy drive in a hurry and stepped through a side door in the big metal barn. "Okay," said Terry to Simon. "You wait here. We gotta unload." And Terry stepped back outside.

Simon looked around him. He was in a fairly big room with a couple of other doors, one with an arm-sized deadbolt holding it shut. There was a tall grey filing cabinet in one corner, an old steel-sided desk with a wooden chair on rollers next to it, and even an old black rotary-dial telephone with function buttons at its base like a row of fake gemstones. When Simon picked it up there was no dial tone – not that he expected one. Simon's theory was taking pretty firm shape – and dead telephone lines, abandoned offices, maimed farm boys, and the particular smell he was smelling all fit that theory fine.

Zoly's restaurant was like one of those wild-game restaurants that charged a fortune for a slice of emu or ostrich or African Rhino on your plate. Only Zoly didn't get his meat from Africa. It came from another place, maybe a little farther away, maybe not – Simon hadn't figured that much out yet. But he had figured out that it was bird meat. That explained the size of the loading doors in back of Zoly's restaurant, and that big refrigerator door that looked like a bank vault.

Zoly's patrons ate the bird meat.

And like Terry had said, thought Simon, the birds eat us.

Simon swallowed. He felt sick thinking about it – shit, he'd eaten some of that bird meat probably! – and the bird-stink of this place didn't help settle his stomach any. Fucking Zoly, he thought angrily. Serves him right, getting eaten by the fucking bird.

Simon stuffed the hammer through a belt-loop in his jeans and rolled his bad shoulder experimentally. It hurt, but not so bad he couldn't move it. That was good – because Simon had no intention of sitting still for Terry and his friends to finish unloading. He didn't know where they came from, or how they got here – but they seemed to be settling in for the long haul, laying in food stock. And he didn't like the way they talked about faggots. He didn't want to be around when they started to work out their own theories about what kind of kid an old faggot like Zoly would bring out to the farm.

Simon walked over to the door with the deadbolt. He pulled the bolt across, and the door swung open into relative darkness.

The smell was stronger here than anywhere, but this time Simon was prepared for it – so his gag reflex only stopped him an instant. He felt around on the side of the door for a light switch but his hand found only bare two-by-four. It didn't matter, though – there was enough light in the space beyond that Simon's eyes could become accustomed to it and make out at least a few shapes – most of them indistinct clumps of block and tackle, beams, and thick chain link fencing. At the far end – maybe fifty feet to his left – grey light filtered through a sagging, shattered roof, and pieces of wood and metal gleamed wetly on the earthen floor underneath: troughs and buckets and benches, broken plywood dividers.

None of it contradicted Simon's theory. If anything, it cemented it.

This place was the factory farm that supplied Zoly's restaurant. Simon had heard of chicken farms like this – at Walter's place, he'd sat through a *60 Minutes* exposé on one in the southern United States – Kentucky or Florida or somewhere. They packed 10,000 birds into long, low out-buildings, bathing in their own shit, and the workers slogged it so hard they all got repetitive strain injury and lost their jobs.

Except from the look of the Terry and his friends, repetitive strain injury was the least of their worries in this place. Eyes and fingers and legs were the price of working a shift at the giant chicken farm.

As if working was why they were here.

Simon stepped into the cavernous coop and let the door swing shut behind him.

The coop had seemed dark enough when Simon had opened the door, but after a few minutes in the dimness Simon found he was seeing just fine. Part of that was his eyes adjusting to the low light – but Simon thought another, more important part was just his eyes opening.

The place was organized in rows of big, steel-barred cages, topped with more bars and chain-link fence. Above these ran plywood-covered catwalks, suspended from the ceiling by thick cables. Simon saw no way to get to them, so he was forced to walk along the ground. His feet clattered through a little stack of mud-covered bones – bones that he would have mistaken for sticks and shards of pottery in brilliant day-light, had his eyes still been closed; had he not worked out for himself exactly what was going on here.

Simon, these other kids – and more kids, the former owners of all these bones – were feed. Walter had given over Simon to Zoly – and Zoly had brought Simon to this farm, to feed the livestock.

But something had happened. The livestock had broken out of their cages.

Simon went to examine one of the cages. It was probably fifteen feet on the side, and one side was a great door on tracks and a pulley system. The door was partly open, jammed a few degrees askew in its tracks. Simon ducked underneath and took a step inside. The muck in here had a different quality – it was mixed with down and feathers, and it clung obscenely to Simon's shoe.

"What the fuck are you doing in here?"

Simon turned. Terry was standing a dozen feet behind him with his arms crossed.

"Did you not learn a fuckin' thing from last time?" he said. "You think that bird that almost got you was a fuckin' special effect?"

Simon didn't answer.

"You want to fuckin' die?" Terry took a step forward. "You want to fuckin' die. Don't you?"

Terry closed the gap between them and grasped Simon's good arm. "Come on then," he said. "I got something to show you."

Terry led Simon out of the cage.

"Where –" Simon began, but Terry didn't let him finish. He pointed to the far end of the coop, where the grey daylight streamed in.

"You're so fuckin' fearless about birds – we're goin' over there," he said. "Have you got any idea what this is about?"

Simon nodded. "This is a chicken farm," he said. "But bigger."

Evidently, Simon had answered correctly. Terry nodded, and looked away for a moment. As they stepped over a fallen stack of two-by-six lumber, he looked back – his gaze bled dry of the contempt it'd had a moment before.

"Have you got a better idea what this place is?" Simon asked.

"I been here a couple months," said Terry. "Left my old man in the winter, figured I'd go to the coast hitch-hiking. Probably not the brightest thing I did – nearly froze my ass off a couple times on the highway, and as I learned, nobody picks up hitch-hikers anymore. Nobody who wants to give a ride and leave it at that, anyway. Managed to ride with a couple of truckers, though. The second one was this

Polack who told me he'd stand me to a meal. Who the fuck am I to say no? So we drive and drive, and finally wind up at this back-in-the-woods kind of diner. Looked like nothing from outside. The place looked closed-up in fact – it had those old-style gas pumps out front and no lights or signs or anything. But it was ploughed and there were a couple of rigs in the lot. Inside – it was a weird fuckin' place. There were only a couple of trucks outside, but the dining room was packed. Filled up with –"

"Old guys in dark suits talking with accents?"

Terry stopped and stared. "Something like that," he said.

"What did he feed you?"

"Stew," said Terry. "Big meat and vegetable stew. Carrots. Onions. And big chunks of meat. Tasted fuckin' great. But I think he slipped something into it. We got back into the cab of his truck, and that was it – I was out."

"And you woke up here. Right?"

"Not right here," said Terry. "In a bed. You haven't seen that part of the place – it's kind of like a hospital, but dirtier and filled with old shit. It's not like the scalpels are rusty or anything. But it's like those gas pumps. Everything's, like – out of date."

"So what – were you sick?"

"Nobody comes here sick."

"So why were you there?"

"To make bird feed."

"In a hospital?" Terry didn't need to answer, though – Simon worked it out. Just because these birds ate people, didn't mean they ate people all at once. "That's how those guys lost fingers and shit – right? They cut them up bit by bit –"

"– to mix it in with the feed," finished Terry.

They were almost at the hole in the ceiling now – the light was better here, and Simon could see the ground in front of them. It was incongruously clear of detritus. Terry put both hands on Simon's shoulders now, and stepped behind him. He whispered in Simon's ear: "A little goes a long way."

Simon's breath caught in his throat, and he reached down for the hammer at his belt. But Terry was quicker, and grabbed his wrist. "You won't be needing that," he said. "I'm not going to hurt you."

Simon believed him. Terry had moved closer to him – really close, so that Simon felt a familiar pressure against his ass. Simon let himself smile – Terry was getting hard.

"I'm willing to bet," said Terry, "that the old faggot didn't take you to the infirmary room right away for a reason."

Simon arched his ass back and up so it rubbed hard against Terry.

Whenever he did this with Walter's old men, they nearly wept with the unexpected pleasure. It wasn't much different with Terry – who, considering recent developments, Simon was now beginning to understand a little better. He was willing to bet that Terry had been at this kind of shit before, in some surreptitious way with some fellow farm boy who didn't have a clue what he was doing.

Simon knew what he was doing. He reached around with his good hand and feathered his fingers under Terry's belt-buckle, squeezed them underneath the tight line of his jeans. It was damp down there, the fabric of his underpants a little stiff. Simon was willing to bet that Terry had blown more than a couple of loads into those shorts and let them dry through the day to make them set that way. Kind of gross, but Simon put it in perspective – at least Terry wasn't a sixty-one-year-old granddad whose ass sagged to his ankles and who liked it with the lights on. Simon found Terry's cock and wrapped his fingers around it with real enthusiasm.

Terry let out a little yowl at that, and Simon leaned back to whisper in his ear: "It feels like someone else is doing it when someone else is doing it."

Terry looked around him – checking for his buddies, no doubt – then let go of Simon and worked his belt buckle undone. His jeans dropped and so did his underpants. "Suck it," he whispered.

On some level, Simon supposed he knew how unwise this was to pursue. Just because Terry turned out to be a barnyard queen didn't mean his buddies swung that way too. And dark and deserted as this place was, it wasn't exactly private – to anyone coming in from that office door, for instance, Simon and Terry would be silhouetted against the light. He didn't know what those other guys were capable of, and he didn't know enough about his situation yet to really fall into anything.

But Simon was getting pretty hard himself – it had been too long since he'd actually had a go at anyone he was attracted to – months, it seemed like – and he'd gotten himself psyched for some pleasure-fucking the night before, when he met Zoly.

So in the end, he sort of compromised. He turned around, fell to his knees, and took Terry's cock in his fist. He stroked the head with his thumb – holding it just an inch or so from his mouth – and stopped, and looked up at Terry.

"So how'd you escape?" asked Simon.

"Ah, fuck," said Terry. "Just do me!"

Simon let go of his cock.

"Tell me first," he said.

Terry didn't know how long he'd been strapped into his bed in the in-firmary when it all happened. He knew he'd seen one guy wheeled out of the room with one arm missing, and come back with a bloody bandage around the stump of his other wrist; another guy left with all his limbs, and came back with a stumpy fist at the end of one arm that would never unfold again – the fingers were snipped off and the ends cauterized.

The room was run by a white-haired man who wore baggy black dress pants held up by suspenders slung over the shoulders of a pressed white dress shirt. He occasionally spoke to one of the other men in the room, but it was in Polish – or the language that Terry had associated in his mind with Polish. Whatever language it was, Terry didn't want to engage the guy in conversation to see if he spoke any English as well. For most of the time it didn't seem as though the Polack even recognized Terry's existence. And as long as the Polack didn't notice him, Terry figured he'd keep all his fingers and toes.

Only at night did Terry talk – but then it was just to the other guys strapped into bed like him, and most of them didn't talk back. They were too fucked up, Terry reasoned, from all the amputations.

It was on one of those nights that the birds broke out of their cages. Terry was trying once again to engage the guy in the bed next to him in something resembling conversation. The guy had obviously been there awhile – he was down to a head, a torso and the upper part of his right arm – and he was harmless enough that the Polack hadn't even bothered to strap him down. Terry was going on about the Victoria's Secrets catalogues he'd cadged from his old man's girlfriend at some length when the kid finally spoke. "Quiet," was what he said. Terry was quiet. The kid was listening for something, so what the fuck, Terry listened, too.

He heard the bird call once, before the window shattered and the curtains carried into the room, propelled forward by the giant shape they wrapped. "Shit," said the kid. And he disappeared. An instant later, Terry heard the clunk as he smacked against the floor.

The bird-shriek came again – this time from the middle of the struggling mass inside the curtain. By degree, the curtain tore and dis-integrated, and what finally emerged was a bird – the first bird Terry had seen.

It was a little smaller than the one that had grabbed Simon, but only a little. It stood high on two legs, its raptor-beak gleaming in moonlight that made its two round eyes into bright silver coins. The thin feathers on its head brushed against the ceiling tiles as it gawked around the room. The armless, legless kid on the floor whimpered in terror, and he was soon enough joined by a chorus of the half-dozen other kids who were still stuck strapped in their beds.

It was a bad hour. The bird went from bed to bed, pecking a bit from here and a bit from there, poking and prodding like some cannibal doctor making rounds in the hospital. As Simon had suspected, the bird took an eye – or most of one – from Terry, various other parts from the other guys. For a while, it seemed like the guy on the floor was going to get away scot-free, but about a half-hour in the bird found him and yanked out a good five feet of his small intestine like a worm from the ground.

The whole thing didn't end with their rescue or anything like that. After about an hour, it seemed like the bird had just eaten its fill, and it left.

The rest Terry didn't remember so well. There were more of those bird shrieks, some screaming from the Polacks, and sounds like gunfire. Terry couldn't do much but lie there and bleed – so he figured he couldn't have been there too long because otherwise he would have bled to death. At some point, the red-haired guy showed up, undid the straps, and pressed a cloth against Terry's bloody eye-socket. "It's okay," he said as he helped Terry up out of the bed. "We cut a deal – we're free."

———

Simon kept his part of the deal with Terry. It really wasn't a problem: Terry came about seven seconds from the time Simon started to work on him, which actually pissed Simon off a little. He would have enjoyed drawing it out a little.

Lying beside each other in the dirt, looking up through the hole in the roof, Terry turned it around.

"I told you 'bout me," he said. "Now you tell me how you got here."

"Suck me if I do?" said Simon, knowing he wouldn't.

"Fuck off," said Terry.

"Then you fuck off." The sky was starting to clear – eggshell blue peeked through tiny fissures in the cloud cover, so bright it made Simon squint. A sound like thunder began in the distance.

"How'd the birds get out? You guys set 'em free? Big revolution in the infirmary? Something like that?"

Terry arched his back, yanked his jeans up over his ass, and sat up. He didn't say anything for a minute, and he didn't look straight at Simon, but he had a look in his eye that spoke volumes. It was like the old contempt had come back now that Simon had done him.

But it wasn't exactly contempt. And it wasn't exactly post-coital shame – which Simon had seen plenty of in his adventures with Walter's old men. It was something else.

Something like the look that Walter had had, when he'd left him with Zoly.

Simon looked back at the hole above them. The hole itself was a circle, thirty feet in diameter. The edges sagged where they'd been torn; water still dribbled here and there.

It was a big hole. Simon swallowed hard. He was developing another theory – once again, one rapidly confirmed by the unfolding events. The thunder roll wasn't stopping – of course it wasn't; it was building because it was getting closer. Simon gripped the handle of the hammer.

"So what kind of deal did you cut?" he asked.

Even as he said it, the great bird's shadow eclipsed the sky. If Terry had an answer, it was drowned out by numbing screams.

***

Terry would have gotten away if Simon hadn't used the hammer on his kneecap. The prick deserved it. He'd lured Simon almost to the middle of the cleared-out area – kept him there and just like one of Walter's old closet queers, had his secret little grope while they waited. And when the bird showed up – the mama bird, the Bird God, the one come to collect its due from the circular little altar the boys had made here – Terry, the fucking bird-cultist prick, was up and ready to run. But Simon had it worked out, and he was pissed, so he swung the hammer – claw-back first – and dug it into Terry's knee.

Simon might have been smarter to have tried to run, too – because the time he'd wasted doing Terry's knee was the time he'd have needed to escape. The bird stuck its head down through the hole, spied them both with its trash-can eyes and plucked both of them up from the clear circle in the corners of its car-sized beak.

"Jesus, fuck!" screamed Terry as they rose up through the coop. He dangled by his leg – his bad leg – just three or four feet from where Simon hung grasped by the chest, hot bird-saliva moistening his ass.

Simon didn't have anything to add. The two of them dangled what may have been fifty feet over the chicken coop. This bird was immense. It could probably tromp the shit out of the coop if it wanted to. Or the van, which sat parked safe and sound like a little toy next to the coop building. Thunder cracked beneath the bird's wings then, and Simon felt a rock sink in his pinned belly as the ground and the truck and the coop-building fell away.

The giant bird flapped and dipped and finally climbed – so high the air grew thin and frost tightened the tiny hairs in Simon's nostrils. The air rushed by with such a roar that it became like silence – Simon couldn't even hear himself draw a breath in the cotton-wrap muffling of the screaming wind.

As they flew through cloud, Simon looked at Terry. The skin was drawn like a drum-top across his face, and his sunglasses were gone. His good eyelid pulled wide open like a surprised old man's; his bad eye a pit of dark, wide to begin with. Simon looked away as they left the cloud – Terry disgusted him now, as much as the knobbiest old man Walter'd made him service. He looked down.

They were high all right – so high he couldn't see the coop or Zoly's house or even the road between the two places. It was all lost in the midst of a great circle of mountains – a perfect circle, like a moon crater. Inside the crater's perimeter, Simon could see green and blue of field and pond, and the rich brown of fertile earth; outside the circle, the land was barren and grey, like the moon itself.

Simon supposed he was surprised – but only at the blunt truth of what he was seeing. Based on his increasingly well-resolved theory, he had expected something like this. Birds this size didn't fly on Earth; the smallest were the size of ostriches. On Earth, if you were as big as an ostrich, there was too much gravity for anything but running across African veldts and sticking your head in the dirt.

And Simon hadn't forgotten his last memory before falling asleep in Zoly's car: a falling feeling in his gut, like the car had driven off a cliff. He was willing to bet a bird like this or maybe one even bigger had plucked Zoly's car from the highway and carried it away, over the peaks, into the crater. Maybe this was the moon – or if not, someplace like it, with craters and funny gravity.

Another thunderclap roared beneath them, and the bird rose higher still, into air that was almost too thin to breathe. The cold was unbelievable – where his skin was exposed, it stung as from a dull-razor shave. He was warmer inside the bird's beak, but Simon had to fight a sudden urge to stay; he'd drown in that warmth, he knew. As surely as he'd suffocate if the giant bird flew any higher. Simon shut his eyes and waited for death.

———

Death didn't come. Instead, by degree the air thickened and Simon's flesh warmed, and he was released amid a great hot blast of bird-shriek, plummeting in space an instant before feeling the sharp impact of rock against his good arm. Thunder clapped; once with near-deafening effect, then again more distantly as its source ascended.

Simon opened his eyes.

The bird had deposited him on what must have been the side of a mountain, on a wide ledge that curved down to a lake of cloud maybe a hundred feet below. It was late in the day and the falling sun pinkened cloud and rock in equal measure.

Simon wasn't alone. Not far from him was Terry – sprawled on his face, his leg horribly askew. Further up the mountain, there were others. Carefully so as not to slide into the cloud, Simon stood up and climbed toward them.

At first, Simon thought he was looking at more corpses – the mutilations on these bodies made Terry's bad leg look like a scratch. But as he climbed past one – not more than a torso, a head and a leg – the head moved and turned to Simon. Its lips moved as if speaking, but the wind was too loud to hear.

He leaned closer to it – as he did, he noted the whisps of white hair poking out through the dried blood. "Say again!" he yelled. "Couldn't hear you."

"The edge," it said, in a heavy accent that didn't surprise Simon one bit. "Help me – to the edge."

Simon sat on his haunches and considered the request for a moment. It wouldn't be a big deal – the thing should be dead anyway. But nothing, he thought, should come without a bargain. Nothing should be unconditional.

So Simon set a condition. "Where's Zoly?" he demanded.

The head looked puzzled. "Zoltan," said Simon, and this time it seemed like the name rang a bell. The head turned and nodded to another body, a dozen yards to its right, near an overhang that was nearly a cave. Simon got up and more confidently this time walked over. Sure enough, there was Zoly. He was in better shape than the head – although not much. His left leg had been gnawed down to the bone below the knee, and his hands were both gone. Simon wondered how he'd managed to survive all the blood loss. Maybe, he thought, there was something in the bird-spit that worked like an anaesthetic, and helped the blood clot. Maybe in the place they were, guys weren't meant to die from a bird-bite.

Zoly looked to be asleep.

"Hey, Zoly." Simon shook him by the shoulder until Zoltan opened his eyes. He blinked in the light. "Remember me?"

Zoly opened his mouth to say something, but Simon brought his good hand down across his face in a sharp smack.

"Rhetorical question," said Simon. He felt a kind of elation at the moment – a charge going through him looking at Zoltan whatever-his-name was lying in front of him. This was the guy who had effectively purchased Simon – not just for a little jiggle in the toilet or a weekend of jiggling in a farmhouse somewhere. But for feed. To feed birds in a factory farm — birds that stayed in that factory farm only as a result of another transaction, with their mother.

Simon slapped Zoltan again. Their contract, whatever its terms or however long it had persisted, had broken down when the boys in the feeder had cut their own deal with the mama bird — a deal that it liked better, but one that still put Simon on the bottom-rung.

"See you, Zoly." Simon got up and went back to the torso. "We had a deal," he said, and rolled the mangled body down the slope and off the edge of the mountain. It became a speck before he vanished in the cloud. Simon watched for a moment, then climbed back up-slope.

Next, he went to Terry. He was still immobile, but as Simon had deduced, dying was more difficult in this strange gravity than it might have been in Simon's world. Terry lived. Simon looped his good arm around Terry's chest, and began the difficult task of hauling him up-slope. Back to the safety of the overhang.

Not much later, the sun vanished beneath the cloud lake, and the wind was joined by the screaming of the birds — coming back to roost for the night and maybe take a snack first. Simon jammed himself deeper into his fissure. He needed to watch and think for some time maybe — to see what they needed, see what they liked. After all, the boys back at the coop had trumped the old men with something.

From where he lay clamped between Simon's legs, Terry began to stir. Simon nodded to himself, and ran his fingers one last time from the edge of Terry's empty eyesocket, up and across the stiff bristle on his goose-fleshed scalp.

NO SILENT SCREAM

Nancy Kilpatrick

 "IS A HUMAN RESPONSE TOO MUCH TO ASK FOR?"

"Excuse me?" the clerk snaps.

"I need to know *all* the ingredients. I have an allergy. To nuts." Tom watches the face of the clerk mask over, and his expression turn steely, the way so many faces have looked to him lately. A small, sharp pain shoots through his head, making him want to scream.

"We don't make it, we just sell it." The clerk's buck-passing is a variation on what they always say. Tom is infuriated, but left helpless.

"Fine." He hands back the box of frozen scallops, then shoves the "light" gourmet dinner at the woman with faded hair, one-two punch style. Then he spins his mini-cart around and heads down the aisle to the checkout.

His shoulders feel heavy. Perspiration causes the fabric at the small of his back to stick to his flesh. The acute pain has subsided, but behind his eyes the continuous dull ache threatens to erupt into something worse. You can always tell when they've labelled you crazy, Tom thinks, but he knows that *they* are dead wrong.

He slams item after item onto the counter, telling himself to ease up, the girl at the cash didn't do anything wrong. Just like the clerk back there couldn't possibly know the ingredients lumped under the category "corn oil and/or other unsaturated oils." And then he hears himself mutter under his breath, "Right! Nobody's ever guilty of anything. That's the whole damn problem, isn't it?"

"Pardon?" The young girl behind the conveyor belt pauses, her narrow eyebrows arching.

When Tom says, "Nothing," the shockingly thin girl, whose name tag identifies her as Rena, turns and jabs her finger onto the yellowed plastic covering the register's buttons for an item that won't scan. Her young face turns stony. Tom suspects the girl is afraid to interact with the lunatic who had the audacity to ask what the ingredients are in a supposedly edible food product.

He decides to try to be nice to her anyway. Besides being young and probably anorexic, he realizes she has her own problems. She's only human.

"These are a good buy." Tom holds up the plastic bag of three oranges and smiles.

Rena says nothing, just zombie-tallies up the rest of the groceries. Tom controls an urge to slash open the bag and hurl the oranges one at a time at the mask that passes for a face.

"Use this," Tom insists, handing over the string bag, but the girl is nearly finished trying to stuff fifteen items into a doubled plastic bag. "The environment," he says.

The hazel eyes open wide, as if she's never heard the word before, let alone has a clue to its meaning.

What? What did I say? Tom wonders. Every week he comes in here, and every week this girl acts as though she's never seen a string bag before. Tom can't stop himself. "You know they're not bio-degradable, don't you?" He nods at the plastic.

The hazel eyes glaze, the head turns, the fingers snatch at new groceries coming along the conveyor belt and are already scanning the bar code on a box of frozen Snickers and punching in the price of a pint of strawberries.

As Tom leaves the trendy air-conditioned market in the city's gay ghetto, the sun's rays lick his skin like flames. "Damn!" he says, rolling down his shirt sleeves. A man he recognizes from the bars passes and glances around to see who Tom's talking to. Hairs on Tom's head warm, and the rays reach between them to his scalp; the flesh on his arms prickles. He looks at the man and offers a smile, despite his discomfort. The man looks away, the smile unreturned.

Tom feels hot, too hot. The sun is a fireball, its light too intense. He drops his eyes earthward. His head begins to throb.

The environment. They're ruining it, letting carbon fluorides destroy the ozone, leaving the ultraviolet to burn through the skin and distort cells. He can feel that happening, destruction just beneath the surface, turning what was once healthy into a violent, cancerous thing that does not deserve to live. He races for his Toyota.

Inside, the car is stifling. He stores the groceries in the back seat, knowing the fresh food will wilt before he makes it home. He would have gone to the health food store and paid twice the price for organically grown lettuce, but the last time they only had one head of romaine and it was pitted with dark holes from the insects that tried to devour it.

He snaps on his seatbelt, reaches over and cranks down the passenger window in the front, then the window directly behind him, refusing to use the air conditioning and contribute toxins in the air. But it's hot, and the air weighs on his brain.

With a heavy sigh, he glances in the side-view mirror, broken because some idiot sideswiped him last month. The image is too distorted. He adjusts the rear-view and looks at himself. The face is lined, the eyes haunted. What was once been a mop of red hair has thinned considerably over the years. He let the grey come in, but he paid for that. Twenty years ago, he was sought after. Now he does the seeking, and the finding costs him money.

His forehead is pink and slick with sweat; he mops up the moisture with the sleeve of his cotton shirt. Then he notices his eyes: glassy, blue marbles with dark pits in the centres like some malignancy. He blinks twice; the pink lids are red-rimmed and sting from the pollution. He watches them turn redder as tears begin to well. He feels the pain behind his eyes ooze out of his pupils.

"They box you into a corner!" he shouts, slamming the wheel with his fist, letting the tears flow. Furious with himself, he turns the key and, with difficulty, listens to the carburetor vomit gasoline into the engine. He knows he is spewing more junk into the atmosphere and feels guilty. "What can I do?" he asks the forlorn face in the mirror. He can't walk ten miles to this store which supposedly sells genetically unaltered food, and it's too dangerous these days to bike through the city. The public transit doesn't stop close enough to his house. He has to eat; he needs the car.

Why do they make life so difficult?

He slams the automatic transmission stick into drive but has the presence of mind to ease out of the parking space, muttering about how there are more metal objects on the planet than people. He knows the headaches make him less reasonable than he should be, than he used to be. He has already again today exceeded the recommended daily dose of Advil.

Traffic is bad and he is forced to wait in line to get into the street. He switches on the radio: "Well, it's just not economically feasible for the big car manufacturers to build gas-free cars; they might have the technology, but they just won't do it. It all comes down to money. Things will get worse before they get better."

Tom snaps off the radio. The heat makes his head pound. If only he could get home, have a cool shower, a nap, maybe he'd feel better. . . .

He and Bill lay side by side on beach chairs, close. Water from the ocean laps at the shore of Bandaras Bay in Puerto Vallarta. The day's delicious heat penetrating their already brown bodies, baking muscles into relaxation, heightening desire. He reaches over and strokes Bill's arm. The muscle beneath the skin ripples at the contact. Bill turns his head and stares with large, sand-colored eyes. Tom smiles at him. Bill turns away.

A horn blares from a car ahead of him, then another, as if that will change anything. Seven cars are lined up to get out of the market's lot.

He aims the nose of the Toyota at the left side of the rear bumper of a large Chrysler with the windows rolled up; he just might be able to squeeze by. But at the same moment the Chrysler pulls left, enough to block the Toyota. "Yeah, add to the pollution!" Tom yells out the window at the driver, who does not hear him, or even bother to glance in his mirrors to see how his action might have affected someone else. "Hope that air conditioning gives you huge gas bills!" Tom snarls under his breath.

The Chrysler is able to pull ahead several metres. Suddenly, a yellow Mazda sneaks into the space before Tom can get behind the Chrysler's bumpers. He blasts the Mazda with his horn, and the driver blasts right back. "Asshole!" he shouts. But its windows too are closed, and tinted.

Several sweltering minutes later, the sun burning the skin of his hand and the left side of his face and neck, Tom jerks the Toyota to a halt at the booth. He opens the glove compartment, but the ticket is not there. Suddenly he remembers he stored the ticket in his shirt pocket; he forgot to get it stamped by the cashier. His entire head hurts, from the base of the skull to the forehead, and he can barely speak.

In front of him, the Mazda pulls out of the lot, expelling a cloud of dark exhaust over the Toyota. "Can't even keep his muffler repaired!" Tom snarls, and turns to the window. The attendant peers down at him, waiting.

"Ticket," the young man says in a dull voice, as if that's all he says all day long. His eyes are large and pale brown, the color of sand. Tom thinks he recognizes him from the baths. They had a night together. Tom paid for it.

Tom hands over the parking ticket.

"Ain't stamped."

"I forgot to get it stamped."

"Four twenty-five."

"What? That's ridiculous!"

"Read the back. If it ain't stamped, you pay four dollars, twenty-five cents."

"But I've been shopping. These are my groceries in the back."

The attendant peers through the back window. "You coulda bought 'em anywhere."

"I bought them at Banyon's, the same as I do every week."

"How come they ain't in Banyon bags?"

"Because I bring my own bags to help cut down on the use of plastic." The word *bitch* almost finishes the sentence, but Tom manages to control his tongue.

"Four twenty-five," the attendant says again.

Something inside Tom snaps. He jams his foot onto the accelerator. The Toyota jolts forward, crashes through the black-and-yellow guard rail, skids onto the street. Horns blare and at the last second Tom yanks the wheel to the left, tires squealing. The car swerves wildly over the asphalt for a moment, then rights itself. Engine roaring, he speeds down the street heading toward the safety of home.

In a flash of consciousness, he realizes his headache is gone. Visually, everything appears sharp-edged. Then he notices his windshield is gouged on the left side. The hood is dented.

Guilt and anger wash over him in alternating waves. How will I ever show my face there again? he wonders. Surely they won't throw him in jail for a few dollars, will they? But he knows *they* are capable of anything. Look what they've done to the environment! And then he remembers destroying the barrier – what would that cost?

He passes a billboard: a man behind bars within a red circle, a slash angled through the circle's diameter, cutting him in two. Underneath: "Crime Does Not Pay!" *I am no criminal*, Tom thinks. They are the ones committing the crimes! *They* should be punished! He checks the rearview, expecting a police car to be following. He listens: no siren. His headache returns full force, as if a knife stabs him behind the eyes.

Tom makes it home in time to hear the telephone ringing. He leaves the front door open and drops his parcels onto the hall table in his hurry to stop the incessant ringing. He pauses. What if it's the police? He picks up anyway, and is greeted by a dial tone.

Slow fury rides his backbone. He slams down the handset. A sound makes him spin around. One shopping bag has toppled to the floor. The carton of eggs lies open. Gooey yolks mix with whites. The mixture coats the string bag and seeps through the bag's mesh onto the parquet tiles.

As Tom stares at the cracked shells, pain pulses through his head. He walks over to examine the mess. Six eggs intact. Six eggs broken. Some of the yolks have a red streak running through them. He becomes dizzy from the pain in his head.

The pain of living suddenly chokes him with nausea. He flies to the bathroom. Only half of what he expels makes it into the toilet. When his stomach is empty and dry heaving, his headache dims. The phone rings again.

Gasping, he rinses his mouth with filtered water from the tap and stumbles back into the living room, catching the phone on the tenth ring.

"Hi there! Ever dreamed of a vacation from life? Make your dreams a reality. Get away from it all, for free. Yes, absolutely free!" The mechanical voice chirps on and on about a dream vacation, available gratis to the first ten people who call the number given.

"You're evil!" Tom yells at the handset. He slams it back into the cradle, knocking the phone onto the floor. The cradle skids across the wood tiles and he hears, *"Picture yourself taking off –"*

His body trembles. His stomach lurches, but there is nothing more to be expelled. Machines are taking over, he realizes. The world is full of mechanical people and their computer lackeys! There are so many of these calls! Every day. Seven days a week! Hundreds a year! Sweat beads his forehead and he feels dizzy again as the pain inside his skull overtakes him.

He collapses onto the sofa, eager for unconsciousness to swallow him. Instead, his head pounds as though a sharp object has been driven down the centre and is wedged there, nearly splitting him in two. He is alive but dead, forced to endure.

Bill carries the last of his things out the door. Tom stares at the closed door, numb. It makes no sense. Twenty years, and now, the end. Why? They survived infidelities before, on both sides. There were no money worries. Neither had contracted HIV, or any other major illness. They had a good life together. How can love simply end? What did he do to deserve this?

He hears the beep of the phone off the hook. Gradually he picks himself up, lifts the phone to the table, and hangs up. He cannot bear this tension. Has he become like *them*, guilty of destruction.

He will call the police, turn himself in, clear the air about the broken barrier. But as he lifts the handset, the phone rings. In his ear, the recording, full of false hope, still going strong: *"... no worries, no responsibilities, you CAN get a free ride ..."*

He grabs the cord and yanks it from the jack in the wall. The pain deep inside his skull eats away at his brain like maggots consuming rot. The image terrifies him. He staggers toward the door.

The air is suffocating, the day too bright. Heat and light cause him to reel. The pain inside his cranium expands until his head feels swollen, about to explode.

By the time he reaches the supermarket, the headache is blinding. The sight of the mechanical ticket dispenser on the other side of the booth floods him with fury. Instead of taking a ticket for parking, the Toyota slams through the entrance bar as it so recently crashed through the exit. The car sideswipes a concrete post, which bashes in the door on the passenger's side.

Next to the supermarket is a strip mall. Too many stores, too many products, too many mindless beings consuming the excrement of inhuman machines. The dry cleaners spewing chemicals into the air; the gas station emitting noxious fumes; the bakery poisoning people with sugar and white flour; the shoe repair dying the hides of dead animals to feed human vanity. . . .

Tom slams on the brake and jumps out, leaving the key in the ignition and the door of the Toyota wide open. The hardware store is just over the parking lot's fence, in another parking lot, which does not connect to this one. He jumps the low railing between lots and runs into the store.

Nails – for coffins. Insecticide – for killing life. Shovels – for burying the dead. He sees a wall of axes, the blades shiny, the handles appealingly natural, and snatches up a small one.

The clerk barely glances at Tom as he grabs a handful of bills from his wallet and tosses them onto the counter. On the way out, he slips the hatchet under his shirt.

When Tom steps back over the low fence, he sees that the exit from the supermarket's parking lot has a lineup. Both the striped entrance and exit bars are shattered but still mechanically lifting and lowering, or at least what was left. He leaves the Toyota where it is and strolls to the booth.

The young man behind the window looks startled at Tom's approach. His thin lips compress and turn down at the corners. "Hey, you're the nut broke the barriers!"

"I came back to make things right!" Tom says, too loudly.

He reaches into his pocket and pulls out four one-dollar coins. He slams them onto the tray beneath the plexiglass window. The guy does not pick up the money.

"Take it!" Tom yells.

"It's four twenty-five."

Tom is stunned. He stares blankly. "What?"

"Parking's four twenty-five. You owe me a quarter. And that's just for the parking."

Tom reaches into his pocket again and finds another dollar. He feels the weight of the small hatchet against his stomach. The wood and metal have taken on the temperature of his skin. The natural caress of a friend in a hostile land. He reaches under his shirt and grips the handle, then pulls the hatchet into the open. The young man behind the glass draws back.

Tom drops the dollar onto the tray. "Take it," he says in a low voice.

Reluctantly, as though his fingers might be chopped off, the young man pulls the five coins toward him. With a trembling hand, he slips three quarters back.

"Keep it! You're the one who needs change!"

Tom gives the pain in his head a voice. A long, hysterical laugh imbeds the sob.

In a flash, he realizes the problem: this is no human being before him. It never has been. Not even a cyborg. This is a non-human entity, a machine, taking up space that once rightfully belonged to those of Tom's own kind. But Tom must be the last of his kind – where are the others? He glances around and sees nothing but pre-programmed automatons. He understands things now. Finally. Why he feels alone. He feels alone because he *is* alone. The simple realization makes the past, the present, and the future crystal clear.

He hoists the hatchet, the wide flat part aimed at the window, as if ready to smash it. The parking attendant pastes himself against the back wall of the booth. His sandy eyes are wide open. His thin lips form an "o." The scream is a silent one, and Tom knows why – machines can't scream.

With a grunt Tom brings the hatchet down hard. The blade cracks the attendant's skull. Bone shatters like eggshells, fragmenting, like a life destroyed. The steel slides easily, naturally, down into the middle of his fiery brain. Cool metal extinguishing the flames as it buries itself in the smoldering ashes of memory.

Liquid coats his eyes, his face, blinding him. All around him, voices. Computer chips squawking sound through a speaker. One voice, though, is familiar. Very close at hand. It is no silent scream. The scream is human.

NESTLE'S REVENGE

Ron Oliver

Valentine's Day, 2000

Her Grace,
The Duchess of Milton,
St Gerome's Home for the Aged,
Welpington-on-Green, UK

Lady Milton:

I trust this letter finds you well and in good spirits. I'm sure the days pass pleasantly in Welpington-on-Green although, having never been to England myself, let alone out of the state of California, I can only assume the recent A&E documentary on your life did the place justice. And while the tone of *Lavinia: The Madwoman of Milton* was surely condescending – indeed, Harry Smith was often so insulting I was surprised you didn't beat him within an inch of his life with your prosthetic arm – it did at the very least present an interesting view of your life. One point in particular caught my attention and, before I introduce myself properly, let me just ask you this:

Do your butterflies still talk?

Please pardon my directness; indeed, I do have to consider the possibility that you've simply tossed this letter into the garbage and continued with your lunch – tapioca pudding and puréed cream corn, if A&E got their facts right. But I'm going to bet you're still with me, good Lady. You see, when I watched your story on the small color television we have here in the common room, something in your eyes just told me you'd believe my story.

And that you'd understand about Nestle.

I'm not exactly sure why Kyle gave his toy terrier a name synonymous with sweet or delicious. It's not as if he wasn't aware of what an unpleasant little beast it was; in fact, as I think back to the night we met, I'm positive he deliberately avoided the topic of pets. But I should have known better; in West Hollywood's hierarchy of required accessories only cell phones outnumber canines, with the rule of thumb being the bigger the muscles, the smaller the dog. And my ex-husband certainly is well-built.

Oh, I see I've slipped a bit and let the cat out of the bag. Or dog, if you'll pardon my little joke. I am indeed, as my Aunt Lillian often said, "a gay." But I suspect a lady of your lineage will barely bat an eyelash at this startling revelation. I believe it was a friend of your mother's, Mrs Patrick Campbell, who uttered the now famous line, "Does it really matter what these gentle, affectionate people do, so long as they don't do it in the street and startle the horses?"

I would hope you share her sentiments as I finally begin my tale. . . .

My dear friend Paris DeLamour, noted astrologer and psychic of the transvestite persuasion, had recently signed a deal to appear in her own weekly television program called, aptly, *Paris DeLamour, Noted Astrologer and Psychic*. Granted, it was only on the local cable access station but for Paris, who had dreamt of stardom ever since her unhappy childhood as epileptic Clark Nesbitt of Puce, Nebraska, this was a cause for celebration.

Her previous forays into show business had been miserable failures, given her suffering from a rare condition known as Chronic Short Term Recall Disorder. In spite of possessing a distinctive, almost pleasant singing voice, she was sadly unable to commit to memory any song lyrics beyond the first she had learned as a child; and, while "I Got Rhythm" is a wonderful tune, it did not give her the sort of repertoire upon which one can build a career.

And so we met that night at Revolver, a local lounge catering to gentlemen who prefer the companionship of other gentlemen, for what was supposed to have been just one drink.

The first thing I saw as I came out of the coma was Kyle's face, staring down at me with that very familiar, disapproving frown. The sickly green tint of the hospital room deepened into focus around him and I could make out a steely-eyed doctor peering at me from over her clipboard, then glancing at a nurse. Nobody spoke. The silence in the room was, as they say, deafening and since I, like nature, abhor a vacuum, I felt compelled to rasp a sentence through my parched lips:

"Did I miss last call?"

I was kept in the hospital for two more days of what they referred to as "observation" but as Kyle told me later they simply wanted to make sure I couldn't score another bump of crystal before my body chemistry had the chance to return to what, in my case, passed for normal. Apparently, there had been some concern about brain damage.

I should pause in the narrative here and, with your kind permission, educate you regarding the subject of crystal methamphetamine, or "Tina," as she's known to an army of wide-eyed championship house cleaners. An intriguing combination of stimulant, aphrodisiac, and hallucinogen, Tina is practically currency in the gay bar scene and with my job as a professional event planner in and around Hollywood I had more than a fair share of it greasing my palm nightly. It became, I'm ashamed to say, my favorite sin and, finally, the proverbial straw which broke my husband's back.

Kyle had delivered his ultimatum with a deceptively casual air, catching me off-guard while he filled Nestle's dinner dish with the obscenely expensive designer dog food the tiny beast demanded. Drugs or marriage, it was up to me. We would leave West Hollywood or we would leave each other. As simple, and as complicated, as that.

I looked around our stunning Doheny Avenue condo, at the evidence of our life together, the sleek furniture from Shelter and Diva, the fastidiously framed black-and-white erotic photographs from Weber and Ritts, the Williams-Sonoma chromed espresso maker. I looked at Kyle; even after a long and difficult day at the bank, managing the accounts of cranky gay men – bitter at suddenly facing the fact that after selling off their life insurance policies for the money they needed to "die with dignity," they were now going to actually live – he was still the most beautiful man I had ever met. His brown eyes were fixed on my face, waiting for an answer as, at his feet, that animated tissue-box cozy smugly devoured the doggie equivalent of dinner at the Ivy.

I found myself wondering two things: one, how much would all this stuff fetch us at the Yard Sale surely looming in the future and, two, where on earth where were going to live?

My dear Duchess, should you ever find yourself appearing as a special guest on one of those television game shows where they ask obscure questions in return for vast sums of tax-free money and should one of those obscure questions be "Where is the World's Largest Thermometer located?" you will now be in luck. You see, I happen to have spent almost eight months of my life staring at said thermometer through the window of our rented two-storey house.

The answer is Baker, California.

Glorious Baker. Population 2,000. Only a three-hour drive from West Hollywood, but at least twelve light years away from the twenty-first century. However, it was not a town without a certain charm; there was always the Dairy Queen.

Kyle had no problem finding a job; a managerial position at the Bank of America's local outpost had opened up, following a particularly nasty double murder/suicide at a nearby trailer park. My situation was, however, considerably more challenging. You may find this hard to believe, but in a town like Baker there are very few career opportunities for a gay man in his early thirties whose sole skill is planning the perfect dinner party.

I tried the entrepreneurial route, taking out an advertisement in the *Baker Gazette* for an "Event Planner," offering my services to make any gathering "a memory to last a lifetime." The single call I received inquired about my ability to "make them little animals outta balloons." When I assured the prospective client that while I could not at that time, I would be more than happy to learn if the price was right, the sound of the phone being hung up was like an arrow to my heart.

I did not renew my advertisement the following week.

Despondent, bored, and more than a little homesick, I tried all the usual remedies. I went to the local gym – "Stan's Workout Center and Hardware Store" – but, upon asking about their aerobics schedule, was met with a stare so blank I found myself unable to lift even a single weight thereafter. I checked out the local library, figuring to make the most of my exile by reading the classics: *Valley of the Dolls*, possibly, or, in a pinch, the new edition of *Mommie Dearest*.

But the town council, with the urging of a local church group, had passed an ordinance declaring any book with "in excess of four profanities per chapter" unfit for community standards. Needless to say, the only literary works left in the place had the words "Jesus," "God," "the Light" or "Flopsy, Mopsy, and Cottontail" in the titles.

And so, as easily as Kyle seemed to adapt to our new life, even going so far as to plan and design a barbecue pit for the backyard – my very soul spiraled into an abyss of afternoon television talk shows and tearful phone calls to Paris DeLamour in a desperate attempt to stay in touch with the outside world.

But through it all, no matter what, there was always Nestle.

Nestle needed to go for a walk. Nestle needed his water dish refilled. Nestle had to be fed. Nestle had to be brushed. Nestle had to be let in, let out, taken to the vet's, picked up from the vet's, walked again, fed again, brushed again: and since Kyle was at work, and since work was *all the way* across town (a five-minute drive, mind you), who do you suppose was left on full alert Nestle duty?

Dear Lady Milton, I am not an animal hater. And despite what many have said about me in the media, especially as they have cast long shadows upon the issue of my humanity, let me assure you that what happened to the dog was an accident.

Just an accident.

You see, I was upstairs in the bedroom cleaning out one of my old knapsacks – well, truth be told, I wasn't just cleaning that knapsack, but it was the last place I had looked in my desperate search to find even a single hit of acid, a grain of coke, *anything* to alleviate the spine-decalcifying tedium of life in Baker. Nestle was at my feet as usual, demanding, in that high pitched *yip! yip! yip!* of his, another walk in the park or perhaps it was fresh water or maybe that I play fetch with him, tossing that ridiculous rubber hamburger Kyle had given him the Christmas before. Whatever it was, I was ignoring it, playing what I had come to know as the "Nestle isn't here anymore" game, the object of which is fairly self-explanatory. And that's when I found it.

A tiny little ziplock baggie. Inside, another little baggie. And inside that. . . .

Enough crystal meth to get me through the summer.

Everything around me seemed to melt away – the Ethan Allen bedroom suite, the clapboard house with its single, hopeless hibiscus tree in the backyard, the whole hideous little town – as I considered my options. I could flush the drugs down the toilet and forget I ever found them. I could take a little bit now and then flush the rest down the toilet and forget it ever found them. I could take a little bit now and save the rest for later.

Or, I could keep my promise to Kyle: to try and stay clean, to give our new lives a chance, to really work at being a better, drug-free me.

I looked at the bag in my hand and felt a lump of shame rise in my throat. Had it come to this? Had the move to Baker caused me to slide so far down the moral chute that my wedding vows, to love, honor, and cherish Kyle as long as we both should live, meant nothing if there was a possibility of satisfying my baser instincts?

I glanced out the window again, where the World's Largest Thermometer was topping 114, and decided to snort the whole bag.

Now before you shake your head in disapproval, good Lady, rest assured that I didn't bend to my addiction that day. I couldn't. Because it was at that exact moment that someone forfeited our game of "Nestle isn't here anymore" by leaping up like a demented kangaroo rat and grabbing the bag of crystal between his shaggy jaws! Before I could even threaten him with the possibility of a future hanging in a Korean butcher shop window, the demonic mutt was out the door!

I chased him along the upstairs hallway and into the guest bedroom, where he scuttled into the tiny bathroom. Cornered against the toilet, he snarled at me, baring his fangs as I reached down toward him.

"Good Nestle . . . just give me the crystal, Nestle, and everything will be fine. Just give it to me. . . ."

He tried to make a break for the door, but I caught him by his silver Tiffany dog collar and held tight. The dog squirmed and struggled against my grasp, but I clamped down on his head, forced his jaws open, and reached into his mouth with my fingers.

His tiny, piranha teeth snapped and bit at me as he desperately tried to fight back, but I just held tighter, digging deeper and finally grabbing a corner of the slippery, saliva-drenched plastic. I yanked it out and let the little beast go. With a bark and a yelp, he scrambled away from me, his claws clattering against the tiles as he fairly flew out the bathroom door, leaving me alone with the baggie.

The *empty* baggie.

His teeth had gouged a good sized chunk out of it, and what little of the drug remained inside was now soaked in terrier spit. I looked around the floor hopefully; the tiles were clean and dry, and there was no sign of my crystal anywhere.

In the parlance of the narcotics *cognoscenti*, a "bump" of crystal is usually a single thin line of the powdery drug, about an inch long and less than a sixteenth of an inch wide. One or two "bumps" is more than adequate for, say, a man of six feet in height and 180 pounds in weight to experience the drug's effects. By my conservative estimate, there were about twenty "bumps" in that baggie.

The average toy terrier weighs approximately fifteen pounds.

Suddenly, from out in the hallway, I heard a strange gurgling sound. I moved out of the bathroom and cautiously stepped toward the hall, already dreading the sight I had guessed was about to greet me.

Nestle. Shaking, drooling Nestle. Now in the full throes of a massive crystal meth overdose, the dog had backed himself into a corner, eyes glazed wide and teeth bared. And he didn't look terribly pleased about it.

"Nestle . . . good boy. . . ." I coaxed.

He growled in return, a thick wave of foamy saliva oozing from his jaws. This was going to be a problem. I glanced at my watch; Kyle was due home soon, and I was definitely going to have a hard time explaining why his beloved terrier was performing selections from the road company version of *Cujo* in the upstairs hallway. But maybe, I reasoned, if I could just get the dog out of the house and lock him in the garage for a couple of hours, he'd dry out in time for his walk before bed. I made a move toward him holding my hand out, palm up, like Kyle always did to soothe the monstrous little throw rug.

"Good doggie . . . how about a nice walk?"

His fur rose on his haunches and he snarled at me again, his ears flattening in attack mode. With no further warning, he lunged at me!

One of the more curious side effects of crystal meth is the user's inability to accurately determine distance or strength. With that in mind, it really should have come as no surprise to me when, instead of hitting me, Nestle launched himself on a remarkably graceful arc about ten feet through the air and sailed cleanly out the second floor window.

The sudden, deathly silence below told me everything I needed to know before I made it down to the backyard.

"Where's Nestle?" was, of course, the first thing out of Kyle's mouth as he came home twenty-five minutes later. I kept my eyes on the pot of boiling angel hair pasta on the stove in front of me, nervously adjusting the apron I had thrown on in a desperate attempt to appear domestic.

Normal. Everything very normal. That was my plan.

"He was out in the backyard a few minutes ago," I replied, which was more or less true.

"I told you not to leave him alone," he retorted, slamming his briefcase on my perfectly set table and knocking an entire basket of breadsticks to the floor.

"It was just for a few minutes," I said, perhaps a little too nonchalantly; it was hard to concentrate with the pasta steam billowing up into my face. "What could possibly happen to him in a few minutes?"

"Coyotes don't get paid by the hour!" Kyle shouted as he hurried out the back door. Still trying to figure that one out I followed, with steaming pot in hand, and did my best Marjorie Main impression at the doorway.

"Dinner's almost ready," I called after him. But by then he was already halfway across the yard, shouting Nestle's name at the top of his lungs. I turned the burner down to let the pasta simmer and, kneeling to pick up the breadsticks, I felt a shiver of cold water run down my spine as I caught a glimpse of my hands. I wondered if Kyle had noticed them.

For in spite of soaking and scrubbing with water hot enough to turn my knuckles red, there were still traces of black earth under my fingernails.

Dirt from burying that scruffy little ditch rat's body under the hibiscus tree.

Kyle scarcely spoke to me for the rest of the night. We ate in silence, he barely touching his meal, and even the slice of key lime pie on his plate – his favorite dessert – was met with only a suspicious glare.

"What's this for?" he grumbled.

"Dessert," I said. "I thought you liked it."

"What I'd like is to know what happened to Nestle," he muttered, getting up from the table without taking a single bite of the pie. And so it went, all evening, until he crawled into bed and turned off the light, plunging me and the new issue of *Wallpaper** magazine into darkness.

"All you had to do was watch him," Kyle snorted, as he turned over and burrowed down into his pillow. "That's all you had to do."

I chose not to reply. What was I supposed to say, anyway? That I had watched him? That, in fact, I'd had a ringside seat as his beloved pet flew out the window and landed in a broken pile of triple digit grooming bills and absurdly expensive dog food receipts on the ground below? I rolled over onto my side and closed my eyes, hoping things would look, if not better, at least more tolerable in the morning.

Three hours later, I awoke to the knowledge that we were not alone in the house.

I wasn't sure at first what I'd heard. But something had definitely reclaimed me from a deep sleep, my body immediately tense, my ears tingling in spite of the silence. I looked over at Kyle, still dead to the world, a trail of drool staining his pillow. Not wanting to wake him with a false alarm – no sense adding insult to injury – I quietly eased my naked body from beneath the covers and padded on silent bare feet out of the room.

I stood there at the end of the upstairs hallway for a moment, listening to the house. Nothing. Only the distant hum of traffic rumbling along the freeway back to Los Angeles; back home. I glanced down at my once gym-trained and pool party-tanned body, now a pale grey in the thin moonlight, and patted my stomach. To my horror, it rippled; not the ripples of muscle, mind you but the ripples of cheese and potato chips, and enough Entemann's boxed cakes to cause a stampede at Jenny Craig.

No question, kind Lady Milton – I was losing it. First goes the career; then the body; and finally, you find yourself standing completely nude in the middle of your house, thinking you're hearing things.

That's when I heard the sound. A dry, scraping noise, like a dead tree being dragged off to a woodpile slaughter, followed by the hollow clink of something metal. I looked over the railing, to the floor below, but saw nothing there. The sound came again, a little closer this time. I leaned back into the bedroom where Kyle slept silently, snorelessly, on; whatever it was, the sound certainly wasn't coming from him. I listened again, as the strange scraping noise became louder, the metallic whisper closer.

It seemed to be coming from the stairs.

Barely aware of being naked, I crept cautiously down the hallway. The moon squeezed through a tiny hall window, bathing the empty landing in silver and leaving the rest of the staircase to tumble off into shadows below.

And it was from those shadows that the sound came. Closer.
Closer.

I tried to move, tried to scream, but somehow my feet had sunk into cement and my voice had fled in terror! The hideous rasping, scratching sound continued until it seemed as if the very walls themselves were alive with it! I could only stand there, naked and shivering, as what I knew to be impossible happened in front of my eyes!

A twisted limb stabbed out from the darkness. Matted fur, claws bent at impossible angles, it slapped at the next step, uncontrollably it seemed, and pulled the rest of the hideous vision into the light.

It was Nestle!

The dog's body, shattered by the fall, forced itself to continue up the stairs, one wrenching inch at a time. Clumps of dirt hung like icicles from its mangy fur, bloodied spittle dangling from the slack jaw. Its head lolled limply at the end of its broken neck, the expensive Tiffany collar tapping against the stairs with that horrendous metallic sound. Yet, in spite of its injury, it reached the top of the landing and somehow managed to turn its demon eyes toward me.

They were completely white, as if the horror of the animal's resurrection had bleached them to their very core. But still the beast seemed to stare with those slick ivory orbs, as if accusing me of its murder. The broken jaw began to work with a ghastly rhythm, the grim keening of bone grinding against bone, and I somehow knew that if I listened it would drive me mad. I clamped my hands tightly over my ears and closed my eyes and waited for what I knew was to come. . . .

Rinnngggggg!

The sound of the alarm clock on the bedside table wrenched me, taut and sweating, from the nightmare. My eyes snapped open, focusing on that damnable – forgive my language, but that's how I'd come to think of it – thermometer in the distance, reading eighty-two degrees already and it wasn't even nine in the morning.

I reached over to Kyle's side of the bed, to wrap myself in his arms long enough to shake off the dream, and found myself face to face with Nestle.

I screamed, a high-pitched wail, and scrambled backwards out of the bed, falling hard to the floor. Kyle rushed out of the bathroom, already in his suit with a toothbrush dangling from his mouth, to find me cowering in the corner.

"The dog," was all I could manage. "The dog!"

Kyle reached down to the bed and picked up a small pile of freshly printed flyers, gathering a few more off the floor where they'd fallen. He held one up for me to see; it was a computer scanned picture of Nestle's face, framed by "Missing Dog" and "Reward Offered" as well as our address and phone number.

"Yeah," he nodded, dropping the pile into my lap. "I made them up this morning. You stick a few up around town while you're getting the groceries today, I'll hand some out at the bank."

I stared down at those beady little eyes, peering out from the nest of its furry face, and felt a wave of nausea pass over me. Kyle didn't notice a thing as he headed back into the bathroom.

"But don't leave until after the landscaper finishes," he said, between spits. "He looks kind of suspicious to me."

"What landscaper?" I asked, still in a daze.

"The one in the backyard."

He came back out of the bathroom, fingers impatiently negotiating a Windsor knot into his tie and I turned so he wouldn't see the blood drain from my face.

"God, what's the matter with you? I told you about this half a dozen times. He's putting in the barbecue today!"

As soon as Kyle left for work, I rushed out to the backyard with a tray of ice cold lemonade and no idea what I was going to do.

The landscaper's muscular form was bent over a wheelbarrow, unloading a pile of bricks and placing them next to his garden tools; shovel, pickaxe, rake. His once-white tank top, dirty with sweat and dust, pulled up with each brick he lifted, revealing a narrow band of his taut tanned waist. His close cropped blond hair glistened with sweat.

"Thought you'd like a drink," I said. He turned and looked at me with crystal blue eyes and suddenly the tray felt just a little heavier. Only twenty if he was a day but let me tell you, Lady Milton, Caravaggio in his wildest absinthian dreams couldn't have painted a beauty like the common laborer standing before me.

"Thanks," he mumbled, hiking the loose fitting workpants up over his thin hips. He wiped at his sweating forehead with the back of his hand and I don't mind telling you that simple action caused enough rising and falling of muscles across his upper body to register on a seismograph. I poured him a glass, babbling.

"It's not store bought. It's fresh. I made it myself. From lemons. Well, lemons and water. And sugar. But not too much sugar. That's the thing people always get wrong when they make lemonade. They put in too much sugar, to make it sweeter. But then why do they bother at all? I say, if you want something sweet, then don't have lemonade."

I laughed alone. He just stood there, looking at me, so I handed him the drink. For a brief moment, as he took it, our fingers touched on the sweating glass. I introduced myself and waited for his reply.

"Harold," he mumbled, taking the drink from me quickly. He downed it in a single, long gulp as I stood there silently, watching the muscles in his throat roll like waves. He lowered the glass and noticed me staring. He held the glass out to me. "Not too sweet."

"Right," I nodded, taking the glass back. This time, he was careful not to let his touch graze my hand.

"You live here. With the other guy?" he asked.

"Yes."

"Alone?"

"Yes."

"Just the two of you?"

"Just us."

He looked at the house. Looked at me. Nodded.

"Thanks for the drink," he grunted, turning back to pick up his shovel. He started to move toward the far corner of the yard.

Toward the hibiscus tree.

"What are you doing?" I asked, maybe too quickly.

"Gotta move the tree," he said, without breaking his stride.

"Why do you have to move the tree?" I asked, urging a calm layer over my voice.

"Cuz that's where your . . . that's where he wants the barbecue."

"No!" I blurted, hurrying toward him. "I mean, you can't move that tree. We love that tree there. It's perfect, right there."

"He said he wanted the barbecue here. He told me to move the tree over there, I'm gonna move the tree over there." He raised his shovel and, in one quick stab, plunged the blade into the soft earth at the base of the hibiscus.

"Wait!" I shouted. He stopped, and turned slowly to look at me. A droplet of sweat rolled down his left temple and he squinted to keep it out of his eye. "He changed his mind. He told me he decided to put the barbecue over . . . there!" I pointed vaguely toward the other side of the yard. Harold shook his head with a smirk.

"Look, buddy. I don't want to get involved in some kinda —" His nostrils flared slightly with distaste. "Some kinda family feud, okay? The guy told me what he wanted done just before he drove outta here this morning, and he was pretty specific. You want something different, you talk to him, alright? Me, I'm moving this tree."

He returned to his shoveling and began to dig around the base of the tree. I backed up slightly, toward the brick pile, waiting for him to find the remains of Nestle, and wondering if I could make it to the bus station before he called Kyle. I bumped into something sharp and metallic and looked down to see what it was.

Don't you find, good lady, that sometimes, fate just comes along and hands you an opportunity? And wouldn't you agree that you ignore that opportunity at your own peril?

The landscaper continued digging with strong, deep strokes, sweat now pouring freely down his face.

"You just put this tree in? Ground's pretty soft around here, like somebody was just digging it or something."

I didn't answer. I was too busy aiming.

"Huh?" was all he got out as he turned to look at me, at the pick-axe in my hand, the sharp end making a wide, sweeping arc down toward him.

He reeled backwards before it connected, but couldn't move fast enough to avoid the blow. The point of the axe glanced off his forehead and skidded across his face, cutting a swath of blood and torn flesh on its way to gliding into his open mouth. His grunt of shock ended abruptly as the axe punctured through the back of his skull.

His body convulsed, limbs lurching wildly, as evidence of a last few coherent thoughts flickered across his face. He fell forward, but the pickaxe handle jammed into the soft earth and kept him from hitting the ground, supporting his body on its knees as if in prayer. Blood spilled from his mouth and down the axe handle, splashing the grass below him as he died, and I decided I'd better pour myself a glass of lemonade.

There was work to be done.

Although the television documentary mentioned your many trips to America, it did not say whether or not you had ever visited Joshua Tree National Park. Situated as it is halfway between those twin islands of high culture, Los Angeles and Las Vegas, I wouldn't be surprised if it hadn't made it onto your travel agenda. However, if you do find yourself in the area again in the future, I would highly recommended stopping by; it is a truly beautiful place. Twenty miles of desert terrain punctuated by breathtaking vistas of giant rock formations and incredible views of distant horizons, one could drive for half an hour without seeing even a single human being. Nothing but the stark, skeletal "Joshua trees," rather optimistically named by the Mormons because they appear to be praying. They couldn't have been more wrong for, in fact, the poor things are actually wrenching themselves upwards toward the heavens in a misguided attempt to find sustenance in the unforgiving sky. Not unlike the Mormons themselves, one supposes.

Still, it is a spiritual place and one where Harold will, I hope, have found some peace. Granted it was probably a rather rough start, what with his corpse being stripped naked and left out in the open on a rock. But the body is only a vessel they say, and I like to think that Joshua Tree was only a brief stop on his way to a better life.

As a side note, Kyle was quite right about coyotes; they don't waste any time at all. Why, I'd barely reached the truck and they were already starting to appear from behind rocks and cacti, drawn by the smell of the freshly dead landscaper.

What's that expression, "It never rains, it pours"? You know, I don't think I really understood exactly what it meant until that day. For no sooner had I abandoned Harold's truck out behind a seedy little bar on the highway, being careful of course to wipe for fingerprints – those years watching *NYPD Blue* paid off after all – and rode my bike the eleven miles back to Baker that the Mormon boys showed up.

I suppose it makes some kind of cosmic sense, really. I went to the Joshua Tree. The Mormons came to me.

I was in the back yard, preparing to dig up Nestle's remains in order to dispose of them once and for all, when the doorbell rang. I ignored it. It rang again. I ignored it again.

But you've got to hand it to those missionary types; they are persistent.

"Hello?" came a voice from the side of the house. I immediately stopped digging and turned to see the two young men tentatively walking into the backyard. One blond, blue-eyed, and lanky, the other a strapping red-haired lad, they both wore the same taut haircuts, short sleeved white shirts tucked into ill-fitting black slacks and clip on ties. They carried leather-bound Bibles, zipped up as tight as their faces.

"Hello," I replied, non-committally, casually leaning on my shovel in a way that blocked any view they might have had of the hibiscus tree. As they approached, I noted their clip on name tags, rather incongruously labeled "Elder Howe" and "Elder Niles" since neither of them were an hour past eighteen years old. They were sweating, dank circles under their arms, droplets of perspiration dotting their foreheads and upper lips, but in spite of their discomfort they summoned the grimly determined smiles of used-car salesmen before they spoke.

"Good afternoon, sir," Elder Howe offered, extending a hand to shake. I ignored it, being neither of the mood nor with the time to suffer these religious fools gladly – no matter how handsome they were. "I'm Elder Howe, this is Elder Niles, and we'd like to share something wonderful with you."

I raised a hand to stop his pitch.

"I already have something wonderful, thanks. It's called a life, and it doesn't need whatever you're selling, so why don't you guys just –"

Suddenly, Elder Niles clutched his stomach and doubled over, grunting in pain.

"Eric!" Elder Howe bent to help his friend, but Elder Niles pulled away, and through his gritted teeth I could make out one word:

"Bathroom!"

Elder Howe looked up plaintively.

"May he use your –"

"First door on the left," I nodded, and without further ado Elder Niles loped toward the house. Elder Howe gave me a sheepish look.

"He's from Iowa," he said, as if that explained everything. I suppose he read my blank face as a lack of understanding, rather than the lack of interest it was, and continued. "He's not used to the food in California. We went to a place called Burrito Villa and I guess it didn't go down too well."

"Yes," I nodded. "I guess it didn't."

There was a long pause as he looked around the yard. He seemed to be thinking, trying to find something to talk about I suppose, as his friend evacuated his bowels in my once-pristine bathroom.

"You live here alone, sir?"

I was about to respond with something sharp and clever, when I heard the noise behind me. I froze. Elder Howe turned to look at me, waiting for an answer. Had I really heard what I thought I heard?

"Sir?"

There it was again. *Yip! Yip! Yip!* A high-pitched, muffled sound. I turned to look at the source. It was coming from the hole behind me. Beneath the hibiscus tree.

I swear to you, good Lady, I knew it was impossible. I knew it couldn't be. But it was. I knew that voice.

It was Nestle.

Yip! Yip! Yip!

I didn't dare to move. Elder Howe looked at me strangely, waiting for me to say something, but I couldn't speak. I just kept staring down into the hole, the dirt, the darkness, dreading what was going to happen next.

"Sir, are you all right?"

Couldn't he hear it?

Yip! Yip! Yip!

It was getting louder now, as the beast must surely have been digging itself up and out of its grave.

"Is there something wrong?"

Of course there was!

Yip! Yip! Yip!

Didn't he hear the barking? Didn't he see the earth was about to move as the hideous thing clawed with its filthy paws, up, up, toward the surface?

Elder Howe stepped up beside me and leaned over the hole, peering down into the darkness. I backed away, letting him take a good look. Any moment now I knew the dead dog's head would lurch up through the dirt and the boy would see it and he would tell the police and they would tell Kyle and then Harold's body would be found in the desert and everything was going wrong so quickly.

"Is there something down there?"

I plunged the shovel into the young missionary's back. The sharp edge of the blade cleanly severed his spinal cord and burst out through his abdomen, taking what looked to me like his liver along with it. He gurgled in shock as he grabbed at his torn stomach, unsuccessfully trying to keep his intestines from spilling out through his fingers. The thick, ropy organs tumbled down into the hole, getting tangled up with the hibiscus roots, and Elder Howe fell to his knees, dropping his bloodstained Bible onto the ground next to him. He turned to look at me, his eyes sparkling with fear and confusion, and for one crystal clear moment I knew how he felt. A wave of pity washed over me.

So I swung the shovel again and cut his head off.

"Feeling better?" I asked Elder Niles as he stepped out of the downstairs bathroom.

"A little," he nodded. He still looked pale and if the stench coming from the tiny room behind him was any indication, he had emptied himself of several weeks' worth of food. "I had one of those burritos you know, the spicy ones."

"Elder Howe told me. This might help," I said, offering him a glass of bubbling liquid. He took it gratefully, raising it to his lips. I gave him my warmest smile. "It works best if you drink it down in one gulp."

He stopped abruptly and looked at the drink with suspicion. The smile on my face froze.

"Is there any caffeine in it?" he asked. "We're not allowed to drink anything with caffeine."

I relaxed. "No. No caffeine." That, at least, was true. To my knowledge, they've never put caffeine in drain cleaner.

He smiled and swallowed the stuff in one gulp.

I was still mopping the blood – and the other – off the floor when the telephone rang. It was Kyle. I could tell he was still angry. After grilling me about the groceries and the flyers and whether or not there had been any sign of Nestle, all of which I lied about with remarkable ease given the circumstances, he told me he was bringing his assistant manager and her husband home within the hour. I was supposed to make dinner. That was it. No "Please clean up the two dead Mormons and then make a nice meal for us, honey, I love you." Nothing. He just expected it to be done.

I hung up the phone and looked around the kitchen. An hour? If we were back home in West Hollywood, I could have called any number of fabulous restaurants and had a gourmet meal delivered in less than thirty minutes. But Baker was strictly KFC territory, and if I dared served deep-fried anything to Kyle I would never have heard the end of it.

No, I needed to prepare a feast, and it had to be delicious. But I certainly hadn't had time to get to the grocery store, what with the murders and all, and there was simply nothing fresh in the house.

Well . . . almost nothing.

So what was I supposed to do? I ask you, Lady Milton, what was I supposed to do?

Dinner was a huge success. Everyone, even Kyle, commented on the delicious meat; its delicate seasoning, the way it literally melted in their mouths. When the meal ended, Tanya, the assistant manager, shyly asked if she and her husband could take some of the leftovers home. She had, she admitted, never tasted anything like it in her life. What was my secret?

Of course I told her. No caffeine.

They left shortly after dinner, spouting all the usual lies of reciprocation, and Kyle and I were alone again in the silent house. He made a few feeble stabs at conversation as he helped to clean up the kitchen, but I could tell his heart wasn't in it. I suggested he take a walk around the block, showing Nestle's picture to our erstwhile neighbors; it was very possible, I lied, that the dog was even now enjoying the hospitality of one of the friendly locals. Kyle took the bait, gave me a peck on the cheek, and left.

I stood there for a moment in the foyer of the dreadful little house, his kiss drying to become an itch on my face, and wondered what had happened to our wonderful life. My husband was grimly wandering the streets of a hick desert town in search of a dog he'd never find, and I was picking Mormon flesh from between my teeth, trying to remember where I'd put the flashlight.

Was this our destiny? Was this to be our future? Where had it all gone wrong?

And where was that flashlight?

Twenty minutes of fumbling through the cluttered garage yielded nothing, not even a decent candle to light the pitch darkness of the backyard. How was I going to unearth the remains of that ghastly dog if I couldn't even see the hibiscus tree? Tears came suddenly to my eyes as I found myself thinking about home. It was nine thirty; Santa Monica Boulevard would just now start coming to life. Wednesday night. Half-price Margaritas at Revolver. Go-go boys at Mickey's. Maybe a floor show at Rage, some comedy troupe or a drag queen.

Drag queen. My dear, dear Paris DeLamour. I missed her quick wit, her clever put downs, the withering stare she could summon at will if one of her less attractive fans became a little too adoring. I could almost smell her perfume, something cheap and French, leftover from her mother's last visit to La Rive Gauche.

"You've only been here a month and already he's making you sleep in the garage?"

I opened my eyes in shock. The smell was real. And so was the voice.

It was Paris DeLamour, right there in Baker!

"Darling," she exclaimed, pulling me into the embrace which had earned her the Nebraska State High School Wrestling Championship two years running. "You didn't tell me you were moving out of the country!"

"What are you doing here?" I sputtered, standing back a moment to take in her ensemble; peasant smock, pigtails, gingham blouse and matching – matching, mind you – gingham pumps. Salvador Dali meets Loretta Young in *The Farmer's Daughter*. The overall effect was stunning.

"I had a vision. I felt you needed me. Plus, they cancelled my show. Got any Ketel One?"

I couldn't move.

"Hello?" she said. "Anybody home?"

And then the dam broke. I began to sob uncontrollably, great whacking gulping sobs, the kind where your eyes feel like they're going to pour right out of their sockets. Paris took me into her arms.

"There, there. It's alright, darling. Stoli will do. But there'd better be mix."

I looked up into her kind face, eyes thick with caterpillars of mascara, her day-old beard growth beginning to poke through the heavy pancake makeup. Backlit by the naked bulb suspended from the garage ceiling, her wig seemed to glow like a halo. I knew then she was an angel. A caring, loving messenger sent from Heaven to make everything all right again. And between crying spasms, I told her the whole story.

The town. The World's Largest Thermometer. The house. The dog. Harold. The Mormons. Dinner.

Everything.

Moments later, we were in the backyard, with me digging beneath the hibiscus tree while Paris held aloft her authentic *Charlie's Angels* Zippo to light my way.

Her reaction should have come as no surprise, really. After a childhood spent clawing her way up through the sewers of midwestern heterosexuality, surviving the vicious taunts and horrendous physical assaults which surely went along with being an effeminate boy in small-town America, Paris had a healthy disregard for common morality. As she explained it, spilling tears over a few less rednecks and religious fanatics was nothing more than a waste of good salt. What I had to do, she insisted, was get rid of the damn dog and forget the whole thing ever happened.

Good friends, dear Duchess, are those who will help you bury the bodies.

Which made what happened next all the more painful. You see, as

I continued shovelling the dirt, making my way deeper and deeper into the hole under the tree, I began to realize there was something wrong. Very wrong.

I had dug almost six feet down but I still hadn't hit the terrier.

"Are you sure this is where you buried it?" Paris wondered, holding the lighter low enough to cast eerie shadows deep into the hole.

"It was right here, right under the hibiscus," I insisted. "I know it was."

"Maybe you were confused, dear heart. I mean, burying your husband's pet dog is enough to make anyone a trifle *désorienté*."

"I'm not *désorienté*!" I shouted, loud enough to echo through the backyard. In the distance, a dog barked and a window slammed shut. "It was right here!"

I began to dig like a madman, ravaging at the earth with the shovel. Paris backed up as I flailed, dirt flying in every direction! I felt the muscles on my arms shriek as I slammed the spade again and again into the sun toughened ground.

"It's here! It's right here! Damn it, I know where I put that god-damnned dog!"

Suddenly, the flame of the lighter flickered out, plunging us into darkness.

"Paris!" I grunted, still digging. "I need that light!"

But there was no answer from the drag queen. Only the strange, rasping sound of breath forced through taut teeth.

"Paris?" I turned to where she had been standing, and peered into the darkness. "Paris, what are you doing?"

A cloud moved away from the moon, casting the backyard in a cold, silver light.

The first thing I saw was one of the gingham pumps, empty, laying on its side on the grass.

And beside that, convulsing on the ground, the former Clark Nesbitt of Puce, Nebraska, now Miss Paris DeLamour of Glamorville, USA was having an epileptic seizure.

I leapt up out of the hole and knelt beside her, trying to calm her down, or at least make sure she didn't break off one of her expensive acrylic fingernails.

"Shh, shh . . . you're okay, you're okay. . . ." I said lamely, my hands on her shoulders, holding her firmly against the ground. "Just breathe . . . breathe. . . ."

Suddenly, her head twisted toward me, her eyes snapping open. Her pupils gleamed with platinum moonlight, boring into me with an un-earthly gaze as she parted her glistening coral lips to speak.

And I swear to you, kind Lady, this is what came out of her mouth.

Yip! Yip! Yip!

It was Nestle.

Somehow, don't ask me by what demonic power, that hellish toy terrier had possessed my beloved friend!

"Paris!" I shouted at her. "It's evil! The dog is evil!! Fight it! Don't let it win!"

But the animal's control of her was complete, its horrendous spirit in command of her every breath. So violent were her convulsions that her scarlet wig pulled away from her skull, exposing the bleached blonde nest of processed hair beneath.

"Yip! Yip! Yip!" she shrieked, her body writhing in pain and terror. "Yip! Yip Yip!"

"No, Nestle!" I screamed. "Let her go! Take me!! Take me!"

It was no use. The beast held her in its ghastly thrall, determined to enact God-only-knew what hideous revenge upon me. She clawed at the grass, her muscles contorting, the tendons along her neck straining as if to burst.

Yip! Yip! Yip! Yip! Yip! Yip!

Dear God, I could stand the yelping no more! There was only one solution, only one way to free the poor transvestite from the clutches of the horrid thing!

I closed my eyes and prayed for forgiveness as I wrapped my hands around the soft yielding throat of my dear Paris DeLamour.

I'm sure you can imagine Kyle's reaction when he arrived moments later to find his husband of four years holding the broken neck of a dead drag queen at the edge of a six-foot deep pit in the backyard.

But can you imagine my shock when I saw what Kyle was carrying in his arms?

It was Nestle.

Claws and fur thick with dirt, but otherwise alive and well, staring at me with those beady little terrier eyes.

I could have sworn it was smiling. . . .

I have spent endless nights trying to make some sense of it all.

From what Kyle told the police in his statement, and from the numerous articles on the subject printed in the *Baker Gazette* – this was, after all, the first interesting thing that had happened in the town since they'd built the damn thermometer – I have managed to put together a theory of sorts.

It is my belief that the wretched hound had never died at all. It simply fell into a coma after ingesting all that crystal meth and, when it awoke, dug its way out of the premature grave. Unable to rouse either Kyle or myself from our sleep, it wandered out into the street and found shelter with our next-door neighbors, a charming Indian couple with utterly unpronounceable names. Not knowing to whom the dog belonged, and with only the most rudimentary command of the English language, they had set out that evening on a quest of their own. It had only been when they met up with Kyle at another house down the street that the entire situation worked itself out.

Well, not entirely of course. There was still the matter of my murders.

I confessed right away to killing Harold and the Elders Niles and Howe; I saw no point in lying, really, as eventually even the dullards employed as police officers in that town would have connected the rather obvious dots. There was one rather interesting moment when I showed them how I had disposed of the bodies of the Mormon boys; apparently Tanya and her husband were finishing off the last of the leftovers when they were told the truth and it caused quite a fuss at their house.

And while I did admit to strangling Paris DeLamour, I tried to explain that in fact I hadn't really *murdered* her *per se*. It had been a mercy killing, I told them; an exorcism to release her from the unholy grip of that devil dog.

As you can see, by the return address on this letter, your Grace, my sanity was immediately called into question.

There were countless hearings and examinations, during most of which I simply let the lawyers argue amongst themselves.

They tossed around meaningless phrases like "disconnected sociopathy and brain damage due to controlled substance abuse," things like that. But I ask you, who wants to listen to all that legal mumbo jumbo, anyway? I was just happy to be getting out of Baker.

I will admit, however, that I do miss Kyle.

Of course he was exonerated of any involvement in my crimes. And while having a serial killer as an ex-husband should give one a certain "cachet," or at the very least the grounds for a best-selling tell-all book, Kyle has declined all offers – he even turned down Larry King! – and has apparently gone into hiding. With Nestle, I assume.

As for me, well, I'd like to think I have been spending my time here at the Center wisely. I'm taking a few courses in art appreciation and history, with an eye toward becoming a teacher when I'm released at the end of my sentence – if, of course, they still have schools at the turn of the next century.

You'll be happy to know I have been working very hard with my therapist to try to work through the feelings I still have about the dog. About Nestle.

Dr McDermid, an extraordinarily patient and understanding man, has helped me to see that the toy terrier was just a symbol, a physical manifestation of my intense fear of relationships. And by acting out around those fears, in my case by burying a toy terrier and then ritualistically slaughtering four innocent victims, I was only trying to communicate a deeply repressed desire to escape from what I perceived to be a suffocatingly "normal" life. We're still trying to figure out why I think Paris barked.

Which brings me, finally, to the point of this letter, kind Lady.

Do your butterflies still talk?

And if they do, is it still in the voice of your late husband, the one you slowly poisoned with the arsenic you slipped into his oatmeal during the course of that overseas voyage from the continent to the West Indies two decades ago?

Or have they stopped, letting you sleep at night without the constant reminder of your crime?

You see, there's this spider in my cell. We've become quite close, actually; he's more of a pet now than a nuisance. And I've been thinking that maybe, just maybe, if I can convince Dr McDermid that I love the spider, he will see that my attitude towards having pets has changed. Then he will know that the therapy is working and perhaps he will make a recommendation allowing me to have a day pass soon.

I would use it to go back to West Hollywood. Just to have one drink, that's all I want. Just one drink as the sun sinks down behind the distant silver castles of Century City. Sitting there in front of Mickey's, say, or Rage, licking the salt from the rim of my dollar margarita and watching those handsome young men walk by. That's all I want. If the spider would just stop making so much noise.

He keeps me awake at night, you see. I've tried asking him to be quiet, I need my sleep, but he doesn't seem to listen. So I was thinking that if you found a way to make your butterflies stop, then maybe it would work for my spider, too?

Now, I know you must be a very busy lady, what with your charity work and I'm sure a very full social calendar at the Sanitarium. But if you can find it in your heart to send a reply to me by return mail, my dear Duchess, I would be ever so appreciative. You see, unlike your butterflies, my spider doesn't talk.

He sings "I Got Rhythm." Just like Paris DeLamour did. Exactly like she did. With her voice.

Don't get me wrong. The fact that he sounds like my late, lamented transvestite friend isn't what disturbs me. It's actually rather comforting.

But the spider . . . like Paris, he only knows the one song. And frankly, it's beginning to drive me crazy.

Please write soon.

Your Servant,

Trevor Bowden
Millwood Center for the Criminally Insane,
Needles, CA

SECOND SHADOW

Joseph O'Brien

HALASZ HAD FIRST HEARD OF SHEBAT'HA DURING a buying trip in Cairo. A minor legend borne of merchants' tales of a land of rare and uncommon treasure, concealed beyond a barrier of impassable mountains and impenetrable mist. He dismissed them at first; they might have been tales of Agartha or Atlantis for all the heed he paid them. But he listened. He listened because despite the great discrepancies in each account, there were also tiny similarities; tantalizing details that, if not forming a larger whole, at least suggested the existence of one. And for a man like Halasz, who had spent half his lifetime in search of beautiful things, the lure of a place shielded from the rest of the world was strong indeed.

And then it seemed to be everywhere. He overheard a passing mention in a café in Istanbul. Saw the name buried beneath an avalanche of kaleidoscopic graffiti on a wall in Hong Kong. Read reference to it in an ancient Greek text. Heard it spoken twice the same day in New York, whispered by a child in a schoolyard and shouted by a madman on the street. *Shebat'ha.*

In the years that followed, it became a pastime, a way to while away the gallery's slow days or fill those weeks when Thomas was abroad. Assembling fragments of folklore into usable information, merging the vagaries of myth with geographical and historical fact. *Shebat'ha.* Where the world held no dominion. And as he slowly wove the threads of legend together, as his knowledge expanded, so too did his desire for the place. And somewhere between the moment he saw Thomas die and the day he laid him to rest, mourned, missed, unavenged, he could think of nothing else.

He surrendered everything they had ever had to find it. Every book, every piece of furniture, every *objet d'art* they had rescued and protected from the ugliness of the world. Everything they had struggled for, the gallery, even the house, was gone now. Every evidence that they had ever been. All of it sacrificed for this one last expedition. And now even that was gone, spent in a year of false starts and bad information and those final precious slivers of detail that had at last led him to the great grey range shielding *Shebat'ha.* He stood before it and stared for an eternity. Past this point no traveler had ever returned.

Either they had found what they sought or had died in the attempt.

For Halasz, who wanted nothing more now than to escape the world, either was acceptable.

He spent days traversing the range. Here his painstaking research paid off again and again; he had built this place in his mind a thousand times, until every detail was known to him. He negotiated each perilous ascent, uncovered every hidden trail with something bordering on instinct. More than once he came across the remains of those others who had preceded him and failed, bodies mummified by the dry, barren cold, their backs broken against the treacherous, unyielding rock or starved on some lonely ledge, skin burnt black by frostbite.

On the eighth day he descended into a thick, clinging fog. Fingertips bloody, skin wind-scoured, willpower nearly exhausted, he was greeted with a sudden uprush of warm air, moist and alien and invigorating, and he pressed on. Within a day he emerged from it and found not rock, but the dense, impossible forest of the merchants' tales. Gargantuan trees twisted out of the brush, sinewy branches stretching upward into a canopy that broke sunlight like a prism, painting the wilderness in dazzling rainbow hues. Even the air was electric; just breathing it seemed to renew him. Light seemed brighter, sounds somehow sharper. He had found *Shebat'ha*.

And as night fell, as the light surrendered to blue-black shadows, he found them. There were predators in this hidden place. But what *magnificent* predators.

They moved just beyond the range of his night vision, their eyes obsidian, reflecting the deep orange of his small campfire back at him. Their movements were quicksilver, like liquid shadows. Sometimes on four legs, sometimes two. Their presence a whisper broken only by the wet snap of bone and the howls of distant victory.

But he would never have seen them, he later realized, had they not allowed it. Invisibility was their survival; *Shebat'ha* was their camouflage from the world, as it now was for him.

Not once did they venture within his circle of firelight. Neither did he breach this tenuous perimeter. He watched each night as they passed, heading into deep forest to hunt, and marveled at the beauty of them. Of all the tales he had sifted through, all the stories of *Shebat'ha*, not one had mentioned them.

But there were, after all, other legends.

He was quick to guess the nature of these creatures on his own, although his words were a crude translation at best. Their language was far more elegant, more descriptive, more perfect; and why shouldn't it have been? They knew themselves best, unlike those Halasz had fled; savages who dreamed they were men. These creatures were purer.

Uncivilized, and so less savage for it.

It was on his seventh night in *Shebat'ha*, black and moonless, that Egren came to see him.

He was naked, his body lean, muscular, and covered with a dozen deep scars. He was hairless, lacking even eyebrows, and it gave his face a strange alien aspect. Only his eyes were unchanged, black as coal, burning from within. He approached Halasz' fire, staying just beyond the edge of the flickering glow.

"You've been watching me for hours," Halasz told him, not looking up. "You're not so quiet after all."

The visitor sat on his haunches. "I am Egren," he said simply.

"Have you come to kill me?" Halasz asked.

The question seemed to puzzle the visitor. "Why are you here?" he asked after a time.

The fire cracked and spit sparks into the air. They glowed brightly for an instant as they ascended, then faded and finally died.

"Do you know love?" Halasz asked.

Egren shook his head.

A long silence passed between them. "Will you kill me?" Halasz asked finally, looking up. But Egren was gone.

———

Halasz slept and dreamt Thomas. He dreamt love. He dreamt the taste of naked skin. He dreamt blood steaming on cold concrete. He dreamt beauty. He dreamt choking on broken teeth.

———

The days passed. Each night Egren would return to his camp, each night subtly changed. His body more massive, muscles thicker, bare skin covered at first with a light blond down that grew darker and heavier as the moon grew fat. Halasz came to realize that their transformation did not come upon them all at once. Their nature was unfixed. They waxed and waned with the moon, their aspect inconstant, changing slowly, fully recognizably human (yet even this definition was imperfect) only for those few days when the sky was dark. Yet even when Egren was at his most bestial, incapable of forming words, he would break from the pack and sit at the edge of the light. On those nights Halasz would tell him of Thomas, and together they would listen to the wild hunt in the distance. And Halasz came to understand the rare and uncommon treasure of *Shebat'ha*.

He envied them the simple perfection of their unfixed nature.

Egren was liquid, never the same from moment to moment. As such, he could never be. Not being, he could never feel. Without love, he would never feel loss. Without loss he would never feel fear. Without fear, he would never feel hate. And without hate, he could never know cruelty. He would never know murder.

Before the moon again vanished briefly from the night sky, envy had become something else. And Halasz made a request of his friend as the firelight died. And Egren left him for the deep forest and was gone for two more days.

On that last night they circled close, Egren and the rest, penetrating the circle of light. Halasz stood silent and naked and unafraid as they fell upon him.

Halasz slept and dreamt falling, and the world ran back. He fell away from *Shebat'ha* and Egren, from the harsh snap of jaws and the spray of hot blood on his face and the pain. They receded away from him, one after the other, left behind.

What is this?

He fell through his journey here and the research that had led to it. He fell through those fruitless, expensive expeditions, through all that time wasted.

He fell through the funeral and a week of tears. Through the living hurt that had owned him, burning from the inside out. And then they, too, were gone.

I'm losing myself. The thought flickered for an instant and died in his mind.

He fell through Thomas lying in the street, in his arms, face broken and bleeding but still managing that last tiny smile as the light faded from his eyes. That last breath. That last whisper. . . .

No. His mind struggled for purchase on that one moment, strained to hang on to the memory, to drag it down with him. . . .

He fell away from the fear. He fell away from the pain. He fell through Thomas. Through years of him. Handsome Thomas, who had shown him love in a world of hate. Strong Thomas, who had lived to shelter cherished things. Protector Thomas, who had died for it. Teacher Thomas, who had shown him the difference between kindness and weakness.

The past no longer is, Thomas had told him. *And the future has not yet been invented. We're simply passing from one nonexistence to the next. There is nothing but this moment. This is all we have.*

He wanted to scream as he fell away from Thomas, as the memory of him crumbled into dust and slipped away. And he was alone as he had never been before. He fell back through his childhood, so awkward, so unsure. He fell back through his parents. Through isolation and a distant, obligatory sort of love. He fell back through his birth. He fell back further. He fell back until there was nothing left of him, and yet still he fell, empty. He fell back into oblivion. He became liquid. He ceased to be.

———————

No traveller who entered *Shebat'ha* ever returned. But its inhabitants had been known to venture into the world beyond from time to time.

There were, after all, other legends.

Halasz – or what had been Halasz – wandered out of the grey range on four legs, retracing steps that had brought it there on two. Even when the moon waned, and the thing approached an aspect not unlike a man – hairless, reborn, with eyes like coal – its thoughts did not return to Thomas, or the city or the things the savages there had done to him. They were lost now. They had never been. But even as it approached the city, and the moon grew fat, a shadow remained. As they had torn at him, as his blood mixed with their own, that last memory had clung to him, fallen with him, refused to let go. That last breath. That last whisper. . . .

Love.

The shadow remembered this last moment alone. Lived for this last moment alone. In this simple passage between one nonexistence to another, the shadow remembered beauty. The shadow remembered love.

And loss.

And fear.

And hate.

And the hunger for vengeance.

CONTRIBUTORS

T.L. BRYERS is a Toronto writer. "You Can't Always Get What You Want" is her first published short story.

ROBERT BOYCZUK is a Toronto writer. He has previously published stories in *On Spec, Transversions,* and *Prairie Fire,* and in the anthologies *On Spec: The First Five Years, Erotica Vampirica, Northern Frights 4, Tesseracts 7,* and *Northern Suns.*

DOUGLAS CLEGG is the author of *You Come When I Call You* and other novels. His collection, *The Nightmare Chronicles,* won both the Bram Stoker Award and the International Horror Guild Award. He lives in the United States and is at work on his next book.

GEMMA FILES is an award-winning short story writer and screenwriter, as well as a film and culture critic for Toronto's *eye Weekly.* Her short horror fiction has appeared in small press magazines and mainstream anthologies, and has received Honourable Mention in every edition of Ellen Datlow's *The Year's Best Fantasy and Horror* since 1993. Her story, "The Emperor's Old Bones," which first appeared in *Northern Frights 5* won the International Horror Guild Award for 1999, and will be reprinted in *The Year's Best Fantasy and Horror 2000.* In 1997, her stories "Fly-by-Night" and "Hidebound" were optioned for teleplay adaptation by Tony and Ridley Scott for *The Hunger,* the half-hour anthology series. Later, she adapted her stories "Bottle of Smoke" and "The Diarist" into teleplay form. Both appeared during *The Hunger's* 1999 season.

MICHAEL THOMAS FORD is the author of numerous books, most notably the essay collections *Alec Baldwin Doesn't Love Me* and *That's Mr. Faggot to You,* for which he won back-to-back Lambda Literary Awards. His new collection, *It's Not Mean If It's True,* was published in 2000. He has also released a spoken-word compilation, *My Queer Life,* and he wrote the libretto for *Alec Baldwin Doesn't Love Me,* a musical based on his work.

BRIAN HODGE is the author of seven novels ranging from horror to crime, most recently *Wild Horses*. He is currently at work on his next, titled *Mad Dogs*. He's also written around eighty short stories and novellas, many of which have been forced at gunpoint into two highly-acclaimed collections, *The Convulsion Factory* and *Falling Idols*, with a third in the works. He lives in Colorado, where he's recently begun an alter-ego recording project called Axis Mundi, with an ever-growing studio of keyboards, samplers, didgeridoos, and digital gear, all of which very much want a room of their own. His website is www.para-net.com/~brian_hodge. "Little Holocausts" previously appeared in *Dark Terrors 3*, edited by Stephen Jones and David Sutton (Victor Gollancz, 1997).

CAITLIN R. KIERNAN's first novel, *Silk*, received both the International Horror Guild Award and the Barnes and Noble Maiden Voyage Award for best first novel. She has recently completed her second, *Trilobite*. Her short fiction has been selected for *The Year's Best Fantasy and Horror* and *The Mammoth Book of Best New Horror*. It has also been collected in the chapbook, *Candles for Elizabeth*, and in the recent collection, *Tales of Pain and Wonder*. Caitlin also scripts *The Dreaming* and other projects for DC / Vertigo. Trained as a vertebrate paleontologist, she dislikes crowds, and lives in a renovated textile factory with her cat and several thousand fossils.

NANCY KILPATRICK has authored over 150 short stories. Her most recent works include the collection, *The Vampire Stories of Nancy Kilpatrick*, and *Bloodlover*, the fourth novel in the *Power of the Blood* series. She has edited seven anthologies including the upcoming *Graven Images* (co-edited with Thomas S. Roche). In 1992, she won the Arthur Ellis Award for best short fiction. Her website is www.sff.net/people/nancyk.

WILLIAM J. MANN is the author of two novels, *The Biograph Girl* and *The Men From the Boys*. His 1998 biography, *Wisecracker: The Life and Times of William Haines*, won the Lambda Literary Award. A study of the gay subculture in Hollywood titled *Behind the Scenes, Between the Lines* is planned for publication in 2001. As a journalist, Mann has written for *The Boston Phoenix*, *The Los Angeles Times*, *Architectural Digest*, and *The Advocate*. A grant recipient for fiction from the Massachusetts Cultural Council, Mann's fiction has appeared in dozens of anthologies, including *His: Brilliant New Gay Fiction* and *Men On Men 6*. He is currently working on a sequel to *The Men From the Boys*. "The Spark" previously appeared, as written by Geoff Huntington, in *Grave Passions*, edited by William J. Mann (Badboy, 1997).

MICHAEL MARANO's first novel, *Dawn Song*, received the two most prestigious awards in the field of horror, the Bram Stoker Award and the International Horror Guild Award. His short fiction is widely anthologized. Marano has a formal background in Medieval history, and has spoken publicly on dark fantasy and horror with particular emphasis on Alchemy and Kabbalah, both of which have figured prominently in his fiction. Since 1990, as "Mad Professor Mike," Marano reviews horror movies on the nationally-syndicated Public Radio program, *Movie Magazine*. His punk/heavy metal style of criticism has been described as "combining the best of *Cahiers du Cinema* with the spirit of pro-wrestling," and he currently reports in horror and science fiction films and TV for national publications such as *Gothic.net* and *Sci-Fi Magazine*. His film and media commentary appear in the award-winning publication *Dark Echo*, and *The Charleston City Paper*. His website is www.mindspring.com/~profmike.

DAVID NICKLE's stories have appeared in anthologies such as *Sons of Darkness*, *Northern Frights* (volumes 1 through 5), *Tesseracts 4, 5*, and *8*, *Northern Suns*, and *The Year's Best Fantasy and Horror*. It has also appeared in magazines like *Transversions*, *On Spec*, and *Valkyrie*, and adapted for the small screen in the television series, *The Hunger*. He is a past winner of the Bram Stoker Award (with Edo van Belkom, for their story, "Rat Food") and the Aurora Award (with Karl Schroeder, for their story "The Toy Mill," later expanded into a novel, *The Claus Effect*). He lives and works in Toronto.

JOSEPH O'BRIEN is co-writer of the epic-length miniseries *Robocop: Prime Directives*, and producer of the animated National Film Board short, *Hoverboy*. He also wrote the screenplay for the atrocious Chris Penn/Michael Madsen thriller, *Trail of a Serial Killer*, and will go to great lengths to avoid talking about it. He is a regular contributor to *Rue Morgue*, where he was most recently responsible for making George A. Romero laugh out loud. Under the alias "WideScreenPig," he can be found on usenet's alt.horror newsgroup saying unconscionably horrible things to Poppy Z. Brite. He is also a shameless name dropper. "Second Shadow" is his first short story, and he's pretty sure it shows.

RON OLIVER denies that his story "Nestle's Revenge" is autobiographical, even though he does despise gay lap dogs of any variety. A longtime West Hollywood resident, the award-winning writer/director has countless television and film credits, but his proudest achievement is his recent wedding to his longtime boyfriend, Anthony. Congratulations and hate mail can be sent to ROliver588@aol.com.

DAVID QUINN was a 1999 finalist for both the Bram Stoker Award and the International Horror Guild Award. He wrote the trailblazing adult horror comics franchise, *Faust*, as well as the screenplay for the 2000 film, *Faust: Love of the Damned.*

THOMAS S. ROCHE's short horror fiction has appeared in such anthologies as *Love in Vein 2*, *Gothic Ghosts*, *Northern Frights 4*, and *Embraces*, among others. He has edited or co-edited seven anthologies, including *Sons of Darkness* and *Brothers of the Night*, both with Michael Rowe. His most recent anthology is the third volume in the *Noirotica* series. Some of his short stories are collected in his book, *Dark Matter.*

BECKY N. SOUTHWELL is a Canadian writer living in Los Angeles, where she writes for film and television.

C. MARK UMLAND lives and writes in Toronto. His non-fiction has appeared in *Fangoria*, and "The Nightguard" marks his fiction debut. Currently he is at work on his first novel, tentatively titles *Interment.*

EDO VAN BELKOM, Bram Stoker and Aurora Award-winner, has published over 150 short stories in a wide variety of magazines and anthologies, including *The Year's Best Horror Stories 20*, *Best American Erotica 1999*, *Robert Bloch's Psychos*, *Northern Frights* (volumes 1 through 4) and *Brothers of the Night.* His novels include *Lord Soth* and *Teeth*, an erotic / horror / mystery to be published by Meisha Merlin in 2001. He is the author of the short story collections, *Death Drives a Semi* and *Six-Inch Spikes*, and three works of non-fiction, the interview book *Northern Dreamers* and the instructional guides, *Writing Horror* and *Writing Erotica.* He lives in Brampton, Ontario, and his home page is www.vanbelkom.com.

Michael Rowe is the Lambda Literary Award-nominated co-editor of two original vampire anthologies, *Sons of Darkness* and *Brothers of the Night*. An award-winning journalist and essayist whose work has appeared in *The National Post, The Globe and Mail,* and *The Next City,* Rowe is the author of two critically-acclaimed works of non-fiction, *Looking for Brothers* and *Writing Below the Belt.* A lifelong afficionado of the horror genre, his essays, articles and reviews have appeared in *The Scream Factory, Rue Morgue, All Hallows,* and *Fangoria.* A member of both PEN Canada and the Horror Writers Association, he lives in Toronto with his life-partner, Brian McDermid, and receives email at Mwriter35@aol.com.

ALSO BY MICHAEL ROWE
Looking for Brothers (1997)
Writing Below the Belt (1994)
When the Town Sleeps (1990)

EDITED, WITH THOMAS S. ROCHE
Brothers of the Night (1997)
Sons of Darkness: Tales of Men, Blood, and Immortality (1996)